ILLEGAL
JOURNEY

ILLEGAL JOURNEY

From the Holocaust to Palestine in 1946

EDGAR MISKIN

DEVORA PUBLISHING
NEW YORK♦JERUSALEM♦LONDON

Illegal Journey: From the Holocaust to Palestine in 1946
by Edgar Miskin

Copyright © 2013 by Edgar Miskin

Typesetting by Ariel Walden

Printed in Israel

First Edition
ISBN 978-965-524-127-3

Urim Publications   Lambda Publishers, Inc.
P.O.Box 52287   527 Empire Blvd.
Jerusalem 91521 Israel   Brooklyn, NY 11225 U.S.A.
                               Tel: 718-972-5449
                               Fax: 718-972-6307

www.UrimPublications.com

CONTENTS

MUSE

The author's unqualified acknowledgment is hereby given to CONNIE GRILLETTE, of the debt owed for her consistent encouragement, support, inspiration, enheartenment, advice, and stimulation through the gestation of this book, from conception to birth.

For my Sons: IAN and CLIVE, from whom no father has the
right to expect more love and support than I have received,
and in whose respective achievements and attainments I
have an inordinate pride, knowing too that they have set
admirable examples to their succeeding generation.

ACKNOWLEDGMENT

The author's thanks are given for the drawing of the ship, the

Helen, to the artist ZULAY ITURRALDE DE FROMMEL.

CHARACTERS IN THE BOOK

BERNE, SWITZERLAND

Olaf Cohen*	*Ship's Captain (Norwegian)*
Claude Daumier	*Aircraft Lawyer*
Jacques	*Manager, Berne Aviation*
Etoile Lambert	*Bank Manager*
Jean-Pierre Muraille	*General Lawyer*
Helen Phillips*	*Linguist, Pilot, Purser*
Peter Romaine*	*Linguist, Leader*
Richard & Alice Romaine	*Peter's Parents*

* The "Three Musketeers"

"ALIYAH BET" PERSONNEL

The Dentist	*Zurich, Switzerland*
Shlomo Daniel	*Ship's Chef, Morocco*
Georg Gunnarsen	*Ship's Engineer, Sweden*

CAMP PIETRO, ITALY

Abe	*From Yugoslavia*
Alex	*From Warsaw, Poland*
Dov	*Camp Manager for Aliyah Bet, Group Manager in Alicante, and "No. 1" on the ship*
Heide	*From Mayrhofen, Austria; Arts*
Jacob	*Linguist: Slav and Romance Languages*
Miriam	*From Gdynia, Poland; Linguist*
Max	*From Lodz, Poland*

THE PILOTS

Chief Pilot	*Helen Phillips, Berne*
The Co-Pilot	*James McDonald, Scotland*
The Additional Pilot	*Derek Davey, UK*

SALONIKA, GREECE

Adonis	*Agent for "Naiad"*
Edward Alachouzos	*Owner, "Gamma" Company*
Alex	*Manager, Aristotoles Hotel*
Joseph Christofolous (Levi)	*Shipping Broker*
Dionne	*Joseph's Wife*
John Thessalonikos	*Lawyer*
Victoria	*Secretary to Alex*
Yanis	*Bank Manager*

KAVALA, GREECE

Jack Niarchos	*Owner, "Delta" Company*
Edwina	*His wife*

ALICANTE, SPAIN

Juan Herrera	*Manager, Palas Hotel*

KIBBUTZ MA'BAROT

Louis	*Kibbutz Driver, from Romania*
Yossele (Joseph)	*Kibbutz Secretary/ Administrator, Palestine*
Avram & Leah	*Members, from Switzerland and Belgium*
Jack & Betty	*Members, from Australia*
Prof. Aron & Ruth Weiss	*Members, from Argentina and Romania*
Rabbi Rogosnitzky	*The Traveling Rabbi*

NETANYA

Francois Leclerc, PhD	*Manager, Bank Hapoalim, born in France*

TEL AVIV UNIVERSITY — TAU

Dr. Isaac Katz	*Dean of Students and Emeritus Professor of Central African Languages*

LATRUN – BATTLEFIELD

General Arnie	*Commander, Latrun Area*
Colonel Avram	*His Chief of Staff*
Lieutenant Francois Leclerc	*Company Commander*
Sergeant Moshe (the giant)	*Second-in-Command, Peter's Company*
Lieutenant Peter Romaine	*Company Commander*

UNIVERSITY OF SOUTHERN CALIFORNIA – USC

Sidney David, PhD	*Dean of Students*
William Jones, PhD	*Dean of Language School*
Nancy, MA	*College Lawyer*

CHAPTER I

A Party at the Romaines'

·

THE YEAR WAS 1960 AND THE LOCATION WAS A PENTHOUSE
on the twenty-fourth floor of a condominium building on Wilshire
Boulevard in Los Angeles, California. A large and boisterous party
was being given by the owners, Peter Romaine and his wife, to celebrate her having recently received a PhD, which she had started
twenty years previously.

Peter was born in Berne, Switzerland in 1920, when his father,
Richard, was stationed there as the British Ambassador to Switzerland. After three years as Ambassador, Richard decided to take re-
tirement from the British Foreign Service and settle permanently in
Switzerland. Independently wealthy, and with his diplomatic background, he had not found it difficult to obtain permits from the Swiss
Federal and Cantonal authorities to live there as a foreign national
and apply for Swiss nationality.

His mother, Alice, was born in 1895 in Hampstead, in northwest
London. Her father had been a cartoon editor of a leading English
magazine and her mother, a surgical nurse. Alice had always wanted
to become a doctor, but in her all-girls' high school, her teachers
explained to her how difficult it was for a girl to enter medicine.
However, she was outstanding in sciences, mathematics, and Latin
and at eighteen, won a very rare scholarship to the University of St.
Albans, a few miles north of London. At the age of twenty-three, Alice became a doctor. In 1919, after a year as an intern, she met Richard Romaine, nineteen years her senior, an ambassador and a very
handsome man. They fell madly in love and married three months
later. Peter was born the following year. Alice never formally prac-
ticed medicine, but in the Swiss village near where they lived, she

was always ready to help out the local doctors who appreciated her medical knowledge.

Richard's paternal forebears had arrived in England in 1066 with the invading army of William of Normandy and had been given land by the king. The descendants continued to live as lords of the manor of Muddyford, a village in Wiltshire, for almost nine hundred years.

However, with the rise of income tax rates in the twentieth century, it became increasingly difficult for the family to maintain its substantial standard of living from the rental income received from the tenant farmers who worked the manor. In 1925, all the land was sold, including the lordship of the manor, to a nouveau riche who was hell-bent on becoming a "Lord of the Manor."

The proceeds were placed in a trust in secure international investments, which gave the family a substantial and virtually tax-free income. The management of those investments was placed in the hands of a board of trustees from four banks. Richard's father, who had set up this arrangement, told his son that the four representatives, unanimously, had to approve all investment decisions. In this way the family fortune would remain in good hands for a long time to come. To encourage the trustees to invest wisely, Richard paid them a percentage of the capital value of the trust at each year end, certified by the external Swiss auditors.

Peter grew up in Switzerland, and until the outbreak of the Second World War, had enjoyed vacations throughout Europe at least once a year. He had a great aptitude for languages. He was fluent in the Swiss languages of French, German, Swiss-German, and Italian, as well as Romansh, a Swiss dialect spoken in East Switzerland. It was clear he was destined to become a linguist. By the time he started work on his PhD in linguistics, he had mastered Spanish ("because it was easy") and Catalan ("because it was a challenge") and was close to having mastered all the nine languages of the Romance group, only needing Portuguese, Ladin, Priulian, and Romanian to complete the whole sub-group of the Italic branch of Romance languages. He had put those four into the back of his mind "to be studied when I've time."

CHAPTER II

The Hospital

IN SEPTEMBER OF 1945, PETER WENT TO VISIT HIS UNIVER-
sity friend, Raoul, in Ward 10 of the Berne City Hospital. Raoul was
a patient there, recovering from an operation for the removal of his
appendix. While they were chatting, Peter learned that an entire
ward in the hospital was occupied by a group of survivors from German concentration camps.

As the Allied armies marched through Europe, they opened the
camps and found the survivors suffering from a host of maladies,
from severe malnutrition to typhus, work-related injuries, and worse.

Many survivors were too ill and frail to make their way back to
their former homes and the Swiss government made an extraordinary, magnanimous gesture in undertaking to accept a number of
the most ill survivors and care for them until their recovery.

Peter was quite ignorant of much of what happened during the
war and after hearing Raoul's descriptions of the Holocaust, he resolved to go and visit these people.

He was sure that with his knowledge of European languages, he
would be able to communicate with them. He made his way to Ward
35 and went in.

He found a large and fully occupied room holding about fifty men.
About half of them were in bed and the rest were seated, in pajamas
and bathrobes, on chairs at the far end of the room. Peter walked
down the ward to the group who, seeing a stranger approaching,
immediately stopped talking and awaited with what seemed to him
trepidation or even hostility. He decided to speak to them in English.

"Good morning, gentlemen. My name's Peter Romaine," he began.
"I'm English and I live here in Berne. I was visiting a friend who is a
patient in this hospital. He told me a little about you and as I'm not

familiar with your situation, I decided to come and meet you. I'm a language student here in Berne and can speak a number of European languages. I hope you won't regard me as anyone official and will think of me as a friend. What do you think?"

The group exchanged looks and it was clear that some of them had not understood him. Suddenly, one of the group began translating his remarks into Yiddish, their common language, which Peter partially understood because of his knowledge of German and Schwyzer Tütsch (Swiss-German). The group discussed what he had said in a babble of words and languages, among which he was able to distinguish German, Slavic, Hungarian, and Polish. After the cacophony of voices died down, one of the group spoke to him in quite good English, saying, "Why are you here, Peter? Who do you represent?"

Peter had been eying the group, trying to decide their ages. It seemed they were in their late twenties or early thirties but it was hard to tell; they were all thin, even cadaverous-looking. He understood from the way they were staring at him that some were suspicious of his approach, distrustful of his motives.

Peter replied, this time in German, saying, "Perhaps if I speak German, more of you will understand me. I want you to understand, as I said before, that I didn't know of your existence here in the hospital until this morning, when my friend in Ward 10 told me about you. I'm just a student in the University here and I want to meet you as a friend, to learn your status and to see if there is anything I can do to help you."

It seemed that most of the group understood German, but one person translated his words into Slavic.

Another spoke to him in German. "My name is Max, and I'm from Poland. How old are you and if you are English, why are you studying in Berne, of all places?"

Peter replied, "I'm twenty-five. How old are you and the others in this group? As for studying in Berne, my father is a retired English diplomat. He decided to move here and I've lived here since I was born."

"I'm twenty-seven," Max responded. "I was born in Lodz, Poland. The others in this ward, including those in bed, are between seventeen and twenty-nine. Many of us look older than our age, but that's because of the wretched existence we've had for the last few years. And if some of us seem reluctant to talk to you, it's because we've had bad experiences with a number of Swiss officials since we were liberated from the concentration camps."

"I would have thought you would be very happy to be in hospital here in Switzerland, relatively safe, after your terrible experiences. What sort of experiences have you had to make you feel so uncomfortable with a well-meaning and neutral stranger such as myself?"

"It so happens," Max said, "that we are sitting here together today to discuss a letter that most of us received yesterday from the Swiss government; once you read it, you'll understand why we're so wary of a strange Swiss resident who suddenly shows up here.

"But first," Max continued, "I want to tell you why I'm here. I was captured by the Germans when I was twenty-four and was in the Buchenwald Concentration Camp for three years. I think it was miraculous that I survived so long and I believe I was very near to death when I was liberated. When the British Army liberated us, I was examined by their doctors and found to have a heart problem as well as problems with my lungs. That qualified me to be brought here to Berne. Believe it or not, this is the first time in five years that I had slept in a bed with sheets. Two years prior to my capture by the Nazis, I had been living in the mountains and fighting the Germans with a partisan group. Now, let me show you the letter we all received." Max produced the letter.

Peter read the letter. It was on Swiss government stationery, dated two days earlier:

Dear Mr. Steward,

As you know, you are a temporary guest of the Swiss Government and we wish to point out the following matters to you. As a result of the kindness and humanity of the Swiss Government, you were allowed to enter into our country for hospitalization and healing from the illnesses from which you were presumably suffering at that time. This was at no cost to you; the cost for your hospitalization is being borne by the citizens of this country.

The purpose of this letter is to inform you that at the end of your treatment, you will not be allowed to remain in Switzerland for any reason whatsoever.

We expect you to show your gratitude to the Swiss Government for taking you in, penniless and ill, by leaving Switzerland as soon as our doctors pronounce you cured of your ailments.

We will provide you with transportation to any frontier town of your choosing, at no cost to you. We will also provide to you, at no cost to you, if you request it, a Nansen Passport, which you will be given as you pass out of Swiss territory at the border. This passport will enable you to travel freely across borders, as its issue is authorized by the League of Nations.

We will also present you with a set of clothing in which to travel, and will give you a travel grant of 350 Swiss Francs to be handed to you as you pass from Swiss territory.

You will be required to sign receipts for everything. Also, you will sign an indemnity to the Swiss Government in which you will certify that in consideration for all that the Swiss Government has done for you, you will hold harmless such Government against all claims by you or by any person on your behalf, of any nature, respecting maintenance, medical attention, and support from the time and date of your entry into this country until the time and date of your exit herefrom.

Please sign and date, within seven business days of the date of this letter, the attached carbon copy, to indicate that you have received it. Your signature must be appended in the presence of two adult witnesses of Swiss nationality, who will also sign and give their Swiss Identification Numbers at that time.

Yours truly,

Peter was silent, thinking over what he had just read, considering the facts and trying to visualize what the effect must have been on these young, sick people.

Max interrupted Peter's thoughts, saying, "What you have to understand is that most of us are seriously ill and, although we've already been here between two and four months, we are really not in any condition to deal with these authoritative demands from the Swiss government. You see, we're in a sort of segregated island, isolated, totally disconnected from our homes and loved ones. We don't know if our parents, siblings, or any of our families are even alive. When we leave here, what is to become of us? Where are we to go? Do our homes exist? We're men from about twenty different countries. Do these countries want us back? You see, we're all Jews here, and we were in concentration camps simply because we're Jews. Some of us actually saw our parents and other family members killed, before our own eyes. To sum up for all of us, what is going to be our future?

"Don't misunderstand us. We genuinely appreciate what the Swiss government is doing for us, and our fearful reaction to the letter we received has not in any way diminished that esteem. But we just can't face such ultimata right now. We need more time."

Peter thought for a moment. "Please ask your friends here if they will allow me to help," he requested.

Max turned to the others and asked the question. Again, the babble of languages broke out for a few minutes. When it subsided, he said to Peter, "They want to know what you think you can do to help us and how you will go about doing it."

Peter replied, "There are a lot of things I can try to do. I'll try to get that seven-day requirement extended to thirty days or more. I'll attempt to contact the embassies of the countries from which you originated to see which may help you return to your homes. I'll approach the International Red Cross to see if there is any way that contact can be made with your surviving families, wherever they may be."

Max spoke to the others, and then turned back to Peter. "They want to accept your offer, but ask two questions: First, they want to know if you're Jewish, and secondly, if you're not, then why are you, a Gentile, willing to get involved in our very difficult situation?"

Peter responded, saying, "No, I'm not Jewish, but I consider myself a humanitarian and if I can help a group of my contemporaries in these very difficult circumstances, then I should. By the way, I hope my father's old diplomatic connections may be helpful in my tasks. Incidentally, I've been in the scout movement for fifteen years and part of our code is 'to help other people at all times.' It would seem that our code was tailor-made for your situation."

Max translated and the doubts of many turned into smiles and clapping. "I think you can see the response, Peter," Max said.

Peter's mind started to plan his next move. "Very well. What I want you to arrange is the following: Please prepare lists for each one of your people, giving their full names, date of birth, city of birth and country, names of both parents, names of any siblings, date when first taken to a concentration camp, date liberated, and date brought to Switzerland. I will come here tomorrow about this time to collect the papers. They can be written in English, French, German, Spanish or Italian.

"Everybody has to be interviewed. And remember that I'm on your side. Also, please make me a exact copy of that Swiss government letter. All that information is going to be necessary if I'm to be able to help you all."

CHAPTER III

The Romaine Family

UPON RETURNING HOME, PETER WENT STRAIGHT TO HIS FATHER's study. He knocked and went in. Richard was relaxing in his big armchair, reading a book.

"Hello, my boy," said Richard, "and how was college today?"

"College was fine, Father, but after class I went to visit my friend Raoul, who's in the hospital, having had his appendix out."

"And how is he getting on?" asked Richard.

"He's doing well," replied Peter, "but he told me of a most astonishing matter." He then proceeded to tell his father the startling information he had received from Raoul and what had transpired later, when he met with the survivors.

Naively, he asked his father, "How on earth did these huge concentration and extermination camps come to exist all over Europe and yet I never heard of them? I felt like an uninformed fool listening to Raoul talk about them. When I was with those young men in the hospital ward, I had to pretend that I had some knowledge of what they had just lived through."

"Well, Peter," his father said sheepishly, "perhaps your mother and I have been overly protective of you. We wanted you to grow up in this beautiful and neutral country, as far removed as possible from the war, the killing, and the ugliness of the outside world. I've never discussed this with you and I'm just realizing that I've been terribly negligent in not having sat down with you years ago to tell you of my ideas and philosophy, with which your mother has come to agree. I now understand that I've erred in that respect.

"As you know, I was in the British Foreign Service from 1898 to 1922, when I retired and we decided to live here in Switzerland. However, you may not know I was also a volunteer in the Reserve

Territorial Army from when I was in college in Oxford. Because of that, I served in the South African War, which we called the Boer War, from 1899 to 1902. That was mainly a guerilla war between the South African Republic and the British Empire and was caused by the Boers refusing to give civic rights to the British immigrants in the gold and diamond fields. Anyway, it was a miserable war between two hitherto civilized European groups who killed and slaughtered each other – men, women and children. I was nauseated and appalled by the terrible and needless loss of life by both parties. Surely they should have been capable of negotiating in a civilized way. I couldn't do anything about it – I was a junior officer in the infantry. I was glad to do my duty, survive, and come home to get on with my life in peace.

"But in 1914, I was called up again and served four years in the trenches in France, the ruddy, muddy, bloody, bungled war on the Western Front. There, I saw wholesale slaughter of an unbelievable magnitude. I was in the Battle of the Somme in 1916. In that battle, the British had 420,000 casualties – apparently 200,000 before breakfast on one day alone! The Germans had 500,000 casualties and the French 200,000. The battle of Verdun the same year produced 340,000 German and 360,000 French casualties. So in one year, 1916, 1,820,000 men were casualties: 840,000 German, 560,000 French and 420,000 British. What a terrible waste of young men – it's always the young men sent into battle by the grey-heads. As a result of my own personal experiences, I became totally anti-war. I left the army in 1918 as a decorated colonel and went back to the Foreign Office for the next four years until 1922 when, at the age of forty-six, I resigned. Your dear mother and I resolved to stay and settle down in this beautiful country, to play golf, bridge, bring up our son and heir, and just rusticate and enjoy the rest of our lives together, however selfish you may think us for doing that. I was fortunate in having the personal means to live comfortably here and, as much as we could, to leave the rest of the world out there.

"As far as possible, I've paid minimal attention to the paroxysms taking place in Europe, Africa, the Pacific, and the Far East. You might ask, 'What about duty to the Old Country?' I felt, and still do, that I had adequately paid my dues to the Old Country by fighting in two wars, being wounded three times in battle and serving in the Foreign Office for twenty-four years.

"For better or worse, we tried to establish a small safe harbor here and a home in which you could grow up and mature. We knew that, in due course, you would make up your own mind up as to what you want to do with your life.

"However, from what you have told me today, I see that the ugly life out there has broken into your own sheltered world with a thundering vengeance. I must tell you that I'm more than delighted to see that you realize you can make a big difference in the lives of all those unfortunate young men. There is obviously a great deal of work for you to undertake in order for you to keep the promise you made them, and if you think I can help you in any way, you only have to ask. Now go and tell your mother what's going on."

Father and son silently shook each other's hands, in a very understated and British way, cementing a new relationship between them. Peter understood how hard it must have been for his father to open up to him on so many levels. At the same time, Peter learned a great deal about his father's life and philosophy, which, until then, had been a mystery hidden from him.

Peter sought out his mother, known in the village where they lived as "Madame La Medicine," and told her the whole extraordinary tale of his sudden exposure to the outside world of Nazism, concentration camps, and ailing survivors. When he repeated how he had selflessly volunteered to help these survivors, his mother's eyes filled with tears of joy and she gently held him to her and kissed him. She told him that she, too, wanted to help him in any way she could.

Peter realized he wasn't going to be alone in handling the formidable task he had undertaken. They constituted a trio of expert, motivated, and vigorous partners in this endeavor.

Alice told him that in medical school at St. Albans, she had been something of a curiosity there to the instructors. They had difficulty in taking her seriously. As a result, she was frequently given the tedious and often daunting task of organizing and writing up all the data. She quickly outlined for Peter how to go about gathering the data he needed. The top of the graph (the x-axis) was to be the ten items of information. Down the left margin (the y-axis) would be the names of the boys. There would be a new sheet for each country of origin. "Prepare the twenty or so sheets with the x-headings," she advised, "then sort the incoming data into countries. Use a pair of scissors to cut the data sheets into countries so that you have twenty piles. Place each country in a folder. Then fill each folder with the data for that country."

He jumped up from his chair, put his arms around her waist and swung her around the room before planting a big affectionate kiss on her cheeks and calling out, "What a clever mother I've got!"

He left the house and went to a local stationery shop in the village, where he bought all the paper supplies he would need including scissors, glue, a half-dozen pencils, erasers, lined paper, paper clips of various sorts, and folders for each country. He went home and started to prepare his country sheets.

When Peter went to bed, he couldn't sleep; he was thinking of how to utilize his father's expertise and connections in Switzerland and elsewhere.

Next day, as arranged, Peter returned to the ward. He was met by a beaming Max who declared, "Well, Mr. Peter, we've done it all. I got four others to help me. We obtained paper and pencils from one of the nurses and we finished it by midnight, filling in all the information of the fifty-two men from our eighteen countries."

The word *men* hit Peter like a thunderbolt. "Why didn't I ask Max about women yesterday?" he asked himself.

"Max," he said. "Were there no girls or women brought to the hospital after you men came in?"

Max replied, "As a matter of fact, I did hear from a staff nurse something about a couple of girls brought in who are somewhere in the hospital. I don't know if it's true."

"Okay," said Peter. "I'll check on that later."

Max placed a large pile of loose papers in Peter's hands, which he quickly scanned. At first glance, he could see that for each person, there was about a half page of information in a number of different languages, including a couple in a language he didn't know. Peter showed them to Max, who smiled and said, "that's Hungarian, and it's translated on the following pages."

Peter thanked the group in German and promised to keep in touch with them and to report any progress.

He went to the hospital office and inquired about the female survivors. He was told the women were in a private ward; however, unless he was a relative, he could not visit them. Peter immediately went to a public phone box and called his mother. He told her his problem regarding the women. He asked if she would come to the hospital and as a doctor, take him to meet them.

She agreed at once, and within an hour, arrived at the hospital and met with Peter. He took her to the hospital office and once she had identified herself as a doctor, she was told to go to Ward 47. Unlike the men's ward, this was really just a small room, occupied by two women. Peter and his mother entered. Alice spoke to the women in English, but there was no response. When Peter spoke to them in German, they both understood at once.

Peter explained why he and his mother had come to their ward. Both women were very pale, undernourished, disheveled, and probably younger than they looked. He told them what he had learned from his meeting with the men and how he was hoping to help them. They both brightened up and started to respond. Miriam was from Gdynia, in Poland, and Heide was from Mayrhofen, in Austria. With their permission, Alice looked at their medical charts. She asked them how long had they been in the hospital and they told her five weeks. They had been in Ravensbrueck Concentration Camp near Fuerstenberg, in Germany, which was a camp for women, liberated by the Red Army on April 30, 1945. The key positions were held by men, but the S.S. Nazi staff was mostly female and they were preeminent in their cruel treatment of the inmates. The camp had become, with the installation of a gas chamber in the previous year, an extermination camp.

When the Soviet Army liberated the camp, there were only about 3,000 very ill and dying prisoners remaining. Miriam and Heide had been there for four years and had probably survived due to the fact that they had worked as maids in the home of the camp commandant and had occasionally been able to share a little food stolen from the kitchen. They had not suffered any sexual abuse, since the camp commandant was gay, in spite of his being an untergruppenfuhrer in the Schutzstaffel (the S.S.), equivalent to a full colonel in the regular army. One of the camp drivers was his lover. The commandant had been wounded while fighting on the eastern front against Russia. He had been given this post as a reward for his efforts.

In pre-war Poland, Miriam explained, Jews generally were forbidden to enter university. Although she was Jewish, Miriam had been able to enter Warsaw University by using the identity papers of her best friend, who had died of leukemia. She graduated with an MA in ethnography. She had even managed to retain her graduation certificate, in her friend's name, by having it enclosed in a waterproof, oiled, silk bag stuck to her back, in case she was searched. She showed it to Alice and told her that she was twenty-five years old. Alice's eyes filled with tears at seeing it. Miriam had the unusual and attractive combination of blue eyes and brown hair.

Heide had an untamed head of blond hair and startling turquoise-colored eyes. She had grown up on her father's farm in Mayrhofen, near Innsbruck, Austria. He was a social-democrat and vehemently anti-Nazi, although they lived in a very right-wing part of the country. Even after the war started, he could not keep from airing his political opinions. Inevitably, he was reported to the police. In 1941 his home was raided by the S.A. (Sturm Abteilung – Nazi Brownshirts), who shot him in front of Heide and her mother. They were both taken away, separated, and sent to different concentration camps. She had no knowledge of her mother's subsequent fate. Heide was nineteen, but looked a lot older.

The two girls first met in the commandant's house in Ravensbrueck, where they both had the good fortune to become housemaids. They had come from different countries with different languages, and from different worlds, but they came to trust each other, first for mutual survival, and then as close friends.

Having told the girls about his proposed actions for the fifty-two young men in Ward 35, and seeing they had received the same letter from the Swiss government, Peter asked if they would like him to try and help them as well, and if they would like to have a visit from one of the boys. They readily agreed, anxious to meet someone who had similar experiences as their own. Peter took the same personal information from the girls as he had received from the boys and then, promising to be in touch, he and his mother left.

They went back to Ward 35, where Peter introduced his mother. Peter asked Max if he would like to visit the girls and he immediately said yes, but didn't see how he could leave the ward. They were virtual prisoners and forbidden to leave except to go for treatment or testing, and then only if accompanied by a hospital employee. Nor did they have any clothing except their hospital pajamas and bathrobes. But Peter was undaunted and told Max he would figure something out.

On the way back from the hospital, Alice told Peter that the girls' charts showed severe malnutrition and that even with their medications, it would take at least three months before they could be discharged.

"Mother," Peter said, "do you think you could let me have a surgical gown so that I might take Max to visit the girls in the guise of a hospital employee?"

"Are you sure that's wise?" his mother asked. "If you're discovered, Max will immediately be thrown out of Switzerland, and you'll be denied any access to your friends."

"I'll discuss it with Max," Peter said, "and see if he's willing to take the risk. It's important that the girls feel they're not alone in the hospital. If he's willing to take the risk, I will too."

After they arrived home, Peter and Alice told Richard all that they had found out. Peter left his parents and reviewed the information that Max and his helpers had obtained. By midnight, with a short break for dinner, he had done as much as he could, and fell into bed.

He had to go to a class the next morning, and afterward, he went directly to Ward 35. He had brought the papers with him to show Max, who had become his assistant and liaison with the boys. There were eight boys who had given incomplete information, so Max and Peter had a meeting with each to fill in the omissions.

The boys were quite impressed with the work that Peter had done in summarizing the data that he had received from his fifty-four "clients" from eighteen countries. One of the boys said to him in heavily-accented English, "Well, Mr. Peter, you seem to be doing a great clerical task – now let's see you make use of it." Peter understood his impatience.

On his return home, he wrote up his missing information and completed his country summaries.

Germany	4	Austria	2*
France	3	Greece	1
Holland	4	Hungary	3
Belgium	2	Bulgaria	2
Poland	11*	Italy	1
Lithuania	4	Yugoslavia	5
Latvia	2	Czechoslovakia	3
Estonia	1	Russia	3
Romania	2	Luxembourg	1

Total Survivors: 54
Total Countries: 18

*One female included from each of these countries.

Next, Peter sat with the Berne telephone directories and copied down the phone numbers of all the embassies and consuls general of the eighteen countries. He also wrote down the phone number of the International Red Cross and the British Embassy.

Then he wrote down the tasks for his triumvirate, and, after meeting with his parents, it was decided to break up the tasks as follows:

1. Richard would contact the Swiss government to try to extend the seven-day requirement for response to the government letter.

2. The embassies were divided between the three of them:

Richard	Alice	Peter
Germany* (cities)	Holland	Romania
France	Lithuania	Austria
Poland	Latvia	Bulgaria
Belgium	Estonia	Yugoslavia
Hungary	Greece	Russia
Italy	Luxembourg	
Czechoslovakia		

* It was decided that as there was no functioning German central
government, to call the mayors of those cities from which the
four boys came.

3. Richard would contact the British Embassy to see if any of the
people would be permitted to emigrate to Palestine.

4. Alice would contact the International Red Cross.

There were three telephone lines in their house. Both Richard
and Alice spoke French reasonably well and if another language was
required, they would call on Peter to help out, but generally, they
found English and French were sufficient to get the job done.

A half-hour after they started, there were excited shouts from
Richard. He told Alice and Peter that at the Ministry from which
the letters had been sent, there was a very senior man whom Richard knew well from his diplomatic days. The fellow listened to Richard's request and, although it wasn't in his power to help directly, he
promised to go to the Deputy Minister in order to push Richard's request for a time extension to be handled swiftly and sympathetically.
He promised to get back to Richard in two to three days.

Soon after, Alice told the men that she had spoken to the International Red Cross (the IRC) and also had good news. She learned that
it had just established an all-Europe system of listing people who
were trying to locate family and friends. This system was already in
place in every DP (Displaced Persons) camp. In order to get everyone into the system, Alice volunteered to go to the IRC headquarters
with all the information. The IRC would then duplicate it and send
it to each of their notice boards all over Europe. She made arrangements to go to Geneva the next day.

Richard spoke to the British Ambassador, a man named John Sutcliffe. He had served under Richard when Richard had been Head of
Chancery in the British Embassy in Mexico City in 1919. Since Sut-

cliffe had been posted to Berne, they had met socially on occasion, and he responded to Richard's call very cordially.

"What can I do for you, Richard?" he asked.

"I'd like to know the current view of His Majesty's Government to the possible requests of a number of Jewish refugees from Hitler's concentration camps, presently in a Swiss hospital, seeking permission to emigrate to Palestine. I seem to remember that back in 1917, Lord Balfour told the Jewish community that HMG looked favorably on Palestine as a future national home for the Jews. However," he continued, feigning ignorance, "since I'm out of touch with current policy on that subject, I'd be obliged for your opinion on the matter."

Sutcliffe was silent for a moment, then said, "You're right on the Balfour letter, but in this government, things have changed. I've no idea why you are concerned with such a matter, old man, but let me tell you that that subject is a very hot potato.

"Suffice it to say that there is absolutely no way for such applications to be considered. In fact, these days, the navy is very much involved in *preventing* ships from bringing potential illegal immigrants from Europe to Palestine. When caught, the illegals are off-loaded and transferred to detention camps in Cyprus, Palestine, or Mauritius, to await better days or some political change. At the present time, Ernest Bevin, the Foreign Secretary and my boss, is absolutely adamant – 'no more Jews may enter Palestine.' So, I'm sorry, my friend, it's no go. I look forward to seeing you in the club one of these days. Goodbye, Richard."

Despite the rejection from the Foreign Office, over the course of the next three days the Romaines managed to complete their assignments. The responses of the cities of their clients to the basic question, "Will you welcome back the Jewish citizens of your country and survivors of Hitler's camps?" were as follows:

Country	Yes	# of People	Cannot Say	# of People Affected
Germany (4 cities)	✗	4		
France	✗	3		
Poland			✗	11
Belgium	✗	2		
Hungary			✗	3

Country	Yes	# of People	Cannot Say	# of People Affected
Italy	✗	1		
Czechoslovakia	✗	3		
Holland	✗	4		
Lithuania			✗	4
Latvia			✗	2
Estonia			✗	1
Greece	✗	1		
Luxembourg	✗	1		
Romania	✗	2		
Austria			✗	2
Bulgaria			✗	2
Yugoslavia	✗	5		
Russia	✗	3		
Totals:	**11**	**29**	**7**	**25**

SUMMARY OF "WELCOMES"

11 countries would welcome 29 persons

7 countries "cannot say" about 25 persons

TOTAL: 18 countries 54 persons

Richard stressed the fact that, while no one said "no," in his opinion, the "cannot say" countries were negatives. He also added that he wasn't surprised at the composition of the list.

Just then, Richard's phone rang. It was his contact in the ministry, who gave him the good news that the response to the matter of the government letter was positive. The government was going to send out a second letter to each person to tell them that the seven days' requirement was extended to thirty days. The three Romaines were delighted to hear this.

Alice traveled to Geneva at once and deposited the personal information of the fifty-four survivors with the IRC. She was promised that within a few days the information would be dispatched all over Europe.

The next morning Alice gave Peter a hospital gown saying, "Please make sure to reiterate to Max that what you propose is extremely dangerous for him. Your consequence will be nothing compared to his."

"Very well, Mother," Peter replied, "I assure you that I understand. I'm doing this for Max. I think both he and the girls will be very interested in making contact with others who have been through the same hell as them. And I promise to get his agreement that he understands the danger before he leaves the ward."

"Thank you, Peter," she said. "You know, I've been thinking of another matter. What if your father writes a letter to that ministry that sent out the letter, asking if the requirements expressed in the letter could perhaps be ameliorated somewhat. Maybe those boys and girls could be allowed to stay in the country to study in an approved institution for a profession, so that they could support themselves after they leave Switzerland?"

"That's absolutely a wonderful idea, Mother," Peter said. "But it will have to pass a lot of barriers in the government. I'm especially concerned with the financial obstacle. It will have to be approved by the Swiss Treasury, since it needs to be budgeted for. Anyway, talk it over with Father and see what he thinks. Now I'm off to the hospital to see the group and tell them what we've achieved so far and what we're up to. And, of course, I'm going to talk very seriously to Max and see where that takes me. See you later, Mother."

CHAPTER IV

Peter Reports to the Survivors

PETER LEFT HOME AND RODE HIS MOTORCYCLE TO THE HOS-pital, making his way to Ward 35. He entered and all eyes imme-diately swiveled in his direction. Max jumped up from his chair to greet Peter, shaking his hand and leading him to a chair.

"Good morning, Peter, we all hope you are well and of course we are impatient to hear whatever you have to tell us. We have missed your visits, but we know you have your own life outside here and are grateful that you make time to see us."

"Not at all," said Peter. "We're grateful for the opportunity. My parents and I have been working on your affairs for the last three days and I've a lot of things to tell you.

"First of all, you are all going to get another letter from the govern-ment to tell you that the seven days is extended to thirty days."

At that, the boys smiled and exchanged glances with one another, as if to say, *This Peter is really moving the government.* "That's very good, Peter," Max said, "and will take a bit of the pressure off us. Thank you. What's next?"

"We have contacted the embassies or consulates general of all your eighteen countries and asked them if they would welcome back Jew-ish citizens of their country and survivors of Hitler's camps and help rehabilitate them. The responses were as follows: The eleven coun-tries that said 'yes' were Germany – which includes your four cities – France, Belgium, Italy, Holland, Czechoslovakia, Greece, Luxem-bourg, Romania, Yugoslavia, and Russia.

"No countries refused outright, but the following seven countries responded that 'they cannot say': Poland, Hungary, Lithuania, Lat-via, Estonia, Austria, and Bulgaria.

"My father thinks that 'cannot say' is equal to a 'no.'

"I've the list here and I made five copies and will leave them with you.

"We called the British Embassy to ask about Palestine. The answer was a strong 'NO!' We also learned that other liberated survivors have been trying to cross the Mediterranean Sea to get to Palestine. Those intercepted by the British Navy have been taken prisoner to the islands of Cyprus and Mauritius or interned in Palestine in detention camps, which are guarded by those same British soldiers who freed many of you from the concentration camps. What a strange world we live in.

"Now, for some good news. We contacted the International Red Cross and learned that they have just been helping to set up a kind of notice board in each concentration camp and DP camp, where information can be put up to help people make contact with each other. Yesterday, my mother traveled to Geneva to the International Red Cross Headquarters and handed them all the information we received about each of you. They are sending it out to all the notice boards. Let's hope you may be contacted by your loved ones."

One of the boys called out, "Peter, what's a DP camp?"

Peter replied, "The allies opened camps for liberated survivors who cannot or will not for any reasons go back to their countries and homes. They are called *Displaced Persons* camps. People can stay there temporarily until they decide to go elsewhere. There are no wire fences and no gates. They can come and go as they please. They have food, beds, blankets, toilets, and showers, provided mainly by the American and British Armies."

Peter then turned to Max, "Do you still want to visit the two girls in Ward 47?"

"Yes, Peter, very much," Max replied, "especially since you said one of them is from Poland, like me."

Peter warned Max about the very real dangers his mother had spoken about. Without hesitation, Max asserted that he was ready to take the risk. "Peter, I took much greater risks," he reminded his friend, "when I was in the mountains night and day, fighting the Germans."

"Very well, then." Peter replied. "My mother gave me a hospital gown for me to wear when we leave this ward." He opened the parcel and put on the gown.

Peter took Max's arm as though he was assisting him and they made their way to Ward 47.

He knocked and they went in. Peter said, in German, "Good

morning, ladies. I want you to meet my friend Max, who is from Lodz, Poland. And Max, please meet Miriam, who is from Gdynia and Heide, who is from Mayrhofen in Austria. They were both in Ravensbrueck. I know you want to talk to them, but first I want to give them the same report as I gave the boys."

The two girls listened quietly as Peter repeated the latest information he had accumulated. Then Peter said, "I know you will need time to think about everything and I will continue to come to the hospital to give you updates. But for now, talk to your other visitor, who is taking a very big risk by coming here."

Max first said "Hello" in Polish to Miriam, then "Hello" in German to Heide, and both girls responded in their own languages. After Miriam and Max had conversed in Polish for a few minutes, Miriam told Max that she understood German pretty well and suggested that the four of them should speak in German so that Heide shouldn't feel left out. Everyone agreed.

Peter observed that Miriam had brightened up a lot and the excitement had brought an attractive flush to her previously pale cheeks. She and Peter exchanged information about their educational backgrounds and were astonished to find that they both were involved in similar subjects. Miriam had been studying Linguistic Anthropology, the relationship between language and culture, based on the study of the Slavic branch of the Indo-European language family.

Peter, in addition to his knowledge of Romance languages, was particularly interested in their phonological topology, the sharing of certain predominant features of grammatical structure in connection with the science of their vocal sounds.

Max and Heide also shared common interests. Heide had grown up on a farm, while Max had been studying Agricultural Economics and Management Science at the Lodz School of Husbandry (also known as agronomics) before the war, using a non-Jewish name and forged papers to get into the school.

Heide had done all the administration and accounting for her father's farm, which grew field crops and had a large flock of sheep. She knew a great deal about the management of a farm as well.

Max found Heide articulate and her knowledge went far beyond what he thought a girl growing up on a farm might possess. She was an amateur painter, using oils and water-colors, very well-read, and loved classical music. She would go to Jenbach or Innsbruck for concerts.

Suddenly, realizing that Max might be missed during the nurses' rounds, Peter grabbed Max and started their nurse/patient act, to immediately return to Ward 35. They yelled a hurried goodbye and promised to return soon.

A moment after they got back to the ward, Peter took off his hospital gown as the evening shift of nurses arrived to give the boys their medications. Peter realized that he had cut their return very fine. If they were ever to repeat this escapade, he had to make sure he knew the routines of the nurses in Ward 35. He asked Max to write down the schedules of all those who came into the ward, including doctors, nurses, cleaning personnel, and those who served the meals.

Peter remained in the ward until the nurses left. One of the patients then came over to where Peter was sitting and brought up a chair next to him.

"Hello, Peter, my name's Alex and I'm from Poland." he said, speaking in fluent German. "We are all very grateful to you and your parents for what you are doing for us, a bunch of strangers with whom you have no connection. You give us great honor."

"I'm pleased to meet you, Alex, and I'm happy to be able to help everyone after what you've already suffered," replied Peter.

"Peter, when I was growing up, I belonged to a Zionist youth organization. Do you know what that is?" asked Alex.

"No, sorry, I don't," said Peter.

"Well, it's an international organization for Jewish youth who learn about and identify with Palestine. They are united by their desire to emigrate to the Holy Land. Now, what you told us about the British Navy stopping boats with illegal immigrants made me think.

"There must be a large number of displaced survivors like us who are either going to get through that blockade and land in Palestine or who will end up in a camp in Cyprus. As for me, I really can't get away quickly enough from this accursed continent where, even before the murderous Hitler and the Nazis, my people suffered anti-Semitism for hundreds of years.

"Peter," he continued, "Perhaps I've an old soul, but I feel the scars of the tortures that my people have suffered for centuries in my being. And I'm not the only one. A lot of the boys in this room have been thinking these things."

"I understand, Alex," Peter said. "But tell me what's on your mind. I'm just here to help you in any way I can."

Hesitantly, Alex said, "I would like you to place me in contact with somebody Jewish who can help me leave Switzerland for Palestine."

Peter thought for a moment. Then, a smile lit up his face and he said, "Yes, I think I know someone who might help you. But I'll need some time to meet with him and discuss such an operation."

"Fine. Thank you so much, Peter." Alex left Peter and rejoined his friends.

CHAPTER V

Peter and Alice have Differences of Opinion

AS SOON AS PETER ARRIVED HOME, HE MET HIS MOTHER.

"Well, Peter, how did you get on? Did you visit the girls with Max?"

"Mother, let's sit down, I've a lot to tell you."

They made themselves comfortable in their lounge and then Peter gave Alice a blow-by-blow account of his adventures with Max in Ward 47. He also told her what a coincidence it was that Miriam and he were so enamored by Linguistics, although in quite different, but related fields. He expressed his satisfaction that the girls were so animated when they arrived.

"Well, of course," said his mother, "when two young men show up after weeks of only nurses and doctors, I'd expect them to brighten up."

Peter spoke about the session with Alex. Alice listened intently and then said, "Listen, my dear, these are all Jewish boys, so I don't for the life of me know why you are even concerned with their political problem. If you want my opinion, don't get yourself involved in this matter or you may only find yourself in a great deal of trouble. After all, they are plotting to try to break through a legal blockade set up by Britain. Don't forget, Britain is the Mandatory Power over Palestine, as set up by the League of Nations."

"I'm rather surprised to hear you take the legalistic view, Mother," Peter retorted, a wave of anger overtaking him. "All of us are working hard to help these survivors put the horrors of the concentration camps behind them in favor of a new, better future. That's why we called all those embassies and consulates general. Where are they supposed to go? They don't have anywhere to go. The only place that will welcome them is Palestine. If it wasn't for Ernest Bevin, the Foreign Secretary of Britain, and, I believe, a known anti-Semite, they would be traveling, from Europe to Palestine, as we speak. Who are we, Mother, not to help them, even if we are not Jewish; they are human beings, each of them with a soul, alive by some miracle, and, I aver, mother, if we have any humanity in us, that we are bound to try to help them in spite of Bevin's blockade."

Alice was shocked to hear her son speak like this. "I'm very surprised to hear you say these things, Peter. We are not Jewish, we are Gentiles and, honestly, the church is one thing, but breaking the law is quite another."

"Mother, I'm not aware of a law having been passed in England that says homeless survivors of Hitler's concentration camps are not allowed to enter Palestine. What's more, I find it hard to believe that any democratically elected Parliament, such as in England, would pass such a law. Of course, it may be that a misguided minister may assume he has the power to do such a thing, but if he does, it certainly goes against every ethical and moral principle that we have been taught in Christianity, or have you forgotten 'Love thy neighbor'?

"Anyway, Mother, on this matter I've made up my mind! I'm going to help Alex and his friends as much as I possibly can. I feel responsible, as their only contact with the outside world, and as a matter of human empathy, to do the best I can for them.

"I know somebody I can contact who may be able to help get this thing going, and I shall start tomorrow."

They parted, Alice to her husband to tell him what had just transpired, and Peter to his room to consider his next move.

Peter remembered a girl who had been in his class the previous year. Her name, which he recalled with a great effort of will, was Helen Phillips. Although he had spoken to her only occasionally, he remembered that she was very attractive, with thick, wavy hair and a lovely smile. At the same time, she had always seemed very modest, wearing clothing that never left her arms exposed, was never décolleté, and always appeared elegant. She also behaved in a decorous manner, unlike some of the other girls in his class. He thought she might have been of the Jewish faith and was trying to think of her characteristics that made him come to that conclusion. He decided that it was probably a mélange of all those things. Anyway, she was the only person he knew who even might be Jewish.

He went to the phone book and found only one entry in the name of Phillips. He called the number. A female voice answered. He asked if he could speak to Helen Phillips.

37

"Yes, certainly," he was told. "Who may I say is calling?"

"Peter Romaine," he said.

"Just a moment, sir," he heard.

Then, "Hello Peter, what a surprise to hear from you. To what do I owe the honor of receiving a call from the Englishman who won all those prizes for outstanding language acquisitions?"

"Hello, Helen," he answered, "it's nice to hear your voice and I'm a bit surprised that you even remember me. Anyway, there is something that I want to talk to you about, but the phone isn't the right medium. Could we meet for breakfast tomorrow morning?"

"Why, yes, Peter, surely," she said. "But this is such a mystery, I shan't be able to sleep tonight for thinking about it. So what time and where?"

"Can we meet at, say, 8:30 at Cafe Quito? That's pretty centrally located, although I've no idea where you live. And by the way, Helen, who answered the phone? She called me 'sir.'"

"Yes, 8:30 at Cafe Quito is fine, Peter, and it's only a couple of hundred meters from my home. And that was my mother's secretary. She's always so polite to callers. So, au revoir, Peter. See you tomorrow."

The next morning Peter was sitting at a strategically located table at Cafe Quito, as far away as possible from other tables so they could have a very private conversation. Helen arrived promptly and for the first time, Peter wondered why he had never approached her for a date.

"Good morning, Helen. I hope you slept well and that my mysterious phone call last evening didn't keep you up."

"Thank you, Peter, I managed to sleep well, but I admit I'm all agog to hear what this is about."

"Let's order first, then we can get down to business," said Peter.

They ordered breakfast, Peter noticing that she was quite frugal in her selection, which he commented upon. She laughed at that and said, "Don't you know that all girls my age and single are deathly afraid of putting on weight?" They shared a smile.

Then Peter said, "I hope you won't think I'm inquisitive or prying when I begin by asking you a very personal question. Helen, are you Jewish? The rest of what I've to say depends on the answer to that impertinent question, so you must know that I've a very good reason for asking."

"Yes, Peter, I'm Jewish, so please go ahead."

"Well," Peter commenced, "I've an interesting story to tell you."

And so saying, he recounted his experiences with Raoul, Ward 35, Ward 47, Max, and what he and his parents were doing to help them. Then he told her about Alex and his plan.

"So, you see why I asked you to meet me, Helen. You're the only person I know in the great capital city of Berne who might be Jewish."

"Yes, I am Jewish," she repeated. "And of course I know about what happened in the concentration camps. My heart goes out to those poor unfortunates. Please, let me know how I can help."

"First, Helen," Peter responded, "what I'm going to talk about is very confidential. Do you know anyone in a Zionist organization who might be able to clandestinely help to bring these survivors to Palestine?"

Helen couldn't contain a smile. "Well, it so happens that I, myself, am a member of a Zionist youth organization and have been since I was ten years old. I'm well aware that there is an underground movement that seeks to help survivors from Hitler's camps immigrate to Palestine despite the tremendous efforts of the British Army and Navy to keep them out. What the British call 'illegal immigration,' we Jews call '*Aliyah Bet*,' the resurgence of the Jews to their land, as forecast in the Bible, and promulgated by Lord Balfour, when he served as British Foreign Secretary.

"So, yes, Peter Romaine, you did find a Jewish person, and lucky for you, she happens to be well-connected with Zionist organizations. I will speak to someone I know, I'm sure he'll be able to help. In view of the illegality of this matter, we must never discuss Palestine on the telephone, only face to face. You and I can call each other up for breakfast or a cup of coffee here in Cafe Quito. Okay?"

"Absolutely okay" Peter quickly agreed. "Of course we both understand that these boys cannot think of going anywhere at the present time. They have to get well from their sicknesses first.

"I've another thought," Peter added. "How would you like to pay my boys and girls a visit? I know that each and every one of them would love it. We would under no circumstances allow them to think of you as my contact with the Zionist organizations. Only a nice Jewish girl who happens to be a friend of mine and wants to visit them to help cheer them up a bit. As far as Max and Alex are concerned, I shall tell them that any contact with the outside world must go through me."

"Just let me know a day or so ahead and I will come and visit. In the meantime, I'll invite you to breakfast or a coffee when I've any news to tell you. And thank you for our first breakfast together."

When Peter arrived home that afternoon from school, it was to find his father in a most ebullient mood. "Ah, Peter, my boy," he greeted him. "I think your mother's idea is brilliant and I've been racking my brains to think how this thing should be started and developed. I considered calling that same deputy minister to whom our first request went to extend the seven-day ultimatum to thirty days.

"So, I made a phone call and, as luck would have it, I got straight through to him. I explained who I am and, more particularly, who I was and why I had any interest in these fifty-four people. And that's where I put the blame on you, son. I said that you became aware of these people through visiting your sick friend in the hospital. Seeing their condition and learning from them something of what they must have suffered for years in the concentration camps, you volunteered to help them.

"And then you brought us, your mother and father, into the matter to help you. I then explained that these young people needed a chance to make something of their lives, study in French or German a year ... etc., etc., etc. Believe it or not, the Deputy Minister bought it! He thought it was a noble and magnanimous gesture that the Swiss authorities would be bound to support. What he wants me to do now is to write him a letter, setting out the facts and the main points, which he will then have his people carry out. He thought there would be no trouble in getting his treasury to come up with a budget. My son, we have a deal here. Go and tell your boys and girls that the government says that both the seven-day and thirty-day letters are null and void. However, when their studies are over, they must leave, which seems proper."

Peter told his father he had done a great job for the survivors, who would clearly be thrilled at the news. He would go there in the morning and tell them.

Then Richard said, "Your mother has told me of your interest in this fellow Alex's illegal plans. I support your mother's point of view entirely in this matter and I hope to hear absolutely nothing further from you about it."

"Very well, Father," said Peter. "That's okay with me. You'll hear nothing more from me about the matter."

Richard was no fool and he looked intently at Peter. However, he decided not to take the matter any further, feeling that if Peter did pursue it, he didn't want to know about it.

Peter understood his father's point of view and knew his position in the Swiss community was such that he could never acquiesce to allowing his son to possibly run foul of the law. Peter realized that if he was going to help his friends, he would have to do it without his parents' further help in the matter.

The next morning, Peter went to Ward 35.

"Well, boys, things are definitely looking up. We have been able to arrange that upon discharge from the hospital, you will receive another major benefit from the Swiss. You will be permitted to stay on in Switzerland to undertake a course of study at a university or other academic institution in a subject of your choice. All this is so you can have the practical means to earn a living after you leave Switzerland.

"Now, the language of instruction in most cases will be French or German. You will be allowed a preliminary twelve-month course of study in either the French or German language to enable you to benefit from the academic study. All costs – including rent, food, and clothing – will be borne by the Swiss government. If you choose not to take up this offer of an education, you will have to leave Switzerland immediately after your doctors have discharged you. This will have to be decided before you are discharged from the hospital. You will be given brochures and information soon about the language and academic courses. By the way, the words 'academic courses' include not only university degrees, but also various trades and technical courses. Now, what do you think of all that? May I say that it was an idea dreamed up by my mother and carried out by my father with a deputy minister of the government."

Everyone was ecstatic.

Peter made his way to Alex and motioned him to step away from the crowd. They walked away a few paces and then Alex said, "Well, that was a fantastic piece of news you just brought us, Peter. We owe you and your parents a great debt for what your family is doing for us."

"Thank you, Alex, but we all feel that after what you have suffered, we should do what we can to help. Now, concerning the other matter you spoke to me about. I've contacted a Jewish acquaintance who is well-connected with the local Zionist organization.

"But after hearing my news, you may want to rethink your plans. If you want to take up the offer of the educational courses, then presumably you will have to defer any idea of joining this "Second Aliyah," as I understand it is called, for some years. Please discuss this

41

with your friends. There's no sense in preparing for a journey that won't materialize for years."

Then Peter got up and asked everybody to be quiet for a minute, as he had something else to say. "There is a young lady who was in my class at university who would like to come and meet you, if you have no objection. She is Jewish, very pretty, and she can speak French, English and German. What do you say?"

There was a roar of "Yes" in half a dozen languages. Then Peter asked if there was anything he could bring with him next time. A few voices called out, "Yes, please, newspapers."

"Of course, I should have thought of that myself," he said. "What languages?"

"Any languages," someone called out. "We're starved for news about the world."

Peter said goodbye and made his way to Ward 47. Miriam and Heide were, of course, delighted to see him and Heide asked about Max. Peter explained that he couldn't bring Max because the boys were busy discussing some news he'd given them today. "This news is important and it applies to you, too," he said. He then proceeded to acquaint them with the Swiss offer of education. They were quiet for a moment, then Miriam said, "Do you think that will also include getting on with my doctorate?" Peter said that he would make that one of the questions they would ask the Swiss authorities.

Heide shyly asked him if it also applied to her, as she had not been to college. He said, "Absolutely. Did you finish high school?"

She replied, "Yes, and with honors, too."

He said, "That's fine, Heide. I expect anybody in your group who wants to take up this educational offer will be allowed to, even if they didn't finish college. The Swiss will waive any academic pre-requirements."

Peter turned to Miriam. "You know, it's so interesting that you are academically at the stage to start your doctorate studies in a branch of linguistics, and there happens to be a particularly great school in Geneva specializing in languages. They have departments in synchronic, diachronic, theoretical, and applied linguistics, and one dealing with psychological and physiological mechanisms in-volved in speech, the social and cultural contexts of language, and the communicative function, too. I know about those details because I'm also applying to that school for my own doctorate and I'm right now considering which department to apply to. If I'm accepted, then

I expect to start there in about three months. Wouldn't it be remarkable if you and I both studied there after meeting *here*, of all places?"

Miriam said, "Yes, of course, it would, Peter, and for me it would be a great opportunity. But, we are really jumping ahead. We don't know if this program would actually cover a PhD course. I understood from what you said initially that it was really intended to give an education to those who didn't have one. I hardly qualify as uneducated, do I? We'll have to see what develops in the coming weeks and months, won't we?"

Peter was watching Miriam, fascinated to see how happy, animated, and vivacious she had become in the short time since he first saw this hopeless and helpless waif cast up by the tide, just a few days ago.

"Yes, Miriam, we'll have to wait a little while, as you say, to see how these things evolve and then we can have a clearer idea how they will affect you."

He made his farewells and left to return to Ward 35, where he found everyone in an uproar. Peter made his way to Max and asked, "What on earth is happening?"

Max replied, "It's all your fault, Peter. The news you brought today has awakened enormous amounts of energy in us. Everyone is making plans, and for the first time, their voices are filled with hope."

Peter shook hands with Max and went over to Alex. "What's going on with you, Alex?" he asked.

"You have given us such an extraordinary parcel of news today, Peter, that everyone is really 'lit up' with it. As for me, I've a question to ask you.

"Well, Peter, you know I'm a Zionist, and I very definitely want to go and live my life in Palestine.

"So my question to you is this: Is it better for Palestine to have me settle there now, after I've been discharged from the hospital, as I'm ready and willing to work at anything, but untrained for any trade or profession, or will I be of greater service to my new country after I take advantage of the Swiss offer and acquire some trade or discipline that I can take with me?"

"That's a tough question, Alex, particularly since I'm not Jewish. What you've told me makes me think that you will do better by going there with some qualification that will help that country to develop. At the same time, I think you should take an active part in promoting the Zionist vision in which you believe. But *you* have to decide this."

"Now, while we're on the subject of Zionism, I would like to learn more about it. What book do you know of that can adequately explain to a sympathetic observer the philosophy of this movement?"

"The founder of modern Zionism was Theodore Herzl," Alex explained. "He wrote a book in 1896 called *The Jewish State* and brought the World Zionist Organization into being in 1897. I don't know if his book was translated into English, but it was, I believe, the founding document of modern Zionism."

"Thank you," said Peter. "Incidentally, Alex, I want you to understand that any approaches by you concerning the Palestine matter *must* only go through me. I promise you that I will do everything possible to link you up with the people who matter. I believe you know from what you've already heard from me that I'm not only a man of my word, but that I do have excellent connections."

"Peter," Alex replied, "I rely on you absolutely on this and other matters too. I give you my word that I will not approach anybody else on this subject of Palestine."

"Fine," said Peter. "Now, please find out how many people here want to go to Palestine as soon as they are discharged from the hospital and how many after they've finished the Swiss Studies Program."

"I'll find out," Alex assured him. "For those who want to go as soon as possible, I'll explain that it may well mean going in an unconventional way, which they will all understand."

Peter went back to Max again and took him aside. "Max," he said, "over the next couple of days, I would like you to go to all the boys and make a list of those who think they want to go with the Swiss Studies Program. It doesn't commit anybody, but I just want to have an idea. Of course, those who don't will have to leave Switzerland immediately after they are discharged from the hospital. But they do have a few alternatives. They can try to go home, they can go to a DP camp and try to contact people, or they can try to make their way to Palestine. I've asked Alex to speak to you about that and to tell you everything he has heard from me about it. Now, I must go. I've a class this morning."

That evening, after he got home, Peter received a phone call from Helen. "Hello," she said, "and how are you?"

"I'm fine, thank you," he said, "and how's life with you?"

"Oh, fine, too, but I'm just a little tired. I went to Zurich today for a meeting and I just got back. How about breakfast tomorrow, Peter?"

"Thank you," he replied. "I'd love to meet you again. I so enjoyed the last time we met. How about 8:00?"

"That's fine," she said. "See you tomorrow."

They hung up.

They met at the Cafe Quito, as arranged. She looked her usual beautiful self.

"Did you have a good meeting?" Peter asked. "Did you drive or fly?"

She replied, "I flew. My mother has an executive plane and I was able to borrow it yesterday."

"Wow," said Peter. "And did you pilot it?"

"As a matter of fact, I did. I've had a pilot's license since I was 17."

Peter allowed a small whistle of surprise to escape. "Very surprising lady," he said. "How was Zurich and your meeting?"

"Actually, I went to Zurich on your business," she quipped.

"I didn't know we were in business together," he joked.

"Have you forgotten that you asked my help in a certain matter?"

"Oh, I'm so sorry, I thought you were joking. I've, of course, been thinking of that 'business' ever since we last met."

"Well, I met with a cousin of mine, told him your story, and asked for a name and phone number of someone who could help us. For security reasons, he asked me to vouch for you, which I did.

"Then, having had my positive reassurance, he gave me the phone number of a lady in Zurich. I called her while Phillipe, my cousin, was with me, and asked to see her. She wanted to know who had given me her name and phone number to which I replied, 'My cousin Phillipe, who happens to be with me at this moment. Would you like to speak to him?'

"She said, 'Yes, of course,' so I put Phillipe on the phone. They spoke for a few minutes and he handed the phone back to me. I spoke to her and yesterday I went to Zurich and met her.

"She's a dentist, so it's quite common for strangers to call her up for an appointment, which covered us in case anybody happened to be listening on her phone. We had lunch together in a very upscale Zurich restaurant and I told her your whole story. She went through the same questions that Phillipe had asked me about your bona fides, and I settled her worries on that score.

"As you have passed all the security checks, I can tell you that there is indeed a large 'Aliyah Bet' operation all over Europe designed to put survivors together who are aiming to get to Palestine. They are brought down to various ports on the Mediterranean coasts of various countries. There, small ships have been purchased by our agents, always under fictitious names, supplied with food and fuel, and manned by volunteers – both Jewish and non-Jewish – acting as crews. Then, they set off for Palestine with the hold full of survivors, everyone on board knowing the possibilities that they may be stopped by the British Navy and transferred to a detention camp, in Cyprus or elsewhere, for an unknown period of time. But the general feeling of the people in the camp is that they would much rather be there, in the detention camp, on the way to Palestine, than in a DP camp with an unknown future.

"Incidentally, while in the detention camp, all sorts of activities take place, even though the British Army is responsible for guarding against exactly these kinds of activities. For example, there are Hebrew classes; lectures on Palestine, its history, ethnography, and religion; and rifle instruction and infantry tactics training. It is also said that they have ways in which messengers are able to go in and out of the detention camp and over to Palestine, under the noses of the guards, so that the underground organization is aware of the number of people and their make-up. They have their own medical facilities, doctors, and nurses in the camp, from among the detainees.

"Furthermore, the British Army guards almost never go into the camp and leave all the administration of the camp to the Jewish internees, who rarely cause any problems to their guards. All this is authentic information and is scarcely ever shared with Gentiles, for obvious security reasons. You are, in fact, Peter, looked upon as a very exceptional person and a friend of our people."

"That is an absolutely fascinating story," said Peter, "but I've obvious questions to which you may or not have the answers. How do the internees get away with it – with being left to administer themselves, with being able to move people in and out of the camp to Palestine under the noses of the British Army?"

"There are a couple of reasons for the success of the inmates in these camps. First, the soldiers and their officers are aware that the internees, just a short while ago, miraculously survived concentration camps where millions of people were slaughtered and burnt, and there is a certain sympathy shown by the guards, who are, after all, human beings. Second, the war being over, many of the soldiers of the Parachute Regiment and their officers have been in the army for four or five years, fighting the Germans, and are now motivated by one thing and one thing only: When will their demobilization index number come up so they can go home to Britain, take off their uniforms, and get on with their lives? So, you see, they aren't going to be too motivated to keep these thousands of internees under strict rules and regulations."

"Thank you so much, Helen," said Peter. "The humanity being shown by those British soldiers stands in opposition to the anti-Semitism of Ernest Bevin and those like him, who have no qualms about using the British Navy to drag those camp survivors off their ships and to put them into detention, again.

"So, now that I'm aware of all those things, how does this relate to my boys and girls?" asked Peter.

"First of all," said Helen, "they have to get well. Then, we have to make a group of them. Then, we'll arrange to meet them as they leave Switzerland. It may be that they will coalesce into a group after they leave Switzerland and find themselves in a border town of a neighboring country. Then we'll send them as a group, through the organization's underground system, to a Mediterranean port. The rest, you know."

"There is now a major amendment to that plan," said Peter. He then told her of the Study Program invented by his mother and apparently approved by the Deputy Minister, who has responsibility for his boys and girls.

"As a result of this, some of my survivors will take the program, some will refuse it, and some number will want to go to Palestine either directly, without the program, or after taking it. I've asked Max to collect the information so we know who wants to study, and Alex on who wants to go to Palestine before or after studying. After I've the various numbers, I will put them in a graph or chart and discuss them with you so we can plan accordingly. I understand that, in any case, nobody is going to be discharged in under three months. That means that three months from now would be the earliest possible time to start assembling a group outside of Switzerland."

"Well," said Helen, "I'm delighted that the government has approved your mother's brainchild, but it certainly throws a spanner into the works of our Palestine planning. Now, in order to stop any action starting from my friend in Zurich, I will inform her discreetly of this delay and tell her to put the idea onto a back burner, and that we'll update her with information as soon as we get it, and deal with the implications accordingly."

"Right," said Peter, "and I think that's all we can deal with at this moment, until I can put the numbers together. Then I'll invite you to another breakfast. Agreed?"

"Agreed," she said, putting her things together as she made ready to leave.

"Hold on," he said, "I'd like to talk about something other than our 'survivors' business, if you have a little more time for me."

"Absolutely," she said, and with a big smile, she let him know that she really *did* have time for him.

"You see, Helen, I'd like to know a little more about you as a person. I've heard a word here and a word there, but I'd really like to know a bit more, if you have no objection."

"That's fine, Peter, just ask away."

"Well, I've heard that your mother has a couple of unusual accretions. A secretary and a plane. May I ask why?"

"Well, Peter, my mother owns a fashion gowns business, although it's been pretty low-key for the last six years because of the war. She does a certain amount of work in her office at home and that's why the secretary answered the phone to you. Why does she own a plane? Well, she is also a pilot and she has had the plane since about 1930. She used to use it to fly around Europe on business, and for pleasure too – day trips or to vacation places with the family. My father died when I was very young and I hardly remember him. He was a banker, the senior partner in a private bank and when he died, in a car crash, the other partners bought out his share in the firm.

"So, that's where my mother had the funds to start her own fashion business. She was the designer and was very good at what she did. At one time, she employed about 100 people. Since the war started, she has been making do with a nucleus of six skilled employees, but now that the war is over, she intends to restart her business, as soon as she sees markets opening up. I've one sibling, a brother, a mathematical semi-genius of twenty-two, who is studying post-doc in the USA. Oh, yes, since I finished college, I've been working part-time with the Zionist Federation and part-time with my synagogue. So, that's the story. Any more questions?"

"Thanks so much, Helen. I really appreciate that you've opened up so much to me. Somehow I had the feeling it wasn't too hard for you and also, nor was it something you do on a regular basis, either."

"Well, you're right there, Peter. I've never told anybody so much about myself and my family in one sitting. Perhaps I should just add that religion is a major thing in my life and mine is an unusual mixture of activities – Zionism and Orthodox Judaism. You see, most Zionists come from the secular or liberal areas of Judaism."

"I owe it to you to tell you of *my* background," Peter said. "Of course, only if you're interested, but if you are, we should save it for another time, if that's okay with you."

"I should like to hear about you very much, Peter, and perhaps at another breakfast."

"By the way, Helen, I told the boys that I've a rather beautiful friend who also happens to be Jewish, and that I might be able to convince her to come along with me to meet them. They expressed their interest with a loud 'Yes,' in six languages, no less. You told me you are willing to go, so please tell me when it would be okay with you."

She said, "The day after tomorrow in the morning, if that suits you."

He said, "Fine. I'll meet you in front of the hospital at, say, 8:30, if that's convenient."

At that, they said their farewells and parted.

CHAPTER VI

Helen Meets the Survivors

TWO DAYS LATER, PETER AND HELEN MET, AS ARRANGED, AT the hospital. Peter escorted Helen to Ward 35 and they went in. As the boys saw the vision of beauty accompanying Peter, a hush spread about the room, and when Peter and Helen reached the group at the far end, there was complete silence.

"Good morning, boys," said Peter, "I want you to meet a friend of mine. Her name is Helen. We met at the university here and she lives in Berne. I told her about you and she wants to meet you, and yes, she's Jewish." He led her first to Max.

"This is my friend, Max. Max, this is Helen."

"Hello, Max," Helen said. "Pleased to meet you. I've heard a lot about you and how you've been helping Peter."

"Pleased to meet you, Helen, but the truth is I haven't been helping Peter. He and his family have done so much for us that by working with him, I feel I'm helping ourselves. We all owe a huge debt of gratitude to the Romaine family for what they're doing. We never imagined such kindness coming our way, especially from a family which isn't even Jewish."

By this time, the room had started to resonate again, although most of the boys periodically stole a glance toward Helen.

Max and Helen chatted for a while, and then Peter directed her attention to Alex. "Helen, I'd like you to meet another friend of mine, Alex."

"Happy to meet you, Helen," Alex said, smiling. "I guess you're of the Orthodox group in Berne."

"As a matter of fact, you're right, Alex, but how on earth would you have guessed that?"

"Well, you dress very modestly and you don't offer your hand when being introduced. I come from an Orthodox family in Poland and, as they say, 'it takes one to know one.' You remind me in your cut of clothing of the ladies of my old city, Warsaw, but I would venture a guess that your style of dress is far more fashionable than that of Warsaw."

"If that's the case, it's because my mother designs clothing for a living and she sews all my clothes. Thanks for the compliment."

Meanwhile, Peter returned to Max and handed him a briefcase stuffed with newspapers from different countries that Peter had bought that day.

"Here you are, Max, newspapers from all over Europe. I'll try to bring more with me whenever I come. Leave a few in the briefcase so I can give them to the girls. Do you have any material for me?"

"Yes. I'll put them in the pocket of the bag. I know that Alex also has papers for you."

At that moment, Alex came over and gave Peter some papers, saying, "It wasn't easy, Peter, but the boys here have done their best."

Peter thanked them both, then said, "I think we should take Helen around to meet the boys who are in bed. Who is the best to do that?"

They both said at the same time, "Jacob."

"Why Jacob?" Peter asked.

"Because he has mastered a lot of languages and is our best translator," Alex answered.

Max signaled to a boy to come over and introduced him to Peter, saying, "Please meet Jacob, who is from Czechoslovakia and who is fluent in Slavic *and* Romance languages."

"Pleased to meet you, Jacob," Peter said, shaking hands. Then he went over to Helen, retrieved her from a group of admirers, and introduced her to Jacob.

"I think it would be very nice if you went 'round to the boys who are bedridden and introduced yourself. Jacob will act as your interpreter."

"Yes, of course, I would like that, but won't you come, too?" she asked, sweetly.

"Certainly," Peter replied, unable to resist her charms. "After that, I'd like to take you to meet the two girls."

"Fine," Helen agreed. Then she, Jacob, and Peter made their way around to each bed in turn, saying a few words to each boy. When they finished, Peter and Helen, in turn, said "goodbye" to everyone, and left.

"Helen, you've made a whole bunch of young men very happy today," Peter assured her as they came to Ward 47. They knocked and went in.

"Hello, ladies," he began, handing them each a newspaper; "I'd like you to meet a friend of mine from Berne. Helen is Jewish and wanted to meet you." Then he turned to Helen and said, "This is Miriam from Poland and Heidi from Austria."

It didn't take long for the girls to begin busily chattering away in German about all sorts of things, as though they were all old friends. Helen was sitting on their beds, showing them her clothing and also the contents of her purse. They were especially fascinated by the make-up. Helen promised to bring some make-up the next time she came or send a quantity with Peter. The two girls were absolutely incandescent with the visit of this modern young woman who was interested in their experiences. It had been a long time since they were able to share their feelings with someone outside their circle. Eventually, it was time to go, something none of the girls wanted to do. They kissed and Helen promised to visit again as soon as she was able.

Peter and Helen left the hospital, both lost in their own thoughts. Helen was enormously moved by the experiences the girls had been through and Peter was amazed at the way she'd provided an elixir of happiness for the usually somber Miriam and Heidi. He put her into a taxi and they vowed to come back soon to visit the girls.

That night, after dinner, Peter sat down with the "option lists" that he had received from Max and Alex and analyzed them as follows:

Alex
25 people whose countries said "cannot say yes"

Want to Study	Decline Study
15 (A)	10 (B)
Later: don't know	To Palestine soonest

Max
29 people whose countries said "yes"

Want to Study	Decline Study
14 (A)	15 (B)

The preliminary summary was as follows:

A. Total to study program   29

	After study –	To go home	7
	–	To Palestine	7
	–	Don't know	15
			29

B. Total decline study program   25

To Palestine	10
To go to DP camp to search family	5
To go home	10
	25

TOTAL   54

Notes: 1. "Soonest" = No study
        2. "Later"   = After study
        3. The girls included in "after study, don't know"

The Final Summary was as follows:

To go home	17 – 10 soonest, 7 later
To Palestine	17 – 15 soonest, 2 later
To go to DP Camp	5 – no study
Don't know	15 – after study
TOTAL	54

The next morning, Peter and Helen met at Cafe Quito and sat down at their regular table. After greeting each other warmly, Helen said, "I've been dying to discuss yesterday's events. They were some of the most extraordinary happenings of my life, to meet those brave and courageous young men – and women, too. There's something so desperate about them, and yet all they've been through has not robbed them of a sense of naiveté, a sweetness I can't help but admire."

She thanked Peter for giving her the opportunity to meet with the boys and girls. She also said she would continue to pay visits to the hospital, and intended to go the following day after she did some shopping for the girls.

Peter told her of his previous night's work in summarizing the survey that his two "associates" had carried out for him. He gave her copies of the two sheets of paper and went through them with her.

He pointed out that the responses he was given were not set in stone and that it was likely some of the people would change their minds, one way or the other. Anyway, these preliminary statistics would give "her people in Zurich" something to go on for the present. Assuming the people would be discharged at different times, they would need to set up a place where the survivors could wait until everyone was accounted for.

Helen told Peter she would take the papers to Zurich herself and pass them on to her contacts. Then, they parted.

Each morning, Peter came with a bunch of newspapers for both wards. Two days after the last breakfast, he accidentally met Helen at the hospital entrance as she arrived after shopping for the girls.

"Good morning," they said simultaneously, and laughed.

"Let's go together to the girls," he suggested. "I'd like to see their reactions to what you're bringing them."

"Absolutely," Helen said, anxious herself to see the look on the girls' faces when they saw the *goodies* she was bringing them. "By the way, I went to Zurich yesterday and delivered your papers. They were duly impressed. I also did my shopping for the girls there."

"Oh," he said, "I nearly forgot that last time I visited the girls, Heide made a point of asking me why Max wasn't with me. I'll drop in at Ward 35 with the newspapers, pick up my hospital gown and Max, and the three of us can visit the girls."

Peter could see the perplexed look on Helen's face. "I wear the gown as a bit of camouflage. It's the only way I can *escort* Max out of his ward and into theirs."

They went to Ward 35. They were met with smiles and greetings from the boys and Peter put the newspapers down on a table. He didn't miss the fact that Alex immediately went to Helen, and she was already greeting him like an old friend.

"What's going on with Alex and Helen?" Max wondered, out loud.

"I don't know," said Peter, "but they're both Orthodox, so they have that in common."

"I see," Max whispered. "Looks like something's brewing between them. Should be interesting to watch how it plays out."

"Exactly what I was thinking about you and Heide," Peter thought to himself. He put on his gown, took Max's arm, and went to Helen, who was still chatting with Alex.

"Sorry to break it up, people, but it's time we went to Ward 47."

"You look positively medical in that gown, Peter. Have you thought of going into the medical profession?" Helen said pseudo- seriously.

"I'm afraid the closest I'll ever get to being a doctor is modeling the gown. The medical profession has two characteristics I can't abide: The love of needles and the willingness to see blood."

They all laughed as they left the ward, Peter carrying two newspapers and Helen carrying her shopping.

When they arrived at Ward 47, Peter knocked, and the three went in. Both girls' faces lit up when they saw the visitors, and Peter realized for the first time that both girls were very good-looking, now that they had filled out a little. They all greeted one another. Helen approached the beds and took out two packages from the bag she was carrying and gave one to each of the girls. They both thanked her and both insisted on giving her a kiss. Then they opened the packages, took out the contents, and put them on the bed sheet, screaming with delight and jumping up and down ecstatically.

Each girl proceeded to analyze the contents of her new-found treasure. They carefully, almost reverently, held the lipsticks, colognes, talcum powder, fine soaps, shampoos, hair combs and brushes. They felt the gift wrap these items came in, time and again, finally folding the wrapping and putting it away as though it were a precious gem. They thanked Helen profusely, tears in their eyes. There were a few items with which neither was familiar: mascara, foundation, and rouge. Helen explained what they were for and showed them how to use each item.

Meanwhile, Peter and Max were silent, enjoying the joyous scene.

After a while, Miriam and Heide finally noticed the boys, apologizing for the oversight, but assuring them nothing short of this unexpected treasure could have diverted their attention from their guests.

"It was worth being ignored to see the happiness and joy in your faces," Max assured them.

"The truth is you girls don't need all that stuff to make you pretty. You're already pretty. Perhaps, Helen, you should return –"

A chorus of "No! No!" met his ears.

"Stop teasing, Peter," Helen said in mock anger. "Even natural beauties need a little help once in a while."

After the girls realized they were being teased, they confided in Helen and the boys that this was the first time in at least four or five years when they could let themselves feel unbridled joy. Helen's eyes welled up with tears as she realized what an effect her gift had made on them.

Helen announced that she had to be going. Both girls said, simultaneously, "When will you be here again?" Everybody laughed as Helen assured them she would return very soon.

CHAPTER VII

Camp Pietro 1

BY THE END OF OCTOBER 1945, THE STUDY PROGRAM WAS established and a Ministerial Committee was chosen to oversee the program. As the boys and girls were, one by one, discharged from the hospital, those who opted to study entered either French or German language classes.

Those who chose not to study left Switzerland via various southern border towns, either to Italy or to French border towns close to Italy.

Peter and Helen arranged for Alex (who was listed on the student program, although he opted to go to Palestine) to meet with Helen's associates in the Zionist movement. They would arrange to help those from the hospital wishing to make aliyah to make their way to a newly established Zionist camp in the mountains, above Lake Como, in the border area between Switzerland and Italy. Now named Camp Pietro, it was the collection point for those who would be part of the illegal Aliyah Bet organization to the Jewish homeland.

Peter and Miriam were each accepted at the Geneva School for PhD Linguistics study to start in January 1946.

By the end of December 1945, the fifteen who declined study were out of Switzerland and in Camp Pietro. Two boys who had started to study quit their studies and joined the exodus to Camp Pietro.

Of the fifteen studying who were "don't know"s, eight dropped out and made their way to Camp Pietro. This number included Miriam, who left her program, and Heide.

Heide decided to join the aliyah movement rather than return to Mayrhofen, because her father had been killed by the Brownshirts and she had no idea if her mother was alive or not, so there was no family to return to. At the same time, she was growing more and more fond of Max and believed he felt the same way about her. Since he was going to Palestine, she decided to take the same route.

Of the five who decided to decline study and go to a DP camp to search for family, three ultimately went with the Palestine group instead.

As a result, by the beginning of January 1946, there were twenty-six boys and two girls in Camp Pietro from the Berne hospital.

In mid-January 1946, Peter paid an unannounced visit to Camp Pietro. This way-station had been actually a military camp, which the Italian army had vacated when the surrender of the German armies took place in Italy and the Tyrol on April 29, 1945. There was a guard at the gate, named Yosef, who was from the Berne group. He recognized Peter at once, gave him a great bear hug, and pressed a button that rang a bell throughout the compound to announce a visitor. The group flooded into the reception area and the words, "It's Peter" could be heard everywhere.

Everyone rushed to shake Peter's hand and give him a warm welcome. His backpack was taken from him and he was shown into a visitor's room, which held a bed and some basic furniture. The room filled and everyone was talking at once, in the usual medley of languages.

"Quiet please, everybody," Peter announced. "I've brought newspapers, which I'll be happy to distribute if you let me get to my backpack."

Someone brought his knapsack and he handed the pile of newspapers to one of the boys, who started to call out the language that each paper was written in. Those who were lucky enough to receive a newspaper quickly left to find a quiet place to sit and read.

Finally, only Max, Miriam, and Heide were left. Peter said, "Well, and how are my friends doing?"

"Your friends, Peter, are doing fine," Max told him. "We talk farming all the time, hoping to live on a kibbutz when we arrive in Palestine. But who knows what the future will bring? At least we are out of the hospital, and in Italy. That's a bit closer to our goal."

"And you, Heide, how are you adjusting to all this?"

"Que será, será," she replied. "I'm a bit fatalistic about my life right now. However, I've a lot of support. Max and I are looking forward to the next installment of my life with great anticipation. But now we have to leave you," she told him, looking at her watch and darting a quick glance at Miriam. "We have Hebrew class to attend." And off went Heide and Max.

"Something tells me Heide was more interested in leaving us alone than in going to a class. What do you think, Miriam?"

"I think you found her out. When we're not talking shop, the conversation between Heide and I usually turns to you. She knows I've a very special spot in my heart for you."

Peter blushed. "You've never said that to me before, Miriam. As a matter of fact, one of the main reasons that I visited Camp Pietro today was to see you again, to see how *you* are getting on, and whether you're as lovely to see as I remember you."

"And," Miriam prompted.

"You're even lovelier than I remembered."

As the silence between them filled the air, Peter decided to change the subject. "Who decided to call this camp 'Pietro'? And what does it mean?"

"Oh, I thought that with all your languages, you'd know that Pietro is just the Italian name for Peter. When we got here, we decided to call it Pietro in your honor. We're all aware that if it wasn't for you and your parents, we would never have gotten this far on the road to Palestine. Actually, the Zionist organization wanted to call it Camp Haifa, but we put up a fuss and they finally relented.

"I know you're a bit uncomfortable with me being so forward," Miriam said hesitantly, returning to their discussion of a moment ago, "but I was so very near to death for such a long period that I don't have the time to waste on ancient etiquette or those games young people play. I simply want you to know how I feel about you.

"And don't feel put upon," she added, taking a deep breath. "You've been brought up English and I understand the English are very proper. You don't have to respond in similar terms. You don't even have to respond at all."

"You're right about the English," Peter admitted. "We don't wear our hearts on our sleeves, which means we don't reveal our deepest feelings very easily. But please don't think I don't share your feelings. It's just that I'm trying to juggle so many things that I'm afraid that if I add one more thing – even a very important, lovely young lady as yourself – everything I'm trying to do will fall apart. Am I being very obtuse?"

"I think I understand. Well, at least we're beginning to understand each other," she smiled, noticing how forlorn Peter looked. Spontaneously, she gave him a peck on the cheek.

Blushing yet again, Peter quickly said, "Now, uh, tell me, what is a good time and place for me to address the whole group on a matter of great importance?"

"I think after dinner tonight would be best," she answered, almost enjoying his discomfort. "Dinner is at 7:00, so about 7:45. Why don't you take a nap for an hour or so now. You must be tired after that steep walk up the hill from the village with that load of newspapers. Don't worry – I'll come and wake you up at about 6:45, which will give you time for a quick wash before dinner."

The compound consisted of a dozen small wartime barracks, each capable of holding about a dozen people. Only the two girls had their own barrack. Heating was by a wood-burning stove.

Each day, one person from each occupied hut had to go out into the surrounding forest and bring back sufficient wood to last at least twenty-four hours, while the remaining people cleaned out the ashes and swept and tidied up the huts, just like an army unit. There was a kitchen, where the work was done by the staff of Aliyah Bet people.

One hut was used as a dining room and two barracks, one for men and one for women, housed the showers and toilets. The group was responsible for bringing the food from the kitchen to the dining hut, clearing up the dining room and the tables after the meal, taking the cutlery, crockery and utensils back to the kitchen, and washing up.

For these housekeeping jobs, a roster was established and as each new arrival to the camp came in, he or she was added to the work force.

Miriam came to wake up Peter promptly at 6:45. He was still groggy from his long trip. She helped him unpack the rest of his things and showed him where to wash up. Then she brought him into the dining room, where the tables were always arranged in one long line. By popular demand, Peter was seated at the head of the table.

The one seated at the other end of the tables was responsible for serving the food from the container on to the plates, which were then passed up. When everything had been served, someone stood up and said, "*Chevrah* (friends), let us welcome our most honored guest, Peter Romaine, but for whose efforts, together with those of his parents, none of us would be here today." Everyone stood and applauded. After a time, they sat down to begin eating.

When dinner was over, Peter stood up to speak. Gradually, the customary uproar in at least a half-dozen boisterous languages began to lessen until there was a hush.

Peter spoke in German. "Hello, ladies and gentlemen," he said. "I

60

can't tell you how happy I am to see twenty-eight men and women, tough survivors of the camps and from Berne Hospital, here in Italy on your way to the Promised Land, the Holy Land, otherwise known as Palestine. I can see that you've organized yourselves very well, with the help of the Aliyah Bet people, who, by the way, deserve a big vote of thanks for what they've done and continue doing to make your stay here as comfortable as possible.

"Right now, nobody knows how long you are going to be here. However, I would urge you all to do the following while you remain here: First, everyone should eat three meals a day, even if some of you were hoping for knockwurst or gefilte fish."

A chorus of laughter filled the hall. It was, indeed, difficult for many to get used to foods so unfamiliar to them.

"Just remember," Peter went on, "in Palestine, food is strictly rationed these days, and you need to build your strength while you're here.

"Next, exercise. We have, as you know, a physical trainer here who will show you how to keep fit."

"And please attend the classes which have been arranged for you. That includes the study of Hebrew, the history and geography of Palestine, social conditions in the Holy Land, demographics, and the special classes designed to make you proficient in the use of arms and history of war.

"Next, I'm going to pass out forms, which I would like everyone to complete. At last, we are talking about coming to the sea voyage that you will take in due course. This calls for the following very important information from each and every one of you:

"Fill in your full name, country of origin, language or languages you speak, and any specific knowledge or experience you may have had which might possibly be useful on a ship. These would include *any* experience at seamanship, in the fields of medicine, management, accounting, carpentry, plumbing, cooking for a large number of people, etc.

"When we get on board our ship, there will be a bona fide captain, but you will substitute for much of the crew. Each of you will be given a job to do. Your knowledge and experience will determine the type of job you receive. Remember, no matter what job you get, you must carry out the work of your duties fully and uncomplainingly. It is expected that the entire voyage will last about ten to twelve days.

"I shall remain in the camp tonight and tomorrow. Please bring the completed forms to me by noon tomorrow so I can start to work on them and find out what talents you have. Feel free to ask me any questions at that time.

"By the way, the form is in German, but you can answer in French, English, or Italian. If you have trouble understanding the written German, please speak with Max.

"Thank you all for listening to me so patiently and quietly."

Alex stood up to speak. "Chevrah," he said, "I think Peter is doing an absolutely fantastic job for us. Let's resolve to fill in his forms quickly and return them to him as he has requested."

There was tremendous round of applause as everyone cleared the hall.

Miriam approached Peter to bring him up-to-date about Heide's mother.

"I'm afraid the news for Heide is not good. The Red Cross was able to confirm that Heide's mother died in Auschwitz, leaving Heide an orphan with no near relatives, the poor thing. I know that most of our group are orphans, but she's become such a good friend that I feel her loss reawakens in me all the sadness I felt when I lost my family."

"I can't begin to understand what you've all gone through, but I admire you all, especially you, my dear, for your ability to overcome so much," he responded.

Peter left and made his way to the Aliyah Bet office to meet the senior man, named Dov. Dov gripped Peter's hand, shook it warmly, and spoke in excellent English, "I'm very pleased, and I must say, honored, to meet you, Peter. I've heard so much about you from your group. They think of you on a level just a little below God. You can't believe how often I hear your name mentioned and in how many languages."

"I can't tell you how grateful I feel, on behalf of the group, for what your organization is doing for them," Peter replied. "I assume you're from Palestine?"

"Yes. As a matter of fact, I was discharged from the Jewish Brigade in the British Army after four years in uniform only three months ago. Then, I immediately volunteered to help bring some of these survivors of the Nazi death camps to Palestine. Although the British are using the Royal Navy to intercept our ships, I absolutely believe that sooner or later, that will stop. Then, our mission of rescuing these survivors from Europe and opening the detention camps on Cyprus will see great success as Jews pour into their homeland.

"Incidentally, Peter, I understand that you aren't Jewish. Is that true?"

"Yes, that's true," Peter responded.

"So did you get into this operation for your own religious reasons?"

"No, I found myself doing this purely for humanitarian reasons.

"It started when I visited the hospital in Switzerland, where I live, having heard that there was this bunch of young men, survivors of the Holocaust. I just went to see if I could do anything to help, and then things just mushroomed from there. It's most satisfying for me to be able to help these very special young men and women to get where they want to go."

"Well," said Dov, "while non-Jews helping Jews is not an unknown phenomenon to me, I find it amazing that a Gentile would actively risk so much to help the Jewish people. Unfortunately, most Jews have only known the horrors of anti-Semitism from the non-Jewish world. I've met up with a lot of anti-Semitism myself in my own life."

"How was that?" Peter asked.

"In 1942, I was sent from Palestine to England to study at an OCTU: Officer Cadet Training Unit. I found that, although I wore a British solder's uniform, the insignia on my uniform clearly indicating 'Palestine' apparently gave my comrades-in-arms a license to discriminate against me. However, when we were fighting in North Africa and Italy, somehow we became blood brothers. I think that when the soldiers realized Jews were good soldiers and not just *victims*, they slowly changed their perception of me."

"Well, Dov, I have to tell you, I had never had any interaction with Jews before I became involved with this group. In my circle of friends, I never heard an anti-Semitic remark. Jews just weren't on our radar. But let's discuss the matter at hand. What's now preventing our group from being taken from here to a boat right away?"

"Many things. First of all, we need to raise the money for this voyage. Then we need to find an appropriate ship and purchase it. We need to overhaul the ship and make sure it's seaworthy. We need to stock it with everything we'll need for the journey and, not least of all, we need to find a skeleton crew that's willing to take this perilous journey. We search for Jewish ex-navy or ex-merchant-marine volunteers to crew the ship. Only when all this is completed do we stand a chance of getting to Palestine in one piece."

"I understand," Peter said, getting up from his seat. "I shall be coming over every week or so to keep in touch with the group. If it's okay with you, I'll just pop in to find out how things are progressing. If there's anything my family or I can do to speed the process along, don't hesitate to let me know."

"Of course," Dov said warmly. "Please do come in and visit. I'll keep you abreast of what's happening. As for helping, you're doing more than your share already. God bless you."

"And you," Peter answered, a sense of pride welling up inside him.

CHAPTER VIII

Peter Loses his Father; the Will

PETER WENT BACK TO HIS ROOM, LAY DOWN ON HIS BED, and awaited events. They were not long in coming. After about half an hour, he heard a voice saying, "Shall I leave it on the table?" He looked at the figure near the door and said, "Please do." Then he pushed himself off the bed and sat down at the table. He checked the form in front of him quickly, just to see that the name of the writer was on it, whether the language was one he could handle, and that something was written in the background section. He wrote the number "1" on the form and sat back, waiting.

During the next three hours, fifteen forms came in. Two, he had to return, as they were written in Hungarian and Serbo-Croat. He asked the two boys to get them translated into either English, French, or Italian via Max and bring them back.

There was a flood of forms in the morning after breakfast, and he received all the completed twenty-eight forms by 3:00 p.m. He started to read them and make notes. He had read eighteen of them by the time he had to leave. He packed, said his goodbyes, and walked down the hill to the bus stop.

When he arrived at Berne Station, he called his parents to let them know he was back in town and would take a taxi home. His mother picked up the phone and in a strange, intense voice said, "Thank God you're back, Peter. I'm so sorry ... but ... I've some terrible news to tell you."

His heart stopped as he waited silently for his mother to continue.

"Peter, your father was killed in a car crash yesterday." She burst into heartrending sobs, unable to continue.

When his mother opened the door, she threw her arms around

him, hysterically crying. He held her closely as they walked to the sitting room where half a dozen of their Berne friends had gathered.

They rose to leave when Peter and Alice came into the room. One by one, they came over to Peter to shake his hand and offer their condolences. They kissed his mother, wishing her strength to face her loss, and left.

Peter was in shock.

"How, how did it happen?" he asked her when they were alone.

"A drunken driver ran head-on into your father's car. Both your father and the other driver were killed instantly." She started to sob again. "So senseless . . . so senseless . . ." she kept repeating.

They hugged and cried together for a time. But Alice was a strong woman and after a while, wiped her eyes, looking up at her only child. "Peter, you are now the head of our little family. I would like you to make arrangements for the funeral and I'll take care of the reception. Pastor Twin will help you, I'm sure. Then you'll have to speak to your father's attorney, Jean-Pierre Muraille, about your father's estate."

Peter nodded his agreement, saw his mother to her room, and went to bed. He'd had an exhausting day and a traumatizing evening. Deep down, perhaps he thought he'd would wake up to discover that his father's death was just a fiendish nightmare.

Next morning, he called Pastor Twin who willingly offered to help Peter in any way he could.

Then, Peter called his father's attorney. He was shocked to hear the news and suggested a meeting at 2:30 p.m. at his office, to which Peter agreed.

Peter and Alice had a very silent breakfast together, broken only by his mother's sobs. After ten minutes, she told Peter she was going back to her room.

Following breakfast, Peter called Raoul, who had been his closest friend since primary school, and Helen. They both were appalled at the suddenness of Peter's father's death. Raoul arranged to visit Peter and his mother that evening. Helen suggested they get together at their regular cafe when he was finished with his lawyer and Peter agreed.

Peter had time before his meeting with the lawyer and decided to walk. It was a sunny and warm day and Peter took a few minutes to relax and survey his surroundings. The park he found himself in was straight out of a Rousseau painting. Neatly cut grass, myriad flowers and the heavy scent of mimosa, trimmed pathways filled with stylish young women pushing baby carriages, birds singing, small boys on their way home for lunch pushing each other about and shouting, as small boys will. Under normal circumstances, these sounds and smells would awaken in him a sense of well-being, but now he found them incongruous with the world he presently inhabited, a world of danger and death and unlimited sadness.

He ate a light lunch, then made his way to the office of Jean-Pierre Muraille.

The lawyer's office was in a turn-of-the-century building of classical architecture in the heart of the business and professional center of Berne, on the top floor. Peter entered the ancient elevator operated by a uniformed youth, who pulled on a rope visible through an opening on one wall, and eventually reached the tenth floor.

From the names engraved on the office door, Peter saw that Jean-Pierre was the second of ten partners listed under the firm's name. He entered and was immediately shown into Jean-Pierre's room.

Jean-Pierre Muraille was a graying, dapper, middle-aged man, with a slight paunch, well hidden by the snug vest he wore. He stood up and held out his hand saying, "How do you do, Peter, we've never met before but, of course, I've heard all about you over the years from Richard, your late father. Please take a seat and let me say at once how sad I am to be meeting you for the first time in such unhappy circumstances.

"You should know that I've been Richard's lawyer and more, his 'homme d'affaires,' ever since he decided to retire from his diplomatic career and settle down in Switzerland. He chose me to be his lawyer, as I was then the youngest partner in the firm and he wanted a lawyer younger than himself, who 'would see him out,' as he put it.

"I would first like to ask you if you represent your mother today. I spoke to her earlier and she was too upset to come in but said you would be her representative. I need your agreement to this."

"I agree," Peter responded.

"Fine. Now, it is a requirement of law I should read your father's Last Will and Testament to his next of kin.

"First of all, you should know that you are appointed to be the sole executor of your father's will. Next, while the gross value of your father's estate is yet to be determined, I believe it to be in the order of fifteen million pounds sterling. Just because I use 'sterling' does not mean it is held in that currency. In fact, *none* of it is in sterling, but it is invested in a large number of foreign currencies and securities of the world, in gold bullion and coin, some real estate, mainly hotel properties in various countries outside of Europe."

Peter could hardly believe his ears. "That's amazing. I knew we were relatively wealthy, but not at this level. Would you know how it is that the property we hold is fortuitously outside of Europe?"

Jean-Pierre proceeded to tell Peter about his family antecedents, going back to 1066, the Muddyford Estate in England, the sale of the Estate in 1925 by Peter's grandfather, and the subsequent investment vehicle operated by representatives of four banks, as well as the provisions for an outside audit and annual certification of value. He went on to describe Richard's subsequent influence on the investment decisions and their geographical distribution.

"Peter, your father wasn't only a diplomat and a highly decorated veteran of two wars, but he was possessed of a keen mind and an almost prescient ability to judge the economic and political climate of the times. For example, in the early 1930s, he foresaw a catastrophic European war resulting from the leadership in Germany. Of course, in the thirties, there were other skilled observers of the political scene who were also visualizing the same thing, but your father had the self-confidence to act on his foresight and protect his family fortune. He convinced the trustees of the estate to re-invest the family's fortune in liquid assets and in properties outside of what would eventually be war-torn Europe.

"Thus, despite the war, the value of the corpus of the trust from 1939 to 1945 has been maintained and actually grew by an average interest rate of six percent. If the trust assets had been invested in average European investments, there would have been a loss of corpus of at least twenty-five percent."

"Now I come to a family secret that I need to divulge to you, since it is mentioned in his will. It is in the matter of James," said Jean-Pierre.

"James?" asked Peter. "I've never heard that name in connection with my father."

"During the First World War," Jean-Pierre continued, "your father was wounded in France and was returned to a hospital in England. He was sent to an officers' wartime convalescent hospital in the south of England, established in the famous country home of a titled family. One of the nurses, who was a daughter of the house's owner, fell in love with your father and they had an affair. Your father, as you know, married your mother late in life. At that time, he was thirty-nine, single, handsome, and a decorated lieutenant-colonel. She was twenty-five, a beautiful Florence Nightingale, tending to his injuries.

"After a few months, he recovered from his wounds and returned to France, not knowing that she was pregnant. She never told him, and persuaded her family not to tell him, too. Her family sent her to live with relatives in Scotland, where in due course she gave birth to James, in 1916. His birth was registered in Edinburgh as James Roman. But I move ahead of myself.

"In 1917, Richard was wounded again and sent back to England for treatment, but not at the same convalescent hospital. At the first opportunity, he called his Florence Nightingale. He asked her why she had not responded to his letters, and she answered that she needed to speak to him in person. He told her where he was and she arranged to meet him that Saturday.

"When she arrived at his convalescent hospital, they found a quiet corner and she spoke to him. She told him that she had been pregnant when he went back to France but she didn't want him to worry about her or even consider his obligations toward her while the war was still on. She told him of the birth of a boy in Scotland and that the child had been put into the care of a fine, young nursemaid, who came to her with high recommendation and credentials. This lady was sworn to secrecy about the boy's mother.

"She had decided not to tell Richard until the war was over, but after he telephoned her, she realized that he had a right to know, now. She also told him that he need not worry about any obligation to marry her. She had made up her mind some time ago not to marry, but rather to set up house with her school friend, Pamela.

"Richard listened to her story with both great surprise, and consternation. Despite her protests, he still felt a tremendous sense of duty to marry the mother of a child he had inadvertently brought into the world. He assured her that from then on, he would be responsible for the cost of the child's upbringing, and that he would supply a monthly payment to the nursemaid until his son was self-sufficient or twenty-five years old, whichever came first. The actual matter of payments would pass between their respective lawyers. He made her write down the name and address of his own lawyer, whom he would brief before he went back to France. He also told her he would remember James in his will.

"So that's the story of James," said Jean-Pierre. "And after Richard retired here in Berne, I've had the responsibility of making the payments to James's attorney in London, each and every month."

"What happened to my half-brother?" asked Peter.

"At eighteen, James received a scholarship to Oxford, and also joined the University Air Squadron. At twenty-one, he graduated in Aeronautical Engineering with a high honors degree, joined the Royal Air Force in 1937, and became a fighter pilot in 1939, just in time for the war. He survived the Battle of Britain in 1940, won a DFC and bar (Distinguished Flying Cross, twice), having shot down twelve German fighters, and, I understand, finished the war as a Group Captain with the DSO (Distinguished Service Order) at the age of twenty-nine. He's now considering joining British Overseas Airways Corporation (BOAC) as a pilot. And that brings you up to date, Peter."

"Thank you very much, Jean-Pierre," Peter said, still reeling from this news of a sibling he had never known. "Does he know who his father is? Who has been paying out for his upbringing and education since he was born? Does he know of my own existence? And does my mother know of James's existence?"

"I see you have the curiosity of your father. To answer your questions, no, James doesn't know who his real father is. Not even his lawyer knows your father's name. James only knows that he's a love-child of two well-born parents who fell in love during the First World War. He knows nothing of Richard's life or of your existence. And yes, your mother was told soon after they were married about the existence of James.

"Now I feel I must give you a piece of unasked advice. I realize you'd love to contact James, but please, put the idea of hunting up James out of your head. Your father went to *great* lengths to keep your family and himself anonymous from James. When I get to that part of the will which deals with the distribution of the estate, you will find out that although Richard makes provision for him, it has to go to him anonymously, again."

"I will certainly honor my father's wishes. I'll discuss all this with my mother as well."

"Of course, Peter. As to the distribution of the assets. There are gifts totalling about 50,000 pounds to individuals and organizations that your father felt committed to. Your mother gets the house and the income from a trust fund of seven million pounds, which after taxes of twenty percent, will amount to about two hundred eighty thousand pounds a year. After her death, the capital of the trust fund goes to you, of course. You will receive seven million pounds outright with a suggestion from your father to set up a trust fund so you get the income for life, as do your future children.

"James gets one million pounds outright. Of course, in order to receive the funds, he will be required to sign a document in which he renounces any and all claims which he may have against his unknown father, his father's wife, or any of his father's progeny. I will send copies of all documents to you, as the executor of the estate.

"Thank you, Jean-Pierre, you have given me much to think about. I want to finish with my father's funeral before I press on with the other matters at hand."

CHAPTER IX

Uncle Olaf will Help Out

AFTER SOME SOCIAL CONVERSATION, PETER LEFT JEAN-Pierre's office. He called Helen to tell her he was finished with his meeting and would now very much like to meet with her in twenty minutes, if she was free. "Fine, Peter," she said, agreeing, "at our usual place."

They met at Cafe Quito. Helen hastened to Peter, who was sitting alone at their usual table. He stood up at her approach.

"My poor Peter," she said, sympathetically. "I was so shocked by your news. It must have been devastating for you to hear that, on your return from Camp Pietro. Please tell me what happened. I'm entirely at your disposition. If you prefer just to remain silent, I will quite understand and we can just be two friends having a coffee together. Whatever you want to do."

"You really are a good friend, Helen," Peter said. "I really want to tell you what is happening in my world. I thought on the way back to Berne that I would recount to you what is going on there, but faced with my father's death, that drove everything else out of my mind."

He told her about his father and what happened, how his mother was helping to take the load off him by taking care of the reception following the funeral. Helen was surprised at how *little* load his mother was taking off his shoulders. It seemed to her that there were so many things he had to do that Alice could have done more to share the responsibility. However, she told herself, it wasn't for *her* to criticize Alice, and most especially, to Peter.

Then Peter spoke about Camp Pietro. He told her that he was working on a plan to reduce the problems confronting his group and, at the same time, speed up the process of getting them all on a ship to Palestine. He told her about the forms and his hope that some of the men and women would be able to become part of the crew. But after reviewing the forms they gave in, he now realized he would need a good deal of professional help.

"Hold on a minute," Helen interrupted. "I think I can help with that."

"Really?" he wondered, out loud. "I didn't know you had expertise in this field, too."

"I don't," she admitted. "But my father's older half-brother, my Uncle Olaf, who is half Norwegian, is the First Officer on a Norwegian cruise ship. My grandfather's first wife was from Norway and she died giving birth to her first baby, Olaf. He was brought up by his mother's sister, who lived in Oslo. He grew up there, served for some years in the Norwegian Navy, then retired and transferred to a company owning cruise ships. He's just arrived here on six months' leave and currently staying with us in Berne. I've no doubt at all that he will be happy to be the technical adviser for this worthwhile effort. When you have some time, I'll be happy to introduce you to him."

"That is absolutely fantastic, Helen. A wonderful coincidence."

"Well, I'm glad to help," she told him. "It's about time you had some help in your project. You've been doing so much for the group on your own.

"By the way, Peter, I want to go with you on your next visit to Camp Pietro. I want to keep in touch with everyone and I'd like to see Alex again and see how he's getting on."

"Ouch!" Peter responded, dramatically, at hearing her special interest in Alex.

"Well, I'm sure Miriam is anxiously awaiting your next visit to Camp Pietro as well."

"What? Why? Do you think?" he stammered.

"Yes, Peter, I think so. I've noticed how she looks at you. There's only one word for it, *adoringly*. And don't tell me that you don't know and haven't noticed how she behaves around you. You're too smart for that – Ah! I can see you're blushing. Well, well, so our dynamic leader, our linguistics expert, is really human after all."

"Whew, that was a bit more than I bargained for, Helen," Peter began. "But before we discuss my love life any further, there's an entirely new, and just as personal subject I want to share with you.

"Our family lawyer read me my father's will. It turns out that my father was a very wealthy man. He has left me quite a sum, taking care of my mother's needs as well, of course.

73

"But this new-found wealth changes a lot, especially as regards our group at Camp Pietro."

"Why? Are you going to upgrade the difficult conditions in the camp?" Helen asked.

"Better than that," Peter said, enthusiastically. "I'm now in a position to *buy* that ship I was talking about, *and* to fit it up to take our people to Palestine, without having to ask the Aliyah Bet people for any help. It means we can leave as soon as we find a seaworthy boat and a captain."

"That is absolutely fantastic, Peter. But wait a minute, Peter, what do you know about buying a ship?"

"That's where Uncle Olaf comes in," he answered. "And if Uncle Olaf can't help us, I'll find someone who will. But first things first. I have to attend to my father's funeral. When all this is over, I'll call you and arrange a meeting."

"I'll await your call," she assured him.

Peter returned home. He found his mother in the drawing room just saying farewell to two old friends.

After they left, his mother embraced him and asked him how his day had gone. He told her he had been informed about the subject of James. She smiled sadly and asked him if Richard had provided for James adequately. Peter could assure her that, indeed, her husband had left him a very large sum. She already knew the details of the rest of the will and was content that she had her home and an adequate income. The next day, Peter took a copy of the will, certified by the lawyer, to the bank, closed his father's account, and transferred some money to his account – sufficient to pay the funeral expenses and city fees. The bank manager, Etoile Lambert, gave Peter a code number to enable him to transfer funds to an account, should the need arise, anywhere in the world.

The day of the funeral arrived, at the British cemetery. It was an overcast and gloomy day with a light rain. Peter thought it was absolutely appropriate weather for such a sad day. He saw Helen in the crowd of about sixty persons, and felt relieved she had come.

He introduced her to his mother, who managed a slight smile, saying, "I've heard about you, of course, Helen, and I want to thank you for being such a good friend to Peter and helping him out so much in the recent days. I'm afraid I wasn't much help at all – I haven't been able to get myself out of the house since Richard died. Perhaps we'll see you back at the house afterward."

Helen replied, "Thank you, Dr. Romaine, that's very kind of you."

After the interment, all were invited back to the house for refreshments. This was a catered affair and most people stayed no more than a half-hour. Helen took Peter aside and told him that she had spoken to Uncle Olaf, who would like to meet him for breakfast the next day. Peter was, of course, anxious to meet Olaf, and agreed.

At 9:00 a.m. promptly, Peter met with Helen and her Uncle Olaf. Olaf Cohen was the very epitome of a Scandinavian sailor. Six foot and four inches tall, with a mop of blond hair and a thick, ginger beard, he was built like a wrestler, with huge shoulders, and a leg-of-mutton fist, which he held out to Peter. Peter hesitantly gave Olaf his hand, expecting to feel a vice squeezing the life out of his fingers. He tightened his face, half-closing his eyes in anticipation of pain, which made Olaf smile as he lightly shook Peter's tense hand.

"Well Peter," Olaf began, "I'm delighted to make your acquaintance at last. I've heard non-stop reports of your activities ever since I arrived at my brother's house last week. I understand you're doing great things for a group of young concentration camp survivors who are aiming to get to Palestine, despite the British government and the Royal Navy's best efforts to the contrary. Is that the situation?"

"You've summed it up quite nicely, sir," he replied.

"Now, Peter, please don't 'sir' me although I'm a lot older than you. You have my permission to call me 'Olaf,' but there's something I've forgotten. I know your father passed away recently and I want to express my sincere condolences to you. It is always sad in the extreme to lose a parent, and I understand that in your case, it was a very sudden occurrence."

"That's very kind, Olaf."

"Well, Peter, as you know, my last name is Cohen. I'm a brother of Helen's father, although we had different mothers. I'm proud of the Jewish half of my make-up and so I was most interested in your activities, particularly as you are a fully fledged Gentile helping this Jewish group of survivors. So, how can I help you? You see, Helen only told me about your activities, not why she thinks I may be able to be of some service."

Peter replied: "Simply put, I need to get a group of people across the Mediterranean to Palestine using a ship and crew capable of sailing from Europe. In order to facilitate the process, I had each member of the group fill out a form focusing on what they could do on a ship that would help us in our journey. I've those forms and would ask you to go through them, helping me determine which of these young men and women might be helpful.

"The next thing is the ship. Thanks to a recent inheritance, I'm able to purchase and outfit a vessel. However, I don't have the slightest idea as to what constitutes a seafaring, seaworthy ship. Nor do I know where to buy a ship, how much I should be paying for a ship, how to have it overhauled, etc."

"How many people will be on this ship?" asked Olaf.

"About thirty people, plus a partial or full crew, depending on the abilities of my group. Which reminds me, I don't even know how to pick a crew for the ship."

"Who's to be your captain, if I may ask?"

"That's a position still open. I'm still hoping that the Aliyah Bet people, who are the overall organizers, may be able to find someone suitable."

"Seems to me, young man, what you lack in talent you make up in energy and determination," Olaf complimented. "I'm glad you've at least started outlining the problems and obstacles of this venture. My philosophy, based on my many years' experience as an officer in the Norwegian Navy, and then as a First Officer on cruise ships, is that the success of any journey, as you describe, is in the details. Incidentally, I've got six months' leave due me now, and I've passed all the qualifying examinations for captain's rank. Unfortunately for me, most of the captains in my cruise company are only slightly older than I am, so a vacancy for captain only occurs at long intervals. I tell you all this so you should know 'where I'm coming from,' as the Americans say. And I've got 'time to kill,' which is another of their quaint sayings."

"I would be most grateful for any assistance."

"So would I, Uncle," Helen added.

"Good. Then, perhaps, Helen, you can convince your mother to give us a room with a telephone, a table, and some chairs so we can plan this adventure together."

"Of course, Uncle Olaf, that will be absolutely no problem."

"Helen, I also give you permission to call me 'Olaf' in future, since we have little time to spare and we should dispense with any unnecessary items like the superfluous word, 'uncle.'"

"As you wish, Olaf," Helen replied, smiling.

"Fine, then," said Olaf. "Helen, you make the arrangements and we'll meet at the house tomorrow morning."

Helen and Peter both agreed. They all left the cafe, and Peter went home to work on his forms in advance of tomorrow's meeting.

They met, as arranged, the next morning. Helen had provided

their workroom with furniture and a telephone. Peter put the completed forms on the table, but also gave the others a summary of the languages most commonly spoken by the twenty-eight people and a list of the skills most likely to be of use on the ship. Those were as follows:

Languages of "Crew Members"

	Country of Origin	# of People	German	Yiddish	English	French
A	Germany	4	4			
B	Holland	2	2		1	
C	Poland	11		11	1	
D	Lithuania	4		4		
E	Latvia	2		2		
F	Estonia	1		1		
G	Romania	1				1
H	Austria	2	2		1	
J	Russia	1		1	1	
		28	**8**	**19**	**4**	**1**

Peter's List of Skills of "Crew Members"

Desired Occupation	No.	Background	Country of Origin (See Note 1, below)	Notes Below
Seamanship	1	Fisherman with Father	F	
Communications	1	Telephone Wireman	B	
Engineering	3	Auto Mechanic	B, D, J	2
Medical/Housing/ Hygiene	2	Scouts Training	H, H	3
Management	1	Youth Leader	C	4
Accounting	2	Bookkeepers	C, D	

Desired Occupation	No.	Background	Country of Origin (See Note 1, below)	Notes Below
Carpentry	3		A, A, D	
Plumbing	1		G	
Electrical	2	Home Handymen	D, E	
Cooking	0			5
—	12	Nothing	A, A, E & 9 of C	
	28			

Notes:
1. Letters correspond to same countries as in previous chart ("Languages")
2. 1 skilled, 2 Apprentices
3. 1 Scouts Ambulance Badge, 1 (Heide) Scout Instructor
4. Miriam – 5 years in Gdynia in youth organization
5. Need a Cook? A – B to provide
6. Need a Captain

Olaf thumbed quickly through some of the questionnaires and laid them down, then eagerly seized the summaries. He only glanced at the "Languages" summary, showing little interest. However, Olaf read the "Skills" summary slowly and carefully, more than once. Meanwhile, Helen had read through both summaries, familiarized herself with the contents, then put them down in front of her and sat quietly, as did Peter, to await Olaf's reaction.

After a while, Olaf stood up, came over to Peter, laid a large but gentle hand on his shoulder and said, "Peter, this is good work. For a man with no experience of the sea, you've done a most impressive job.

"These summaries will save us a lot of time. I think we're ready to start expanding Peter's 'Desired Occupation' listing."

Olaf wrote an additional list of jobs that would be useful on a ship. Then he asked Peter for the questionnaires of the twelve boys who left the "experience" section blank. After he looked them over again, and thanks to Peter's ability to translate into English, Olaf made some notes and announced, "I must go to Camp Pietro to meet with these people of some skills and to interview each of them. When can I go?"

"I've got to go tomorrow. Is that soon enough?"

Olaf nodded.

Helen said, "Don't forget I want to go as well, Peter."

"Okay," Peter said, "then the three of us will go tomorrow."

CHAPTER X

Camp Pietro 2: Olaf Visits

THE NEXT DAY, THE THREE OF THEM WALKED UP THE HILL TO Camp Pietro. They walked to the entrance and as soon as they were seen, shouts of "Peter and Helen are here" rang around the camp.

Miriam came running to Peter, flung her arms around him and hugged him closely to her.

Alex arrived and greeted Helen, with more decorum, but with a broad smile as they shook hands.

Max and Heide arrived simultaneously. They shook Peter's hand and hugged him warmly.

Peter tried to introduce Olaf, but there was such a crush of people that it was impossible. Dov, the head of the Aliyah Bet contingent, came up to Peter and greeted him with a warm handshake and a hug. Peter introduced Olaf to the small group.

"This is my friend Olaf. He's Helen's uncle and is just what he looks like, a Viking sailor." They all smiled. "You may smile now, but I think you'll find he's the man of the hour. I'll fill everyone in at lunchtime. Alex, please take Helen and Olaf around the camp and show them the extent of our preparations for going to Palestine."

"Absolutely," Alex replied, giving him a friendly punch on his upper arm.

"Oh, my God," Peter shouted in mock pain, "the Zionists are attacking me!"

"Don't worry, Peter," Miriam said, in a calming voice, "I'll look after you, and Heide will help me. We both took first aid courses in a previous life, and if it's broken and has to be removed, we know where to find a good saw."

"Thanks, you're both gorgeous Nurse Florence Nightingales, but I hope I never need your services." Still smiling, Peter couldn't help but notice how much better both Miriam and Heide looked. They had both filled out, looking very attractive, with fresh, healthy, complexions.

He also noticed that Miriam's wavy, chestnut hair was shiny, and full-bodied. Heidi's long, blonde, shining hair looked golden and resplendent.

He shook himself from this rare reverie, an extravagant waste of his time these days. Then he said to Max and Heide, "Will you both be good enough to fix up the seating arrangements for Olaf, Helen, and me at lunchtime and our sleeping quarters. Helen should bunk with Miriam if at all possible, and be near you, too, Heide, so she feels comfortable in these strange surroundings."

"Of course," they both said, and went off make the arrangements.

That left just Miriam and Peter.

"That was most skillfully done, Peter," Miriam said.

"What are you talking about?" he asked innocently.

"You very definitely know what I'm talking about," she replied, laughing, "and I also definitely approve. I like it that you've arranged a moment or two for yourself and me. Am I right or not?"

"Yes, you are absolutely right," he responded, also laughing.

Miriam led them to a hut, which was a storeroom for the camp's fire-fighting equipment and surplus camp beds.

Once inside, they sat down side by side on one of the camp beds. Peter put his arm around her and she allowed her head to rest on his shoulder. They sat quietly for some moments, both of them enormously enjoying the closeness and peaceful feeling of being together, in that way, for the first time.

Peter spoke softly to her. "Miriam, I've got to tell you a few things. First of all, my father was killed in a street accident last week and the funeral was just two days ago. My father was a man of property and I've been busy with all the city and state formalities and all the arrangements for the funeral. Helen was an enormous help to me during those awful days and even came to the funeral and stood by me. She proved herself a real friend, but *not* in the way I've come to think of *you*. Which brings me to my next point.

"Miriam, I want you to know that I think I'm beginning to fall in love with you, that I want to spend more time with you outside the camp, and get to know you better.

"Now, I'm quite sure that in such a close community as this one, it can't have escaped anyone's attention that you and I have something going on between us. Am I right?"

"Yes, of course," she said, "but everybody has been very kind about it and a number of the people have told me that I couldn't have a better man in the whole world. You're the cynosure of all eyes and so, if you only look and smile at me, as you have done from time to time, they see it and a picture is painted."

"Very well," he said, "I shall have to stop looking and smiling at you, immediately."

"Do you want to break my heart, Peter? I don't want you to change anything, though publicly I want you to deal with me in the same way that you deal with everybody else."

The lunch gong sounded. They picked up Olaf and then Helen, from their respective huts, and walked over to the dining room. As they entered, the room became silent and everybody present stood up to greet the guests. Max was the host. He showed Peter to the chair at the head of the table, Helen on his right and Olaf on his left. Miriam and Max went to their usual seats. Then suddenly everybody was clapping their hands and shouting "Welcome, Welcome," in a dozen languages. Tears were rolling down Helen's face. Even Olaf's eyes were glistening. Eventually, the applause died away, the food appeared, everybody composed themselves, and plates were passed out.

"Tell me why you cried, Helen," said Peter.

"That was one of the most tender moments I've ever experienced," she said. "That these boys and girls who survived the hell of the concentration camps should applaud *us*, that they should compliment *us* in that way, that was almost too much for me to bear." Tears flowed down her cheeks again and she tried to regain her composure.

"She's quite right," Olaf added. "If that applause had gone on for another minute, I would also have joined Helen in shedding tears."

Dov and his kitchen staff had exceeded themselves that day – the lunch was the best the boys and girls could remember. When the plates had been passed down the table and taken away and everybody had his or her cup of coffee or tea in front of them, the conversations died off and the company sat back, looking with expectation at the visitors' end of the table.

At length, Peter rose to his feet and said, "Good evening, chevrah." He felt proud that he had had remembered the Hebrew word for "friends."

"You've all met Helen before, when you were in the hospital. She insisted on coming with me to see you all here. I'll ask her to say a few words to you all when I've finished talking, although I didn't warn her beforehand. She's a very smart lady and I'm sure she'll speak to you from the heart.

"Before I introduce our first speaker, I want to tell you some bad news followed by some good news. Tragically, my father died very suddenly last week. Actually, I wasn't sure until the last minute whether I'd have to remain at home to take care of my mother for a while. But, she's a strong woman and insisted I visit my boys and girls."

Murmurs of condolences were heard coming from all the company.

"Thank you. Now for the good news. My father left me a considerable amount of money. I've decided to use some of that money to purchase a ship and overhaul it so that, after we find a crew, you can set sail for Palestine."

A round of applause filled the dining hall. Everyone understood that with Peter financing their escape to Palestine, the endless waiting would be over sooner.

"Now, I want to formally introduce Commodore Olaf Cohen from Norway, Helen's uncle. He served as an officer in Norway's Navy, then after he retired, he joined a company which owns cruise ships. He's the second-in-command on one of those ships and is now on a six-month leave.

"Thanks to Helen, Olaf has agreed to be our nautical and technical advisor, supervising our plans to sail to Palestine.

"After lunch," Peter continued, "we want to start making use of Olaf's expertise at once. He has seen the questionnaires which you all filled out and he wants to talk to a number of you. We'll call out names before we break. Those who are called please go to Hut 17."

"Now, I want to call on Miss Helen Phillips to say a few words to you."

Shyly, Helen stood and looked along the table, meeting everybody's eyes, one by one. She then took a deep breath and spoke in German.

"My dear chevrah, I won't speak for very long, but there are just a few things I want to say. First of all, I feel that God has given me a wonderful opportunity to be able to help you, especially after what you have gone through in your young lives.

"Next, I want to say that despite what you've suffered and experienced, *you* also have been *blessed* by Providence in that you met up with Peter. Peter possesses special qualities, not the least of which are

82

his extraordinary compassion and leadership abilities. The fact that he's a Gentile makes this all the more extraordinary.

"Finally, a personal note. As a result of your example, and my own love of Zion, I've decided to join you, in whatever job Olaf decides I'm best suited for, to make Aliyah and live in Palestine."

Everyone applauded wildly. They had previously seen Helen as a beautiful, upper-class Jewish-Swiss lady who always tried to make them feel that she was one of them, but a few felt she was of a different social level, and possibly too different to really be one of them. Her decision to make Aliyah was a much-needed shot in the arm for those who now understood that her heart was, indeed, in the right place – Palestine.

Peter was on his feet again. "Helen, this is wonderful. I hardly know what to say. We're proud to be in your company."

Peter took a deep breath and continued.

"Sorry, Commodore, but I doubt that anything you say can top that. But please, do tell us what you envision for our small group."

"Shalom, chevrah," Olaf began, his large bulk towering over Peter. "When I heard from my niece Helen about your group, where you had been, your eighteen countries of origin, your quixotic intentions of illegal immigration to Palestine, past the British Royal Navy, well, to tell you the truth, I thought she was dealing with a group of lunatics. But having met Peter and Dov, I now realize that the survivors of Hitler's "Final Solution" deserve all the help they can get to reach their goal. And I'm proud to be part of this group.

"But the problems are enormous. As you've been told, I'm starting work after lunch to try and put together a ship's crew. It may be that I will eventually need to interview every one of you to see where I can best fit you in our crew. I say *our* crew because I can see that while it is logical for me to be your naval consultant and technical advisor, it is an absolute, personal decision that I take upon myself the role of captain as well."

Everyone began to cheer.

After the noise quieted down, Peter stood up yet again. Everyone wondered what was left to say. Peter thanked Olaf and Helen profusely, reminded the group that sixteen names were going to be read out, then said, almost matter-of-factly, "Oh yes, and by the way, *I'm* going to sail on my ship, too, and *I'm* going to Palestine, and *I'm* going to live there with all of you. I *was* going to tell you even *before* I heard the news from Helen and Olaf."

There was a feeling of euphoria about the group. What could be better than a professional captain, a benefactor, and a woman of valor to lead them?

As they entered Hut 17, Olaf said, "After studying the jobs list, I gave it a little thought and came up with a few more."

"Well, I'm not the slightest bit surprised" Peter responded. "What are they?"

"Radio operator, bo's'n, helmsman, lookouts, navigator."

"What's a bo's'n?"

"He's a kind of head sailor. He's in charge of all the deck activities and equipment on the deck areas – cables, chairs, life-saving, etc. – and also calls people to duty or shifts. His real title is "boatswain," shortened to bo's'n."

"Do we have time to train people for some of these jobs?" asked Peter.

"If we work creatively, I think we can fill some of the spots. For instance, an ex-scout or youth-club member might know Morse Code and be able to work as a radio operator. Any intelligent person can be taught the job of helmsman in a half-hour. Lookouts only need intelligence, binoculars, and motivation. And so on. Each job is different, but intelligence and motivation can sometimes make up for the lack of experience. Other jobs may need a greater technical background."

Olaf, Peter, Helen, Max, and Alex were seated in a half-circle, with an empty chair in front of them for the interviewees. It had been decided that that was the friendliest way to arrange themselves so as not to give the people the impression of a tribunal.

"Who has the list of the sixteen people waiting in the dining room? And who's going to call the others one by one?" Olaf asked.

Peter said, "Here's the list. As each one is finished here, they can go to the dining room and call out the next one."

"Fine," Olaf agreed, picking up the questionnaires. "Now, the first to be called is Miriam."

They started at 2:00 p.m. that day, with Peter and Olaf both making notes about each person interviewed. They found every interviewee open and frank. Olaf knew how to ask questions with politeness and patience, and also had that unique ability to ferret out information that sometimes the interviewee himself didn't know he had.

At 6:45 p.m., Olaf suggested they should break and get ready for dinner. They had dealt with eight people in just under five hours. Olaf calculated that the semi-skilled people were taking about thirty-five minutes each. The unskilled ones would be quicker, so he estimated it would take another three hours after dinner and a full day tomorrow to interview all twenty-eight (thirty, including Peter and Helen). While everyone was pretty exhausted, Olaf, despite having led all the questioning, seemed fresh and energetic. Helen asked him how he managed it and he told her that he was always stimulated when faced with a new challenge. "I was greatly impressed by the average quality of these young men and women and I'm becoming somewhat optimistic that we can put together a good portion of the crew with perhaps our friends at Aliyah Bet filling in the vacancies."

After dinner, their group managed to interview six more people before breaking for the night. Peter went to his hut and found that his luggage had been unpacked, his clothing placed in drawers, and his toiletries lined up on top of the small camp chest of drawers. He didn't have to think hard to realize that Miriam must be looking after him. With that thought in mind, he fell asleep almost instantly.

He was awakened by the sound of his door being closed. He became aware that somebody was sitting on the side of his bed but nothing was said.

After a few minutes, he found there was sufficient light through his window from outside to identify Miriam as the one sitting on the bed. Still not a word had been said. After a few moments, a voice whispered to him, "I thought you would never wake up and I was getting colder by the minute sitting here. I sincerely hope you don't have any objections to my being here."

Before he could answer, she continued –

"You know, Peter, you appeared, suddenly, like a fairy godfather into my life, after which a lot of miraculous things happened to me. And now your decision to sail away from here *together with us*, with me, to live in Palestine . . . It's as though God kept me from dying so that I could survive and be with you. As though you were waiting for me to enter your life, and you to enter mine.

"I can't mince words at this point in my life. I've learned that every day is a gift I hold very dear. Peter, I am deeply in love with you, have been from the first day we met. And why it might not be tactful, or ladylike to say this, I don't think that I could ever find, nor would I want to find anyone else, even if you don't feel the same way about me.

"And now I'm going to stop, to let you get a word in. But before I do, just like a woman, I want to say one thing more. I'm sitting on your bed for the first time and there is nothing in the world to prevent us from getting closer, except our own self-control."

A silence hovered between them.

85

Peter didn't know how to begin. He was very attracted to her, felt deeply for her, but he barely knew her. She professed love for him, but was it love or a loneliness, which so many victims of the camps were likely to have suffered from? In the end, would she tire of him? And what about him? Weren't his feelings for her tainted, at some level, with the same sense of pity he felt for all those who went through such a terrible ordeal?

At last he spoke. "Miriam, first let me say how much I admire your frankness and honesty. Your forthrightness takes my breath away.

"I have deep feelings for you. I can't deny that. But we hardly know each other. And while you profess love for me, you have to admit that your seeing me as a savior of the group greatly clouds your knowledge of the real me. The solution, as I see it, is that we have to spend more time together; we need to know the different sides of each other's personality. It will take time, but dear Miriam, we'll have time, time to plan and discover whether what we're feeling now is, indeed, love."

"I understand, and, as always, you're thinking is clear, honest, and to the point," she told him, a hint of disappointment in her voice. "I'm not taking this as rejection. Quite the contrary. I'm taking this as a new beginning between us, a time to explore each other's feelings and to create the bond that people in love need to have. I think that's where I'm weakest. The years most girls discover love, I was discovering hatred and suffering. Now's my chance, and you can be sure I will take it – with open arms."

"Hello, Miriam," said Heide, as Miriam entered her hut. "Your timing is perfect. Five minutes earlier and you might have run into *my* visitor!"

"I think your visit was much different than mine," Miriam replied. "But what I need now is some sleep."

"Me too," Heide said. "We'll talk later."

At 7:00 a.m. Miriam and Heide reluctantly crawled out of their beds and stood looking at each other. They were both haggard, exhausted, unable to open their eyes more than a sliver. Lack of sleep had taken its toll. They stared at each other a moment later and then broke out into wild laughter, throwing themselves on each other's shoulder.

By 7:45 a.m. they were both showered, dressed, and made up (using very little make-up – they were conserving their supplies), and sitting on their beds waiting for the 8:00 a.m. call. There was a knock on the door. They both called "enter" in two languages and the door opened to admit Helen. She had two packages, one of which she gave to each of the others.

"Well, good morning, you two," she said, looking at them. "Did either of you go to sleep at all last night?"

Both Miriam and Heidi laughed. "Does it show that much?" Miriam asked Helen.

Helen said, "Well, yes, but fortunately, I've brought you fresh supplies of make-up. Do me a favor, and use it. Now."

They thanked Helen and began using the toiletries at once, under her supervision.

Breakfast was a noisy affair. Those who had been interviewed yesterday were being asked by the others how the interviews went and what kinds of questions to prepare for.

When Peter got wind of this, he stood up and knocked on a water glass with a knife for attention.

"I understand that there is some worry about the interviews. Let me make it clear: This is no pass/fail exam. This is the only way we can help Olaf determine who does what on the ship, when we get one. When he has finished seeing each of you, he, and only he, will make up a provisional crew list. It will only be just that for now, since some of the crew requirements will depend on the sort of ship, its size, and so on. There is nothing to be worried about. You will all be on the ship, every man and woman, and you will all be given a job and the duties of each job will be explained to you, in your own languages, so that you will all understand what part each of you will play in this project. So, stop worrying.

"Our program for today is this. There are fourteen who have been seen. That leaves sixteen, including Helen, myself, Max, and Alex, who need to be interviewed. You know who you are and you'll be called, one by one, as quickly as we can."

The interview team finished speaking to twelve remaining people by lunch. The last four would be dealt with later.

After lunch, Olaf publicly thanked the twenty-six people whom he had interviewed. "If the last four people are finished lunch, I'd like to interview you now and then create a provisional crew list. Tomorrow, we'll let you know what position you are best suited for and tell you what comes next."

With that, the last four and Olaf went to Hut 17. When it was Peter's turn, he delineated his background, ending with, "I think that's it."

"Peter, you've forgotten something, haven't you?" Helen asked.

"What could I possibly have forgotten?"

"Don't you ride a motorbike?"

"Yes," he admitted. "I forgot to mention that, but I can hardly take that on the ship, can I?"

Olaf intervened. "On the contrary, Peter; if possible, you should take it with us. It might be useful to take ashore once we reach port and you never know what use the Haganah might have for it."

"Very well, Olaf. But I think Helen forgot something as well," Peter retorted, unable to conceal a smile.

"And what could that be?" Helen asked.

"You can fly," he pointed out.

"That's hardly going to help our voyage, is it?"

Olaf intervened again. "You never know, Helen, and as the captain, I should be aware of it.

"Now, if no one has forgotten anything else, we need to assemble our notes and commence our crew list."

For the next two hours, they worked non-stop. Once the list was made, Olaf released Peter and the rest of the group. He would have to make the final decisions himself. After all, he understood the jobs involved, and, after the interviews, had a good idea of the kinds of people he was dealing with.

After dinner, Peter said to Miriam, "Would you like to go for a walk with me, out of the camp, for a little while? We can just chat and get to know each other a bit more, like we said we needed to do."

"Yes, of course, I'd love to. Just wait a couple of minutes please, while I go back to my room for a sweater."

"Fine," he said. "I'll meet you at the entrance gate."

She hurried off and Peter strolled over to the gate.

She reappeared a few minutes later and they went out and started up the road. They strolled together with arms linked in the dusk until it became night. They were together for about two hours, walking up and down the road to the camp, talking non-stop. They exchanged their personal views on a host of subjects.

She talked a little about her time in Ravensbrueck Concentration and Extermination Camp and she continued to marvel at the fact that she had survived. She talked fleetingly about the mass murders she had seen, the overcrowding, malnutrition and physical abuse. Peter was very curious and pressed her for details, but after a time, she said she couldn't talk about it anymore, at least not now. She agreed to talk to him further about her experiences in the future.

Peter, for his part, admitted how very little he had personally known about what happened in Europe and how his parents had insulated him from the realities around him. He told her how, just a few months earlier, he had had been shocked to learn of the existence of concentration camps and extermination camps, and how angry he had felt at his parents for keeping that knowledge from him.

Miriam found it very difficult to understand how such a smart, intellectual, and curious person could have failed to be aware of what terrible things were happening in Europe.

Peter kept apologizing, but explained that there was almost nothing about the camps in the newspapers he read until 1945. But he admitted that he was to blame as well. He was so taken up with his studies and his love for the Scouts that he didn't think that the occasional rumors were true and he didn't really relate to things going on a continent away. He spent all his spare time working as a Scoutmaster, with the forty boys under his guidance.

"So it seems, Miriam, your hero has but feet of clay," he said despondently.

Miriam was silent, thinking what a blow to his ego it must have been to admit these things to her.

"Well, my love," she said at last, "I prefer to love a man who isn't afraid to admit he's human than someone who feels he can do no wrong. At the same time, I should tell you that no matter what you did or didn't know, all twenty-eight of us here consider you our hero in the real sense. And the dozens of others who chose different paths all considered you their savior as well. So don't be too sad.

"Brrrr! It's dark and I'm getting cold and I want nothing more now than to hold your hands. I've given you a hard time today, but you wanted us to get to know each other better, and we'll both have to accept the bad with the good if we want to truly understand the other."

Next morning at breakfast, Olaf said to Peter, "I finished my work, we have a crew list and here's a copy for you. I suggest we discuss this after breakfast with Helen, Max, and Alex, then brief everybody after lunch."

"That's fine, Olaf, so long as we all are in agreement. Then after the briefing, can we go back to Berne?"

"Absolutely, Peter. Here's the list. And here are the general steps that need to be taken as soon as possible."

Peter read:

1.   Find a ship to buy.
2.   Arrange overhaul.
3.   Arrange to stock it for a trip.

4.   Do some planning for training the crew.

Peter took Miriam aside after breakfast and told her what Olaf had just told him. "So, I'll be leaving this afternoon, Miriam, I'm sorry to say."

"Oh, and I'm so sorry, too, Peter. When will you be back?"

"I can't say, but it will be as soon as possible, to spend more time with you. But while I'm away, you may be sure I'll be working with Olaf to procure a ship."

After breakfast, Olaf, Peter, Helen, Max, and Alex met and Olaf presented his list, headed "Olaf's Crew." He had made copies for the others.

The first thing he said he would need were two professionals, a ship's engineer and a ship's chef. He would speak to Dov to find one of each through the Aliyah Bet. These were obviously necessary and not available from the group. He then explained a few things:

Miriam had the most organizational experience, so she would work with Peter on the work rotations, administrative work, and paperwork, bills of lading, and other matters.

Heide had been a first-aid instructor in the Scouts for five years and would be in charge of medical and hygiene with three assistants for cleanliness and toilet hygiene, etc. – a very important task (seasickness, etc.) on board a ship.

Helen would deal with all money matters.

Olaf had found one of the boys, from Rumania, who had studied geography, and he would be the navigator.

Olaf explained the duties of the bo's'n, and the one boy from Estonia, who had been a fisherman, would have that job.

The only three in the group who knew Morse Code were himself, Ivan the Russian, and Peter, so they would be called on when necessary.

The lookouts would be seven boys: six would do eight-hour shifts, the seventh would relieve all of them, as necessary, for meals and toilet breaks, but there had to be two on duty at all times, one fore and one aft. This was a very important job. Five were from Poland and two from Lithuania, and they all spoke Yiddish, so changeovers would be simplified.

Five of the boys would be trained as helmsmen. Four would do six-hour shifts, and the spare man would relieve them as necessary.

The actual names of the group personnel for each job were then marked on the "Olaf's Crew" sheets.

It was agreed that after lunch, Olaf and Peter would leave to go back to Berne. Max would read out the ship's jobs to the group, with assistance in translation from Alex. Helen would arrange to have copies of the crew list, with names of individuals, given to everyone. Helen was to stay another week in Camp Pietro.

Olaf's Crew – Captain: Olaf Cohen

Job	Group			Aliyah Bet
	How Many	Who*	Notes	
Radio	2	B,J	Morse Code: Olaf, Ivan, Peter	
Engineering	4	A,A,B,H		
Chief				1
Pipes				
Electrical				
Carpenter				
Medical/Hygiene	3	H,A,D.	Heide in charge	
Cargo/Admin.	2	Peter, Miram		
Purser	1	Helen		
Chef	2	C,E		1
Helm	5	C,C,C,C,E (4 × 6-hour shifts + 1 spare)		
Navigation	2	D,G (G = Geog. Student)		
Bo's'n	2	A,F (F = Fisherman)		
Lookouts	7	D,D,C,C,C,C,C (6 × 8-hour shifts + 1 Relief)		
	30			**2**

* Letters represent same countries as listed on "Languages of Crew Members" chart

After lunch, Olaf spoke to Dov, telling him they would need a ship's engineer and a ship's chef from Aliyah Bet, but all the remaining crew jobs could be handled by the group. Dov said he would need at least two weeks' notice to supply the people needed. Olaf said he would let Aliyah Bet know in due course where those two people would have to report.

Olaf told Peter that as soon as the ship was bought, they would want the engineer and chef to join them so that the engineer could supervise the overhaul and the chef would start to plan to order the food, fuel, and kitchen supplies. Together, they would order the ship's spare parts and accessories with Olaf.

The pair arrived back in Berne. Peter was to meet Olaf at Helen's house the next morning.

CHAPTER XI

In Berne and Salonika 1

PETER AND OLAF SAT DOWN IN THEIR WORK ROOM.

"So, what's the order of business, Olaf?" Peter asked.

"Before we start on the ship, there's something else that's bothering me," Olaf told him. "Yesterday, in the camp, I was looking at our group and trying to think of them as a seaworthy crew. But you know, they don't *look* like a crew. What happens if we're boarded? Everyone is so thin and pale. It's impossible to mistake them for a ship's crew."

"You're right, Olaf. And I've an idea how we can handle this problem. Suppose we take then to a hotel for a few weeks, somewhere where there's sun, and have them just laze around, soaking up the rays. At the same time, they'll relax and eat three solid meals a day, which should fatten them up. During that time, we'll finish with the ship. What do you think?"

"I think it's a perfect answer to this problem. I may know of just the hotel. We'll have to time things so that the Aliyah Bet people send us the engineer and chef before we actually set sail and integrate them with our crew, who also need hands-on training. I also need to know what routes have been tried already, how successful the operations have been, and what dangers, besides the British, may lurk in the waters. Perhaps you can speak to the Aliyah Bet people about this."

"Done," said Peter.

"As to the hotel," continued Olaf, "I was in the City of Alicante in southeast Spain recently. It's on the Mediterranean, has good beaches, and a few decent hotels. Spain usually has warm weather by about May, which is three months from now. I doubt we'll be able to set sail much before that."

"Sounds reasonable, but I'll leave these kinds of logistics up to you," said Peter. "But I've been thinking, it's quite a trek from here to Spain. Helen's a pilot. Perhaps we can find a plane and she can ferry everyone to Spain."

"Good man," Olaf declared. "You do that while I go to my room for my address book to see who I can call to start looking for a ship."

Olaf left and Peter got on the phone. In a few minutes, he was speaking to Dov at the camp and he asked for Helen.

"Hi Peter, what's up?" came her usual cheerful voice.

"Remember when you told me you thought your pilot license was irrelevant to our journey? Well, we're now in the market for a pilot. What kinds of planes are you licensed to fly?"

"I'm qualified to fly one- and two-engine planes and to fly by day and night. I've been checked out on about a dozen aircraft."

"Good. Can you come to Berne so I can brief you for a very important job?"

"Of course, Peter, though Alex will be disappointed that I'm leaving so soon after my arrival here."

"Well, remind him of the English saying, 'Absence makes the heart grow fonder.' I'll look forward to seeing you here very soon."

"Will do, Peter."

Olaf re-entered the room just as Peter was finishing with Helen. "What's going on?" he asked.

"Well, I found out that Helen's qualified to fly one- and two-engine planes, so I asked her to return as soon as possible. She's the best person to help us buy a suitable aircraft. We'll use it to bring the gang to Spain and take it along with us to Palestine. It will certainly find use there."

Olaf gazed at him with renewed appreciation. "For an academic, you're a very logical businessman. Just the kind of leader we need.

"Meanwhile, I've found the phone number of a close and old friend of mine named Frederik. He's Norwegian and was in the navy with me, before the war. He married a beautiful Greek girl whose family are ship brokers, among other things. After the war was over, we reconnected. He told me that he was back in Athens and in business again."

He took the phone and called Athens.

When it was over, Olaf turned to Peter, saying, "That was a useful call. He told me that he doesn't know of a ship for us, but there's another ship broker he knows, in Salonika, and he's going to call him. If he knows of a ship, the broker will call me."

Soon after, Helen called to say she could meet with Peter the next day. Then, a Joseph Christofolous from Salonika called. Yes, he had heard from Frederik. He believed he might be able to find the ship being sought. Olaf and Joseph arranged to meet in two days, in Salonika. Joseph said he would reserve two rooms in a good hotel and told him how to get in touch with him.

"When I see Helen tomorrow," Peter told Olaf, "I'll ask her to go to Zurich, to the Aliyah Bet woman she already knows. That will help start the ball rolling. I'll try to be ready to join you in two days' time. Meanwhile, you may want to think of what cargo we should be carrying, if any."

Peter made another call, this time to Spain, to the Hotel Palas in Alicante. He wanted to be sure the hotel could handle a party of thirty, given just a few weeks' notice. They said they would be delighted to welcome the party in due course, and told Peter the rate, which was in pesetas and seemed eminently reasonable.

When they all met the next day, Peter reviewed their present situation, including the upcoming trip to Spain.

"A group of thirty traveling together on trains through Italy, France, Spain is very noticeable. There are undoubtedly British spies at the stations and ports all the way along the North Mediterranean coast specifically looking out for potential illegal immigrants to Palestine, so we need a more clandestine route to Alicante.

"So we want you, Helen, to find a plane we can purchase, which can take us all. Now that the war is over, there are probably a lot of planes on the open market.

"You'll also have to go to Zurich to see the *dentist*. We need to know previous routes, alternate routes, and the best recommended route to Palestine. We'll also need radio frequencies and codes to contact people in Palestine, when the time comes. Find out who to contact, and how, in order to bring the ship's engineer and chef to the appropriate port immediately after we purchase our ship. The engineer has to supervise the complete fitting out of the ship and the chef has to work out how much kitchen and food supplies we will need and how much the ship can hold.

"Any questions, Helen?" Peter asked.

"My goodness, you've certainly been diligent," she told them. "I'm just glad you've left me something to do," she teased. "Don't worry, I'll handle everything."

Olaf and Peter met at Berne airport at 8:00 a.m. the following morning, for a flight to Rome. In Rome, they had to wait four hours for a plane to Athens. There, they took old, cold, slow, trains that stopped at every station on their way to Salonika. They arrived at 9:00 p.m. and managed to find an aged taxi, which took them to their hotel on Aristoteles Street. At last, they were in a warm, welcoming environment. They were shown to their adjacent rooms. Olaf made a phone call to Joseph, who said he was coming over right away, bringing a bottle to celebrate their meeting. Olaf invited him to have dinner with them in the hotel.

Olaf and Peter had only just entered the dining room when Joseph showed up. He was very tall, even taller than Olaf, and emaciatingly thin. Peter was reminded of how some of the boys looked when he first saw them in the hospital. Joseph smiled and put a bottle of cognac on their table.

"Shalom Aleichem, Mr. Cohen," Joseph said, sitting down.

Olaf was astonished. "Do you speak Hebrew?"

"I'll explain in a minute," Joseph said. "First, I want to meet your associate." He shook hands with Peter. A waiter brought a chair and three glasses, opened the cognac, and poured three measures. They each drank.

"I think you gentlemen should know something about me if we are to enter into a meaningful business relationship. First of all, my family name is not Christofolous, but Levy. It was changed when Greece was occupied by the Germans, in 1941. With the help of the mayor of the town where I was born, I had a complete set of documents made for me in a good Christian name. However, in the end, it didn't matter. The Germans had a nasty habit of making a man drop his trousers whenever they suspected he might be Jewish. When they saw I was circumcised, I was taken away.

"That happened in 1943. I was sent to Auschwitz with 60,000 Jews from this city and I somehow survived. But only 2,000 of us managed to survive and return to our beloved Salonika.

"I decided to retain the name Christofolous, which I knew would help me with my business colleagues. I met your friend, Frederik, in Athens just before the war, when I was just married and trying to set up in business for myself. Frederik was very kind and helped me learn the business. He had also just married, so we had a lot in common. After the war, I got in touch with him again. He had returned to Athens and was delighted to know I had survived. He agreed to send any business he couldn't handle my way. So, Frederik passed you on to me and it is my sincere intention to help you in any way I can.

"I know I sound a bit long-winded, but the prospect of doing business with a fellow member of the house of Abraham is both exciting and satisfying for me. Now, please tell me how I can help you. It goes without saying that anything you tell me will be held in the strictest of confidence."

Olaf and Peter exchanged a glance, each nodded positively to the other, indicating that they were both generally satisfied with Joseph's presentation and that he could probably be trusted with their secret requirements.

"Thank you very much," Olaf said to Joseph. "We very much would like your help and accept everything you've said. By the way, I want to let you know that Peter is not Jewish, but is the originator of the story which I will now tell you.

"Peter lives in Switzerland and became aware a few months ago of a group of young people, almost entirely Jewish, who were survivors of concentration camps in Auschwitz, Ravensbrueck, and elsewhere, in a hospital in Berne, the capital of Switzerland. He befriended them and since then has been their mentor, guide, and is now the leader of a group of thirty of them who aim to immigrate to Palestine, despite the efforts of the British Royal Navy.

"As for me, you know my name. I'm a Norwegian, once an officer in the Norwegian Navy, now qualified as a ship's captain. I act as this group's consultant and advisor. I will act as the ship's captain on its voyage to Palestine.

"We are here to look for a seaworthy vessel of any sort, capable of carrying thirty people, from our European port of departure to Palestine. We'll buy the ship outright without the need for a mortgage, arrange for its "as needed" overhaul, provision it with fuel, food, and other necessities for a voyage across the Mediterranean.

"We need you to represent us; to find a ship and help arrange for any necessary overhaul or maintenance work on the ship and engines, electrical systems, all instruments and communication equipment, satisfactory accommodation and facilities, separate quarters for the captain and the owner, lifeboats, and all lifesaving equipment.

"Finally, you must accomplish your task without disclosing anything about our group or who is paying for the ship. We assume that all ports around the northern Mediterranean may well have British spies, alert for any signs of Jewish 'illegals' going on board a ship heading for Palestine.

"I've some ideas in my head of what course we might set to avoid the Royal Navy, but that will depend on the location of the port of departure. What do you say, Joseph?"

"I believe I'm the perfect man for this job," he replied. "Having grown up in Salonika, I know absolutely everybody in the maritime business in this city, and in many other cities as well. I've previously carried out the tasks you need, for others, so I know what has to be done and how to keep it confidential. As for my fee –"

"Yes," Olaf interrupted. He had been looking for an opportune time to broach the subject and was glad that Joseph had brought it up.

"My charges would be as follows: For finding a satisfactory ship, you will pay me ten percent of your purchase price. For finding and supervising a maintenance and overhaul company to make the ship sea- worthy, I will expect a commission of 12.5 percent of your payments. For arranging provisioning of fuel and food and all galley requirements, a commission of 7.5 percent on all payments. Furthermore, I undertake to attempt to get the lowest possible prices for everything you will buy. The suppliers will bill me and I will bill you plus my commissions. I will expect my bills to be paid in sterling, dollars, or Swiss francs at the rate of exchange on the bill date, within seven days of that date. Any local bank can inform you of the rate of exchange against the drachma, on any day. I will provide a standard maritime contract, written in French, if that's not a problem, for you to examine."

"Fine," Olaf said. "We'll talk over these matters and I suggest a meeting tomorrow at, say, 11:00 a.m., if that's convenient. By the way, the French is no problem. Peter is a linguist."

"That will be fine," said Joseph. "Shall we meet here in the hotel? They have a good private room which we can use and it will save you having to go out."

"Excellent," said Olaf, "and you can stay and have lunch with us here tomorrow."

After dinner, Joseph left. Olaf and Peter were exhausted and went to their rooms, agreeing to meet again at breakfast to discuss the matter further.

The next morning, Olaf and Peter sat down to eat, but it was clear neither had had much sleep.

"It's clear that Joseph was in a concentration camp. I saw the number on his arm," Olaf pointed out. "But it's unlikely that he's been in business for more than a year. He was very young when the war broke out, so how much experience could he have acquired in his working life?

"On the other hand," he continued, "I trust Frederik. He has good instincts. And Salonika is a bustling port city. If Joseph was in the shipping business at any time in his career, it won't take long to renew acquaintances and make new contacts."

They agreed to go along with Joseph for the time being, but to keep alert. Unfortunately, neither of them knew the Greek language and so they had to be particularly vigilant at such meetings unless they could be conducted in a language that either Peter or Olaf understood.

They decided to negotiate the fees. So soon after the war, it was unlikely that Joseph could be very busy. The considerable commission percentages that Joseph requested were probably just his "wish list." Therefore, it was decided that Olaf should offer a five percent commission on the ship's purchase, no more than a five percent on maintenance and overhaul work (because they would have their own engineer supervising the work), and five percent on food, fuel, and galley requirements (as they would have their own chef ordering most of those items). Basically, they would offer him a flat five percent on all purchases and expenses.

It was 9:00 a.m. by the time they finished a leisurely breakfast. Peter decided to ask the hotel manager, Alex, for the name and address of the most reliable bank in Salonika, in order to open an account. The manager gave him the name of the "Bank of Greece and the Cyclades" and offered to call the bank manager, Yanis, to introduce him, as he knew him well. He had served in the Greek army during the war, in the same unit as Alex.

Alex called Yanis, explaining that Peter was interested in opening an account at the bank. Yanis said he could be at the hotel within the hour.

"Nice to meet you," Yanis said, bowing slightly to Peter and Olaf. He was a balding, slightly overweight gentleman of about forty, finely dressed in a suit and bow tie.

They sat at a table in the lobby.

"If you don't mind me asking, what is the purpose of your business in Salonika?"

"We're here to buy a ship. If all goes well, I will transfer funds from my account in Switzerland to your bank. At the moment I don't know how much that will be, but needless to say, purchasing a ship is a costly venture."

"I understand that ships, like aircraft, are usually sold in American dollars. The bank has a number of clients in the shipping industry." Yanis then opened his briefcase and took out some forms, written in Greek, that would get the process of opening an account moving forward. Peter wanted to open accounts in drachma, Swiss francs, and US dollars.

"You'll need code numbers to activate your Swiss account," Yanis told him after he had signed the documents. "If you need to transfer francs to drachmas or dollars, a simple phone call to me will be sufficient."

Before leaving, Yanis advised Peter that if he ever wanted to exchange currency, he would do best to use the bank and not money changers or even a hotel for the accurate and best rate of exchange. He further suggested that with inflation rising in Greece and the political situation there becoming unstable, he would be advised to exchange foreign currency to drachma only as needed, keeping the balance of his funds in a hard currency such as Swiss francs or US dollars.

Joseph arrived at 11:00. Peter and Olaf were still at the same table.

Olaf wasted no time in explaining that he felt the fees were too high. He also let it be known that they had met earlier with someone who also had an interest in helping them find a boat. Clearly, Joseph hadn't thought his clients would try to negotiate his commission, nor shop around, and took a few moments to recover from his surprise.

They bargained for a short while, but Joseph soon realized that they were not going to budge from the five percent they offered. On top of that, he had not made a sizable sale since he started his business and he was afraid that if he asked for time to think about their offer, he would be out of the loop.

"Gentlemen," he said, regaining his composure, "you drive a hard bargain and what you offer is less than I would expect for the services you ask for. However, to close the matter, I accept your offer."

All three stood as Peter and Olaf shook Joseph's hand. Then, Joseph said, "I'm going outside to hail a taxi, which will take just a few minutes. Unfortunately, my car didn't start this morning. I think you'd enjoy a short tour of the port, which will give you the lie of the land, as it were."

When Joseph went outside, Peter couldn't resist complimenting Olaf on his business acumen.

"Thank you, Peter," said Olaf, with a smile. "I've had to learn a lot about business since I retired from the navy. I'm just happy that

I was able to justify my position with you as your consultant. But from now on, I'll be the sailor and you can be the contract man. By the way, I strongly suggest you get a lawyer's advice before you sign either the forms or any contract with Joseph. Now, let's go and join Joseph in his taxi. I wonder if he even has a car?"

They went outside and found Joseph standing by a taxi. They got in, Joseph sitting in front with the driver.

"I'd like to show you Salonika's port first, gentlemen. There's been a port and a city here since before Jesus was born."

He then proceeded to direct the driver all around the north of Thessaloniki Bay, from Kolochori to Kalamaria, first to orient them to the maritime boundaries of the city, then back along the waterfront from east to west, stopping at the various docks and wharves, so that Olaf could see the amount and type of activities being carried on in the port area.

When they finished the tour, Olaf thanked Joseph for pointing out matters of port interest to them, then said he would like to visit some of the port victualers and ships' chandlers, and finally, the repair and overhaul companies.

"That's fine. Let's break for lunch now," Joseph suggested. "I've hired the taxi for the day so we can eat at a leisurely pace. And I know just the place."

Olaf and Peter readily agreed.

The driver took them to the restaurant that Joseph had recommended. They had a delicious meal, washed down with ouzo. Peter had changed a small amount of money at the hotel and insisted on paying for the lunch despite Joseph's offer to do so.

The driver was waiting when they emerged. Joseph directed him to a number of ships' chandlers and victualers, with Peter taking notes about each establishment. Then they visited three shipyards, where they could see a number of ships in dry dock undergoing repairs and overhaul. Olaf spoke to the managers of each dockyard, to learn of the types of work they were capable of doing.

At the end of their tour, Olaf said, "Joseph, I can't help feeling that your silence about a ship that would be suitable for us means you already have something to show us and are just waiting for the right moment. Am I right?"

"You're not only a tough negotiator, you're a mind reader as well," Joseph told Olaf. "Yes, I've one ship to show you today and one for tomorrow. The second one is moored up a creek about forty kilometers from here and the first one is here in the docks. So I'll take you to that other one tomorrow."

"That's fine. Tell me about the first one."

"Well, it's what we call a 'coastal' or 'tramp steamer.' It's been used to take cargoes along the coast to the various ports and small towns and is owned by a company in Athens. I spoke with them on the phone this morning before I came to your hotel. They've had it about ten years and just replaced it with an American wartime ship – I believe it's called a Liberty ship – maybe you know of them, Olaf?"

"They're a miracle of American invention," Olaf stated. "They were prefabricated in sections by various companies in various cities in the USA and sent to an assembly dock on specific days in a special sequence. There, they were welded together in a matter of seven days by men and women who worked three eight-hour shifts and were usually launched within seven days from the receipt of the first parts of the ship. An amazing operation."

"But what about the details of the ship?" Olaf inquired.

"Well, from the information I've received so far, I can say that it probably had an operating crew of about ten men, and included women on board, usually wives of crewmen, as well. I don't know the condition of the ship. There is an agent who looks after the ship and sees to it that there is always a watchman on board. The Athens office has already told him to expect us. We'll be there in about ten minutes."

"Do you know the age of this ship?"

"No, I don't, but we can find that out from the agent."

"What about the price?"

"You haven't given me a budget, so I went after a ship I thought met all your other requirements. You'll have to negotiate price through me. Oh yes, one other thing, I was told it was registered here in Salonika. Would you require a change of registration?"

"No, I don't think so, that will save us a big job of transferring it."

"Yes, and you'll require a local agent here."

"We understand, and when we find the right man, we'll appoint him as our registered agent."

Joseph smiled, knowing that he would have the job if they bought the ship.

When they arrived at the dock, there was a car parked on the wharf at the gangway of a ship. The name of the ship, *Naiad*, was visible on the bow. As the taxi stopped, the occupant of the car emerged and greeted Joseph, with much back patting and playful arm punching, which Peter and Olaf were to see repeatedly in Salonika. Joseph introduced the maritime agent, named Adonis. It turned out that Adonis and Joseph had been in the same class in school as boys.

Adonis told them that he didn't know the condition of the ship. He represented the owner, who was selling her "as is, where is," without guarantees. The ship had only come on the market a week ago, when the owners took delivery of a Liberty ship. Adonis offered to take them over the ship and Olaf agreed.

Olaf saw that the forecastle contained ten cabins with bunks for one in each, but enough room to install two bunks, if necessary. The bridge had a small captain's cabin off the chartroom, but below the bridge there were four cabins of reasonable size, which could hold two bunks each. Aft of the bridge, there were two small cabins with one bunk each. The chain locker could be adapted to take two double bunks, if necessary. Thus, the ship could be adapted to hold thirty-five persons, including the captain.

They inspected the hold, which was quite large and could take substantial stores. With some minor alterations, it could additionally be made to hide a number of people.

He was satisfied with his cursory inspection, but it would be the professionals who would decide whether the ship was seaworthy.

They thanked Adonis and left the *Naiad*. Upon re-entering the taxi, Joseph immediately asked Olaf, "So, what did you think of her?"

"Seems decent enough," Olaf replied warily. He didn't want to seem too anxious. "Let's wait until we see tomorrow's ship before making any decision. What time do we start tomorrow?"

"Would 9:30 be convenient?" Joseph asked. "I would want to call the owners first to tell them we're going to examine their ship. I'll pick you up from the Aristotle Hotel."

Joseph left and Peter and Olaf went up to their rooms to freshen up for dinner. When he had showered and changed, Peter knocked on Olaf's door.

"Before we go for dinner, I want to show you something," Olaf told him, letting him in.

Olaf showed Peter a revised schema of the *Naiad*, indicating accommodations for thirty-five people. "I've worked out that we'll be a total of thirty-three souls on the ship. There's the original twenty-eight of the group, plus you and me, plus Helen, the engineer, and the chef. That's thirty-three. So if you buy it, we have enough room for all of us."

"I'm impressed," Peter said. "What about the price?"

"Subject to inspections, I think this ship would be perfect for us, but I wouldn't tell Joseph just yet. Let's see what else he has for us. As long as each owner is aware that they have a competitor in the field, we are in a better bargaining position."

"Absolutely. But what about price?" Peter persisted.

"I'll try giving you a rough figure, but please don't hold me to it. If I was the seller, I would take the gross tonnage of the ship and multiply that by the price per ton of steel scrap. That would tell me the scrap value of the ship. Then I'd estimate the value of the equipment on board and the difficulty of procuring such a ship in the current market. For example, we've heard from Joseph that these two ships are the only ones of about our size requirement in the Salonika area at present. The war took its toll on every country's fleet. Nevertheless, in the United States, there must be a large surplus of vessels, making it a buyer's market."

"You'll get no argument from me. But can you give me some numbers to work with?" Peter was a lot less interested in the rationale for estimating the price of the ship than the price itself.

"Okay, I'm just trying to show you how I come to my conclusions. I know the ship weighs 5000 tons. The last time I heard, the price of steel scrap was nineteen pounds sterling a ton. We multiply those numbers and we get to 95,000 pounds.

"Now, we add the value of the equipment. That's engines, electrics, ventilation shafts, electric cables, plumbing, pipes, navigation items, lamps, chains, and a host of other things, large and small. The largest element is the engines, of course, and I would estimate that if they are in good working order, that cost would be not less than 100,000 pounds.

"There's an added value associated with putting it all together, which is usually twenty percent, so add twenty percent of 195,000 pounds and you have 39,000 pounds sterling.

"Then, there is the scarcity value, which is hard to estimate. But we know we're in the second-largest city in the country and there are only two ships of decent size on the market. So let's say we would have to pay one-third more for that, which adds 78,000 pounds. All told, the ship would cost 312,000 pounds or, in US dollars, $1,310,400.

"To that, we'll have to add the cost of the inspections, then the cost of surveying the ship and pricing the cost of all the repair work that the survey indicates, then the cost of outfitting the ship to our requirements. I think that will be limited to installing eighteen additional wooden bunks and something that I think will be helpful in the hold, namely, a steel wall at the stern of the hold, like a bulkhead, to create a secret room. Here, our 'surplus crew' could hide in a big hurry if the Royal Navy was about to board us for inspection. Access would be by sliding down a few metal tubes like giant ventilation shafts, the openings to which would be disguised. We would install pneumatic mattresses at the bottom of the shafts to soften the landing, and there the 'surplus crew' would remain, absolutely silent, until the danger passed. Egress into the rest of the hold would be by doors only able to be opened from the inside."

"That's brilliant," Peter said. "Now, can you add the cost of the remaining items to the previous total?"

"Well, there's inspections, surveying, repair work, and bunks plus the bulkhead." He was quiet for a time thinking of the costs. "I'll give you a wild estimate of say 50,000 pounds for all those items.

"That will bring the final total cost to about 362,000 pounds or US dollars $1,520,000. The question now, my dear friend, is: can you afford that, and do you want to?"

"Well, Olaf," Peter replied, "a couple of weeks ago, before my father died and left me much more money than I thought I'd ever have in my lifetime, the possibility of paying out such a sum of money wouldn't have been even remotely possible. But now it *is* possible; have no fear about that.

"I'm humbled and grateful to be your friend, Peter, and blessed to have been able to take part in this enterprise. And now, before we start to blubber on each other's shoulders, let's get some dinner."

The phone rang. It was Joseph, reminding them that they had an appointment at 10:00 the next morning to leave to see the second ship.

Promptly at 10:00, Joseph picked them up driving an old, white, exquisite Jaguar s.s.100 of pre-war vintage. While driving the forty kilometers from Salonika, Joseph spoke to them.

"Good morning, gentlemen. You see before you a very happy man, behind the wheel of my own car today. When I got home after dinner last night, I found my mechanic waiting for me to give me the great news that my car was now ready to renew its life.

"You see, when the Germans took me away in 1943, my wife placed my car in the hands of my faithful mechanic, who hid it, cared for it, and returned it to me in 1945, in perfect condition. Since then, he lavishes such attention upon it, even visits it weekly, making sure it's in top form. I know it sounds like an absurd story, but it's the truth. The car is recognized by the local populace and my mechanic is known in the city as my car's nurse.

"But back to the business at hand. We're going to see a trawler named *Demetrios*, which has worked in the local fishing fleets of the Adriatic since I was a boy. The ship had a well-known captain named Homer, who was both a famous fisherman and a famous drinker. While under the influence of alcohol, he was quite uncontrollable and unpredictable. Two months ago, out at sea, Homer drank even more than usual and shot the ship's cook dead for not bringing his dinner to the bridge in a timely manner. He was arrested when he returned to port, but managed to overpower his police escort, grab a policeman's gun, and shoot himself in the head while still in the police car.

"Homer had been a half-owner of the ship *Demetrios*, together with the widow of his ex-partner. After Homer's death, the two widows had no interest in continuing to own it, so they placed it on the market for sale. The townspeople are superstitious and no fisherman wants to buy a ship with that kind of history. This should work in your favor. I don't know how much the ladies want for it, but with the information I've just given you, you should be able to negotiate a good price."

"That's quite a story, Joseph," Peter said, "but I'm not happy with the idea of buying a ship with such a sordid history."

"I quite agree," Olaf seconded. "Especially, since sailors, myself included, are very susceptible to stories like that and may hesitate to work on the ship. But let's wait and see."

In due course they arrived at the creek, which was actually an inlet of the sea between two mountains, about a mile across, with a busy village on their side of the water. As Joseph drove them around a bend in the road, they could see numerous docks with a few ships in and alongside them. Joseph drove to the *Demetrious*.

They alighted and approached the gangway. A man appeared on the ship and hailed Joseph. Joseph introduced Peter and Olaf to Damon, the local agent. He spoke no other languages than Greek and Turkish, so all their questions had to go through Joseph.

Damon told them that the ladies who owned the trawler had not set a price, but rather, afraid of asking too little, wanted the potential buyer to make them an offer. As of now, no one had made a bid for the boat because of its history. Olaf said that before they would consider making a bid, they needed to see the condition of the ship and Damon began to give them a tour.

As they started around the ship, their nostrils were assaulted by an extremely strong smell of stale fish.

"Hard to ignore the smell, isn't it?" Olaf said, noticing Peter wince. "Once the ship is steam-cleaned, it should be much better. That's what happens when a boat isn't properly cleaned after a voyage."

The *Demetrios* was a lot bigger than the *Naiad*. The trawler had an enormous hold and many cabins, significantly more than most other ships where two or three sailors bunked together.

"This boat took long voyages and, as you can see, had a very large hold for the fish they would catch," Olaf explained. "But because of the extended time at sea, instead of giving the sailors crowded cabins, each sailor got his own cabin. There was probably quality food served as well to make up for the long, cold months at sea."

After the inspection of the ship was complete, Joseph returned the pair to their hotel. Olaf promised to call Joseph when they had come to some decision.

They arranged to have lunch in the hotel and sat down in a quiet location in the dining room.

"I don't know what you feel, but I'll tell you that as far as I'm concerned, the *Demetrios* is out," Olaf began. "For two reasons: First, it stinks, literally, and I wouldn't want our group to live in that environment for a couple of weeks or so. Second, I think it's much too big for our thirty-three people. That ship could take 200 people. We'll be working doubly hard just to keep the ship trimmed."

Peter leaned back on his chair and thought a moment. "I quite agree. That stink is unbearable. I don't know if the cleaning you have in mind will really lower the level of stench enough for all of us to survive weeks on the ship. And of course, it's ridiculous for us to spend more money than we need to and the *Demetrios* is absurdly too big for our needs."

"So it's back to the *Naiad*," Olaf said. "But let's make an offer on both ships, subject to the repairs and inspection we need for each. We'll make a real offer for the *Naiad* and an extremely low offer for the *Demetrios*. If the owner accepts our offer, it may be worth our while to take the *Demetrios* if only for the value it will have to those in Palestine.

"Now, as to the offer on the *Naiad*, using the numbers I talked about previously, *before* taking into account the repair/maintenance work plus our work and inspection costs, we came to a total of $1,310,000. Suppose we make an offer to buy *Naiad* for, say, $1,000,000. The $310,000 we talked about for extras will remain constant. If we decide that we won't pay more than say, $1,400,000 for the boat itself, then we know our limit and we'll walk away from any counter offer that exceeds this amount. My experience tells me that the boat is worth between $1.3 and $1.4 before repair and maintenance."

"I'll leave the bidding up to you," Peter responded. "My strength may be in negotiating the terms of the agreement."

"Fair enough," Olaf nodded. "Now, the *Demetrios* is about triple the size of the *Naiad*. On that basis, the value for the *Demetrios* would be about $4,000,000. That is the figure that we should calculate the market worth of the *Demetrios*. If we're correct, that's the figure they would come to. So, what's our ridiculously low offer on the *Demetrios* that is probably going to be rejected?"

"I'd say at fifty percent of the calculated value, say $2,000,000."

"I'd agree with that, Peter. Now, I've thought of the answer to your question. If we can buy a ship worth $4,000,000 for $2,000,000, we can offer it to Aliyah Bet for the same $2,000,000. They might well jump at it. They could use it to carry 100–200 people.

"If they decline to buy it, and I don't think they will, we'll buy it for $2,000,000, overhaul and sell it when we reach Palestine, as you suggested. If we have the time, and the price is right, we can even purchase both ships, sail the *Demetrios* to Marseilles with a hired crew, sell it for, say, $4,000,000, thus recouping the money you will have spent for the *Naiad*, and probably come away with a tidy profit. You can pass on the profit to the Aliyah Bet people or offer some financial help to the volunteers we're taking to Palestine."

"Or do both," Peter added.

"Exactly. Now, I'll call Joseph to come meet us in the hotel, and to bring the contract we need to sign with him. *Then* we'll instruct him to make *two* offers on our behalf, for the *Naiad* 1,000,000 US dollars and for the *Demetrios* 2,000,000 US dollars.

"This way, he'll tell each owner that we have other bids out and the pressure will increase. He'll be told that if we buy either one or both ships he gets his five percent. He'll have a terrific incentive to try to see to it that we get both ships and he'll certainly get us the lowest prices possible. Do you have that paper you told me your bank manager gave you to confirm how much money you have at your disposal?"

"Yes."

"I don't want to see it, it's none of my business, but I want you let Joseph see it, to prove that we are not men of straw. Will you do that, Peter?

"Wait, I just thought of something else," Olaf continued, eyes wide. "Suppose you get a taxi right now and go see Yanis with your bank paper. Let him take a copy of it. Ask him to contact *your* bank manager in Berne to confirm the letter. When that has been done, *Yanis* can confirm to Joseph that you possess sufficient funds to finance these deals. How's that?"

Peter smiled. "Brilliant! I'll call just to make sure he's there and then go to his office."

Peter confirmed that Yanis was, indeed, at the bank and took a taxi.

It was in a very old building and, set in the wall above the entrance, Peter could see a heavily ornamented carved stone tablet on which was displayed the date 1439 CE in Roman numerals (MCDXXXIX). He went in, asked for Yanis, and was promptly shown to his office.

Yanis greeted him warmly, offering him coffee, and then they sat down at a low table.

Before starting, Peter asked, "That date, Yanis, on the front wall over the entrance to this building intrigues me. Can it be that this building has been around for over 500 years?"

"Absolutely. It's just as it was after the city was taken by the Turks in 1430. In 1913 it became part of Greece."

"And before that?" Peter prompted.

"Before the Turks, it belonged to Venice and before Venice, it was part of the Byzantine Empire, starting from 1261. So you see, Mr. Romaine, our little city has had quite a long history, and even before the Byzantines, it had been owned by Normans, Bulgarians, and others, even the Romans. Our city became the capital of the Roman province of Macedonia in 315 BCE."

"Wow," said Peter, "that *is* a history."

"Are you a historian of sorts? You seem to be so interested."

"Well, I've always had a passing interest in the immutability of things. Some cities pass from hand to hand for centuries and yet manage to give the impression of never changing. But let me tell you why I'm here. I've a document to show you." He handed to Yanis the letter from his Berne banker.

Yanis read it slowly and as he came to the amount of money available to Peter from his father's estate, his normal banker's imperturbable features changed and his eyebrows rose slightly signifying he was quite impressed.

"Very good," he said, handing back the letter to Peter. "Tell me how I can be of service to you, Mr. Romaine."

"I would like you to phone my bank manager, Mr. Lambert, who signed this letter, introduce yourself and ask him to verify, both by phone and by wire, that this letter is authentic. Once you have this confirmation, I want you to be ready to confirm my financial soundness to those I will be doing business with in Salonika."

"I don't see any problem with that. I will deal with it at once. What else can I do for you?"

"I would like to use your telephone in a private room to make two phone calls to Switzerland, if you don't mind," said Peter.

"No trouble at all, Mr. Romaine. Please use my office. Take as long as you like. I shall be outside if you need any help. I'll tell our telephone operator to connect your calls immediately."

Peter's first call was to Mr. Lambert, his bank manager in Berne.

"Good day, Mr. Lambert. This is Peter Romaine. Do you recognize my voice?"

"If you will use the code I gave you, I will recognize you."

Peter gave him the code.

"Thank you, Mr. Romaine. How can I help you?"

"Two things, Mr. Lambert. First, I'm in a bank in Salonika, the Bank of Greece and the Cyclades, where I'm opening a foreign currency account. Please send $50,000 to that account. Next, the bank manager here is going to call you to ask you to verify the letter you gave me in which you mention the amount of money currently at my disposal. Please confirm it both verbally and by telegram."

"Very well, Mr. Romaine. I will do those things and I will remit the money at once."

"Thank you, Mr. Lambert."

"At your service, Mr. Romaine. Goodbye."

Peter's second call was to his mother to say he was well, in Greece, and would be back in a few days.

Peter took a taxi back to the hotel and found Olaf in the small sitting room, where he promptly reported his discussions at the bank. Olaf told him that Joseph would be arriving soon to sign the contract for his services.

Joseph arrived and handed the contract document to Peter who glanced at it and told Olaf that it was in French. Olaf then requested Peter to read it to him and translate it into English, as precisely as he could. It proved to be a short, straight-to-the-point agreement and Olaf seemed satisfied that Peter should sign it.

Joseph then said, "We should go to a Notaire Publique who will read the document, decide if it is, in his opinion, a fair contract, and then witness our signatures. I know this seems strange to you, but in Greece, as in some other European countries, the notary does a lot more than just witness signatures and record them in his register."

Peter asked the hotel manager for a notary nearby and the three of them walked to his office. The notary was a charming gentleman of the old school, who put Peter and Olaf at their ease immediately, but read the contract very carefully, asking both Joseph and Peter if they understood the meaning of certain words and sentences. It took over half an hour before both signed and the notary finished the process. Peter paid a very small price for the transaction, and they returned to the hotel where they settled down in the sitting room.

Olaf told Joseph their decisions regarding purchasing both ships and the maximum amount of money they would pay for each. Their offers would be valid for thirty days. Olaf also told Joseph that he wanted each seller to know that there was another ship being considered very seriously.

"One final point to you personally," Olaf concluded, "We wish to remind you of your promise when we first met, that anything you learn about us will forever be held in total confidence. We wish to point out that it is *imperative* that nothing about us or the use to which the ships are to be put may be divulged to *anybody*. Any breach of that will result in a cancellation of our purchase of either or both ships and we will take you to court for all costs incurred as well as the loss of our potential profit.

"We wish you to put these offers into the Greek language, to transfer them to the sellers within seven days of today, and to insert the date of transfer in the last sentence of the offer referring to thirty days' validity."

"About keeping quiet," Joseph began, a bit overwhelmed, "there's no problem with your mention of taking me to court, though I'm a little hurt that you would even think it necessary to say it, but I *do* understand. You don't know me. However, let me assure you that I know how to keep my mouth shut when necessary and I am acutely aware of how this transaction will reflect on my reputation and my income now, and in the future.

"I would like to ask something to you, Mr. Peter: Are you really prepared to buy two ships? I understood from our original discussion that you are seeking a ship to carry about thirty people. I showed you the *Demetrios* in order to give you a choice of ships, but I certainly didn't think you would want such a big ship. And now you're telling me that not only would you purchase the *Demetrios*, you would take both ships. Have your plans changed?"

"It's really very simple, Joseph," Olaf responded. "We need one vessel for our group, and that could be either ship. But we are working with certain organizations whose goal it is to bring groups of survivors to Palestine. If we do purchase both ships, one would go to these organizations for their use."

Olaf could see that Joseph had a number of questions, but he decided not to divulge anything more.

"Well, Joseph, I think that about wraps up our instructions to you. I see you've been making notes, and that's good, as we didn't give you written instructions. There's one final thing. You may well need to satisfy the sellers that Peter has the money for these two purchases. Please contact Yanis, the manager at the Bank of Greece and the Cyclades for any references you may need."

"So that's it for now, Joseph," said Peter. "Would you like to have dinner with us tonight in the hotel here? We'll probably be leaving tomorrow to return to Switzerland for a few weeks while the owners are considering our offers. You have our phone numbers in Berne. Please call us to confirm that you have given both our offers. After that, feel free to call us with any further news."

"Thank you," said Joseph. "I'll decline your kind offer of dinner tonight. It so happens that it's Dionne's birthday and I'll be taking her out to dinner at our favorite restaurant, but thank you anyway."

Joseph left. Peter went off to call Yanis, who told him he had already spoken to Mr. Lambert and received verbal confirmation. He was awaiting a wire to confirm in writing, and had received a wire transfer of money, which he had put to the credit of Peter's account. Peter told him he was returning to Berne tomorrow but would be back in Salonika in about five weeks.

Peter called Helen, who was excited to hear from him. They agreed that the "Three Musketeers," as Peter referred to the three of them, would meet the next evening for dinner. Helen offered to pick them up from the airport.

CHAPTER XII

The Three Musketeers

"I'M SO HAPPY I'M ONE OF THE THREE MUSKETEERS," HELEN told Peter, as they entered her car.

Olaf's ears pricked up. "Are you two keeping something from me?"

"Why would we keep anything from you, Uncle?" she asked with a winsome smile.

"Well, if we three have become the Three Musketeers, then if there *is* a secret between *two* of you, surely the *third* one, myself, should be let into the secret, especially if it may have an effect on the business of the Three Musketeers."

"We have no secrets from you, Uncle, and if you suspect some romantic entanglement between Peter and me then you are dead wrong. Peter and I are extremely close and good friends and for your own ears only, as a fellow Musketeer, I can tell you that we each have a romantic entanglement elsewhere, and again, for your ears only, both in our special group."

"Well, well, well," said Olaf. "Thank you for the confidence, which I shall keep under wraps until and unless it becomes available for public consumption."

Helen dropped off Olaf and drove Peter home. On the way, Peter summarized their Salonika affairs for her. She was amazed at what they had accomplished in the short time they had been away.

"So now we're buying two ships?"

"Yes," Peter said, "but I hope not, and I hope we are able to buy the *Naiad*. And I've an idea, to rename it, if we do buy it, as the *Helen*. She was after all, the most beautiful woman of Greece, and that is a perfect match with you, my beautiful, dear friend. I don't think Olaf would have any objections, for Helen of Troy was the patron deity of sailors."

"Well," she said, "I will only agree to your naming it "Helen" if we tell everybody that it's in honor of Helen of Troy and the patron deity of sailors and only a coincidence that it's my name, too."

"Very well," he said, "but just a secret between you and me, I thought of it to honor you because we could not have done the things that we've done without your help. You've been the drive, if not the driver, that has brought us to this remarkable point in all our lives."

"What can I say, Peter. Not too many women have had a ship named for them. So, again, dear Peter, thank you."

They reached Peter's home and Helen told him the name of the restaurant they were going to meet at and its location and drove off.

Alice was delighted to see her son after his mysterious and quickly-arranged journey to Salonika. She had a million questions for him, but he stopped her flow of talk and told her he was going out for dinner to meet his two friends and might be home late, as they had a lot to talk about. However, he promised he would bring her up to date the next day.

A few hours later, the Three Musketeers met in The Troubadour (an extraordinarily apt name for a place for them to meet) one of Helen's favorite restaurants. Helen had asked for a table in a quiet alcove where they could talk privately. After they had all been seated, Peter said, "On the auspicious occasion of the dining together of the three of us, I'm going to order a bottle of a good champagne, which, I regret to say, wasn't grown or bottled in Switzerland."

The bottle was duly ordered, approved, opened, poured, sniffed, tasted, and pronounced potable. A toast was proposed by Olaf in honor of the three of them, and, as he said, "particularly in honor of his two younger partners in their enterprise, whose wisdom is beyond their years."

Helen commenced the discussion. "There were two main tasks you gave me: To find a plane and go to Zurich to the 'dentist.' I'm happy to report that I found a plane and I went to Zurich.

"I spoke to my old flying instructor. He pointed me in the right direction and after a few false starts, I actually managed to find a DC3 for sale here in Switzerland, in Geneva. A DC3 is a two-engined plane, it will fly at about 200 mph, has room for thirty passengers plus two pilots and a hostess, and has a range of 1,500 miles. The price, I understand, is about $100,000. The one in Geneva is maintained by a local company and the engines are rated "zero hours," which means the engines have not flown any hours since they were last overhauled. The plane is up-to-date regarding all manufacturer's recommended equipment modifications. Any questions?"

"Yes," said Olaf, "who were the previous owners and why is it on the market?"

"That gets an interesting answer. The previous owner, who bought it new from Douglas, was the US government. When the war was over last September, the plane had just landed in Geneva, en route from England to Tokyo via India, carrying some foreign diplomats who were to attend the Japanese signing of their surrender. However, the signing took place on September second and these diplomats had literally missed the bus. The plane was ordered on September second to stay where it was, the diplomats were told to go home, and for some time, nobody knew what to do with the plane. Then, next, a local company was hired to carry out maintenance. Finally, a few weeks ago, it was placed on the market.

"So, to summarize, the plane has only had one owner, the US government. I've made other inquiries and I can find no other plane in the area or on the market which will carry our group. I've not been checked out on a DC3, but if we decide to buy it, I can go to Geneva, spend a week there, and get checked out on the plane by a licensed instructor. Then we would be ready. I recommend we purchase it."

"I agree," Peter seconded. "We should buy this plane at once, arrange insurance and send Helen off to Geneva to get herself checked out."

"Agreed," said Olaf.

"Well, Helen, are you ready?" Olaf asked

Helen looked a bit stunned. "How on earth can you make that decision so quickly? Purely on what I've told you?" she asked.

"That's how we've been working," Olaf replied, "and since you are one of us, you have our complete trust and confidence both as to your common sense and in the technical knowledge in your subject."

"Very well," she said. "I've prepared a schedule but am prepared to modify it." She presented her schedule of flight movements for the coming weeks.

"I presume that Peter needs to go to Alicante to check out and confirm hotel arrangements and that it is close enough to the beach. I'm also assuming that Salonika remains our headquarters until the ship leaves. I've made the intermediate refueling stops at Rome or Milan to put any potential spy off our trail. Rome and Milan are major cities and our plane will be less noticeable in large cities with lots of air traffic than in a smaller city.

"Regarding a second pilot: I inquired whether I should have a second pilot with me. The answer was yes. I made inquiries and have found an English pilot named Jim McDonald, who is familiar with the DC3. He's an ex-RAF pilot who has recently retired, is presently awaiting being called to his new permanent civilian job, and has been doing stand-by flying work for some months. I met with him, checked out his flying experience, and I believe we can rely on his confidentiality about our group. He will be available for flying with us at forty-eight hours' notice. He currently resides in London.

"I went to Zurich and met my dentist friend. I told her of our plans and in return, she gave me the information you requested. From August last year to March 1946, they have sent out eleven ships. The first six got through, then the British Navy got busy and out of the next five ships, four were stopped and the people arrested, and one was beached. From that ship, 252 people came ashore by a rope bridge. The other ships were all caught within 100 miles of the north Mediterranean coast. Nine came from various Italian ports, including Bari, Taranto, and Vado, one came from France, and one from Greece (Piraeus).

"So far, out of those eleven ships, 1,021 people were landed safely and 1,912 were arrested, either at sea or when they landed. Those arrested were either taken to one of the detention camps on Cyprus or to a detention camp under canvas near the coast at a place in Palestine called Atlit."

Peter was impressed, as was Olaf.

"Thank you so much, Helen," Olaf said, "for bringing us such valuable and detailed information. It will prove useful in plotting our course from Europe to Palestine. I already have an idea or two of where our route should be and I'll tell you when I've gone a bit further.

"By the way, I think it is remarkable how the 'dentist' shared that confidential information with you."

"Oh, I should tell you of that," Helen replied.

"You have no idea how highly we are regarded by the whole Aliyah Bet organization. We are the first in a whole bunch of firsts. The *first* survivors to find their own friend to buy a ship. The *first* group to come to a 'Camp Pietro' en masse with a common background. The *first* group to organize their own crew for a ship and the *first* to find their own captain. It turns out the Aliyah Bet people are very grateful to *us* for having saved them from spending a great deal of time and money for a ship and crew.

"They consider us an outstanding group and particularly so, of course, since Peter the Gentile is our leader. They told me they are looking forward to meeting with Peter in a free Palestine, or whatever it will be called once the British leave and they are convinced every time a ship-load of so-called illegal immigrants arrives in Palestine, it not only greatly increases the morale of the existing Jewish population, but at the same time tells the British that there is an extraordinary and tremendous urge among survivors of Hitler's camps to face that perilous journey to their Promised Land."

"Excellent," said Olaf. "You know, it's like a shot in the arm for even me and reinforces my own feelings about what we three are doing. Now, let me tell you how my thinking is going.

"The fact that most ships have left from Italy, with just one from France and one from Greece, tells me the Royal Navy is going to concentrate on the central Mediterranean. There are just two ways to avoid the navy: The first is to crawl from our starting port, sail west parallel to the French and Italian coasts, down the east coast of Spain, past Majorca down to Gibraltar, then along the North African coast past Morocco, Algeria, Tunisia, Libya, and Egypt before getting to Palestine, about 1,500 miles of unfriendly coastlines along the North African coast, apart from the northern coast of the Mediterranean.

"The other way is to go stealthily south down the Aegean Sea and west coast of Turkey, east along its southern coast, then south past the coasts of Syria and Lebanon to Palestine, about 1,000 sea miles from Salonika. If our ship has hold capacity, we should carry some cargo suitable for delivery to Lebanon, with all the Bills of Lading appropriate to that cargo.

"After she is prepared for sea, we would leave Salonika and sail her 'round the coast eastward to a Greek port city called Kavala, which has a commercial harbor. This city was Turkish till 1912, when it joined the Kingdom of Greece. We would get our ship's maintenance work done in Salonika, and our own special requirements, for security reasons, done in Kavala. Then, after Helen brings in the group from Spain to Salonika, I want it to be met by one or more buses at the airport and taken straight to our ship in Kavala. I don't want our ship, while in Salonika, to be linked with this group. Our ship will leave Salonika after our special work is fully prepared in Kavala. It will then be installed on the ship before the group arrives there from Spain.

"We may have to hire one or two seamen from Kavala to help me and the engineer to sail the ship to Kavala. What do you Musketeers think of my little scheme?"

"How long do you think it would take, Olaf, from Kavala to Palestine?" asked Peter.

"Well, it depends how much advantage I will need or want to take of the very broken coastline on the west coast of Turkey. You see, one of those early ships from Aliyah Bet did come from Piraeus in Greece, which would be just the other, western, side of the Aegean Sea. I'm aware it wasn't caught by the Royal Navy, but I'm assuming they would have found out later where one ship, which got through the blockade, began its journey.

"Going in and out along that very broken coastline of Turkey and sailing only by night could easily multiply our journey by a factor of three, which would make our journey between 1,000 and 3,000 miles. Taking an average of 7.5 knots and traveling 2,000 miles would take about eleven days. But there are many variables involved.

"The most helpful thing we could get would be the very latest information about the British Navy from our friends at Aliyah Bet, just before we sail. Perhaps we could set up a code to use by telephone from Kavala. After we set sail, I want to have wireless silence, except for emergencies, so as not to tip off the Royal Navy that there is one more illegal ship on the way. We would keep listening on a pre-arranged wireless frequency until we're close to Palestine and receive a final signal where we are to land our passengers."

"Apropos," Helen cut in. "I discussed wireless frequencies with one of the dentist's friends, as well as codes. There will be a codes list for each possible place on the Palestine coast where our ship could land its passengers. The actual place will only be decided upon twenty-four hours before the landing night. Following the code word, there will also be one letter of the alphabet sent to us and that will be the code for the time we should aim at arriving at that place.

"As far as wireless frequencies are concerned, there will be the one basic listening channel, which will be on the hour for fifteen minutes. There are two back-up frequencies at fifteen minutes and thirty minutes past every hour, respectively. The language used for the words and letters will be French, German, and Italian for the hour, the hour plus fifteen and the hour plus thirty, respectively. Is that all clear?"

Both Olaf and Peter said, "Clear."

"When and how will we get the codes list for the locations and the letters list for the time?" Olaf asked.

"We are to tell them by telephone of our port of departure and day of leaving, seventy-two hours prior to departure. They will send us a messenger who will ask for Olaf, Peter, or me. After passwords are exchanged, he or she will give us a sealed envelope with the codes and frequencies information inside. For identification, the messenger will say, "Pegasus," which was the mythical winged horse of the ancient Greeks. Our answer will be "Bellorophon," who was the mythical rider of Pegasus.

"We must not leave the port even if it takes more than seventy-two hours before the messenger arrives because they cannot send the information by wireless and we must have it before we leave.

"And finally, when we are within two or three days of getting to Palestine, we are to send just one word on a special frequency, at forty-five minutes past the midnight hour, in Morse Code, the word is "Herzl."

"You did two fabulous jobs, Helen," Peter said. "But what about the engineer and the chef?"

"Yes, Yes," she said, a trifle petulantly, "I dealt with that, of course. As soon as we know where the ship will be and the name of the ship, I will phone my dentist friend and tell her the city and ship's name, and hang up. They already have two professionals lined up and they will send them at once."

"Well, Peter," said Olaf, "the third Musketeer has well and truly qualified as one of our triumvirate."

"Absolutely, Olaf," said Peter, getting up and going over to Helen and giving her a hug and a kiss on her cheek.

"Thank you, Peter," she said, "thats the first hug I've ever had from you."

Not to be outdone, Olaf also got up from his chair and gave Helen an affectionate hug.

The next day Peter and Helen made their way, on his motorbike, to the office of Daumier, the lawyer who was responsible for selling the DC3. Helen had received his name and address from the aircraft maintenance company that was looking after the plane. She found that the office was in the same building as that of her cousin, Phillipe.

They were shown into the office of Claude Daumier, the attorney. He was a dapper, short, middle-aged man with a pencil-thin mustache. He was dwarfed by his modern office, with post-impressionist prints on the wall and every piece of modern communication and reproduction equipment available at the time. Claude was seated behind a desk supported by one great tree-trunk in the center of the see-through glass top. He was gratified that they were impressed by his office.

"Yes, it's not like a standard Swiss lawyer's office, is it? It so happens that I spent ten years in a Washington, DC attorney's office; I so enjoyed being among modern designs that when I returned to Switzerland, I decided to furnish my office in a modern style."

Helen and Peter smiled and Peter made a motion with his hand towards her, hinting that she should start the conversation.

Helen complimented Mr. Daumier on his office.

"We understand that you represent the United States government in the ownership of a DC3 aircraft now reposing in Geneva airport."

"Yes, as I told you on the phone, the United States government is interested in selling the plane, among others."

"Well, Mr. Daumier," Peter began, getting the lawyer's attention. "I've a mind to buy it. So please tell me what is involved."

"Well, as you may be aware, a fair price for an aircraft of that make, year, and maintenance condition, would be $150,000."

Peter could see that the lawyer realized he didn't know much about planes. But of course, he also didn't know about Helen's expertise in these matters.

"Mr. Daumier, I'm going to ask Helen Phillips to discuss that matter with you. She is my pilot and my associate in this matter, making her own inquiries on my behalf. I've been brought up to date on the subject but I think it better if Helen talks to you, if you have no objection."

"Of course, of course," he hastened to reply. "It is a little unusual for a young lady like yourself to have the knowledge to discuss the technical matters such as the purchase of an aircraft, but if you feel you're up to it, I'm quite happy to do so."

Helen couldn't believe this Swiss imitation of an American lawyer was talking so condescendingly about her, and she opened up with guns blazing.

"Mr. Daumier, as you probably know, the engines are zero-hour but the body is not and is due to have a major overhaul after just another 5,000 flying miles. That will be a very expensive job. And consider, as far as I know, there is no package of spare parts involved in this sale, not even a single spare engine. The cost for the items mentioned would easily be in excess of $60,000 so I'm authorized by Mr. Romaine to make you an offer of $90,000 for the aircraft 'as is' with full insurance to continue until the date of sale. This offer is non-negotiable. Mr. Romaine has a letter in his pocket from his

Swiss bankers, which he will show you and allow you to copy. That should allay any question you have as to his solvency."

On cue, Peter nonchalantly pulled a long envelope from the breast pocket of his jacket, extracted the content letter, glanced at it as if to check that it was the right one, and then handed it to Mr. Daumier. Then he sat back silently, as did Helen, neither of them glancing at the other.

Mr. Daumier read the letter slowly. He raised his eyes, as if to speak, but decided against it. Instead, he took the letter to his document copier and made a copy. He returned somewhat unsteadily to his chair and returned the letter to Peter.

"You understand, Mr. Romaine," he said apologetically, "that after you leave I shall have to verify this letter by communicating with Mr. Lambert."

"I understand, Mr. Daumier," said Peter, coolly.

"Mr. Daumier," Helen said, "I shall expect a phone call from you within the next seventy-two hours from now to let us know if we have a deal. By the way, we'll not require a transfer of registration if it is registered in Switzerland, as I assume, since it is being offered for sale here. Is that the case, Mr. Daumier?"

Daumier looked stricken. "I don't know, Miss Phillips, I'm sorry to say, I'll check on that at once."

"Very well, Mr. Daumier. If it is not registered here in Switzerland, then that *is* required before completion of sale. The sale, of course, will be for cash, no mortgage, and I assume it is free and clear of any liens and charges. But you will be able to check that, of course, when you verify the current registration at the Ministry."

"Yes, of course," he said, weakly.

Peter and Helen rose, thanked Mr. Daumier for his kind attention and left.

As they made their way out of the building, Peter whispered, "Not a word until we are well away from here, if you please, Helen."

They mounted Peter's motorbike, he started up and they rode up the street and around the corner by a small park. They got off the bike, walked into the park, still both silent, and sat down on a seat side-by-side. They sat for a few moments then turned to each other and, as their eyes met, they exploded.

"Did you see his face when you raised the subject of registration?" Peter said between paroxysms of laughter.

"He didn't know what Ministry!" Helen gleefully shouted.

"He didn't know you could have a lien on an aircraft!"

"And what about the zero-hours and the body overhaul? He'd never heard of them!"

"But the best was when you gave him seventy-two hours to respond. He turned absolutely white. That will surely be the last time in his life he belittles a 'young lady' who he doubts has 'the knowledge to discuss technical matters.'"

They laughed all the way home.

For the next three days, there was no action needed by the partners for the operation. Peter went to school and Helen went to work with her mother.

Olaf sat and drafted out the metal work that would be required to install a false bulkhead, behind which there would be a hidden space in which at least twenty of the group would hide if their ship was boarded by the British Navy. The remaining people would take up working positions around the boat.

On the second day, there was a phone call for Olaf from Joseph in Salonika to tell him that he had prepared the two offers in Greek and *had* presented them to the representatives of the two owners. The only reaction he could report was that the lawyer for the owner of the *Demetrios*, having seen the amount being offered, had used a Greek expletive meaning "nonsense." He told Joseph that the offer price was a good fifty percent of the owner's idea of its value, but, of course, he would pass the offer to the owner.

On the third day, at 1:30 p.m., a call came to Olaf from Mr. Daumier. He made a half-hearted attempt to get Olaf to raise the price but Olaf said, very firmly, that he understood that Miss Phillips had made it clear that the offer made of $90,000 was non-negotiable and so that was the final offer. After a few moments of silence, Daumier came back to the telephone and said he accepted the offer. Olaf then said that Daumier would receive a check the next day for $9,000 as a deposit, together with the name of Mr. Romaine's lawyer, and the two lawyers should then arrange for the sales contract and the change of registered owner to Peter Romaine. Daumier agreed.

Olaf told Helen they had bought the DC3. She was delighted to hear it. He then phoned Peter at home and told him that Peter was now the owner of a DC3, subject to a contract being signed. He also told Peter that he needed to give a check to Daumier for $9,000 as a deposit, the next day, and to notify Daumier of the name of his lawyer, who would handle the contract for him.

The next morning, Peter called his attorney, Jean-Pierre Muraille, to ask him if he was knowledgeable about the subject of transfer of ownership of an airplane. Jean-Pierre replied that if Peter had asked him that question three months, ago he would have had to answer in the negative. However, he had since acted as attorney for a similar transaction by another buyer, including re-registration, and felt confident to be able to handle Peter's request as well.

Peter told him he was buying a Douglas DC3 presently in Switzerland, which was represented by Claude Daumier. The price was $90,000 and he needed to give Daumier a check for ten percent of that today. How should they proceed?

Jean-Pierre told him to bring the check at 10:00 a.m. and he would take care of everything.

He then briefed Jean-Pierre on the insurance, asking him to arrange insurance from the date of completion of the transaction and to arrange for registration or for re-registration of the plane, in his name, in Switzerland.

He then made a phone call to Helen, inviting her to lunch. They met at "Quito," where Peter said everything was going smoothly and he wanted her to get herself checked out on the plane in Geneva and then to bring it to Berne and take him for a flight. She happily agreed.

"You told me," Helen said, "how your mother and father tried so hard to bring you up as an English gentleman, with all those so refined attributes, in so cultured, so civilized, Switzerland, and here you are now, playing the part of a bushwhacking international adventurer, and, what is more, doing very well at it, and, I believe, enjoying every minute of it. For a highly educated linguist whose future seemed to be in the ivory tower of university life, you are certainly going off at a mighty tangent."

"Fate is funny that way. I feel like for the first time in my life, I'm really living. Not long ago I would have been afraid to have so many people depending on me, and to be dependent on so many people. But now, your warm friendship, and the friendship of the others has overshadowed my earlier linguistic ambitions and I'm anxious, determined, to continue this journey and complete it successfully."

"That's my Peter," Helen said, squeezing his hand.

Two weeks passed with no fresh news. Then, Joseph phoned to say that the owners of the *Demetrios* had decided to reject Peter's offer on the grounds that it was ridiculously low and, knowing that it was a non-negotiable offer, confirmed that the matter was null and void as far as they were concerned.

Both Olaf and Peter gave a huge sigh of relief that the potential problem of having to handle the ownership of two ships had now dissipated. However, the fate of the *Naiad* was still undetermined. Helen, too, was delighted, and admitted that she would never, herself, have taken the gamble of making an offer on both ships, especially knowing that the *Demetrios* was definitely not suitable for their requirements.

Soon after, Peter had a call from Jean-Pierre Muraille, saying that after having had to push Daumier for action, the plane contract was complete. It turned out that the DC3 had always been registered in the USA, not Switzerland, and that the US authorities had worked with unusual speed in getting the plane de-registered in the USA. It seemed that the government had informed all its agencies that wartime equipment listed for sale should be disposed of with the utmost celerity. This was to eliminate the heavy costs of maintaining equipment in good working order, so that it could be disposed of at a good price, as well as to liquidate such surplus material for cash quickly. The authorities still remembered the embarrassing affair of discovering the large quantities of First World War surplus equipment filling warehouses desperately needed during World War II.

Jean-Pierre had arranged to re-register the plane in Peter's name in Switzerland, and that matter had now been completed.

Peter called Helen to give her the news, requesting that she contact Jim McDonald, the second pilot, to tell him that we now had the plane, and to invite him to come to Switzerland to inspect the plane, fly it a little to get to familiarize himself with it, and to meet the owner.

During this time, Peter was also busy at the university, working on his PhD and was gently reprimanded by his supervising professor on his frequent absences. He was told that if he wanted to deal with his PhD work properly, then he must concentrate on it and reduce or eliminate whatever activity was taking him away from his studies so much.

Peter had to tell Professor Dupont that he was engaged in a major life-saving activity that would quite likely take him away from his studies for perhaps quite some time. However, he was determined to complete his PhD studies when time permitted and would let the professor know more in due course. Professor Dupont was unhappy to hear this and told Peter that he had already recommended Peter to be appointed a full professor, after completing his PhD, in a new department of language education at present being formulated, and in addition, in due course, as Professor Dupont's successor in his own chair, a towering appointment.

Peter was quite stunned to hear of these two appointments lined up for him, and he told the professor that he was enormously honored to hear these things, but his commitment to his other activity was paramount at this time, and he must take a leave.

"Well," said Professor Dupont, "all I can say is that knowing you, this 'life-saving activity,' which may well eliminate you from consideration for those two appointments, must be extraordinarily important, at least in your eyes, and does you great honor. I wish you good fortune and a safe return in due course, to these halls of academe."

Peter was greatly moved by Professor Dupont's words. However, Peter left the good professor with a feeling of relief at having parted from his studies under such circumstances and with his reputation intact. He knew he could count on Professor Dupont for good references should he need them in the future.

The feeling of relief was also due to the fact that for some time, he had experienced a guilty perception that while he was doing his best for the group matters, his work in the university was suffering, and that when he *was* concentrating on that work, his concentration on the important group activities was suffering because he wasn't giving *it* his full attention. Now he could concentrate wholeheartedly on his position in the Musketeers.

Two weeks later, Olaf received a phone call from Joseph. Twenty-nine days after presenting their offer on the *Naiad*, he had received a written counter-offer from her owners of $1,200,000. What should he do? Olaf immediately replied that Joseph should counter-counter and offer in writing the amount of $1,100,000 and request a response within seven days.

Olaf then immediately called Peter, told him what he had done, and asked if Peter approved. Peter did so, and thanked Olaf for not unnecessarily delaying the reply by calling him first.

"It would seem that their counter-offer of $1,200,000 indicates we *have* a sale, the price being somewhere between $1,000,000 and $1,200,000. Do you agree?" Peter asked.

"Absolutely," replied Olaf, "and, of course, subject to inspections and costs. So within another seven days, we'll know the price.

"By the way, have you heard from Helen in Geneva?"

"Yes," Peter replied. "I heard from her yesterday. She's checking out the plane, and Jim McDonald has arrived from London and the two of them will be flying to Berne tomorrow. She has also arranged that

a company called Berne Aviation, at Berne Airport, would be handling the plane and doing all required maintenance. I'll call Helen at
her hotel tonight and finalize arrangements."

"Fine with me, Peter," said Olaf.

That night, Peter called Helen in her room at the hotel in Geneva.
She talked about Jim McDonald, who had been there for two days.
She said she had to stop herself from being too overwhelmed when
he told her of his RAF flying experience and showed her his pilot
log books and licenses. He was apparently a single man and quite
available for the upcoming trips, even at short notice. He knew the
DC3 plane well and was perfectly happy to be her co-pilot despite his
extremely extensive experience. He just loved flying and was looking
forward to doing that as his life's work.

She told Peter they had arranged to leave Geneva at 11:00 a.m. and
would be landing in Berne about 11:30. "By the way," she said, "he's an
English gentleman, but grew up in Scotland and prefers to be known
as a Scotsman."

"Very well," said Peter, "and tomorrow I'll take you and our Scotsman for lunch and then in the evening, we'll have dinner with Olaf,
just the Three Musketeers. Oh, and by the way, it looks as though
we're buying the *Naiad* – they made a counter-offer and we gave a
counter-counter offer, so we'll know in a few days if we've got it.

"Also, as soon as we know we've got the *Naiad*, I'm planning to go
to Camp Pietro for a day or two to brief the group. Do you want to
come with me?"

"Of course I do, Peter, you know that," she replied, animatedly,
"and why don't we fly there in your plane to, say, Milano and then
take a train to Camp Pietro. We can take Jim with us. He'll stay in
Milano for a couple of days on his own, then fly back with us to
Berne before going back to London."

"That's fine, Helen. But there's a thought that's been in my mind
ever since I learned from you that the DC3 needs to have two pilots –
How do we explain what we're doing to the hired pilot? Give it some
thought and we'll discuss it tomorrow night at dinner."

Next day Peter drove out to Berne Airport and went to the Berne
Aviation Office. He asked to meet the manager. The manager, named
Jacques, knew he would be coming.

"I'm very pleased to meet you Mr. Romaine," he said, "and I know
your plane is due in here soon. I had a nice conversation yesterday
with your pilot, Mlle. Phillips."

"She's also my associate in business, Jacques," Peter told him. "Anything she says about the plane to you may be taken as coming from me, and I confirm that I'm the owner of this DC3. Are you familiar with that aircraft?"

"Yes, I am. There's a local company which flies two of them and we look after all the maintenance, repair, and overhauls."

"Good. Do you have your own hangars?"

"Yes, we actually have two. One for the DC3s and one for the little planes."

"Now what's the procedure today?"

"The plane will wireless in when it's on its way and we'll tell the pilot how and where to taxi to our hangar. There it will be met by our representative and an official from the Police and Passport Office, who will deal with landing procedures. He may or may not inspect the plane, although, as your plane is a new arrival, he may want to give it a once-over."

Just then one of the employees came to Jacques to tell him that the DC3 would be landing in ten minutes. Peter said he would like to meet the plane.

They walked to the hangar, where Jacques pointed out to Peter a plane flying in. "There's your DC3, Mr. Romaine, coming in slowly and steadily."

Peter stood there by the hangar entrance and for the first time, saw his plane. It was an interesting moment in his life. He never thought he would become the owner of this huge airplane. At about fifty yards, he could see a white-gloved hand waving through the window of the pilot's compartment and he waved back. Then the plane stopped, then started again, very slowly, in order to enter the hangar, and finally stopped.

"We have to let the Police/Passport Officer on first and wait for him to complete his formalities before we go on board," Jacques explained.

Wheeled steps were pushed to the plane and Peter watched the official walk up as the aircraft door was opened from inside. He saw Helen at the same moment as she saw him and they exchanged a broad smile and then he blew her a kiss.

The Police/Passport Officer was aboard the aircraft for about ten minutes, then left. Jacques indicated to Peter that they could now board. Peter climbed the steps and entered *his* plane. It was a most exciting moment for him. He was met by Helen, who gripped his hand firmly and then planted a gentle kiss on his cheek, saying,

"Welcome aboard, Peter, and first, I'd like you to meet your co-pilot, Jim McDonald."

She turned and indicated a man standing behind her wearing a fur-collared flying jacket that half hid his face.

She said, "Jim, this is Peter Romaine, the owner."

Peter and Jim shook hands. Jim said, "I'm very pleased to meet you, sir, and I want to tell you right away that you have a fine aircraft here, and in excellent condition."

"And I'm happy to meet you too, Jim. We'll talk later at lunch, but meanwhile, I'd like Helen here to show me the plane, then I'd like you both to take me on a short flight."

"Come this way, Peter," said Helen. She then proceeded to show him around the plane and its equipment and finally the cockpit and its instrumentation. Peter found it all immensely fascinating, asking her innumerable questions until finally Helen said, "That's it, Peter, you've seen it all. And now we'll take a short flight. Will half an hour suit you?"

"Certainly. I just want to have the experience of being flown in my own plane for the first time, so let's go."

She sat him in the central seat of the front row from which he could watch the two pilots in the take-off procedures.

Helen was very conversant with the topography in the region and as they flew around, she pointed out the various mountain peaks to Peter and to Jim, who was unfamiliar with the region.

As he was sitting there, observing the flight and the interplay between the two pilots, Helen and Jim, Peter had a rather strange feeling, as if he recognized Jim from somewhere, a sort of déjà vu experience. For some reason, as Jim turned sideways, Peter could swear it was his father's face looking out the window. He felt the hairs on the back of his neck stand out as he sought to understand his reaction.

He heard Helen ask him through a kind of fog if that was enough for his first flight and he heard himself say, "Yes, thank you, Helen, it has been a wonderful flight and we can now return to the hangar." But it felt as though he was speaking outside himself.

They touched down and taxied to the Berne Aviation hangar. The engines were switched off and silence descended on the plane.

"So, Mr. Owner," Helen said, turning to face him, "how did you enjoy your first flight in your own plane?"

"I must admit, it was exciting and I thoroughly enjoyed it. Now," he added, "I'm inviting my two pilots to lunch at the Brasserie Restaurant."

"What do you say, Jim?" asked Helen, "Are you free and shall we accept the owner's invitation, because if we don't, we might get fired. What do you think?"

Jim played along, "Hmmm . . . Seems like the prudent thing to do. And as I ate over six hours ago, I can't help but feel that a resounding 'Let's eat' is in order."

"Good thinking," she said. Then, turning to Peter announced, "Sir, your wage-slaves are cognizant of the honor you are showing them by inviting us to eat with you and we gratefully accept."

"Well, thank goodness that's over with," Peter said. "For a second there I thought I'd be able to save money and eat by myself."

They all laughed good-naturedly.

Helen led the way off the plane. Jim handed the plane over to the Berne Aviation personnel, told them to fuel it up, give it the daily maintenance, and then garage it. Helen translated his instructions to the ground crew.

CHAPTER XIII

Jim's Background

THE THREE OF THEM LEFT THE AIRPORT FOR THE BRASSERIE Restaurant in Berne. When they arrived, they ordered drinks and lunch and relaxed.

"I'd like to have a little background about you," Peter began, turning to Jim, "but I must tell you, you bear a remarkable likeness to my late father. I had quite a feeling of déjà vu when I first saw you, and it still remains with me. But I suppose that my father dying so suddenly and recently has made my mind play tricks on me. I'll probably see other likeness of my father over the next little while. Anyway, I understand you were in the RAF until recently."

"Well, sir," Jim began.

"Please, Jim," Peter interrupted, "call me Peter."

"Certainly. I grew up in Ayr, went to prep and public schools, Oxford, did a degree in Aeronautical Engineering, joined the RAF in 1937, became a fighter pilot, and was able to battle my way through the war. When I left the RAF, I went to work for British Overseas Airways Corporation as a pilot, and I will join them in about four or five months' time for training on their long-distance aircraft."

"That's a lot to digest in one go, Jim. Maybe backtrack a bit and tell me about your people. I assume they were comfortably off if you went to a prep school, then a public school, and then to Oxford. Helen, in England what is called a 'public school' is in fact a private school and to go to Oxford is also very expensive."

"You're right, Peter," Jim answered, "but to tell you the truth, I don't know who my people are. I was born in Edinburgh in 1916 and my official name is James Roman. I was brought up by a lady in Ayr named Janet McDonald who was, for all intents and purposes, my adoptive mother, and when I was sixteen, she asked me, and I agreed, to change my last name from Roman to McDonald. Locally, everyone believed I was the illegitimate son of Janet's sister, Maisie, who lived in London.

"However that wasn't the case. Janet had been sworn to secrecy when I, as a baby, had been given to her. All I was told was that I was the offspring of two well-born and well-connected people. Money was paid to Janet monthly by her solicitor to cover my upkeep and hers, and to keep her in a fair degree of comfort until she died. There was also money for all my school fees and uniforms and so on. As far as Oxford is concerned, I won a scholarship, which covered all fees. When I was in public school at St. Paul's in London, I lived with Maisie, Janet's sister. All my holidays I spent in Scotland with Janet.

"At Oxford, I joined the University Air Squadron. When the war broke out, I, and most of my graduating class, joined the RAF, I became a pilot, was commissioned, and had a busy war."

Peter thanked Jim and then briefly recounted his own birth in Switzerland, his academic work, and the subject for his PhD on which he was presently engaged "when I'm not messing about with a DC3 purchase."

Peter went on to add that "I'm now going to say something which is in every sense highly confidential. The purchase of this plane is totally legal and it will be used for humanitarian purposes. However, the end result to our adventure may raise some eyebrows and you may be asked questions by the British authorities. We want you to give us your solemn word that anything you understand or see during your employment as my pilot will never to be talked about to anyone outside our group, a number of whom you'll meet over the next short while."

"You have my word of honor and my assurance that if this is a humanitarian project, I will be in the forefront of helping you anyway I can."

"Good. By the way, is Janet McDonald still alive?"

"I'm afraid not, Peter. She was killed in 1942 during an air raid on London when she was visiting Maisie. I lost them both at once. It was a terrible loss to me. They were the only links to my own blood."

After lunch, as they were leaving, Helen reminded Peter that they were going to fly to Milan in a day or two on their way to yet another meeting. Peter offered to find accommodations for Jim and put him on salary at once. Helen then took Jim to find a suitable hotel.

Peter took a taxi back to the airport to pick up his motorbike and went home. His mother was out and he sat quietly reviewing that day's events and, in particular, Jim's history. There were a number of things that coincided with his father's history, as told to him by Jean-Pierre Muraille. It was worth making a call, just to be sure that this fellow was not somehow linked with him in other ways besides their business venture. He picked up the phone.

"Jean-Pierre," Peter began, suddenly realizing this might sound strange to someone who hadn't actually seen Jim, "I'm curious about James, my father's illegitimate son. Can you give me some additional information about him?"

"Of course, Peter. Let me take out the file. Ah, here we are. What would you like to know?"

"What was the name of the Scottish nursemaid?"

"Let me see. Janet, I believe."

"And the sister's name?"

"Sorry. I don't know."

"James's year of birth?"

"1916."

"And his family name at birth?"

"It's not written here, but I should think it would be your father's family name."

"Where was he born?"

"Edinburgh."

"Anything else you can tell me about him?"

"Well, Peter, he graduated Oxford with a degree in engineering and I believe – yes – he joined the RAF soon after."

Peter could barely contain himself. There were too many coincidences here. James and Jim had to be the same person.

Peter thanked Jean-Pierre and hung up.

But what was he going to do with all this information? His father had gone to great lengths to keep the knowledge of James's blood secret from everyone. Did he have the right to disregard his father's wishes in order to be able to call James his brother? Certainly, he could help James surreptitiously without having to annul his father's wishes.

Another thought struck him. "If and when he found out that Richard had died and left that huge estate, what effect would that have on Jim? Would he claim an equal share in the estate?

And what effect would this revelation have on Alice, his mother? It was one thing to know that your husband had fathered another child and quite another to find that child at your doorstep. How would she handle this so soon after her husband's death?

He hated to be dithering over a decision and wondered if there was anyone who could help him come to a decision. He thought of Jean-Pierre, but remembered how he had already warned Peter *not* to pursue it. He considered Helen. She was an extremely bright person, perfectly capable of being trusted to keep concealed this family secret, and she possessed a great deal of common sense. But since she would be working with Jim, was it fair to burden her with this intense family conundrum?

In thinking about all this, Peter recalled that Jean-Pierre had also said that James's legacy of one million pounds would be paid to him only after he agreed to sign a document renouncing all future claims to his father's estate. Peter wondered how secure that document would be if James decided to sue. Peter couldn't ask Jean-Pierre's opinion without telling him all about Jim.

And how would this potential legal battle affect his present commitments? Could he accomplish his mission with all this hanging over his head?

He decided to let all these questions stew inside him as he left his house to meet Olaf and Helen for dinner, as they had arranged.

After they had ordered, Helen said, "Peter, I'm dying to hear your reactions to your maiden flight in your new acquisition and to our co-pilot, Jim McDonald."

"Sorry to intervene," Olaf interrupted, "but I've some red-hot news for you from Salonika. Just before leaving the house, I received a call from Joseph. He told me the *Naiad*'s owner has come back with $1,150,000 as a final offer and he wants to know what to answer.

"I worked out the percentage and told him to accept the offer plus an expense cap of 18.25 percent. He'll give us the information regarding to whom and where to send the deposit. In short, we have a ship!"

Everyone was ecstatic. Peter signaled their waiter and ordered a bottle of champagne.

"Well, my friends," Peter said, "we now have a plane and a ship. I suggest that tomorrow we three will fly to Salonika. I'll give the deposit to Joseph, and we'll book in at the hotel on Aristoteles Street.

"Helen, we'll take you to see the *Naiad* and then you can let your dental friend know that we have a ship and are awaiting the engineer and the chef. And you, Olaf, please get busy arranging the inspection and find a company to overhaul the ship.

"When we get settled in the hotel, I'll rent a room, which will be

Helen's office, and get three phones put in. Helen, you'll set it up with the usual office equipment.

"After a couple of days, I'd like to go to Camp Pietro with Helen, leaving you, Olaf, in Salonika. We'll fly to Milano, leave the plane and Jim there and take a train to Camp Pietro to brief the gang and Dov. We'll stay there a couple of days.

"We'll return to Milano then fly to Alicante, inspect the hotel and beach, then return to Salonika. At that point, we decide whether we can send Jim home, leaving the plane in Salonika. Okay everybody?"

"Okay" They both agreed.

"Now, to answer your question, before Olaf so rudely interrupted – but I must say, with very good news – I was really very excited, in my own repressed, English way, and it was exhilarating to take a flight in my new plane. Thank you for all your hard work, Helen.

"And as for Jim, I'm sure he'll keep our work confidential, and when it's all over, I'll give him a nice fat bonus to remember us by."

"By the way, Olaf," Peter added, "when we get the *Naiad* to Kavala, I'm going to change her name to the *Helen,* and, as I've already explained to Helen, it's in honor of Helen of Troy not for your niece. After all, nobody has fought a war for her – yet!

"And, finally, it dawned on me that since Helen is a pilot, it stands to reason that she must be highly experienced in maps and may be of use to you on the ship as a part-time navigator. Aside from you, I don't think anyone else is as competent in map reading as Helen, am I right?"

"Absolutely, Peter," came the immediate reply.

After dinner, they agreed to meet at the airport at midday the next day.

Helen phoned Jim to tell him they were flying tomorrow and to prepare the plane. Then she made a list of what office equipment she would need to buy for the Salonika office, which she would set up in the hotel and then transfer to the ship.

Peter arrived home to find his mother still up and joined her in the family room. She greeted him warmly and, as he bent over to kiss her, she whispered, "Hello, stranger, it's so nice to see you, Peter. Do you want something to eat?"

"No, thanks, Mother," he answered. "But I'm glad you're up because I'm leaving tomorrow and I want to tell you some things."

"Yes, of course, Peter. So, please tell me what's going on in your life."

"Well, Mother, I know that you and Father said you didn't want to hear any more about my association with those Jewish survivors, so you haven't. But the fact is, I am deeply involved with them. I'll gladly tell you what I'm up to, but if you prefer not to know, that's okay with me too."

His mother looked at him sadly.

"Peter, at first, I was delighted that you had the compassion and sympathy toward those unfortunate young people and the maturity to want to help them. Then, as you know, your father and I did what we could to support your efforts, whole-heartedly, until we felt you were getting yourself in over your head. From what we understood, you were pitting yourself against the Royal Navy and plotting to break the law."

"That's true, Mother, but remember my telling you that, in my opinion, although we are Gentiles, there are moral and ethical principles involved here, such as we have been taught in Christianity to 'Love Your Neighbor,' which, incidentally, comes from the Old Testament. And as to whether Ernest Bevin is legally in the right to blockade Palestine, that's a question of law and I'm not sure that British policy and British law are exactly the same thing.

"In any event, and I'm not going to change my mind over this, I'm committed. So, please tell me whether you want to hear about my activities or not. If I tell you about them, you must hold that information totally confidential, not because I believe them to be illegal, but because I believe what the British are doing is illegal."

Alice Romaine was silent for some time before she spoke.

"I don't want to hear about your activities, Peter, for the reasons I've already given you. I'm sorry that it has come to this and it doesn't mean I don't love you. You are, after all, my beloved only child and I shall always love you, but over this matter, we shall have to agree to disagree."

"Very well, Mother, that's settled, then. Tomorrow I'm going away on a trip, as I said. I'll call you from time to time from wherever I shall be, and I'll be back here in due course. Goodnight, Mother, I'll see you before I leave." With that, he left the room.

CHAPTER XIV

Salonika 2 and Camp Pietro 3

THE FOLLOWING DAY, OLAF, PETER, AND HELEN ARRIVED AT the airport within a few minutes of each other. They went aboard the DC3 to find Jim doing his pre-flight check in the cockpit.

Peter introduced Olaf. They shook hands and then Jim said to Helen, "Where are going, Captain?"

Helen smiled and said, "That's the first time I've had equal billing with Olaf, even though for different professions. So Jim, please plot a course for Salonika and when we're all settled in, I'll tell Flight Control."

Helen saw that Olaf and Peter were comfortably seated in the middle seats of the first row and that all the luggage was stowed, then she returned to the cockpit, went through the pre-flight checks, talked to Flight Control, and they were off.

"We have a name for our ship," Olaf said to Peter, "why not a name for our plane?"

"I'd be happy to give her a name," Peter replied, "if the Musketeers can agree on one. Do you have a suggestion?"

"What about 'Pete's Pet'? It's short, snappy and even truthful. What do you think?"

Peter said in reply, "Actually, I've quite another suggestion. Since it was my father's money which bought us the plane, I'd like to name it for him – perhaps *Richard's Renown*.

"Seems fitting," Olaf said. "But let's also ask Helen. I'll pass her a note."

Helen read the note, smiled and nodded back to Olaf.

"Helen approves," Olaf said to Peter. "We'll put her new name on the plane as soon as possible."

They landed in Salonika and agreed to meet at the Aristoteles Hotel.

Peter met the manager, Alex, at the hotel and told him they needed four rooms, plus a room for an office. He then asked Olaf to check with Joseph as to when the check would be needed. For his part, he was going to ask his bank manager to recommend a lawyer to handle the contract and other formalities for the purchase of the *Naiad* and the marine insurance for the ship.

When Peter got to his room, he called Yanis, the bank manager, and arranged to go and see him later in the day.

The group met Joseph in the lounge about an hour later. Peter asked Joseph for the name in which the check was to be made out, which he gave him on a slip of paper.

As Jim got up to leave, Olaf asked him, "Why is it that the Dakota needs to have two pilots? I'd have thought one pilot was sufficient to fly a plane."

"It may be for most planes," Jim answered, "but in the case of the DC3 and some others, like the Lancaster and the B17, there is a need for two pilots. The co-pilot keeps the pilot from over-speeding the engines or under-shooting the required power settings. In other words, the pilot concentrates on controlling the aircraft and the co-pilot fine-tunes the throttles to ensure the proper setting. The pilot pushes the thrust levers to the approximate take-off setting while the co-pilot tweaks them to the pre-calculated take-off power setting.

"Also, in some planes like the DC3, the throttle levers have a habit of not staying on full power at take-off but slipping back, and so the co-pilot grips and holds steady the throttle levers, as the pilot needs both hands on the control wheel to pull the plane off the ground. There is also the fact that the pilot can leave his seat to go back into the cabin if he wants to, for any reason, and the co-pilot simply takes over control from his own seat. The co-pilot is also available to assist the pilot at all times if asked to look at maps or to use the wireless, etc."

"That's certainly a detailed answer," Olaf said, smiling.

Everybody then left the lounge, including Jim, who got hold of Alex to ask about places of interest in or around Salonika. Alex found some copies of pre-war maps of the town and surroundings, one of which he gave to Jim and pointed out a number of interesting sites. He also promised to find him a taxi-driver who spoke English for a tour of the city.

A half-hour later, Helen and Peter were off to meet their banker.

They found Yanis hovering about in his foyer. He shook hands with Peter and then said, "Don't tell me, Mr. Romaine, that this quite incredibly beautiful lady is the business colleague of whom you spoke. I wouldn't expect somebody who looks like this lady to be involved with anything so mundane as business."

Peter listened to this flowery speech with alarm. He hadn't expected Yanis to be so flattering and condescending to Helen, at the same time.

"Yanis, I trust you don't fall at the feet of every beautiful woman who enters your bank like this," he said, reprovingly. "Allow me to present the Princess Helen Phillipa of one of the oldest royal families of Switzerland, in fact since the year 1291. Yes, she is a lady, but also my business colleague, my chief pilot, my accountant, the executive colleague in all my business affairs, *and* the love of my life, so I trust I shall never find you making even the slightest personal move in her direction. One rather special thing about her. She absolutely abhors the thought of touching the hand of any strange man, especially one who is not equal to her in family lineage."

As he listened to Peter's words, Yanis became pale. He realized that he had seriously overstepped the limit of what was acceptable banter and had put in danger the business relationship of the bank with this remarkable Englishman. He, therefore, for the first and only time in his life, being a proud Greek, in order to mollify Mr. Romaine's obvious displeasure, made a deep, deep, bow to Helen, saying, "It is a great pleasure and a distinct honor, Princess Helen, to welcome you to the bank of which I'm the General Manager, and to offer you all the facilities of this bank as I do for Mr. Romaine. Please forgive me if I've offended you in any way. Will you both kindly come into my office?"

Peter and Helen could barely keep straight faces. The same thought came to both of them at the same time: If Yanis was Japanese, he would have produced a Samurai sword and fallen on it – he was so outrageously embarrassed.

"Now then, Yanis," said Peter, "I would like to get down to business."

"Of course, Mr. Romaine. I'm at your service. What can I do for you?"

Producing the slip of paper with the name on it, he said, "I need a banker's draft for $115,000 from my account in favor of this company. I will give you a check from my account in favor of the Bank of Greece and the Cyclades."

While he was writing out the check, Helen asked very sweetly of Yanis, "Would you please explain what 'The Cyclades' signifies?"

"Of course, Princess," he said, at which point Peter, who was bending over his checkbook began coughing. Helen to hit him hard on his back, while suppressing her own urge to roar with laughter.

Totally unaware of the barely contained merriment which his use of her spurious title had engendered, Yanis continued to explain:

"The Cyclades are twenty-four islands in the Aegean Sea, which are the submerged peaks of the mountain ranges of Greece. In antiquity, they were the center of a Bronze Age culture, the Cycladic, known particularly for its white marble idols. Virtually all of these islands have some archeological interest, especially Santorini, which happens to be the island where I was born. The islands all produce and export raw materials, mainly various ores, but also wines, brandy, tobacco, and other agricultural products. I suppose when this bank was incorporated, 250 years ago, somebody wanted to give the impression of longevity. The bank now has branches in many cities of Greece, including Athens."

"Thank you so much, Yanis," said Helen, "that was very illuminating."

Peter handed Yanis his check and, in a few minutes, received the bank draft for the same amount, which he handed to Helen.

"Is there anything more I can do for you, Mr. Romaine?" Yanis asked.

"As a matter of fact, there is," said Peter. "I'm in the process of buying a ship and I need a lawyer who is experienced in the buying and selling of ships. Can you recommend someone to me?"

"Of course, Mr. Romaine," he said. "There are a number of lawyers skilled in that business in Salonika and the one thought to be the best is John Thessalonikos. He also is a customer of the bank and I'm happy to recommend him to you. Would you like me to call him to make an appointment for you?"

"Thank you, Yanis, I would appreciate that," said Peter.

Yanis made the call and spoke to the lawyer. He then asked Peter if he was free right now. Peter nodded. Yanis finished the call and wrote the address on a piece of paper. Peter thanked him and then he and Helen left the bank amid goodbyes from Yanis, together with a half-bow to Helen, and profound promises of future service at any time.

They walked up the street about three blocks to the offices of John Thessalonikos. They found him to be a pleasant man of middle age who welcomed them into his office. It was a traditional office; the walls were covered by engraved certificates attesting to his lawyerly ability and university distinctions, as well as a multitude of family pictures. Peter and Helen both felt this was an office of a straightforward professional who was also in touch with his family.

Peter introduced himself and Helen, speaking in English.

"I am sorry," Mr. Thessalonikos apologized, "that my English is very poor."

They found, however, that all three were equally comfortable in French.

Helen produced the bank draft in favor of the owners, with whom the lawyer was acquainted, and he explained the formalities required in Greece to transfer title, which were not excessively complicated. As Thessalonikos explained, with a twinkle in his eyes, "In this country, with its very long history of ship-building and ship-owning, we have come to a system that employs minimum bureaucracy and allows transactions to be completed in a surprisingly short space of time."

"Such as?" inquired Helen.

"About three days, generally, if there is no mortgage to pay off, which I understand is the case here."

"Wow," said Peter, "that's really remarkable."

"You see," he said, "registration can only be made in Athens and here in Salonika, the second largest city. It so happens that the Registrar of Shipping here in Salonika is my younger brother, so for me, that makes for a very speedy transaction!"

After a short discussion of the legal and filing fees, which, to Peter and Helen, seemed eminently reasonable, Peter signed an application to transfer the ship and, following his request, also an application for a change of name from *Naiad* to the *Helen*. The lawyer said the change of name would be registered on the day after completion of the purchase.

"One final question, Mr. Romaine," he asked gently, "are you possessed of the funds required for the balance of the purchase price?"

Peter said, "You may call Yanis, the General Manager of the Bank of Greece and the Cyclades for confirmation of that, and I'd like you to do that right now so that we can leave with that inquiry out of the way."

Thessalonikos made the call. It was interesting to Peter and Helen to watch the lawyer's face change its expression from professional coolness to one of impressed listener as Yanis told him about Peter's financial status and Helen's title.

After the call was completed, John Thessalonikos smiled and said that any questions he had were answered and he would take care of everything immediately. He would notify Peter at his office in the hotel when the final papers were due to be signed and the balance monies paid. With that, they left.

They returned to the hotel and met up with Olaf. They told him about the bank, the lawyer, and the new title (strictly for use in Salonika) of his niece and the pending change of name for the *Naiad*. They found Jim and told him that after lunch they were flying to Milano, where Jim would be left for a couple of days while they went on by train to their next meeting.

Before lunch, Helen met with Victoria, the secretary to Alex, the manager. Helen gave her a list of the equipment and stationery she needed for her office in the hotel, and Victoria promised to purchase everything in the course of the next day or two and to have it all in the office, ready for her return.

They arrived at the hangar to see Jim in his right-hand seat of the cockpit of the DC3, but as they mounted the steps, they saw painted on the fuselage just forward of the door, the words *Richard's Renown*. They both smiled at the sight and as Peter said to Helen, "Did you arrange this?" she said, "Look what Jim arranged, Peter."

On board the plane and in the cockpit, Helen became very much the Chief Pilot and went through the pre-flight check with Jim in her usual professional way.

When it was over, Peter came to the cockpit and said, "Thanks, Jim, for the paint job."

"It was a pleasure, and I'm glad you like it," he responded.

They flew off after the usual formalities and came in to land at Milano after an uneventful flight of about four hours. Jim had been told of a good hotel in which to stay while there, so that they could get in touch with him on their return to the city. He was left to arrange for refueling, basic maintenance on the plane, and parking, and then his time was his own for a few days.

Peter and Helen took a taxi from the airport to the central train station and started their train and bus journey to Camp Pietro, arriving there at about 6:30 p.m.

As they walked through the gate, they were quickly spotted and the cry rang around the camp, "Peter and Helen are here!"

They were surrounded in moments by a noisy, welcoming crowd, who swarmed around them, and Peter had to tell everybody that he would talk to the group after dinner and tell them all the news, "and there was plenty." The big crowd dissipated leaving Max, Alex, Miriam, and Heide with the new arrivals.

Miriam and Heide threw their arms first around Helen, kissing her warmly, then each kissed Peter. Miriam whispered in his ear, "I've missed you so much, Peter."

Peter found Dov in his small office and the two men greeted each other. Peter told Dov that he had bought a ship in Salonika.

Then he went to his room and found Miriam there, just putting the last touches, having unpacked his bag for him. She had also managed to find some empty glass jars from the kitchen, picked some flowers, put them in water, and placed them around in his room, a rather lovely and feminine touch to an otherwise sparse soldiers' hut. Peter went over to Miriam, put his arms around her and kissed her lovingly.

Just then they heard the dinner bell sound. They pulled themselves apart, tidied themselves up, and went to the dining room.

As before, they seated Peter at the head of the table. He sat Helen on his right and Miriam on his left, with Alex, Max, and Heide next. Helen told Miriam and Heide that she had more supplies for them and they should collect them from her room after dinner.

When the dinner was over and dessert was being eaten, Dov came in and found a place to sit at the table. Peter tapped a water glass with a knife a few times to get everybody's attention.

"Good evening, chevrah."

A heart-felt "Good evening, Peter," was everyone's response.

He recounted all the events up to that point. Everyone became excited at the prospect of finally moving on with their lives. Then Peter left them and returned to his room.

He found the room in darkness, but the ambient light through the windows was sufficient for him to see a female form, fully clothed, lying on his bed.

"It *is* Heide, isn't it?" he asked. "Or is that you, Helen?"

He managed to catch the pillow which was flung at him with great force. and he heard.

"You are a horrible, horrible, man, and I don't know why I waste *any* time on you. Even if you were only joking, that is no way to welcome me into your room. How can you be so heartless? Thank God, not all men are like you."

He was laughing uncontrollably, knowing full well that this supposed anger was also in fun. He leaned down and kissed her gently on her forehead.

"Miriam, to continue where we left off last time, I've come to the same conclusion about you, that I'm not only in love with you, but that I'm sure that I want to spend the rest of my life with you. I know it took me a lot longer to understand the depth of my feelings for you than you might have liked, but I can tell you, without hesitation, that I will henceforth think of you as my future wife, and after we have gone through this unstable period and are able to settle down somewhere together, we will make it official, if you'll have me."

"My darling Peter, do you doubt it? You've made me the happiest woman in the world. And I don't need a public announcement or an engagement ring or any other outward declaration. It's enough that I know how you feel about me."

That night, two mature, but inexperienced adults, very much in love with one another, very gently and lovingly came together. When it was all over and they reposed in each other's arms, each one said how much they loved the other.

When the breakfast gong sounded, Peter left his hut and went to the dining room. Miriam had left a short while earlier. When he looked at her seated next to him, he saw that her face was actually *glowing*. She said to him quietly, "Heide took a look at me this morning and said immediately, 'So you finally consummated your love for each other, am I right?' and of course, I had to admit it. I asked her how she had known and she said 'you haven't seen yourself in a mirror this morning, my dear.'"

After breakfast, Peter stood and answered everyone's questions with patience and grace. Peter said he would be there all that day and overnight and if anybody had any other questions for him, they only had to ask.

After they dispersed, Peter wandered around the camp, reviewing the activities in the camp. There were lectures by Aliyah Bet people, rifle instruction and infantry tactics by Dov, the ex-army captain, cooking in the kitchen, trash and bathroom pick-up. Food was delivered from the village down the hill daily. It was, in fact, a highly organized and professional operation, planned and operated by Aliyah Bet, and he visualized it taking place all over Europe, in temporary camps, to be opened and then closed and vacated after its specific raison d'être was satisfied.

Peter found himself in front of Miriam's quarters. He knocked. Heide opened the door.

"Hi, I've come 'round to see if Miriam wants to go outside for a walk. What do you say, Miriam?" he asked, walking in and looking at her. "It's a lovely, sunny day."

"I'd love to," she replied. "Would anybody else like to join us?"

Heide said, "Thank you, but no thanks, I'm going to meet up with Max to talk about sheep diseases, of all things, which he wants to learn about!"

Peter and Miriam then left the hut and went outside the camp for a stroll. They walked up and down the road for a couple of hours, talking nonstop about Palestine, how and where they would be living in the future, and so on, until it got chilly and they decided to return to the camp.

"I know where we could go where it's warmer," said Peter, innocently.

"And where would that be?" asked Miriam, just as innocently.

"I'll show you, if you promise to keep it a secret," said Peter, as he led her to his hut.

On the way there, they bumped into Helen. "Just the person I wanted to see," said Helen.

Peter replied, "It's a great privilege to be wanted by you, Helen, so how can I help you?"

"I wanted to know if you want to leave tomorrow to go to Alicante or do you want to stay another night and leave the morning after."

Peter said, "I think we'll stay another night because I want to stay as long as it takes for all the group to thoroughly understand our complicated plans."

"Thank you, Peter," Helen said, and went on her way.

Miriam said to Peter, "I'm wondering, my love, if you told Helen the whole truth about you staying another forty-eight hours."

He said, "What I said was the truth and nothing but the truth, Miriam."

"Ah," she said, "but I didn't hear you say, the whole truth.'"

Peter said, "You've caught me again, you clever thing. You're quite right, you know. I decided to be self-indulgent for once, and stay over to have an extra night with you here.

"And as a matter of fact, if Olaf had completed all the preparations, there would have been a phone call from him to Dov to send out the engineer and chef and I would have been informed."

"Thanks for the explanation," Miriam told him with a smile. "While it sounds a bit like rationalization to me, I do appreciate your explanation. I've also been thinking. Is there any way you could take me with you on your flight to Spain? I've never yet flown on an airplane, and, I'm terribly jealous of your going to Spain with beautiful Helen flying you, and, who knows, maybe spending a day or two, *and* the *nights*, in a hotel in Alicante, and me waiting here in Camp Pietro. As I said, I hope you're not going to be upset with me for asking that question, but I think if you've learned anything about me it's that I don't hold back from telling people what's on my mind."

"A straight question deserves a straight answer," Peter responded. "First of all, Helen and I are the closest of friends and have been so ever since I met her. But there has never been any romantic relationship between us because she met Alex and I met you. So, even though I will be in Spain for a night or two, that doesn't mean the friendship that Helen and I share will therefore suddenly blossom into something else. Besides, her Orthodox style of Judaism precludes her from having the kind of liaison that we have.

"Second, even though people in Camp Pietro know that you and I've got something going on between us, I don't think this is the time to be taking you on a trip for any length of time. Remember, I'll be gone for a number of weeks and the camp needs you here even though there's no question that I want you with me.

"In addition, showing this kind of favoritism will hurt my ability to work with the group. If you can go with me, then perhaps Max and Heide should be able to take off together for a time, or any of the other couples in the camp. You see, there are a lot of potential problems which could arise."

"Okay, my dear," she replied. "I understand completely what you say and perhaps it would have been better not to ask. But please remember when you're in Spain with Helen that I'll be on your shoulder watching every move you make. I can't help but be jealous."

Peter smiled, kissed her and said, "I wouldn't have it any other way."

They parted then and Peter returned to his own hut. After a half-hour or so, the door opened quietly and Miriam slipped in. She looked over at Peter who was engrossed in a book and had not heard her entry. She locked the door silently, then crept behind him, put her hands over his eyes and said, "Now guess who *this* is, Peter Romaine."

He said, "This had better be the woman I'm in love with, because if it's somebody other than the one I'm in love with, you should know my darling knows everything I do. See," he said pointing to his shoulder, "she's right up here watching."

At that, she took her hand away, moved around to face him, removed his book, then lowered herself on to his lap, put her hands behind his head and gently pulled his head down to her as she brought her lips into contact with his. They sat together in that position for some minutes.

"That was absolutely . . . ," he started to say.

"Shhhhhh," she commanded and placed her lips on his again so that he had to stop trying to speak and concentrated on sharing the embrace with her.

At length, as they separated, Peter rose from his chair and adjusted his position so that his arms could envelope her and hers could enfold him.

And thus they stayed, for a long, long time, until they heard the gong of lunch, when they had to separate, very reluctantly.

After lunch, Peter arranged for Dov to come and talk to the group about what sort of action was likely to take place after they arrived at their destination, and how speedily they would be required to get off the ship so that the ship could sail away.

Peter made a sketch of his ship and the layout of the bunks and cabins for the group to have an idea how they were to be accommodated on board the ship. He also told them that the ship he had bought was originally named the *Naiad* but was to be renamed, the *Helen*, not after Helen, their beautiful pilot, but after Helen, the most beautiful woman of Ancient Greece, and the cause of the Trojan War.

After Peter had finished some hours of an additional session with the group, Dov asked to speak to him privately. They went to Dov's office where he told Peter he would like to come along with him on his ship to Palestine. He was, after all, an experienced soldier and would be needed in the upcoming battles. Peter readily agreed.

Then Dov wondered out loud how the ship would avoid capture once they landed the crew. Would it make sense to sail to Turkey and leave the ship there? Peter could then have the option to do with the ship as he pleased, even give it to the Aliyah Bet organization, who would use it to bring more people on aliyah. Olaf would have no trouble in leaving Turkey and the three Aliyah Bet men might have another task for themselves or return to Palestine, one way or another. What did Peter think of these plans and ideas?

Peter admitted that he hadn't given it much thought, but Dov's plan seemed well thought out and as long as his ship could be useful to Aliyah Bet, he was all in favor of the idea.

"Dov, you can inform your people that, assuming Olaf agrees, which I'm sure he will, your organization will be able to take over the ship in Turkey and use it as you please."

"Thank you very much, Peter, on behalf of Aliyah Bet. I've no idea how long Britain is going to sit it out in Palestine, but there has to be an end to it. And certainly then, if not earlier, your ship will be very useful to us."

The next day, Peter was approached by some of the members who wanted certain details of their future involvements made clear yet again, and so, with exemplary patience, he ran over the plans once more, in various languages, which, this time, required him to bring in Jacob as a translator of Romance to Baltic languages. Peter realized it was very necessary to make sure the boys really understood what he was telling them when he was using German, and made sure those who did not understand that language wrote down the technical words so they would become familiar with them and react immediately on the ship.

Peter made it his business to attend some of the lectures and demonstrations given by the Aliyah Bet people and also some instruction in the Hebrew language.

He arranged with Helen to leave after breakfast and, as before, they were accompanied out of the camp and down to the village by a number of their friends who carried their luggage for them and waited with them until the bus arrived, then waved to them until the bus was out of sight.

CHAPTER XV

Alicante and Helen

AFTER LEAVING CAMP PIETRO, PETER AND HELEN TOOK THE bus and train to Milano, getting to the airport about midday. They found the Dakota, *Richard's Renown*, and Jim McDonald easily enough; the plane was fuelled up, and Jim, with his maps, was all ready for the flight to Spain. The two pilots went through the pre-flight routine and they took off.

Their course was first south to the Ligurian Sea, then west, parallel to the south coast of France, then later, southwest, passing between Barcelona and the Balearic Islands of Minorca, Mallorca, and Ibiza, and finally to a smooth landing at Alicante.

Helen taxied the plane to a parking area and then they were boarded by a customs/police officer, who carried out a perfunctory check of the aircraft, congratulating Peter and Helen on their fluency in Spanish despite their British and Swiss passports, respectively.

Peter told Jim the name of the hotel to which they were going and left him to arrange to refuel the plane and normal post-flight checks, and to follow them there. Peter and Helen took a taxi to the Hotel Palas, where they were met by the manager, who greeted them with pronounced cordiality, aware that Peter was going to bring thirty or so visitors to the hotel to stay some weeks.

It was now sunset and Peter and Helen arranged to have dinner together on the hotel restaurant balcony, which overlooked the Mediterranean. They met as arranged, each ordered a manzanilla, and sat quietly together to relax after the busy day they had both been having. They each took a sip of their drink, swallowed, and breathed out a long sigh of contentment.

"What a marvelous –" Peter said, just as Helen said, "What a fabulous –"

They laughed together.

"I must tell you something of interest," Peter began. "Although Miriam knows what close friends you and I are, with no romantic relationship between us, she told me how terribly jealous she is going to be of us spending time together in Spain. If she was aware of this heavenly spot and you and I sharing it together, I think she would really blow her top."

"What you just said is most interesting because Alex said something on similar lines to me," Helen responded. "Alex had the temerity to claim that he hoped I would be a 'good girl,' as he said, 'when being away in Spain for a day or two' with you."

Peter said, "and how did you respond to that?"

"I told him that you and I are as close friends as a man and a woman can be, short of going to bed together, and that he doesn't have the right to tell me to be a 'good girl.'"

"And he said?"

"Well, Helen, and have you and Peter gone to bed together?'"

"And you replied?"

"I told him he doesn't have the right to ask."

Peter smiled. "Well, I'm now one-hundred percent certain that he believes we have been to bed together."

"What makes you think so?" she asked, somewhat startled.

"Because that's how men think."

"What do you mean by that?"

"If you couldn't reply to his question with an emphatic negative, he would think that your reply that 'he didn't have the right to ask' meant you didn't want to admit it and didn't want to lie."

"Wow," she said, "so that's how you men think, is it?"

"Well," he replied. "That's how I would think, in his shoes."

"And now tell me, my good and close friend, Peter, have you ever wanted to go to bed with me?"

"Absolutely, my beautiful and wonderfully close friend."

"Really, Peter? When?"

"Almost always, whenever we are together."

"And why did you never approach me with that thought in your mind?"

"Because, at the beginning, I didn't want to risk being turned down, and, later, didn't want to risk losing a great and close friend, my dear."

"And what is it that makes you want to go to bed with me?"

"Because you are beautiful, no, gorgeous, very smart, very sexy, and always perfectly turned out."

She sat quietly for a few moments, relishing his words but mainly surprised at the inclusion of "sexy." She said, "Peter."

"Yes, my dear," he responded.

"Please tell me –"

"I bet I know your question," he interrupted.

She said, "How could you."

He said, "Will you bet me?"

She said, "Yes, what are the stakes?"

He said, "If I guess correctly, will you admit it?"

She said, "Of course I will. What are the stakes?"

He said, "You have to go to bed with me. Is that agreed?"

She thought for a minute. There was, after all, no way he could know what was in her mind as a question. "Very well," she said.

He said, "You wanted to know how I meant it when I said you were very sexy."

She went quite white, but composed herself immediately. "Hmmm. Why would you think that?"

"It's very simple. You certainly know you're beautiful, and it's hard to imagine you don't know you're smart, and you dress, as the Americans say, 'To the nines.' So that leaves sexy. Now, it was surprising to you that I would use that adjective to describe you, and probably I'm the one close friend who might be so open as to say that to you, because you have never thought of yourself as sexy. So I knew you would want to ask me what I mean by that. Now, tell me honestly, was I right, Helen?"

She had now recovered her color and was blushing. She knew if she agreed he was right about the question, she had just agreed to go to bed with him. On the other hand, she didn't want there ever to be a lie between them.

In order to gain some respite, Helen said, "Let's go out on the terrace and order dinner, shall we? We can continue there."

"Very well, Helen, let's do that," he agreed.

They moved out on to the terrace, selected a table and sat down. The maitre d' brought a wine menu and Peter ordered a bottle of the best wine of the area. Their glasses were filled and Peter offered a toast.

"Here's to the girl with the high-heeled shoes, who spends your money and drinks your booze, and then goes home with her lover to snooze: Here's to the girl with the high-heeled shoes."

She joined Peter in laughing at the toast, and they both drank.

"Now," she said, "there's no point in procrastinating any longer, Peter, and the answer is Yes!"

At that moment, Jim McDonald appeared on the terrace and approached their table.

"I'm not intruding, I hope, Peter. Just wanted to know if we're flying back tomorrow or the next day."

Peter stood up and led Jim away from his table saying, "No flying tomorrow, Jim. You have the day off and I'll let you know by tomorrow evening if we fly the following day. Enjoy yourself."

"Thanks Peter, and goodnight to you both," and off he went.

Peter returned to the table and Helen.

"What a convenient interruption *that* was," Helen said. "I don't know for the life of me what I must have looked like to him when he appeared."

"You looked your usual beautiful and sexy self," he said with a broad grin, "and anyway, he was looking at me, to get his orders for tomorrow.

"May I top up your glass?" he asked.

"Thank you, Peter," she replied. "Are you trying to get me drunk?"

"Do you think you need to be, in order to settle your bet?"

"It hadn't occurred to me that I would need some liquid relaxation to pay off my bet," she said, looking him straight in the eye.

"Fair enough. But let me ask you, Do you really want to go to bed with me, or are you doing this just to settle a bet?"

"First of all," she said, matter-of-factly, "I've always believed that a bet is a bet is a bet, and that no one should ever back away from paying his or her dues when losing. And secondly," she lowered her voice, "in the same way that you told me you were attracted to me I can freely tell you that I was attracted to you in exactly the same way and have remained so since that time. From the time you first phoned me up, which started this whole Zionist/Aliyah Bet thing, I've had much more feeling for you than would be accounted for by our close friendship, of which we profess to each other all the time. So, my dear Peter, when do you want this to come about?"

"Well, I believe the decision of 'when' should come from you, because I'm always ready to make love with you whereas I've always felt that women need to be in the right mood."

"You're right, Peter. But I must tell you that this is a romantic location and I'm in the right mood. But I do have one reservation."

"And that is?"

"That whatever happens between us tonight does not in any way affect our close and affectionate friendship in the future, which I value so highly. And yes, you may top up my glass, Peter. It would be a shame to leave any of this delicious wine in the bottle."

And with that, they finished the bottle, Peter signed the bill and they left the restaurant. Going up in the elevator, Peter summoned up a nonchalant tone in his voice as he asked, "Your room or mine, Helen?"

"Mine, in an hour, if you please, Peter. I'm in 301, by the way."

An hour later, having taken a bath and changed, Peter went to room 301 and, finding the door slightly ajar, entered.

Helen was sitting up on the furthest side of the bed with a couple of pillows behind her. The night table on the side furthest from the door held the reading lamp which was alight. She was wearing a beautiful lace-topped nightgown. The light from the bedside lamp shone through the gaps in the lace top. The bed sheets covered her up to her hips, thus showing her very slender waist wrapped by the closely-fitting silk nightgown.

He found he had stopped breathing as he took in the sensual scene before him. He exhaled deeply and closed the door.

He took a couple of unsteady steps toward the bed and sat down. He looked at her and was silent for a few moments. Then his shoulders shook and he couldn't suppress a smile.

"What's so humorous, Peter?" she asked in an unhappy voice.

"It's just that a couple of hours ago I was doing my darndest to define 'sexy' and here before my very eyes is the absolute epitome of the word. You, my dear, are the most beautiful, gorgeous, desirable sight that a man could ever dream of. It's like a dream come true."

"Well, then, Peter, isn't it time you took off all those superfluous clothes you're wearing and come to bed? Or, do you intend to spend your time here fully dressed?"

He was silent for what seemed to Helen to be an age, but she said nothing, waiting for him to speak. She started to have a premonition that all wasn't as it appeared. As the seconds passed, she felt a dread and her heart began pounding. She gently drew up the cover around her.

"Helen, my close and wonderful friend" Peter began, and Helen knew what awaited her. "This has to be one of the hardest things I've ever done. I've never wanted anyone as much as I want you, but in my heart I know it's not right.

"It's clear to me that Miriam and I are soul mates and that we will one day, perhaps soon, marry. Even though we're not even technically engaged yet, I would always feel – you and I would always feel – that we betrayed Miriam's trust in us. And, just as importantly, I realized that our friendship *will* suffer and that's something that, at this point, I can't live without.

"I know this is shocking behavior. So, before I leave here I need to know that you're not so angry with me that you won't continue our friendship, as it was."

Helen found, much to her surprise, that as a result of his heartfelt words she too felt relieved.

"Peter, as difficult as this was for you to say, I want you to know I respect you more than ever. I suppose that would be a reversal of roles for some people. But you really are a man of integrity and that's very important to a woman. Miriam will be lucky to have you for a husband and I, I'm lucky to have you as a friend. So please, come 'round to my side of the bed so that I can give you a *friendly* good night kiss before you go back to your room to get some well-earned sleep."

They exchanged a kiss, then Peter left her, lost in his own thoughts.

The next day dawned bright and sunny and he looked on a placid ocean as he walked on to the balcony for breakfast, to join Helen and Jim who were already seated.

They all greeted one another. Peter looked hard at Helen, who met his glance with nothing more than the usual open, warm, smile that he was accustomed to receiving from her. She had not a hair out of place and looked her usual beautiful self.

After breakfast, Peter excused himself and took a stroll around the interior of the hotel, then he went outside to the beach and the street alongside the hotel. He had remembered that he was, after all, in Alicante to check out its suitability as a vacation location for his group, and he'd better do it.

The Hotel Palas was one of the great, old luxury hotels of Europe. It was located right on the sea front, next to a walkway, which was, itself, on the edge of the sand beach. The guests were protected from the outside by large, glass windows, through which they looked out and the passers-by looked in. The beach itself was about 150 meters deep at that point, between the hotel and the Mediterranean. Next to the hotel was a street called "Calle Cervantes," along which, about 100 meters down, was the City Hall of Alicante. As he could see from the hotel, the beach was a large stretch of unbroken golden sand. To the right of the beach, southward, was the beginning of a yacht marina with about a dozen sailing boats moored there, then a little further was the commercial port of Alicante.

He walked out on to the sand, and turned around to look at the hotel. He could now see that beyond the hotel there was a busy street. To the north, there was a great rock hill and on the very top, the remains of the battlements of a castle.

He returned to the hotel and found the manager in the reception area.

"Good morning, Mr. Romaine. I trust you slept well. My name is Juan Herrera and I'm at your service. I'm sorry I didn't introduce myself to you when you arrived last evening, but I could see you and the lady were looking tired and obviously wanting to get to your rooms to relax. So, what can I do for you today?"

"I've just been outside to look around the location here and I noticed what appeared to be the battlement walls of a castle on top of the hill. Tell me something about it."

"That's the remains of our Alicante Castle and we love it. It's been there, gently falling into desuetude over the centuries, since the fourteenth Century, actually."

"Is there a pathway up?" he inquired.

"Yes, indeed. It starts about 200 meters north of here. There's a sign pointing the way. It's a fairly rigorous walk to the top and takes about one and a half hours to do it each way, assuming you're fit for such a walk."

"Thank you, Juan," Peter said. "I might try it later, and maybe my colleagues will join me."

"At your service, Mr. Romaine," said Juan as Peter started to move away.

"Oh, yes. I almost forgot," Peter added. "When my group gets here, they will be spending a lot of time on the beach and in the sea. Where can they change their clothes for swimming?"

"We have changing rooms for gentlemen and ladies," he replied. "The entrance to them is just around the corner, on Calle Cervantes, and they can also be reached from inside the hotel. When people are wet, they can use the Calle Cervantes entrance to avoid coming into the hotel in such a condition. Other than that, we don't have any onerous restrictions here."

Peter rejoined Helen and Jim. He told them of his explorations. He also told them that after breakfast tomorrow they could all take the hill walk up to the castle with a picnic lunch. They both agreed.

Peter had obtained a recommendation from Juan Herrera to a

good restaurant near the hotel and Herrera made a reservation for them for that evening.

Peter knocked on Helen's door, as arranged, at 8:00 p.m. She opened the door to him and he came in and closed the door. She came to him, put her arms around his neck and kissed him warmly.

"Helen, my dear," he was just able to say, "what's this all about?"

"This is, dear Peter, just to show you that we are continuing to be close and non-romantic friends and so, are you ready to go out for dinner?"

He managed to adopt a causal and cool mien as he said, "Very well, Helen, my dear, and if *you* are ready to go out then perhaps we should."

So they left the hotel, with Helen casually taking Peter's arm, making Peter feel very comfortable and warm.

Arriving at the restaurant, they were shown to a very good table, with a view of the ocean and of the passing people. They ordered a bottle and with some recommendations from the maitre d', they ordered dinner.

Peter told Helen of his plans for the immediate future, which included flying back the next day to Greece. Helen asked him if he had informed Jim, which he had *not* done, and she told him he ought to do it right away so that Jim was fully prepared for the coming flights.

From the restaurant he phoned to the hotel to speak to Jim. Peter told him they would leave Alicante the next morning at 11:00 a.m. and fly to Rome, where they would refuel, then fly on to Salonika. There, barring any further change of instructions, the plane would be parked for a few weeks and Jim could return to England until recalled for the next flight.

When Peter returned to the table, they finished their meal and returned to the hotel.

After breakfast the next morning, Peter picked up a packed lunch for three persons and a borrowed backpack to put it in. Jim promptly volunteered to wear the backpack and they set out.

Peter told the other two that he wanted to see what degree of fitness and effort was required to take the walk up to the castle. He wanted to use this track as a fitness activity for his group when they arrived.

They found the path and proceeded to walk up. They reached the castle after an hour and a quarter of walking, and after a rest and lunch, they walked about the battlements, parapets, and turrets to explore what must have been at one time an impregnable fortress.

They walked back down with a leisurely step, taking an hour to return to the hotel, where they were met by Juan.

"Did you enjoy your walk?" He asked. "I'm curious as to how long it took you?"

"It took an hour and a quarter up and an hour down," he informed the manager, "and we stopped once on the way up and then at the top to have our very delicious lunch, which we enjoyed very much. Thank you, Juan."

"I'm very pleased to hear that, Mr. Romaine," Juan replied.

"I wouldn't be surprised if some of our group will want to do that walk after they get here, especially if they have that delicious packed lunch to look forward to at the top."

"It will be our pleasure to provide that and to look after your group in due course," said Juan.

They then went to their rooms to freshen up and pack for their flight. Meanwhile, Peter told Juan he would like him to be especially attentive to the group, as they were young people who had suffered greatly during the war and were coming to the Hotel Palas to rest up and recuperate, although none were ill. The manager was very sympathetic and promised to do his best.

The three flew off in the dusk, first to Rome, to refuel, then on to Salonika, which they reached at about midnight, parked the Dakota, and then returned to the Aristoteles Hotel. Jim said he would go out again in the morning to arrange for refueling and engine checks.

CHAPTER XVI

Salonika 3 and Camp Pietro 4: Contracts

AFTER THEY ENTERED THE HOTEL, PETER WENT DIRECTLY to Olaf's room. Olaf opened the door and ushered Peter in. He gave Olaf a full report on the Alicante hotel and its accommodations.

"So now, Olaf, tell me, what's going on with the ship?"

"We're doing very well. I contacted the largest firm of ships' inspectors and found they are licensed to check everything: lifeboats, engines, electric systems, hydraulics, navigation equipment, power transmission, propellers, and communication equipment. They obviously wanted the work badly, for within an hour of my signing a contract, they had twenty-five men on board doing the inspections.

"I hear that the contract for the ship purchase is now completed and agreed between the lawyers. It is ready for you to sign and pay the balance of $1,035,000 into an escrow account at your bank, pending settlement of the expense cap we added.

"I took it upon my own responsibility to phone Dov and tell him to tell Aliyah Bet that it's now time to send out the ship's engineer and the chef since we're making good progress. Also, the engineer can start by working on my sketches of the engineering work to be done in Kavala.

"By the way, I went to Kavala yesterday with Joseph and I decided on a marine engineering company there to do our special 'hold' work and they are, of course, waiting for final drawings from our engineer.

"When in Kavala, I made inquiries about the fuel and supplies and found an adequate company for our chef to work with, although we could buy some supplies in Salonika. I also found a clean, small, hotel for the chef and the engineer to stay in, close to the dockyards.

"Finally, I also contacted a labor contractor who will find me two or three seamen to help me sail the *Helen* from Salonika to Kavala when the repair work here is finished."

Peter then told Olaf of his discussion with Dov about his joining them to become a crew member, then after the off-loading of the group, helping to sail it to Turkey, with Olaf's agreement.

"It's a good idea, Peter, and it will complete my part of this incredible adventure, after we get to Palestine."

They both said good night and Peter went back to his room.

The next morning, at breakfast, Peter told Helen they needed to visit his bank and then the lawyer, to sign the ship purchase agreement and to pay the balance check into an escrow account and he needed a "Princess" to look after him. He also summarized for her the reports he had received from Olaf and asked her if she had checked in on her office and if it was all as she had requested.

She told him that she had, and that it was all set up and in such a way that when the time came for her to transfer it to the ship, it would be easy. They then went to Helen's office, where he called Yanis and then his lawyer, John Thessalonikos.

After he hung up, Helen said to him, "You are quite amazing, my friend, how easily your have clothed yourself in the skin of a polished and efficient businessman from just an ordinary genius of Romance languages."

They took a taxi to the bank, and found Yanis in the lobby. He greeted them, bowing ever so slightly to Helen.

"It's a pleasure to see you again Princess," he said, "and you, Mr. Romaine. Now how can I help you?"

"I need a bank draft in the amount of $1,035,000 to complete the purchase of a ship. Please tell me how we can arrange it, Yanis."

"Well," he answered, "I assume you don't have that amount in your account here at present, so first, you need to top up your dollar account to at least that amount, then give me a check for that amount, made payable to my bank, and I will then give you a draft for the same amount, made payable to your required payee."

"Thank you. May I make a call to my bank in Switzerland to arrange to wire the money to you at once?"

"Of course, Mr. Romaine. I will go out of the room and tell my secretary to arrange the call. You may, of course, take as much time as you need." So saying, he left his office.

The phone rang after a few minutes. Helen answered it and told the operator the Berne bank number. In a few moments, Peter was speaking to his bank manager in Berne, Mr. Lambert.

"Mr. Lambert, this is Peter Romaine and I've a code number for you—."

"Thank you, Mr. Romaine, and what can I do for you today?"

"How quickly can you send $1,100,000 to my bank account here in Salonika, to which you have previously sent dollars?"

"I can send it now by 'special express high value money wire transfer' (SEHVMWT*) but it will cost you $250 to do so," he replied. "Do I have your approval? It will take between fifteen and twenty minutes to arrive from our central transmission office in Zurich."

"Yes, you have my approval, Mr. Lambert and thank you," said Peter.

"Can you believe that, Helen?" he said to her. "That amount of money to get here in twenty minutes."

"That is certainly remarkable," she said.

They left Yanis's office and found him in the front of the bank.

"Yanis," said Peter, "the Princess has arranged to have some money sent to my account within the next twenty minutes. While we are waiting, we'll go out and get a coffee and then we'll be back."

They left an astonished Yanis, and went outside to find a cafe.

They returned to the bank after a half-hour to find Yanis waiting for them.

"I've never even heard of such an incredibly quick transfer from another country," he said. "It arrived ten minutes ago."

Peter responded coolly, "Don't forget it was from Switzerland, Yanis, I suppose not all countries have that ability and efficiency."

Yanis responded, "If you will let me have your check, as you said, I will give you the counter-draft to the name as you direct me."

In five minutes, the check was written and handed to Yanis by Helen. He took it away and returned a few minutes later with the bank draft, which he gave to her.

Peter then prevailed on Yanis to allow Helen to use a phone to call John Thessalonikos, to tell him Peter was ready to call on him. John told her he was free now and would look forward to seeing them again.

They walked to the office of Thessalonikos, who greeted them and produced the ship purchase documents, which were in the Greek language. He went through them carefully, answering various ques-

---

* This money transfer system is but a figment of the author's imagination.

tions that Peter and Helen directed at him. At length, it was done and Peter signed a number of papers, including the change of name from *Naiad* to the *Helen*.

John Thessalonikos then said to Peter, "I suppose you have a bank draft for me?"

"No," Peter answered.

John suddenly looked shocked.

"What?"

"My associate has it," he answered with an amused smile.

"Well, I'm glad someone has it."

Helen handed the draft to John, with a big smile. John examined it carefully and said, "Thank you very much. I will deposit it today in an escrow account in the joint names of myself and the attorney for the seller, to be released to the seller after the condition is met, that is, after the certification of the expenses cap.

"In the meantime, I will give you a receipt for this draft, and as a matter of fact, it is going to be deposited into the escrow account in the same bank that issued the draft."

Peter said, "How interesting. I could just have deposited my check into that escrow account."

"No, Mr. Romaine, that's not how it works. It had to be done as we are doing it. Now, you are the ship owner for all practical purposes and I wish you luck in your enterprises."

They thanked him, left his office, and returned to the hotel.

They found Olaf in their office, just completing examining a pile of papers before him.

"Well, you two," he said, "I'm pleased to say I've now received the nine inspection reports I've been waiting for and I've just finished reviewing them. They are all acceptable, that is to say, every negative point raised is minor and so nothing is reported on which cannot be fixed quickly and properly by whichever engineering company we use. I'm now going to make three copies of these reports, then call the three contracting companies and invite them formally to make a bid for the work we require and give them a time limit for submission. This last item is what I'm now considering – I want it speedily, but realistically, and in English."

"That's great, Olaf. Now tell me how we can help."

"Well, if you can take care of the copying process, I'll get on the phone to the three engineering companies, invite them to bid, and fix a time for each to come and pick up a set of the reports."

"Give them to me and I'll go and get them copied," Helen said, picking up the pages and rushing out. She went to Victoria Nixos – the secretary to Alex, the hotel manager – and asked her how she could get the papers quickly copied. Victoria told her there was a printing company along Aristoteles Street, who had a very modern American machine that could take pictures of each sheet and then make as many copies as needed. She offered to go along with Helen to arrange it.

The two girls went out and were back in less than an hour with the three additional copies of each paper. Helen made up three sets of the inspection reports, each of which she put in a prepared file folder, with a printed name on the cover, "Peter Romaine, Société Anonyme" to look professional. She gave them to Olaf, who thanked her for such a business-like approach.

Olaf also told Peter and Helen that he had received a call from Dov. Dov told him he had heard from Aliyah Bet, using their code word "Abie," meaning Aliyah Bet (AB), that the two people they had had standing by were on their way to report to Olaf at the Aristoteles Hotel. They were expected to arrive within three days.

By dinner time, Olaf was able to confirm that all the reports had been issued to the engineering companies and all had said they would be able to bring in their bids in English within five working days. Peter told Olaf that he had completed the purchase contract of the ship and paid the balance of the purchase price. The ship was now his.

While Olaf was to stay put in order to brief the AB people and supervise their work, Peter wanted to return to Camp Pietro to brief the group on what was happening. Helen would accompany Peter, but Jim would stay in Milano until Peter went back to Salonika.

With that, the Three Musketeers parted to go their separate ways. Peter went to his room to read a book, Olaf and Helen to the office to finish some work.

The next morning, Jim went to the airport to prepare the DC3 for its next flight. Helen and Peter packed, went to the airport, and found *Richard's Renown* all ready to go, with Jim in the co-pilot's seat. The weather forecast was excellent for their trip to Milano, where they parted from Jim.

They arrived at Camp Pietro just in time for lunch. Peter sat at the head of the table, Miriam sat next to him, barely able to keep her hands off him. When lunch was over, as usual, Peter tapped on a glass with his knife and said, "Shalom, chevrah." The group replied in unison, "Shalom, Peter."

He told them of the progress in Salonika and Alicante. He said they had completed buying the ship and were now dealing with the overhaul. He had been to Spain and checked out the hotel, which was perfect, next to the beach, near shops, and close to an old castle.

They would each get an increase in allowance and just in case they didn't know, Dov would be going with them on the voyage. Peter said he would be at the camp for the next four or five days and available for any other questions.

When he had finished and everybody was leaving, Miriam whispered to him, "Please come to your hut." He managed to get away and went to his hut. After he came in and closed the door, Miriam, who was already inside, threw her arms around him and said, "Peter, I had to hold you, right now, I couldn't wait for tonight" and covered his face with kisses, which he eagerly returned. She said, "I missed you so much, my love, especially because you were in Spain with Helen."

"There was no reason to feel jealous of Helen – you know we are just very good friends. I missed you, too, and now I'm here for four or five nights – I told the group four or five days, but with you, my love, I much prefer the nights, which I'm looking forward to very much. But for now, and until tonight, I must behave myself, in order to maintain your reputation. And anyway, I've invited anyone who has any questions to come to my room now to discuss things."

Miriam said, "Can I stay to unpack your case and put your things away, my sweetheart? At least, I could be doing that now, if anybody comes to visit you."

"Of course," he said. She opened his case, and as she started, there was a knock on the door.

"Come in," he said, seeing she was already putting his clothing in drawers. Two of the boys entered, one, he knew, was from Yugoslavia, plus Jacob.

The Yugoslav boy, whose name was Abe, spoke Serbo-Croat and wanted to know the best way to spend the pocket money they were going to get. Peter said, "I would recommend you buy a swimsuit first and some sunglasses – the sun there can be very strong – and then some sun-repellent cream to protect your face and body and to very gradually expose yourself to the sun. You will be told about this again and again, later on; I don't want anyone getting burnt by the sun, only browned.

"But I now have a question for you, Abe," Peter said. "Do you know how to swim?"

"No, I don't."

"We'll have to do something about that," replied Peter. "Since I'm sending you all to the sea-shore in Spain, I'd better make sure that somebody teaches the group to swim. I wonder if anybody in the group is a swimming instructor? I'll ask when we are at dinner today."

After everyone had left, Peter turned to Miriam and said, "You see, my love, how important it was that you were doing something *for* me and not doing something *with* me when those two boys came in."

"Yes, yes, I see," she said. "I'd better leave now, just in case you have any more visitors, since I've finished unpacking your stuff and I'll see you later, at dinner."

After dinner, Peter stood until the room quieted. Then he spoke.

"Chevrah," he said, "in the near future, you are all going to be in Spain with a mission: to eat, lie in the sun, swim, and take some exercise. I learned today that at least one of you does not know how to swim, which concerns me, because I'm the one who is taking you to the sea-side. Now I want you to raise your hand if you do *not* know how to swim."

After translations, fifteen hands shot up.

"Now," Peter continued, "is there anybody in the room who has had experience as a swimming teacher and/or lifesaving?"

There was silence as everybody looked around. One hand was slowly raised. It was Dov's.

"I was raised on a kibbutz," he explained, "on the shore of the Sea of Galilee, the Kinneret, as we call it. All the kids of the kibbutz were taught to swim when we were very young and some of us went on to learn to be instructors to the younger children and some of us also qualified in lifesaving. It so happens that I did both. So, I'm at your service, Peter."

"That's wonderful, Dov," said Peter. "I think that you should go with the group to Alicante, as my deputy, to teach all the non-swimmers to swim."

"With pleasure, Peter. As you know, my plan was that as soon as your group has left Camp Pietro, my people and I would close the camp down, and send the equipment to our depot. Now, if I'm to go away with the group, my assistant will take over from me and close the camp down. No problem."

Everyone gradually dispersed to their various activities for the evening. Dov and Peter had a long chat about the voyage to Palestine. Peter was certain that Olaf would be very pleased to have Dov on board to take some responsibility for crew activities. Peter then left him to go to his hut.

Arriving at his hut, he went inside. A quiet voice said to him out of the dark, "Well, good evening Peter, my love, get undressed and come to bed at once, and explain, if you can, why I had to wait so long to get another hug and more kisses from you." He hurried to join her waiting arms.

They eventually fell asleep, until, in mutual shock, they heard the sound of reveille. They kissed again, with more affection than passion and then Miriam silently slipped out of his room.

The next day Peter attended four lectures: on infantry tactics by Dov; on elementary Hebrew by a native-born Jewish Palestinian girl, who had completed her education at the London School of Economics and was now a volunteer cook with the AB people; on the political status and political structure of Palestine by an erstwhile lecturer from the Hebrew University of Jerusalem; and on the ethnology of the area by a retired professor from Tel Aviv University. He also put his name down for the next day's lecture on the geography and geology of the country, on the archeological findings in the country, and on the relationships among Jews, Arabs, Druse, Assyrians, Christians, Roman Catholics, Eastern Orthodox, Protestant, Methodist, Ethiopian, Coptic, Armenian, and others.

He was amazed at the quality of the Aliyah Bet volunteers who had been allotted to such a small group of potential immigrants and the diversity of the subjects being offered. There were no AB volunteers there who were not also academics. He also learned that the volunteers teaching these courses had no hesitation in working as cooks, camp trash collectors, maintenance people, and any other menial job required to keep the camp functioning healthily and efficiently, as their personal contributions to the Aliyah Bet organization.

Day followed day as he studied voraciously these new subjects, making copious notes as he met each new challenge, including a new language, Modern Hebrew, which, he was amazed to learn, was almost identical with the ancient classical form of two and a half millennia ago, although the form of the letters had changed somewhat over time.

After a week, on Thursday, the long-awaited phone call from Olaf finally arrived, informing Peter that he had received Georg the engineer and Shlomo the chef, and that both appeared well qualified. He also had the three bids for the engineering work in Salonika. He was going through them with Georg and analyzing them, and was ready to go through them with Peter when he arrived.

Peter told him he would return right away and be ready to sit down with Olaf tomorrow morning. Peter found Helen, told her the news, and asked her to phone Jim in Milano to prepare to fly back to Salonika that day. He also arranged with her what time they would be packed, ready to leave.

He told Miriam he had to leave right away. She immediately said she would pack for him and did they have time to be together before he left? He declined that most tempting offer, saying he had to speak to Dov before he left. They hugged and kissed warmly before parting.

When Peter arrived in Salonika, he immediately sought out Olaf, who was in their "office" with Georg and Shlomo.

Georg Gunnarsen was from Sweden and looked the part. He was as tall as Olaf, shoulders like a barn door, slim-waisted, blond hair cropped close to his skull, and brilliant, blue eyes. Despite his appearance, he was Jewish, had served in the Swedish Navy as an engineering officer for ten years, and this was his first mission for Aliyah Bet. He held a master's degree in marine engineering and Olaf's opinion was that he could not have had a better man for the job, especially since Olaf and Georg could understand each other's language (Norwegian/Swedish) and Georg also spoke a good English.

Shlomo Daniel was the chef. He was slim, forty years old, dark, and had been a chef in the French Navy on a frigate for five years. He was from Algeria and he, too, was Jewish. He had successfully smuggled himself into Palestine from Egypt, had joined an underground organization that had passed him on to AB, as he wanted an active job. He spoke French and Arabic fluently. He felt confident that he could handle feeding the crew and passengers of the *Helen*.

Olaf introduced both men to Peter, who shook hands with them and asked them to tell him how they were getting along with the work that Olaf had given them. He knew that people are more ready to talk about their own work rather than unrelated subjects and that this was the best way to know what kind of enthusiasm they would bring to their jobs.

After that, Peter told Olaf that he would sit down with him after breakfast tomorrow, as he was feeling tired and needed sleep.

"You look as though you didn't get much sleep in Camp Pietro," Olaf observed. "They certainly are running you ragged."

Peter went to his room, unpacked, while thinking of Miriam having packed it for him just a few hours ago, and prepared for bed. Just then there was a knock on his door and before he could say "come in," the door was opened and Helen entered. Closing the door behind her, she came over to him and, putting her arms around him, she gave him a warm, close kiss.

Then, standing back a little and examining his face, she said, "My dear Peter, you must have had a hard time in Camp Pietro on this last visit. Did Miriam take so much out of you?"

"What are you talking about, Helen?" Peter said, confused.

"Peter, my dear, you look as though you have not slept properly for a month, although, of course, I know we've only been away in the camp for a week. You look totally exhausted and, as your friend, I want you to have a very good night's sleep tonight and rise tomorrow morning quite recovered from whatever excesses you have been enjoying."

"The midnight activities at camp don't seem to have had any deleterious effect on you, Helen. Your beauty hasn't lessened one iota from when we were together before Camp Pietro," he observed.

"To tell you the truth, Peter, I didn't enjoy any of those activities you may have participated in."

"Really?" he said, "and why was that? Or am I asking something that I shouldn't?"

"Perhaps we can talk about it later. As I said, I want you to go to sleep *now*." Having said that, she went over to him, gave him a full-mouthed kiss and went out.

Peter reflected on her remarks about his appearance, while remembering that Olaf had also remarked that he didn't look as though he had slept much when he was away. Peter glanced in his bathroom mirror. He *did* have dark circles under his eyes and his normally healthy complexion seemed to have been replaced by something like pallor. He didn't like what he saw, but he remembered the extreme pleasure that he had experienced. "It was well worth it," he decided. Feeling good about himself, despite his tiredness, he prepared for bed and within five minutes, was in a deep and restorative sleep.

At breakfast, next morning, Peter found Helen's eyes checking him out, as she said brightly, "Good morning. If I may say so, you look like a new man today and I'm sure that somehow your body rests and sleeps better here than it does in Camp Pietro. Isn't that so? The hours you put in at night took their toll, didn't they, Peter."

Peter was beginning to feel a little ruffled at Helen's relentless leg-pulling but he gave her his most imperturbable look, saying "Maybe you're right, Helen, I shall have to take care of myself a little better the next time I go there."

"Or perhaps I shall have to take care of you there myself, to see you get enough sleep, Peter." She responded, dead-pan.

"Or maybe you should take better care of me here in Salonika to see I sleep enough," he answered.

"What nonsense are you two talking so early in the day?" Olaf interrupted. "Or perhaps," he said mischievously, "you two are talking in a code known only to yourselves, and not for public, or *my* consumption."

"My dear Olaf," Helen said, "as though Peter and I would even think of tricking you. I wonder what must be going on in your mind for you to think we are saying anything but what our words profess. And I think I speak for Peter as well when I say, dear uncle, that trying to fool you would be no easy matter. You are a man who has seen and heard too much of the world to be bamboozled.

"But you're right. It is a bit early in the day for such trivial chatter."

A half-hour later, in the office, Olaf opened up a file labeled "Ship Repairs, Bids, etc." which had previously been prepared by Helen.

"So here they are," he said. "I've called the three bidding companies by the first three letters in the Hebrew alphabet, aleph, bet, and gimel, to avoid repeating their difficult Greek names each time we refer to them."

"Excuse me, Olaf," said Peter. "It seems to me that considering our present location, we should consider alpha, beta, and gamma for the three companies."

"What do you think, Helen?" asked Olaf.

"I agree with Peter," she answered. "I think the Greek letters have a more direct relationship to those companies than the Hebrew letters."

"Very well, then," said Olaf, with a twinkle, "that's it. Our committee has voted on a most important matter.

"Now here's the first company, Alpha. I'll give you the bottom line first: their bid is $150,000 and they say six weeks from start.

Here's company Beta: bid is $125,000, time, eight weeks. Company Gamma's bid is $145,000, time is four weeks."

"How do we relate the different costs to the amount of time each needs to complete their tasks?" Peter asked.

"We need to understand the indirect costs incurred during the different time periods. That means the hotel cost in Alicante and the hotel cost here in Salonika. Helen, can you give us those figures?"

"Sure," she said. "The Alicante weekly cost for the group in the hotel will be about $37,000/week. The Salonika cost for us three, plus two new men, is about $4,400 a week. To summarize:

	Alpha	Beta	Gamma
	6 weeks	8 weeks	4 weeks
Alicante expenses	$222,000	$296,000	$148,000
Salonika expenses	26,400	35,200	17,600
Spending money	17,000	17,000	17,000
Total Indirect	$265,400	$348,200	$182,600
Direct Contract Work	$150,000	$125,000	$145,000
Total	$415,400	$473,200	$327,600

"From this, we see that although Gamma's bid is $20,000 higher than Beta's and although Alpha's bid is only $5,000 more than Gamma's, when we factor in the indirect costs occurring because of the added time it will take Alpha to finish the job, we see that Gamma's bid is most cost-effective. That's assuming the quality and details of the bids are somewhat the same."

"I understand," said Peter. "I think you've saved me a lot of money. On my own, I'm fairly certain I would have gone for the lowest bid, all things being equal."

"That's the problem with bids," Olaf told him, "All things are rarely ever equal."

The three agreed that the Gamma company would get the job and Olaf said he would go ahead and get the Gamma owner in, clear up any small points, and arrange a daily bonus or fine price for early/late completion of the job. He would also call the Alpha and Beta companies to tell them they had lost out.

They agreed also to use John Thessalonikos to do the repair contract, as he had done a good job for them with the ship purchase agreement.

Peter and Helen would do a number of administrative jobs, let Dov know that the group would be leaving soon, and tell Jim that his services would be required to take the group from Italy to Spain, then to fly back to Greece.

"I suggest that eventually we send our plane to Berne to be stored there," Helen said. "They did a good job for us at a reasonable price, and they already look after two other DC3s."

Both men agreed.

A half-hour later, Olaf asked Peter and Helen if they would like to meet with the boss of the Gamma company, Edward Alachouzos, who was on his way over to meet him. Both declined, realizing Olaf was the man for this job.

They met Olaf later, after his meeting. He told them his visit with the director of Gamma had gone well. The company could start in ten days. The director, somewhat reluctantly, agreed to the daily bonus or fine.

"I then called the Alpha and Beta companies," Olaf said, "to tell them they had lost out and they told me they appreciated the fact that I called them."

"What about Georg's work?" inquired Peter.

"He has taken my draft paperwork and went off to the *Naiad* with Joseph, to reconcile my draft work with the actual ship and to complete the specifications, which he and I and Joseph will take to Kavala as soon as it's ready to hand over to the Delta company there. We'll also require a contract to be signed and when the specifications are done, we'll go to John Thessalonikos to make up a simple contract to take with us to Kavala.

The flow-chart for the ship's sail-away date from Kavala was as follows:

Olaf's Flow-Chart

A1	Olaf, Peter, and Helen to John Thessalonikos to brief him to prepare CONTRACT I with Gamma
B1	Georg to spend time on *Naiad* and prepare specification as basis for contract with Delta
B2	Olaf, Georg, and Helen to John Thessalonikos to brief him to prepare CONTRACT II with Delta
A2	Olaf to call Edward Alachouzos of Gamma to come to sign CONTRACT I
A3	Shlomo to intensify work on Fuel/Supply Lists, half for Salonika and other half (for A6) for Kavala
B3	Olaf, Georg, and John Thessalonikos to go to Kavala to see

Niarchos of Delta for him to quote on CONTRACT II and specification

B4   Receive quote from Delta

B5   Olaf, Georg, and John Thessalonikos to Kavala – Delta to sign CONTRACT II, fix "start of manufacture of parts," fix "completion," fix "installation/completion" dates

A4   "Start Date" for CONTRACT I – Georg to supervise

A5   "Completion Date" for CONTRACT I. Helen to move office to *Naiad*

A6   Shlomo to receive in Salonika first half fuel and part supplies on *Naiad*

A7   Olaf to receive three deck-hands, from Kavala contractor: to be housed on *Naiad* in chain locker bunks.

A8   Olaf and Georg move from hotel to *Naiad*

A9   Olaf, Georg, and Shlomo, plus three deckhands to sail *Naiad* to Kavala with Peter and Helen – Delta to receive ship

A10   Delta to start installation of parts and rename ship to "Helen"

A11   Shlomo to receive half fuel and balance supplies in Kavala

A12   Receive group on board

A13   Sail from Kavala

"All quite professional," said Peter. "Okay, Olaf and Helen, are you both ready to meet the lawyer?"

They both said, "Yes."

Peter then called John Thessalonikos, who said he would make himself available and looked forward to his visit.

The Three Musketeers took a taxi to John, where Peter introduced Olaf as the partner who had negotiated the contract with the Gamma company. They wanted John to put it into legal form as soon as possible and to phone their office when it was ready to be picked up. John looked through the paperwork and said he could not see any real problem and thought he could have it ready in three days, but he pointed out that it would have to be in the Greek language. He would go through it in detail with them in a more understandable language, and he would try to keep it simple. They thanked him and left.

Returning to their office in the hotel, they found Georg hard at work. He had gone over the ship using Olaf's drawings. With a few changes in regards to disguising the secret entrances to the exit tubes down which the crew would slide, fixing the steel wall in the hold, and the one-way egress by the doors, he could now proceed to prepare final drawings, which would take about three days, so that Delta could quote a price. Georg was told to go back to his room, with light-hearted instructions from Olaf and Peter, to work and not to take time off for extraneous things like eating or sleeping.

Olaf made a note to remind himself to instruct Shlomo to buy six inflatable beds and to speed up his work on listing supplies.

Peter needed to acquire false Bills of Lading for goods to be delivered to Sidon, Lebanon. Olaf told Peter to talk to Joseph about the bills and that they should acquire ten crated wooden boxes of varying size filled with rocks, simulating the weight of machinery. Olaf would arrange with Jack Niarchos of Delta to pack the boxes and load them, after the false wall was installed in the hold.

When Joseph arrived at the office, he was very surprised to see a bedroom turned into a business office. Peter found him a chair and asked him about Bills of Lading.

"Glad you asked me," Joseph said. "It just so happens that I bought a number of those forms today, which, when expertly and properly filled in, become official Bills of Lading. I can help you to fill them in, in French. If you had told me on the telephone that this is what you wanted, I could have brought them with me."

"I wouldn't talk about them on the telephone," Peter told him. "Please bring them tomorrow morning, about 10:00, so we can work on them."

"Very well, Peter, I'll be here," Joseph said, and left.

"I don't have a good feeling of his ability to be sufficiently discreet regarding our affairs," said Peter.

"I'm sorry to say I agree with you, Peter," Olaf seconded. "However, I recall that when we established relations with him and discussed the confidential nature of our affairs, we put the fear of litigation in him. Since he has a miser's love for money, I'm of a mind to give him the commission due him tomorrow, which is $57,500. That should be quite an incentive for him to keep him mouth shut."

"Right," Peter said. "Now I think we're almost ready to send the group to Spain. So, if you agree, the time is coming for Helen and me to go to Camp Pietro, for the last time, to make sure the group is ready to leave and to verify that the Hotel Palas has room for our people which, with Dov, will be thirty-five. I also have to see how many double rooms we can organize; the more, the better as far as cost is concerned."

"Peter, we still have two unknowns," Olaf reminded him. "We don't know how long it will be before Gamma finishes Contract I or how much longer it will take Delta to finish the Contract II work in Kavala. If we're lucky enough to have the Delta prefabrication work finished in Kavala by the time the Gamma work is completed in Salonika, then it will only require the installation and welding work to be done after the *Naiad* arrives in Kavala, which I guess may take about two weeks, and only after that, we can get our group on board."

"How long do you think the group should stay in Alicante?" asked Peter. "You see, we can't have everyone getting sunburned. The process of getting a nice tan takes time. The last thing we need is the Royal Navy coming on board and seeing either a bunch of pale or sunburned sailors. With the efforts and cost being invested in this enterprise, we have to take great pains that it doesn't come to naught once a Royal Navy or Marine officer sees our people."

"Fair enough," Olaf responded. "In any event, I would expect the two contracts to take not less than six weeks, start to finish, and maybe an unknown amount of additional time."

"That should be just enough time for the group to get a tan," Peter said. "Once we have more accurate information, I'll start the process of bringing the group to Alicante. It seems we'll always have at least six weeks from the moment we acquire the time data.

"In the meantime, Helen, you and I can start to put another flow-chart together, for money payments, transfers, etc. and administrative matters not covered by Olaf's flow-chart. I suggest we start that tomorrow."

Peter met the others for breakfast. Olaf looked at him and said, "You look awful, Peter, just like you did when you got here the last time from Camp Pietro. Are you having trouble in sleeping?"

"Yes, I've been tossing and turning all night, worrying about all those details we have to deal with before we sail away."

"Well, you can count on me and Helen to help you in every way we can," Olaf offered. "And I think you'll find Helen especially helpful with the technical matters that seem to preoccupy you."

About an hour later, Joseph joined them in the office. He announced proudly that he had brought the appropriate forms. He then sat down with the Musketeers and with their input, he was able to turn a bunch of blank forms into Bills of Lading, making reference to the ten crated and boxed "machinery" cargo, which would be simulated in due course by Jack Niarchos of the Delta company as coming from Salonika, Greece, and going to Sidon, Lebanon. The crates were to be numbered SAL/GR SID/LE one through ten. Joseph finally affixed his agency stamp, then another consular stamp he had "borrowed" at the cost of $100.

Peter then asked Helen to make out a dollar check to Joseph for commission on the ship purchase. "Let's see, Joseph, how much is it?" he asked.

Joseph pretended to do the calculation. "Let's see, how much did you pay for the *Naiad*?" he asked.

Peter said, "$1,150,000."

"Very well," said Joseph. "That number times five percent is er, er, er, er $57,500, I believe. Is that right?" he asked Peter.

Peter said, "That's right! Helen, will you please make out that check for $57,600. That will include your disbursement to the Lebanese Consul," he winked at Joseph.

"Oh that," said Joseph, "I wasn't going to charge you for it, as a matter of fact. But how did you know it was the Lebanese Consul?"

Peter answered, "I'm a linguist. I read the wording on the stamp."

"Oh, I see," Joseph said, obviously deflated.

Helen wrote out the check and gave it to Peter, who signed it, and gave it to Joseph.

"Thank you all," said Joseph, and with a flourish, left. "Shall we sit down together now and start on that flow-chart so that I can stop worrying and get a good night's sleep?"

"Yes, of course, Peter," responded Helen, absolutely dead pan, to Peter.

Peter's Chart

A. AIR MOVEMENTS

    A1. Salonika to Athens – Refuel

    A2. Athens to Milano – Meet bus from Camp Pietro and pick up group and Dov

    A3. Milano to Alicante – Leave group there

    A4. Alicante to Rome – Refuel

    A5. Rome to Salonika – Peter and Helen to work

    A6. Salonika to Milano – Refuel with Peter

A7. Milano to Alicante – Pick up group

A8. Alicante to Rome – Refuel

A9. Rome to Salonika – Drop off group

A10. Salonika to Berne – Jim and Co-Pilot (Refuel) to Berne
Aviation

B. BUSES

		Who to Book	*Reimburse*
B1.	Camp Pietro to Milano Airport	Dov	Helen
B2.	Alicante Airport to Hotel Palas	Juan	Pre-Pay Helen
B3.	Hotel Palas to Alicante Airport	Juan	Pre-Pay Helen*
B4.	Salonika Airport to Kavala/*Naiad*	Joseph	Pre-Pay Helen*

C. OTHER BILLS TO PAY

C.1. Joseph

C.1.1 – 5% Supplies in Salonika/in Kavala*
C.1.2 – 5% Fuel in Salonika/Kavala*
C.1.3 – 5% Engineering in Salonika/Kavala*

*Helen to pay.

C.2. Juan: hotel stay, by Peter

C.3 Yanis: to prepare 29 packs of 150 pounds in pesetas

C.4. Berne Bank: Lambert: to pay:

C.4.1 periodical DC3: Mtce/Storage by Berne Aviation
C.4.2 Periodical Storage/Mtce of the *Helen* in Turkey
C.4.3 Jim to end; Co-Pilot Salonika to Berne; Bonus
Jim. Notify Lambert of Pilots' daily rate.
C.4.4 Periodical – Joseph: As Salonika registry repre-
sentative of the *Helen*

D. Confidential (Peter's Notes)

D.1 Reminder: Peter to make Will with John Thessalonikos

D.2 Legacies: $1 M: × 4

   $½ M: × 3

   A total of $5,500,000

D.3 Balance: Trust for all who came in this crew

   (28) = 875 K/ea. Trust total of $24,500,000.

When they finished, they were alone in the office, as Olaf had gone to see how Georg was getting on. Peter and Helen sat back in their chairs, sighed, and then Helen laughed out loud.

"My poor Peter," Helen said sarcastically. "'He looked so awful, just like he looked when he came from Camp Pietro last'; isn't that what my uncle said? 'Hadn't been sleeping well.' Well, of course not, the poor dear. 'Tossing and turning all night.' Why not, his mind is just filled with important thoughts and fantasies. 'Worrying about all those details.' Not sure everyone would call them 'details.' Peter, you are just a fraud, my friend, your indulgences are just doing you in, as they should. And that poor girl in Camp Pietro – you must have worked her –"

Just then, Olaf returned to the office, looking excited. "I've got good news," he said to them. "Georg worked round the clock and will finish in half an hour. Looks like he took you literally, Peter. We can now make an appointment to meet with John Thessalonikos to brief him on Contract II with 'Delta.' Peter, will you call him now?"

"Yes, of course, Olaf." Peter picked up a phone and called him. After he hung up, he told the others that they were to meet him in his office at 10:00 a.m.

John Thessalonikos said he had been just about to call them to tell them he had the Gamma contract finished and that if they were agreeable, he could give it to them now. He also said he could finish the new contract within a few days. After he gave Olaf the contract, his secretary presented a bill to Peter.

"There's no hurry to pay me, Peter," John assured him.

"No, no, John," Peter said, "we'll dispose of it right away." He gave it to Helen, who took a checkbook out of her briefcase, made out a check, gave it to Peter, who glanced at it and signed it, and then gave it to John.

He said, "Thank you very much, Peter. I don't remember the last time I produced a bill and was paid on the spot."

"If you can speed up the Delta contract, we'll see if we can do this again, John."

They returned to the office and Olaf, at once, made a call to Edward Alachouzos of Gamma. He told him that he had their agreement ready. Alachouzos said he would come in at 2:30 p.m. to sign it.

"Just a moment," Helen said, "I haven't seen a bill from the inspections company yet – have either of you?"

"Oops," said Olaf, "this came in yesterday and I forgot to give it to you, Helen."

She quickly looked at it and saw it was in the ballpark of what they expected to pay, then promptly made out a check, which Peter signed.

"One thing which occurs to me," said Helen, "why didn't we have John go through the Gamma contract with us?"

"The contract cover sheet just says what they have to pay and when" Olaf explained. "The inspection reports are the details of what Gamma has to do and those reports are an attachment to the agreement. I looked at the face of the agreement and read the amount in drachmas equivalent to the dollar figure of $145,000, which is what we had agreed to pay."

"I see," said Helen.

After lunch, Olaf received Edward, who read through the contract cover sheet and verified that the drachma figure shown was as he had bid. He was ready to sign. Olaf phoned Peter and asked him to come to the office to sign the Gamma contract as well.

Peter and Helen came in. Olaf introduced them to Edward, and in due course, the contract was signed. Edward's last words before he left were, "I'm getting geared up to start work in seven days."

For a few days, there was no activity at the Aristoteles Hotel, then there was a call from the secretary of John Thessalonikos to say the Delta contract was finished and, as Mr. Thessalonikos understood it was urgently wanted, they could either pick it up or it could be mailed to them. Olaf said someone would come and pick it up that day, and Helen did so.

Olaf then phoned to Jack Niarchos of Delta and made an appointment to go and see him to present a proposal and specifications for a contract for him to quote on. An appointment was arranged for the next morning, for Olaf, Georg, and Joseph to go to Kavala to meet with him. They went in Joseph's car.

On his return, Olaf met with Peter and Helen and informed them that while Niarchos knew he wasn't bidding against any others, nevertheless, he also realized that Olaf was aware that he was very short of work and expected him to come up with a fair bid, quickly. When Olaf spoke about the dummy cargo, he said he would supply it at no charge. All in all, Olaf believed he had been dealing with an honest man who would come up with a fair bid, and quickly. Peter suggested they should bring Shlomo to their office to find out his progress.

Shlomo duly showed up and presented lists of foods and fluids for thirty-four people for up to a five-week period – two weeks while in Kavala and three weeks of estimated time to sail to Palestine by a secret route, yet to be divulged by Olaf.

Olaf was quite familiar with the vast quantities of food that ships had to buy at the onset of a voyage, and this one was minuscule in comparison with what he had seen in his sea-going life, but for Peter and Helen, it was an eye-opener.

Shlomo pointed out that thirty-four people times three meals a day times thirty-five days meant almost exactly 3,600 meals to be provided for. Besides the six bottles of alcoholic drinks, the soft drinks, including water and milk, constituted a considerable quantity needing storage space. He had already gone aboard the *Helen* twice to check on refrigerator and dry goods storage capacity. He had also found where he could take care of fuel needs, both in Salonika and Kavala. He would also give them a list of payment terms for each vendor.

Two days later, Olaf received a call from Jack Niarchos of Delta that he had a price for him and he was ready to discuss dates for "start of manufacture of parts," "completion of manufacture date," and "date for installation completion," and when could Olaf go to Kavala?

"Tomorrow, at, say, 10:00 a.m.," Olaf responded.

Olaf called Joseph and told Georg, and next morning, Joseph appeared with his car and picked up Olaf and Georg for the meeting.

While there, Jack signed two copies of the agreement, which Olaf brought back with him for Peter to also sign. The contract called for "start of manufacture" in one week, "completion of manufacture" in four weeks, and "completion of installation in four weeks after arrival of ship in Kavala."

The next morning, the Three Musketeers met in their office to consider the overall situation and prepare a short "time chart." They also outlined the activities for those actively involved in moving the process along.

CHAPTER XVII

Salonika to Kavala, Peter's Will

1. Dov to stay with group from Camp Pietro – Alicante – Kavala [Olaf to appoint Dov to a crew job when on board].

2. Peter to go with DC3 to Milano and with group to Alicante to help move them in, and to distribute peseta packets (34) to group on plane, return with plane to Salonika, stay there pending the flight to pick up the group from Alicante, fly them to Salonika, and move them to Kavala by bus.

3. Helen to move office from hotel to ship at any convenient time in the radio room adjacent to the chart room, after equipment installed there and captain's cabin finished.

4. Georg and Shlomo to move onto ship when their cabin is finished, to continue to supervise work, to record the arrival of supplies and to assist in sailing to Kavala.

5. Olaf to move on board at his discretion.

6. Jim to receive co-pilot in Salonika then both to fly *Richard's Renown* to Berne, park with Berne Aviation, thus ending their employment.

Note: During the 2-week period of the *Helen* in Kavala with all group and staff aboard, Peter and Helen can finalize all bill payments and instructions to:

Etoile Lambert – Berne, Re Berne Aviation, Joseph, Jim, Turkey.

Berne Aviation – Re: DC3.

Hotel Palas – Alicante.

Hotel Aristoteles – Salonika.

John Thessalonikos – Send Will to Jean-Pierre Muraille, Peter's lawyer in Berne.

When the time chart and personnel jobs were completed, Olaf told the other two that it was time for him to share the big secret of the course to be set when the *Helen* leaves Kavala.

"As you both know, all our efforts until now have been designed to not leave a trail of what we were doing and where we were going, should anybody get curious. The goal is to be able to leave suddenly and quietly using a route I've outlined after examining the maps of the eastern shore of the Mediterranean Sea. What I propose is that we sail down, north to south, the Turkish coast. It is very serrated, rather like the western coast of Norway, and the fjords with which I'm very familiar. So, it is my plan to sail south, in and out of the Turkish fjords, to sail by night and hide by day, to be minimally visible to Royal Navy eyes.

"Then, having gone all the way down the Turkish coast, we sail east along the southern coast of Turkey, then south a few miles off the coast of Syria, continuing south off the coast of Lebanon, where we have to move carefully even during the day. At that point we should get a signal from our friends in Palestine, who will tell us where and when to go to discharge our passengers.

"We'll most likely have to stop the ship a couple of hundred yards off the shore to meet the small boats that will carry off the group, including you two, to the shore. Once on dry land, you will be scattered throughout the country among the villages and kibbutzim.

"I will then sail the ship, with a crew consisting of Georg, Dov, and Shlomo, back to Turkey, and then arrange to have a local shipping company look after it, billing monthly to your lawyer in Berne. When that is all properly fixed up, the four of us will leave Turkey and go about our lives."

During the previous four weeks, Peter had arranged a flight to spend a "long week-end" in Camp Pietro lasting four nights, in which Miriam had demonstrated her love for him, and in which neither had enjoyed much sleep except for a couple of hours just before dawn. On the return flight, Helen confided to him that she had allowed Alex to go further than she had intended.

On Monday of week six, in which Gamma was due to complete, Olaf called to Edward Alachouzos to find out how they were getting on. Edward replied, "Very well, Olaf, and I expect to finish by Friday, the latest."

Olaf then called Jack Niarchos of Delta in Kavala to find how *they* were doing. He was told that the last pieces of the eighteen-inch trunking were to be welded together that day and that all the metal sections and metal doors were finished.

Olaf reported this to Peter and Helen, saying, "It's now time for the group to go to Spain, as I expect the Salonika work to be finished this week and manufacture of the Kavala parts and trunking, too."

Peter called Juan Herrera at the Hotel Palas in Alicante and verified that the accommodation would be available on Wednesday. He then called Dov in Camp Pietro and told him they would pick up the group on Wednesday at Milano Airport, and that Dov should arrange the bus to pick up the group on Wednesday morning to take them to Milano, as planned.

Helen spoke to Jim in London and told him to come to Salonika the next day, Tuesday. They would be flying on Wednesday to Milano to pick up passengers, then to Alicante to drop them off the same day, then on Thursday, they would fly back to Salonika. After that, Jim would be free to go home for about six weeks. Then he would come back to Salonika, they would fly to Alicante, then back to Salonika. On the final leg of the journey, he would fly with a hired co-pilot to Berne, where he would be paid off and sent on his way.

On Wednesday, Helen and Jim, with Peter in his accustomed place in the first passenger row, flew *Richard's Renown* to Milano Airport. A bus rolled up to the DC3, Peter went aboard and welcomed the group. He led them onto the DC3. Everyone was excited. Except for Dov, none of them had ever been on an airplane before.

Peter pointed to the name on the plane and explained that it was his father's name. After they were all aboard, Peter went around to hand out the packets of pesetas, each of which was equal to 150 pounds. On each envelope, he had attached a printed slip that said, "Buy sun cream, swim suit, and sunglasses, and tan very slowly" in four languages. After they took off, Peter also drove home the fact that they had to be careful not to burn in the sun and to use plenty of sunscreen.

They were flying non-stop to Alicante, but Peter couldn't resist pointing out some of the landmarks as they flew westward over the northern Mediterranean, roughly parallel to the coasts of Italy and France, then to Spain and the Balearic Islands, where he got Helen to fly a figure eight around the three islands so the group could see everything from both sides of the plane.

At last, they landed at Alicante airport, and found the bus waiting to pick them up. It took them to the Hotel Palas, where they found Juan Herrera waiting expectantly in the lobby. The group was led to a lounge, where hotel personnel served them with cold drinks and sandwiches, while they arranged for the rooms.

Dov was placed in charge because Peter and Helen had to leave the next day for Salonika. Then everyone was given their keys and went to their rooms.

Peter had arranged additional rooms for himself, Helen, and Jim. He had also managed to tell Miriam *his* room number, before she went off to share a room with Heide.

After things quieted down, Peter took Dov outside, walked him along the beach and showed him where the trail started leading up to the castle. He also showed him the section of the beach where he had been told it was safe to swim, as well as one area where there was an undertow, and therefore not safe.

They returned to the hotel, where Peter met Miriam sitting in the lounge, looking very sad.

"Why are you looking so unhappy, my dear?" he asked.

"Well, Peter," she said, "you whispered your room number to me, I put my stuff in my room, then went to yours; I knocked, no answer; I came down to the reception and asked and they told me you had gone out with Dov. I didn't know *where* you'd gone and didn't know *how long* you would be away and *that's* why I looked unhappy. But now," she said brightly, "I feel happy again because I'm *with* you. I just want to say I love you very, very much and I've missed you *so* much since we were last together. And I want to say one more thing – I know I have absolutely *no* right to complain to you, in this way. After all, we aren't married, or even engaged, and I feel I've over-stepped my bounds. Please forgive me."

"Please, Miriam, think nothing of it," Peter said. "If you remember my room number, let's meet there now. I'll go up first."

A short while later, they were locked in each other's arms. Then suddenly, a thought struck him.

"What on earth is it, my love?" she asked him.

He answered, "I forgot to tell Juan that evening meals for everybody should be put on the bill and I forgot to tell everybody that their evening meals as well as breakfast and lunch are covered. I don't want them spending money on food. I've to speak to Juan immediately." He picked up the phone on the bedside table and spoke to Juan, asking him for his best price for meals for the group. After some haggling, they agreed on a fair price.

"Just one thing more, Juan. Please send a notice to every room of my group telling them that I'm covering each meal as long as they are staying in the hotel. Send the notice in Spanish, English, and any other language you can manage. And please do it at once, before dinner time today."

That done, he turned his attention back to Miriam.

"Now Miriam, what about you? Do you feel like something to eat? I could have some food brought up to my room."

"Maybe later, Peter dear."

"I'm going back to Salonika tomorrow, my dear, because I've a lot going on at my headquarters at the moment and it will remain so until I move on to the ship, and *that* won't take place until at least half the engineering work is completed. I know very well how much we'll miss each other, but this bond we feel for each other makes us a very fortunate couple, one that has found their 'opposite number' in life.

"Someone once told me of a most beautiful word, which epitomizes this experience. It's a word which I've never forgotten. Bashairt. I wonder if you've ever heard of it?"

"Yes," Miriam replied, "and you described it exactly as I know it. It's a word that every Jewish mother uses or thinks of when visualizing a perfect mate for her child. I truly believe *you* are *my* bashairt and I want to spend my life taking care of you, looking after you, and sharing all the adventures on the long road of life down which we are now traveling, together."

Peter's eyes welled up.

"That is the most beautiful thing anyone has ever said to me, Miriam."

Just then his bedside telephone rang. It was Dov, passing on a question from one of the boys.

"If I had already gone off to Salonika, how would you deal with that question?" Peter asked him.

"But you're still here," Dov answered.

"I told everybody that you were in charge here in Alicante, and you are," Peter explained. "If there's something you absolutely don't know or can't handle, then come to me. But even while I'm here, you need to pretend that everything is your responsibility and yours alone. It was your background as an army officer that gave me the confidence to appoint you the leader here. Rest assured that I will back you, unless the handling was quite perverse, which I wouldn't expect from you."

"Okay, Peter, thank you very much. I understand perfectly."

"Heavens!" exclaimed Miriam, who had heard Peter's side of the conversation. "You certainly let him have it. He obviously doesn't yet understand how much you trust him to let him exercise the authority we all put in you."

"I know. Perhaps I was a bit tough, but he has to learn," Peter said. "I think we should get downstairs now."

They went down and saw Helen and Alex, who were just sitting there and chatting. Peter said to them, "Miriam and I were just going out for a little walk. Would you two like to join us?"

Helen and Alex looked at each other, then Helen said, "Yes, thank you Peter, we'd like that."

Peter led the foursome outside and they walked north along the beach. After about 200 yards, Peter stopped and pointed out the start of the trail, which led up to the castle that they could see from the beach.

They returned to the hotel, everyone going their own way.

Miriam went to her room and found Heide there. She told Heide that she would be elsewhere that night so that Heide had the room for herself. Heide was very happy to hear that. She also told Miriam how much she liked the food at the hotel. "Only I'm afraid I'll put on so much weight over the next week."

"But that's exactly why we're here, Heide," Miriam exclaimed, "to put on weight after the camp, the hospital, and Camp Pietro. Here we are to get good civilian food to beef us up, to lie on the beach and catch some sun, and for you to learn to swim. Only then can you look big and brown like a real sailor."

"But maybe I don't want to get fat, Miriam."

"There's a difference between the recovering state that we're in now and filling out in the way men like, and just being *fat*," Miriam assured her. "You don't have to get *fat* to look like a sailor, but let's look in the mirror right now, and you'll see."

They stood side by side in front of a mirror and took off their clothes above the waist.

"Look at yourself, Heide," said Miriam, "you're white and skinny. Take if from me, men want more meat on their women's bones. Your ribs can be counted. Has Max ever seen you in the light without clothes?"

"No."

"Well, Heide, I strongly suggest you put on some weight before you let him see you like this, my almost-sister, or he will surely run away," she said, smiling.

"No he won't," Heide insisted. "He likes me as I am."

"Well, that means he's either a very spiritual person or he hasn't seen you any way but fully dressed. In either case, he's the exception to the rule for men. And just in case things don't work out between you, believe me, adding a few pounds to your body will go a long way to fleshing out your potentially terrific body."

"When we came out of Ravensbrueck Camp, you were as skinny as me. How did you do it?" Heide asked, pouting.

"I ate whenever I could, Heide, but I was careful about it. My bashairt, as I like to call him, still thinks I should put on a few pounds, and I don't have to tell you that he's seen what you're seeing now in the mirror. So, while I'm here, I'm going to make the effort to eat a little more than I really need and put on a little more weight. And you should do the same, my dear sister, as well as getting some sun, but very carefully and very slowly. And tomorrow you and I are going shopping and we are going to buy swimsuits, which we can let out as we gain weight, and sun-cream and sunglasses, all as we heard from Peter.

"Now Heide, I'm going to take a quick bath, put on a little make-up, and then I'm getting out of here. I will phone you to let you know I'm coming back so that you can send Max back home, and he's not embarrassed to run into me."

Next morning, by arrangement, Jim left early to go to the airport to prepare the DC3 for the flight back to Salonika. Helen and Peter had arranged an early breakfast, at which Alex and Miriam joined them, as a little farewell meal. There were unshed tears in Miriam's eyes as she kissed Peter goodbye in a corner of the breakfast room. She whispered into his ear, "You're my bashairt and don't forget it."

They refueled in Rome and then flew on to Salonika. Helen had asked Jim if he was available to come out again in three weeks if called, and he said yes, but he would need a couple of days' warning. Helen promised to notify him well in advance and apologized for previously calling him to duty on very short notice.

On arrival in Salonika, they went directly to the office, where they found Olaf on the phone. He greeted them and gave them the latest reports.

"The Gamma company has completed its work. Three deck-hands are en route to Salonika. The bunks are installed and waiting for the deck-hands. Shlomo has fueled the ship and taken all the Salonika stores on board. Georg and Shlomo are moving onto the ship, so from now on, we'll always have someone on board.

"Helen, if you want to move the office on board now, that can be arranged. The radios are in and the charts have arrived for the chart room.

"All the work prepared in Kavala for manufacture has been completed, and they are waiting for the ship to arrive so they can do the installation and change the name of the ship to the *Helen*.

"One last thing. Since the ship will be in Kavala for about seven weeks from the time it arrives, per the schedule, I think we should rent a room in a local hotel with a telephone installation, in Kavala."

"Okay," Peter immediately agreed.

"Done. My friend Jack Niarchos of Delta will arrange it for me. He can also help us with any other 'housekeeping' things we need."

"When are you going to leave Salonika and sail to Kavala, Olaf?" asked Peter.

"I thought by the end of the week, say, Friday, which will give us time to finish things here." said Olaf.

"Right," said Peter, "then Helen and I will go on board on Thursday with the office files etc., if that's okay with you, Helen."

"That's fine," she said, "and we'll sail to Kavala, continue to do the office work there, and come back to Salonika by land. Then fly to Alicante in two weeks, and finally, bring the group from Alicante."

"One thing, Olaf," said Peter. "Did Georg properly supervise the Gamma company's work on board and finally sign off on all their work?"

"Yes, he did, and he also did a most professional engineering set of drawings for the Delta company work, especially the circular trunking for the emergency personnel escapes to the hold and the disguised trunking trap doors in the cabin closets.

"If the Delta company does as good a job in making and installing the equipment, we'll be fine. By the way, I checked that Shlomo bought and received on board the inflatable mattresses to give our group a soft landing in the hold.

"As you know, Georg will also be doing the same supervision of the Delta installation work in Kavala. We've got a first-class marine engineer and we're making good use of him. I'll be joining the ship on Thursday. Helen: as the navigation officer, I'd like you to review the charts with me on Thursday, to help set a course for Kavala."

"Of course," Helen agreed.

Peter replied, "Good. My next move is to visit John Thessalonikos tomorrow and make my will. The next stage of our adventure may become a bit dangerous and I want all contingencies taken care of."

The next day, in John's office, Peter gave instructions for his will.

His legacies were as follows: One million dollars each to Helen, Miriam, and Heide and to the Aliyah Bet organization. A half-million dollars each to Georg, Dov, and Shlomo. The balance to be placed in a trust for those on board who came from the hospital in Switzerland, which would come to about $875,000 per person.

The will was quickly done and Peter signed it the next day. The following day, Thursday, both Peter and Helen packed up their personal possessions from the Aristoteles Hotel and the office boxes and files and took them to the *Naiad* after paying the bill at the hotel.

Peter and Helen moved into their individual cabins, side by side, just aft of the bridge, numbers 15 and 16, respectively, and took the office materials to the radio cabin.

"This is so convenient for you and me," said Helen to Peter. "You can slip into mine and I can slip into yours so easily."

"Yes," said Peter, "until the group comes aboard from Alicante. I don't think Miriam and Alex would be too pleased."

"Right," said Helen.

"However," he said, "we'll have to be very careful of Olaf. He's the captain and captains are trained to be aware of what's going on aboard their ship."

"That's all very well," said Helen, "but we're adults, after all, and what we do with our time is our business and not his."

"Yes, that's true and I've thought of something else, too. I'm the owner of this ship and I also have rights, correct?"

"Of course, my dear. So don't forget, you never need to be embarrassed by Olaf."

"Yes, I know," he said, "but we still need to be discreet about our movements, since he is *also* your uncle and we don't want him having a questionable opinion about his favorite niece."

"Good point," she said.

That afternoon, Helen had a session in the chart room, next door to the radio/office room, with Olaf, and they plotted the course to Kavala. It was a new experience for her, but her familiarity with maps stood her in good stead. The only new subject for her was determining the depth of water under the keel. The actual course was quite straightforward until the entry into the channel where Delta company was located. They also planned the route they would take when leaving Kavala by night to start their major voyage.

The three deck-hands stayed in the chain locker bunks, and Georg and Shlomo were in Cabin 12.

Peter gave Helen a copy of the numbered cabin layout. She examined it and saw at once that Alex was to be in Cabin 13, which was very close to her Cabin 16, and that Miriam was to be in Cabin 11, which was close to Peter.

"How interesting," she said, "those cabins are virtually exactly as I would have laid them out. I wonder who made this layout?"

"I wonder, indeed," he said straight-faced.

That night Shlomo made a great meal for Olaf, Peter, Helen, Georg, and himself, which they had in the dining room below the bridge. Everything seemed to be redolent of some form of alcohol, including an apple pie that he had prepared for dessert. He had also made a meal for the deck-hands, which they thoroughly appreciated. Everybody went off to bed in a good mood.

Later, Peter visited Helen in her cabin and the two found that they could have a civilized chat as friends, marking their changed relationship.

After breakfast and promptly at 9:00 a.m. on the Friday morning, there was the ringing of a bell from the bridge and everybody moved to their pre-arranged places.

The propeller was engaged, the mooring ropes were released from the bollards, and the *Naiad* slowly moved away from the quayside to which it had been attached for a long time, heading southwest through the Thermions Bay and out to sea.

As night approached, Olaf took the *Naiad* into a quiet stretch of water between the first and second promontories and lay off the land to the west, near the town of Palini. He dropped anchor, on a good, rocky bottom at 15 fathoms (90 feet) and they spent their first night there, rocking gently in the swell.

The next day, Helen told Peter she had feared being seasick at night, but she was pleased to learn that the the gentle motion helped her to fall asleep, very much "rocked in the cradle of the deep."

Olaf weighed anchor and they resumed the voyage. He told Peter and Helen that Georg had reported to him that the engines and transmission system were working perfectly.

By 3:00 p.m. that day, Olaf radioed to the Delta company that the *Naiad* would arrive that evening by 8:00 p.m. and requested instructions for arrival. Jack Niarchos, whose company would be completing the engineering in the ship, spoke with him and gave him details of where to berth the ship, and then watched with critical approval the masterly way in which Olaf brought his ship alongside the quay.

During the next two weeks, Georg supervised the installation of the parts made in Kavala and Peter and Helen dealt with bills and arranged for payments due after the *Naiad* would disappear from Greece forever. They were receiving bills in Kavala sent on by the postal authorities via the notified address change from the office in the Aristoteles Hotel to "care of" Jack Niarchos's office in Kavala. The latter had willingly agreed to forward any mail received later to Etoile Lambert, Peter's banker in Berne. Lambert had instructions to open all mail, pay all bills, destroy all junk mail and if anything was controversial, to discuss it with Jean-Pierre, Peter's lawyer, who would take it from there.

Helen had called to Jim McDonald to go to Salonika. She and Peter took the bus from Kavala to Salonika, where they flew *Richard's Renown* to Alicante to check on their protégés.

This time Jim had come with a fellow pilot he knew from the RAF, as he wanted Helen and Peter to meet him and check him out. This man, Derek Davey, had paid his own way to Salonika in order to meet Jim's employers. Helen duly checked out his credentials and allowed him to fly with her for part of the trip to Alicante. Peter also talked with him. Later, in Alicante, Peter and Helen decided he was eminently satisfactory. Although he had not come to Salonika at their invitation, Peter decided to pay his return airfare and to arrange for him to share Jim's room at the Palas Hotel in Alicante. Derek was also a decorated RAF ex-pilot with a few months to go before taking up a job with Qantas Airways in Australia. Helen had seen his letter of appointment. They thanked Jim for taking the initiative to bring him out to Salonika to meet them.

That evening, when Peter and Helen arrived at the Palas Hotel in Alicante, they were struck by the immense change in the appearance and personalities of the entire group after only three weeks. The whole Spain operation was obviously highly successful. The group was uniformly tanned, they were filling out physically, especially Miriam and Heide, and they all seemed happy and much more relaxed, open, and chatty. Dov reported that everyone could now swim. There was, however, a permanent poker game running every night among a number of the boys, but the stakes were minuscule. Dov thought it was therapeutic, as there was not much of a night life in town.

"The manager has been wonderful, catering to our every whim," he concluded.

"Good," said Peter. "I'll talk to Juan and thank him for all he's done. I'll speak to the group after dinner."

Peter found Juan in the lobby and conveyed his appreciation for all his help. Very hesitantly, Juan asked Peter if he would mind explaining how it was that so many people from so many countries were vacationing here. He was curious as to where they were going after their vacation.

"These young people have suffered great deprivations during the war and I brought them to Spain to rest and enjoy some peace and quiet before they start their journeys back to their homes, what are left of them. I don't know if you're aware," he explained, "that this group represents the tiniest fraction of the literally millions who have suffered at the hands of the Nazis."

"I understand," Juan said. "And I want to thank you for giving me and my hotel the opportunity to host these survivors. They are the first we've encountered and deploy themselves in an exceptional manner. I understand that you are doing this out of your own pocket. I applaud you and hope you receive the satisfaction you deserve for your magnanimous work."

Peter was more than a little embarrassed to have received a compliment for that which he felt was only his duty to perform.

"Thank you," he said, and left.

Miriam accompanied Peter when he went to check out the room he had been given by the front desk. As soon as they entered the room and closed the door behind them, Miriam threw her arms behind his head and pulled him over to the bed, where they both fell with their arms around one another and with their lips locked in a long, long kiss.

When they separated at last, Miriam whispered into Peter's ear "Oh my love, how I've missed you. Each time you have to go away from me it gets harder and harder to bear, and only when you come back to me can I start to live again. Tell me how long it has to be before we can stay together in the same place."

"Soon," he whispered, "very soon."

*

After dinner Peter spoke to the whole group. He told them of the change of name of the ship from *Naiad* to the *Helen*, hastening to explain that although their own Helen was a wonderful partner in this adventure, the ship was actually named after the beautiful Helen of Troy.

He also reviewed the schedule, while noting that while some in the group usually needed time for the translators to put his German into the native languages of some of the group, many of these young people, especially those who spoke Russian and Polish, were already catching on to the German language and the process of translation was taking less and less time.

He finished by telling them he would be staying at the hotel for at least two days more and was available if anyone wanted to ask any more questions.

When he was finally able to get to his room, he found that Miriam had again taken over. She had unpacked his things and was impatiently awaiting Peter's arrival at his room.

The next two days Peter spent quietly on the beach with Miriam, soaking up some sun, but taking proper precautions against getting burnt.

On the third day, Jim, Helen, Derek, and Peter left Alicante for Salonika. Jim and Derek were released to go home, while Peter and Helen took the bus to Kavala and made their way to the *Helen*.

Once aboard, they put their luggage in their cabins and went up to the bridge to confer with Olaf, who reported to them about the progress by Delta on the installation work.

He said it was going well and very much according to the time schedule that Delta had set themselves. They had planned to finish the job in four weeks and it looked as though they had now completed just about a half of the work. Olaf invited them to go down into the hold to see the false wall taking shape, and another two gangs installing the trunking and entry access points.

"I would like Georg to show you 'round the work," Olaf had said after they arrived, "since it is all based on his detailed engineering drawings, he knows more about the whole job than I do."

Georg introduced them to the foreman in charge who explained that it was a unique piece of work and constituted a technical challenge, but all the parts and sections had been made and were ready to be put together. For Helen and Peter, it was an eye-opener to see the ingenuity of design used to hide the access places to the chutes into the hold.

During the afternoon, a messenger from Jack Niarchos brought a note for Olaf, inviting him and his associates to dinner at his home that night at 8:00 p.m. where Edwina, his wife, would be presenting a Turkish/Cypriot banquet.

That night, at Niarchos's home, the Musketeers were guests at a wonderful dinner prepared entirely by Jack's wife, Edwina, in the Turkish style, but with overtones, as she described it, of Byzantine herbs and spices. She told them that although Cyprus had been, from antiquity, occupied and captured by many armies and had even once been sold to the dispossessed King of Jerusalem by the British, the Byzantines had occupied it for 700 years and had left their culinary imprint on Cypriot traditional cooking.

When the sumptuous repast was finished, Niarchos said to Olaf, "I've a question for you, my friend. I examined carefully those excellent engineering drawings which you presented to me. I prepared all the sections and parts which were called for and I arranged for those mysterious crated boxes, yet I cannot fathom what all this work is for. I know what it is not: it is not to prepare an ordinary trading ship for the high seas, and these additions, as far as I can tell, don't improve its seaworthiness, nor increase its capacity to carry trade goods. So will you do me a favor and tell me what all this activity is about?" He finished his long question by looking straight into Olaf's eyes, sitting motionless in his chair, while waiting for an answer.

Olaf thought rapidly. As the ship's captain, he surely must know what the work was for. Niarchos was an intelligent businessman, an engineer, experienced in his profession, who could not be fobbed off with any story that didn't make sense to him.

Olaf glanced at Peter and Helen, who met his look with sympathetic consternation. They couldn't help him. They didn't have the expertise to convince this engineering expert that what he saw in front of him was just add-ons for some non-sinister purpose.

After an uncomfortably long period of silence, Olaf spoke. "Jack, the best I can do is give you a partial answer. While I'm the captain of the ship and Peter is the owner, we are responsible to others, and it is for them we are preparing this ship. We can't tell you who we're working for since we've been sworn to secrecy. What I will only say is that those for whom we are currently working have a vested interest in seeing that what happened during this war must never, never, happen again.

"I'm sorry. Over the recent period of time you and I have become somewhat closer than just customer and contractor, more like friends, and I should have liked to have been capable of being more forthright and straight-forward with you about this. I hope you understand."

"Of course I do," replied Niarchos, "and since this is clearly a confidential matter and one that affects a wider audience than I imagined, I regret deeply that I've put you and your associates in an embarrassing position. I trust you will all overlook this breach of good manners and put it behind us in our remaining time together before you sail."

"Think nothing of it," Olaf assured him. "There was no way for you to know our situation."

Soon after, the Three Musketeers left to go back to the ship where Peter and Helen congratulated Olaf for "lies brilliantly told," before they parted to go to their cabins.

CHAPTER XVIII

The Group Boards The Helen at Last

AFTER TWELVE DAYS OF INTENSE WORK BY DELTA COMPANY, Jack Niarchos came on board to say that they would be finished within twenty-four hours.

"I would like to present my bill soon after we're finished, if that's okay with you. I know you're anxious to leave Kavala as soon as possible."

"Absolutely," Olaf said. "But rest assured we'll be in our present location for another two weeks, while the passengers come aboard."

"Ah," said Niarchos, "so you're taking on passengers, are you?"

"Yes," said Olaf, "is that something unusual for a ship with the bunk and cabin capacity that you've seen?"

"No, no, of course not," said Niarchos, stammering a little at having been, once more, too inappropriately curious.

When Olaf told Peter and Helen of the conversation, the Three Musketeers had a discussion and decided that Peter and Helen would fly back to Alicante and bring the group to Alicante on Monday. If someone as seemingly friendly and trustworthy as Jack could be so curious, others might be curious as well. Best to be safe than sorry and bring everyone on board and depart as soon as possible.

Peter called his lawyer and banker in Switzerland, informing them he was leaving Greece and would contact them in due course. He also called his banker in Salonika, Yanis, to close his accounts and remit any balances to his bank in Berne.

Now that things were moving at a faster pace, Helen couldn't help but think about her feelings for Peter. She realized she loved him, but also knew that Miriam had befriended him first. And anyway, she was like a sister to her. How could she ever contemplate trying to take Peter away from her?

The next day, Peter spoke to Juan at the Hotel in Alicante, asking him to give Dov a message, namely, to get the group ready to depart on Monday and that Peter would arrive on Saturday to help get everyone prepared.

Peter and Helen both called their mothers to tell them they were about to leave Greece on the next installment of their travels and would contact them in due course from their next port of call.

Shlomo called the dentist in Zurich to report. Georg called to his "nearest and dearest" as he said, which turned out, on inquiry, to be *his* mother too, and so all the staff had left word that they were moving along.

At noon, Friday, Jack Niarchos met Olaf at his cabin, where they each had a glass of whiskey in celebration of the successful completion of the work. Then Niarchos reached into his pocket and presented a final bill.

Olaf scanned the bill and then solemnly said, "I'm very sorry, but I can't pay this."

Niarchos was quite taken aback, protesting, "But you assured me there would be no problem about paying it promptly, Olaf. What does this mean?"

"It means, that while I won't pay you, Helen, who handles all our finances will!" Olaf said, barely able to contain his laughter. "I'm sorry, my friend, I just couldn't resist. You should have seen your face."

"You should have heard my heart," Jack countered, smiling. "I've always prided myself on being a good judge of character, but what you said made all my self-confidence disappear, in an instant."

"Well, don't despair. If we are anything, we are honorable people. I'll just bring this bill to Helen, and be back in a moment."

Olaf left and returned shortly. After a few minutes, Helen knocked and came in. She paid Niarchos, and both Helen and Olaf invited Jack to stay for lunch on board, which he gladly accepted.

Soon after lunch, a message was brought to the ship from Niarchos's office for Helen. It was from Jim, who called to say that the DC3 was fueled and ready and that he would be at the plane by 8:00 a.m. tomorrow.

That evening, as Helen and Peter were chatting, she tried to explain a little of her misgivings about the way her life was turning out.

"My life now is so different from that of the community I used to belong to. I've moved so far away from the way I was brought up, and not because I hated my religious life or ever really thought of leaving it, but because I've been exposed to a world, a new world that holds great promise for me."

"How so?" Peter asked.

"I'm not sure I can make you understand the imbalance I feel inside me. At one moment I feel foresworn to my religious upbringing, and the next moment, to my love for Alex. I've come to love him, emotionally, physically, intellectually, but at the same time I can't help asking myself, have I become a promiscuous woman? Have I lost my sense of self, my Jewish sense of self?"

"My dear Helen, while it's true we come from different worlds, I want to tell you how I view your situation. You were a young woman, ladylike in every respect, proper in every way, but at the same time, naturally curious about life, and love.

"When you met Alex, it wasn't to sleep with him, but to be with him. What happened between you was a natural outgrowth of your feelings for each other. Those feelings, in my estimation, transcend the demands of religion, but they don't negate them. You're still a good Jewess and you're certainly not promiscuous in any sense of the word. Your love is pure and, in my eyes anyway, beautiful."

"Thank you Peter," Helen said, with tears in her eyes. "You are indeed a good friend. I have to think about what you said, but one thing is clear to me from your words, even if Alex and I have a lot of hurdles to overcome, if we do love each other, as I feel we do, the obstacles in our path will disappear."

They said good night and parted.

Helen and Peter left Kavala for Alicante and the Hotel Palas the next morning. They met Juan Herrera at the front desk and he confirmed having given Peter's message to Dov. Then they went outside, to the beach, where they saw the whole group enjoying themselves.

When the group saw them, they ran over, yelling, "Peter and Helen are back!" Dov came over to say that they were in the in the middle of a mini swimming gala and everybody would be pleased if Peter would start off the next race with a "one, two, three" in Hebrew.

"I much prefer you hear how Hebrew should be spoken from Helen," Peter said.

"Okay. Let's go," she said at once, pulling off her sandals and running toward the starting point of the next race. Then she called out, *"Achat! Shteim! Shalosh!"* and the 100-meter swimming race was on.

When the races were over, almost everyone went back into the hotel to have showers and get dressed before dinner. A few lingered on the beach with Helen and Peter, in order to catch up on what was happening. Eventually, they all went inside.

Peter had been in his room hardly five minutes when he heard a polite tap on his door. When he opened it, Miriam was there. She came in, wearing just her swimsuit, then flung her arms around his neck and they collapsed together on the bed, each kissing the other without a word being said.

Peter gazed lovingly at her new full and bronzed appearance. "Miriam, I'm almost at a loss for words. I've never seen anything so beautiful in my life. Alicante has been very good for you."

"Well, I've been working *very* hard to look the *very* best I can, just for you, and I'm so glad you appreciate it," she bent over and kissed him. "But now I must leave you. I've got to shower and dress, so you can see me looking my best at dinner."

She quietly left the room. Peter lay back on his bed with his eyes closed, just remembering the appearance of this bronzed, gorgeous, beautiful woman who, a moment ago, had been in his arms. "It certainly was well worth the trip from Kavala to Alicante today," he thought to himself.

Another visitor, Dov, knocked on the door and was duly admitted. Peter saw immediately that he was nervous and quite tense. He waited for him to speak.

"Well, Peter, I have something of importance to report to you" Dov began, clearly relieved to be getting something off his chest. "Three days ago, Max came to me to say that he had observed a man lounging about outside the hotel watching our group on the beach. Then, he saw the man go into the hotel, so Max followed him to find this man talking to Mr. Herrera in a rather animated fashion.

"After two or three minutes, the man left the hotel and walked away. Max followed him discretely up the street and past the City Hall, where he climbed into a parked car and drove away. Max saw that nobody else was in the car.

Max returned to the hotel, found Mr. Herrera, and asked him who the man was, to which Mr. Herrera replied that he had asked about our group, inquiring if they were locals or people from outside the area.

"Mr. Herrera had the presence of mind to ask the gentleman why the group was of such interest to him. The man said he worked for a film production company and was looking for some good-looking young people to act as extras in the beach scenes they were shooting. When Mr. Herrera pressed him regarding the name of his film company and where they were from, the man suddenly broke off the conversation and left. Mr. Herrera said the man spoke a good Spanish, possibly with a Madrid accent. He also said he didn't like the look of the man and wasn't about to reveal any information to him."

Peter was startled to hear Dov's report and assumed it must have been someone from the British government who had gotten wind of their group and sent an agent to check out what these multilingual, sun- bronzed young people were doing in Alicante. As they were leaving on Monday, less than two days from now, unless the agent made another appearance, there was no use in panicking, so he told Dov to continue as usual and not worry anyone.

Nevertheless, Peter was worried. If the police came and questioned Juan at any point after they were gone, he could only tell them that the group went to the airport to return from wherever they had come from. If they really pressed the hotel manager, the worst he could do is tell them that a philanthropic individual had seen fit to give some survivors of the concentration camps a well-deserved trip to enjoy life. And even if they "followed the money" back to Switzerland, there was nothing they could learn about him except that he came from a good non-Jewish family.

Peter thought of talking to Juan Herrera, but he didn't want Juan to think the group had anything to hide. Since it was clear that Juan didn't like the person, there was little chance he would divulge any information of his own volition.

After dinner that night, Peter tapped with a fork on a water glass and stood up. The room gradually quieted and finally became silent. The door was closed after the dining room staff left.

Peter started by greeting them all with a "Shalom, chevrah." First, he reported that the ship was ready to go, which brought a round of applause from the group.

"On Monday morning, we'll have breakfast at 8:00 a.m., a bus will be waiting for us at 9:00 a.m. to take us to Alicante airport. The plane will be waiting for us. We'll go aboard and fly to Italy first, for refueling, and on to Salonika in Greece, where we'll disembark and get on a waiting bus, which will take us on a two-hour drive to Kavala, where we'll board the ship. During the flight, you will each be given a paper with your cabin number and a small diagram of the ship so you can find your own cabin.

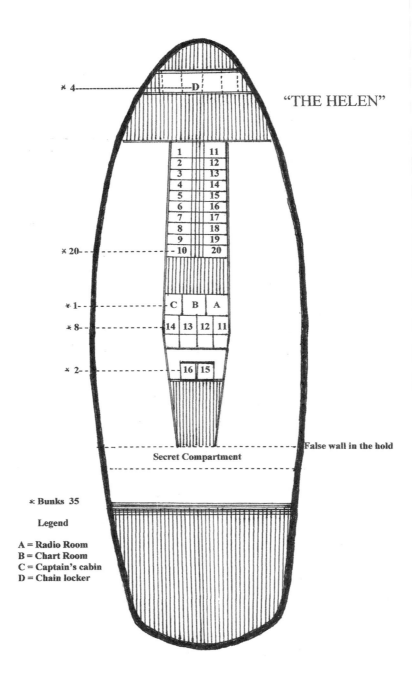

"THE HELEN"

✳ 4

✳ 20

✳ 1

✳ 8

✳ 2

False wall in the hold

Secret Compartment

✳ Bunks 35

Legend

A = Radio Room
B = Chart Room
C = Captain's cabin
D = Chain locker

"Make sure you show the on-board steward your cabin number so we can make sure everyone is accounted for. Soon afterward, you'll start your orientation around the ship. We'll remain two weeks in dock as you become familiar with your jobs. Any questions?"

After the questions were dealt with, the group dispersed.

That night was a night of intense romance for the three couples. They knew that tomorrow would be their last day in Europe and for all of them, except Peter, this was going to be an absolutely unique moment in their lives, a matter they knew they would remember all their days, the chance to be rid of the last physical chains that bound them to the horrors of the camps. They celebrated it, one and all, in their love for one another.

For the entire group, neither the sea voyage, nor the prospect of being arrested by the British Navy was too disturbing. They had all discussed these matters interminably in the group and had come to a number of conclusions.

First of all, as survivors of the German concentration camps and the charnel houses of Europe, they had the wonderful belief that in leaving Europe they would, thankfully, never have to suffer such cruelty, sadism, and humiliation again because wherever they would be going, nothing could compare to where they had been.

Secondly, they had the perception that even if they were arrested by the British Navy and interned, the British were a much more civilized and refined people than the Germans, and undoubtedly would treat them in a more humane way, even if they were to be imprisoned. After all, they had all had been given to read the letter of Arthur Balfour, the British Foreign Secretary, who, on November 2, 1917, wrote to Lord Rothschild, the head of the British Zionist Federation, the following:

"*His Majesty's Government views with favor the establishment in Palestine of a National Home for the Jewish People and will use their best endeavors to facilitate the achievement of this object . . .*" . ."

The next day, Sunday, Juan Herrera came into the dining room when they were having their breakfast. He found Peter and asked to speak to the group. Peter tapped on a glass and introduced Juan, "who wishes to say a few words to us."

"Thank you very much, Mr. Romaine," Juan began. "Ladies and gentlemen, please excuse me for interrupting your breakfast. I just want to say what great satisfaction it has been for me and the whole hotel staff to have had the pleasure of looking after you for the last few weeks. I understand that you have all had a very difficult time in the last few years and came here to recuperate. You have been perfect guests and I just want to wish you all well – good health and success in your future lives. I hope you will look back on these weeks in Spain with warm feelings.

"As you pass out of the dining room after breakfast, one of my staff will be standing at the door to give each of you a small souvenir from the Hotel Palas and Alicante. Thank you very much, ladies and gentlemen."

Peter stood up, shook Juan's hand, and thanked him for his kind words. As the group applauded, Herrera left the room, and many of the group rose to shake his hand as he passed through the tables.

"That was so unexpected and so nice of Mr. Herrera," said Miriam to Peter. "It also shows you that this group of young people, even after having been treated like animals by the Germans, can still appreciate, in a civilized way, when someone shows them a kindness."

As they left the dining room, one of the waiters gave each person a small leather bag containing a metal object in bronze, a representation of Alicante Castle, with the word "Alicante" inscribed on its base.

Peter went to Herrera and thanked him for the presents. He told him that everyone would treasure the gift enormously as a symbol of their time in the wonderful country of Spain.

That day, Sunday, the whole group went swimming in the ocean.

Two of the boys had pooled their remaining pesetas and bought a Box Brownie camera, and they insisted on photographing everybody, on the beach, in small groups. They wanted Helen, Miriam, Dov, Heidi, and Peter in every picture. Peter told them that while they were in Kavala for the next two weeks, he would get them printed and copies made so that every one of them would have a photo set of their own.

By the evening they were all talking very excitedly of the following day's journey and everybody found themselves getting to bed relatively early.

Next morning, the whole group were picked up by the bus, as arranged, and by 9:30 were boarding *Richard's Renown* at Alicante airport.

They left Spain and took off at 10:00 a.m., amid happy cheering from the group, who were now feeling they were all *at last* starting their much-anticipated journey to Palestine. Peter distributed their cabin numbers and ship diagram.

At 7:00 p.m., they touched down in Greece at Salonika, to be met by the bus, as arranged. Peter thanked Jim for his services and handed him a handsome bonus check. Some of the group told Peter that they wished they could see something of Salonika, as they had heard so much about it for months. Peter got the bus driver to drive around the city, including the port area, before they set off for Kavala.

Two hours later, the bus rolled into Kavala and along the quay to stop at the gangway. Peter told everyone to go up the gangway, show their cabin number to Georg, go to their cabins, and choose their bunks. They should leave their possessions there, and wait for a signal, which they would recognize from Camp Pietro, and go to the mess deck, where Shlomo, the chef, who they also knew from Camp Pietro, had a welcoming dinner for everybody, and a glass of wine for anybody who wanted one.

Heide and Miriam were delighted to be sharing a room together again and that their young men were so close. Alex was also very happy to discover that Helen was close by as well. They all knew they had Peter to thank for this.

After putting his gear in Cabin 15, Peter knocked on number 16, next door. Helen called, "Come in," and he entered, leaving the door open.

"Just wanted to see if my neighbor was happy with her accommodation, and to remind you that the walls of the cabins are not sound-proof." he said.

"There you go again," she said, smiling, "always looking after my welfare. And, much as I love Miriam, I hope I don't hear her in the middle of the night, since the non-sound-proof walls go two-ways."

"I'll remember that," he said with a wink as he left her room.

He found the rest of the group in the fo'c's'le all well organized. Apparently, there had been a couple of changes, but that was their business and not his. They all seemed satisfied with their lodgings.

He then went along to the three boys who were sharing the chain locker. He had been told that this was the poorest space on the ship, but was surprised by its roominess and heartened by the very positive attitude of its occupants. They had become friends, all being from Poland, and quite happy to be sharing the space with each other. There was even a surplus bunk which they could use.

Just then, there was the familiar and welcome sound of Shlomo banging two pieces of metal together, and everybody found their way to the mess deck, which was amidships and below the main deck.

Inside, there was a long refectory table such as they had had in Camp Pietro. Olaf was sitting at the head of the table having just put out the four seating cards marked "Georg" and "Dov" on one side of the table and "Peter" and "Helen" on the other side. All the rest of the seats were without cards.

Miriam quickly took a seat next to Helen, while Heide sat next to Dov; Max sat next to Heide and Alex sat next to Miriam. The rest of the group sat along the length of the table.

After everyone was seated and quiet, Olaf rose to his feet and said, "Shalom, chevra" to which everyone responded, "Shalom, Olaf."

"As you know, I'm the captain of this ship, and since we only have one table on this mess deck, this is the "Captain's Table," and it is the captain's prerogative to chose who he wants to sit at his table and where. You are all, of course, welcome to my table, but the people sitting at this end are the ship's officers, whom I would now like to introduce to you.

"First of all, the professional engineer of the ship is *Georg*. He is from Sweden and it was he who was responsible for supervising all the repair work on the ship.

"Next to Georg is your friend *Dov*, a real Palestinian, ex-captain in the British Army, one of your leaders in Alicante and now, I'm happy to announce, the first Lieutenant, my second-in-command on the ship. He will be known as *Number One*.

"On my right, of course, is *Mr. Peter Romaine*. He is the administration officer, as well as the owner of the ship. But most importantly, he is the one who is making our trip to Palestine possible.

"Then, we come to *Helen*. You may know her as the lovely lady who came to visit you all in the hospital in Switzerland, but she wears quite a few hats, including chief pilot of the plane you came in on, as well as head accountant of this operation. On this ship, she is the navigation officer, who will be telling me where to go and how long it will take us to get there.

"Last, but my no means least, is our Master Chef, *Shlomo*, who has prepared a great dinner for us, which I know he is impatient to serve. Will the two boys whose job it is to help in the kitchen please get up and report to Shlomo so we can start eating." The two boys got up at once and joined Shlomo in the kitchen and the meal proceeded.

"Well, Captain," Peter said, "I'm glad you made the introductions and that everyone will know the chain of command."

"Thanks, Peter," Olaf said, "I hope you understand that there can only be one person in operational command on a ship and it has to be the captain. And while I recognize that you own the ship, I must still have the last word."

"Absolutely, Olaf, and I assure you that I've no intention of usurping your authority or giving any orders on board – that's exactly why you're sitting here."

They found that Shlomo had prepared a delicious dinner for them. Following cock-a-leekie soup, a Scottish soup of chicken, leeks, and barley, there was a stew of diced beef, potatoes, onions, carrots, and peas. Dessert took the form of a delightful, sweet apple pie. There were a few bottles of beer and wine on the table, too. And finally, a choice of tea or coffee.

When it was over, Helen insisted on sending for Shlomo, who came into the mess deck innocently, asking if there was anything wrong with the meal. In response, everyone clapped and shouted their approval of the sumptuous meal he had prepared. One young man went so far as to ask, innocently enough, "Is this what we get every day?"

"Sorry, everyone, we have neither the time nor the storage space for such a daily meal, but I assure you I will do my best to make each meal tasty and nutritious."

By the time dinner was over and the table cleared, it was nearly midnight and everyone on board was very happy to go to their bunks.

The next morning, at 8:00 a.m., reveille was sounded and the day officially began.

When breakfast was over, Olaf got to his feet and explained the day's program. Everybody, except Peter and Helen, would be divided into two groups, with one group led by Olaf and the other by Georg. They would tour the ship in order to become familiar with where everything was located. The trip would include the secret chutes, where they were located, and how to use them. There were five of these secret places, two in the f'o'c's'le, one in Cabin 12, one in the mess deck, and one in the chain locker. Every day, while everyone else hid, Olaf, Peter, Dov, Georg, Shlomo, and Helen, plus four others on a rotation, would remain visible as the crew.

Olaf explained about the emergency drills that would take place, and the lifeboat drills, which were very important. Every drill had to be taken very seriously and always had to be thought of as the result of a real inspection by the British Navy. He pointed to Dov, saying that as No. 1, he would be in charge of the drills and hiding places.

Olaf then asked everybody to split into two groups according to which side of the table they were sitting. Those on the port side would be Olaf's group. Those on the starboard side would be Georg's group.

The groups saw everything, including the engine room and the hold. One of the boys in Olaf's group asked about the crated boxes in the hold.

"Oh, that's our cargo," said Olaf, with a straight face.

"What's our cargo?" asked the boy.

"Rocks," replied Olaf.

"What do you mean?" asked the boy.

"These are boxes of worthless rocks, equal in weight to the machinery, which is what we are supposed to be carrying, for which we have certified bills of lading."

"If the British come aboard, will the papers fool them?" he asked.

"That remains to be seen," said Olaf, leaving everyone a bit uneasy.

Both groups finished up at the captain's cabin and were then shown the chart room and the radio room.

After lunch, the real work started. Olaf, Georg, Dov, Heide, and Shlomo prepared themselves for the instruction work of the afternoon and picked up their groups.

After three hours there was a break for a coffee and tea with cookies and then the thing for which they had all been waiting – the alarm call that meant they were to slide down the chutes into the secret room in the hold. That was something they all enjoyed. The hold was fairly barren, but had lighting that made things less nerve-racking. They were told to wait there, silently, until they heard the "all clear." After a few minutes, Dov came down a chute, to applause, opened a door, and let everyone out. However, he had made sure the four boys on the rotation for that day knew who they were and would therefore not take part in the chute slide for that day.

Everyone came up on deck and were standing around chatting when Dov suddenly called out, "British Navy." All the group had learned that this was the alarm call and immediately scattered to the chutes, except the four on that day's rotation. Dov timed the operation, and when they were all able to assemble afterward on the main deck, he told them that they needed to cut their time by at least fifty percent. He also explained that the four remaining sailors had to look busy swabbing the deck, cleaning the lamps, and adjusting ropes. It didn't matter what they did, but they had to be doing something and when that job was done, they had to seamlessly start doing something else. If they ran out of jobs to do, they should go down to the engine room for a few minutes, then reappear.

Then the dinner gong sounded and everyone went to the mess galley to eat. They were in the middle of eating when Shlomo came rushing in to say, "British Navy." Immediately, everyone left in a hurry to get to the chutes and Shlomo and the remaining four cleared the table of the plates and put them quickly into buckets so that there would be no sign of the twenty-four extra hands that were now running to the chutes.

Over the course of the next five days, training for the ship's duties went on daily, interrupted only by meals, lifeboat drill, and Royal Navy alarm practice. As the group became more familiar with their routine, they shortened their disappearing act until, finally, Dov pronounced himself satisfied. Olaf, who had had the job of teaching the positions of helmsmen, lookouts, and deck duties also gradually came to feel that he could rely on the boys to do an adequate job. Just to be sure, he and Dov would spring surprise checks on the lookouts, as well as the others, both day and night, to make sure they were on their toes.

Peter had not forgotten to get the photographs taken in Alicante, printed in Kavala in multiple sets so that each person had received copies of all the pictures taken, which delighted everybody.

Peter asked for an officers' meeting with Olaf, at which time he got together everybody with a supervisory job to find out if they were satisfied with their people.

Heide said she was happy with the routines she had established for hygiene control and the rudiments of first aid in her three assistants. The mess deck was to be the ship's hospital.

Olaf was delighted with the five boys who had learned the basics of the compass and helm, and he and Dov felt that the two bos'n boys and the seven trained as lookouts were doing a good job.

Georg was content with the four boys to assist him with ship maintenance, including basic electrical and carpentry.

Shlomo was very happy with his two assistants for the galley and mess deck.

Olaf felt that the group was cohesive enough to set sail. This being a Friday, he proposed setting sail on Sunday night at midnight. Helen produced the charts and Olaf showed the route they had plotted.

They would start sailing due south, then turn east toward Samothrace and then to the coast of Turkey. He estimated they would arrive at Gallipoli in Turkey by about Tuesday. Then they would sail down the Turkish coast, going generally south-southeast, into a fiord by day and sailing by night, until they turned east, then south, past the coast of Syria, then Lebanon, to Palestine.

Turning to Dov, Olaf said, "I think you should hold your first alarm situation at 4:00 a.m., after we've departed. It's important to see how everyone reacts once we're underway. There's seasickness to contend with and a chance that some of the people may become a bit disoriented."

Dov agreed, and the officers disbanded.

That day, the messenger from AB arrived, and following the exchanges of "Pegasus" and "Bellorophon" passwords, the envelope containing the codes and wireless frequencies was handed to Olaf.

The next day, Saturday, by arrangement, Dov went ashore to the office of Jack Niarchos to make a phone call to his colleagues in Aliyah Bet in Switzerland, to inform them, using Hebrew slang, that "the bird would leave its nest the next day at midnight." He also checked that there was no mail awaiting them in the office.

At midnight, the *Helen* weighed anchor, the captain signaled "slow ahead both" to the engine room, and the ship eased itself away from the Kavala quayside and very quietly slipped away into the night. The ship's lights were on and a phosphorescent trail followed in her wake, but to anyone looking, she was just one of dozens of ships setting out with her cargo to points unknown.

Four hours later, the alarm was sounded throughout the ship and the newly trained crew got out of their bunks and went down the chutes to the hold room. There was a certain amount of grumbling, more annoyance than anything else, but on the whole, they proceeded in an orderly manner. Then came the "all clear" and they went back to their cabins to complete their interrupted night's sleep.

Late on Sunday morning, they changed course due east and six hours later, the captain announced over the ship's public address system (PAS) that they were now passing on the port side the island of Samothrace. They could see its central mountain, which was a little over 5,000 feet high.

At 6:00 that afternoon, the forward lookout called out "ship on the starboard bow." Olaf trained his binoculars on the unknown ship and, a moment later, called over the PAS, "British Navy, this is not an exercise. I repeat, this is not an exercise."

Peter, who was on the bridge, went into Olaf's cabin. "What is it, Olaf?"

"It's a Royal Navy destroyer, Peter. Stand by the radio."

Peter moved back quickly to the radio cabin in time to hear the ship's wireless hail the *Helen*. He answered and was asked where they were from and where were they headed. He replied, "Salonika, to Tyre, Lebanon."

"Heave to, please, we're coming aboard."

"Very well."

He went into Olaf's cabin. "We're to heave to, they're coming aboard. I've acknowledged it."

"Okay, Peter," said Olaf. "I'm going to see if it's all in order on the ship."

Then he signaled down to Georg, in the engine room, "All engines stop."

Helen appeared in the radio cabin.

"So this is it, Peter?"

"Yes, my love. Do we have the bills of lading here?"

"No, Peter, they're in the chart room cupboard."

"Very well." Then he said, "look, they're on their way."

She looked over and saw a small boat from the destroyer heading toward them.

"What's that boat?" she asked.

"That's a cutter," he answered, "it's carried on the destroyer for short trips."

Olaf returned to the bridge. "It's all quiet below and the four deck-hands look busy, cleaning. So far, so good."

The cutter came alongside and Olaf threw a rope ladder down.

Olaf, Peter, and Helen saw a Royal Navy officer climbing the ladder, leaving three men in the cutter. He was a young sub-lieutenant, very serious-looking, with a holstered pistol on his hip. He came up on the bridge and saluted the three of them.

"I'm Lt. Wilson, Royal Navy. Who is your captain?"

Olaf replied, "I'm Captain Cohen, Lt. Wilson. Why have you stopped me to board my ship? We are, as you know, in international waters."

"Yes, I'm aware, Captain. We are carrying out a blockade and looking for illegals attempting to enter Palestine. May I see your ship's papers and bills of lading?"

While they were talking, two more uniformed men arrived on the main deck. These were Royal Marines; a sergeant and a corporal. Both were armed. The corporal remained at the rope ladder and the sergeant accompanied the naval officer. That left one marine in the boat, attached to the side of their vessel.

Olaf said to the officer, "Yes, certainly, Lieutenant, come into my chart room. And Helen, will you please come in, too?" The three all squeezed into the room.

Olaf said, "Helen, please get out the ship's papers and our bills of lading."

Helen reached for the documents and gave them to Olaf, who said, "By the way, Lieutenant, this is my niece Helen, who is traveling with me."

The young Naval Officer, who had not taken his eyes off Helen since he first saw her, said, "How do you do, Miss Helen, it's a pleasure to meet you."

Olaf checked the ship's papers and Bills of Lading and handed them to the officer, who ignored the ship's papers but examined the Bills of Lading carefully.

"Captain, how many does your crew consist of?" he asked.

"Well, there's me, my niece, who is supernumerary, the wireless operator, the engineer officer, the ship's cook, and four deck-hands, a total of nine persons."

"Thank you, Captain. Now, I'd like to examine your cargo of machinery and machine spare parts as described in your Bills of Lading."

"Certainly," said Olaf, "follow me."

The officer, carrying the Bills of Lading, followed Olaf off the bridge and down the ladder to the main deck, his sergeant in tow. Olaf opened and raised a hatch cover and led the way down into the hold. There, he pointed to the crated cargo, indicating the index numbers prominently displayed on the crates and boxes within.

Lieutenant Wilson carefully compared the reference numbers on the Bills of Lading with the numbers stenciled on the crates and boxes. He found they matched perfectly and said, "Well, Captain, everything looks shipshape and in order, but what would you say if I asked you to open a crate and the box inside it in order to compare the contents with the information on the Bill of Lading?"

Olaf looked at the young officer, noticing his determination. He also saw that the sergeant had overtly placed his hand on his side-arm.

He was about to cavil at the lieutenant's request when he noticed that the officer was clenching his teeth, as though he were apprehensive at what he had asked of Olaf.

"Aha," Olaf thought, "so he's under great tension. I wonder, why? Maybe he knows he's exceeding his orders, trying to bluff me. Well young man, let's see what happens when I call your bluff."

"I don't think you have the authority to demand that of me, Lieutenant Wilson, now have you?" Olaf said, speaking in the terse, commanding voice he had learned to use during his years in the navy. "And I think you're aware of paragraph H2(b)(i) of the Hague Convention, referring to the prohibition against opening sealed containers on a Common Carrier. If you were to force me, under duress of the arms carried by you and your sergeant, you know the consequences, don't you Lieutenant Wilson?"

Lieutenant Wilson, all twenty years of age of him, first went white, then, as Olaf continued, turned bright red.

Olaf was silent.

After a minute or so, Wilson answered, but his voice had gone an octave higher than his normal range. "Hmm, and what would that be, Captain Cohen?"

"Why, Lieutenant Wilson, that would the equivalent of pillage of goods on the high seas, a step short of piracy, something I'm sure the Royal Navy does not practice, does it?"

Lieutenant Wilson was thinking furiously, wondering about the Hague Convention and not quite sure what pillage meant. At length, he came to a decision.

Handing the Bills of Lading politely to Olaf, he said, "That's fine, Captain. I shan't trouble you any further."

With that, he led the way up to the main deck again and he and the marines prepared to leave.

"Good day to you, Captain, and to you, miss, and I hope you have a fair voyage to Lebanon and no more impudent stoppages like this."

The Lieutenant and Olaf smiled at each other, two fellow sailormen, each doing his job in difficult times, and then the visitors were gone over the side, into the cutter, and back to the destroyer.

Dov appeared. Olaf asked him to go down to the secret room and let the group out, but only into the hold for the time being, until the naval ship was out of sight.

From the bridge, Peter and the others could hear the sound of quiet conversations as the released crew tasted fresh air after being locked up in the secret room for two hours. They stayed there until the destroyer was over the horizon.

A short while later, Shlomo let them know that dinner was ready and the group sat down together on the mess deck, now very relaxed and comfortable after that incident.

After dinner, Olaf stood up and congratulated the whole group on the perfect way they had responded to this real emergency and how the training had proved itself. He then asked Peter to report on the Royal Navy visit. Peter said how well it had gone because of the preparations they had made. He also referred to a question he had received a couple of days ago and could now respond: "The paperwork they had prepared in Salonika had worked perfectly, and had fooled the British Navy completely." Peter finished by saying, "The visit terminated with the British officer hoping we would have a fair voyage to Lebanon with no further interruptions by the Royal Navy." This brought huge applause as the various translations took place.

The voyage continued that night and as dawn broke, they sailed into a small harbor near Gallipoli. They were now out of Greek and international territorial waters and in Turkish territorial waters. The *Helen* was sailing according to the charts, as Olaf confirmed. He decided to switch Helen, who was on duty every night, with Dov, who agreed.

After that first visit by the Royal Navy, there were no repetitions and so, day after day, the *Helen* took shelter in another Turkish fjord for a harbor. Night after night, she sailed covertly but steadily, easterly then south, first along the Turkish coastline opposite Cyprus, then out to sea, but parallel to the Syrian coast, then the Lebanese coast.

At last, it was time to send a coded wireless signal to the Aliyah Bet people in Palestine, who were anxiously awaiting news of this remarkable ship.

The signal told the Aliyah Bet organization exactly where they were as they approached Lebanese territorial waters and their rate of speed, so that the operatives in Palestine could work out when and where the *Helen* was to arrive.

It had been decided that they should bring the ship close to shore at a beach near the town of Nahariya, which is a little north of Haifa and just south of the Palestine/Lebanon border.

Olaf stopped the *Helen* at midnight about 250 yards off shore, but didn't cast the anchor, to maintain silence. Immediately, six small boats came out, and each took five passengers. The ship then reversed out to sea immediately and sailed as fast as possible to Turkey. The remaining crew was Olaf, Dov, Georg, and Shlomo.

Olaf was prepared for a British raid. In that event, he would beach the *Helen* and the passengers would have swum to shore.

Once ashore, the group was met by representatives of various villages, kibbutzim (voluntary collective communities, mainly agricultural, in which there was no private wealth), and moshavim (cooperatives, combining some of the features of both kibbutzim and private farming). These village representatives each took small parties of two or three people. Peter and Miriam, Helen and Alex, and Heide and Max were able to keep together as couples, although each went to different places from the other couples.

As the village representatives took each party to transport them away, Aliyah Bet people carefully recorded the names of the new clandestine immigrants and the villages to which they were being taken.

In traveling through the night to their destinations, likelihood of being stopped by the Palestine Police or British Army was considerable, and the new immigrants had to look as much as possible like regular Palestine Jews living in the country. Clothing and headgear that looked European had to be removed and more indigenous clothing put on. The newcomers were told to keep silent if their vehicle was stopped by the authorities.

The operation was managed so well that within twenty minutes from the time the first immigrants arrived on shore, all the new arrivals were whisked away. The *Helen* was gone. The beach was silent and deserted once more. The thirty new arrivals were on their way, in a variety of vehicles, trucks, cars, and taxis, on many minor dirt roads and desert tracks, in the darkness, to their new homes. The Aliyah Bet staff, too, hid the small boats and then melted into the night. The only sound was the quiet lapping of small waves.

CHAPTER XIX

The Kibbutz

PETER AND MIRIAM WERE CARRIED AWAY FROM THE BEACH in an old Hillman car to a kibbutz, inland of the coastal city of Netanya. When the car stopped, Peter, Miriam, and the driver got out and by the light in the kibbutz center, they could see their driver for the first time. He was a husky young man who spoke French, so they were able to talk to him. He asked them where they were from. Miriam said "Poland" and he shrugged, but when Peter said "Switzerland," his eyes widened and he told Peter he was the first person he had ever met from there. His name was Louis and he was from Romania. Peter asked him where they were and was told they were in Kibbutz Ma'barot.

He led them in the darkness to a room in a small row of huts, which he said were used for visitors and occasionally, volunteers. He asked Peter if one room was okay for them and Peter said, yes, they were together as a couple. Louis then said, "It's about four a.m. now. I'll return at six to take you to breakfast. Afterward, you'll meet the kibbutz secretary, who is responsible for administration of the kibbutz. The toilets and washrooms are that way" (he pointed).

They thanked him and entered the room. It was simply furnished. There were two single beds with one small bedside cabinet between them. There was also a broken window, and a pile of cardboard boxes of different sizes in a corner. There were blankets, sheets, pillows and pillowcases folded up on the beds. They closed the door, tossed their few belongings on one of the beds, then threw their arms around one another in a very long, long hugging embrace.

After a while, still clasped in each other's arms, they fell together on one of the beds. When they separated, they said, simultaneously, "At last."

"I'm going to block up that broken window with some of that cardboard," Peter said.

"While you do that, I'll make the beds," Miriam told him.

Thus, they started their life together.

For Miriam, it was an impossible dream come amazingly true, while for Peter, this was the conclusion of stage one of a most extraordinary adventure.

While brushing his teeth, Peter ruminated on how exceedingly remarkable, and unlikely, it was that he, a student, a Gentile, an Englishman, living very quietly in Switzerland, should have become so incredibly involved with this group and with their Zionist aspirations. But perhaps the most surprising thing that had happened to him, besides falling in love with this beautiful and cultured young woman, was that he had decided to throw in his lot with her in her quest to become part of the new Jewish homeland.

What did it mean to him? Did it mean that he was psychologically becoming Jewish? No, he answered himself, he didn't know what being Jewish meant. Back in Berne, he had done a little reading about Zionism, but that was focused on the need for refuge from European anti-Semitism. What he needed to know was the fundamental philosophy, theology, history – indeed, the raison d'être of the Jewish people. Especially now that he was living among them. Only then would he have any idea what it was to be a Jew.

At 6:00 a.m., there was a knock on the door and Louis's stentorian voice was saying "*boker tov*" (good morning). Miriam answered by responding, "boker tov" and opening the door to him. He came in, cast an approving eye at the temporarily repaired window, and said he hoped they had slept well during the night.

They all laughed at that, but Peter thanked him for the first time for picking them up at the beach, bringing them here in the middle of the night, and missing his own night's sleep as a consequence. Louis brushed that aside as a matter of no importance, but said he regarded his trip to the beach and return to the kibbutz as a "mitzvah," a meritorious act, although he wasn't a religious person, despite having had a religious upbringing in "the old country."

Louis led them to the dining room of the kibbutz and explained the systems they had to follow in order to pick up their food and to return the crockery and cutlery afterward. They sat at one of the long tables with a number of the members. Louis told the others who Peter and Miriam were and they were greeted by smiles and "Shalom"s (welcome) from them. Some of them spoke languages familiar to the couple, including one woman who was from Poland and greeted Miriam warmly. There was general disbelief that a young man from Switzerland would want to brave the perils of the sea to get to Palestine, but Peter indicated that if one had such a beautiful girlfriend as he had, then it was surely understandable. There were smiles all around, and Miriam, overhearing what he said, smiled demurely.

After they finished breakfast, which had consisted of a vast selection of fresh vegetables ("grown on the kibbutz," he was told) plus cheeses, eggs, and fish, Louis led them to the office of the kibbutz secretary – whose nickname was Yossele and whose real name was Joseph – introduced them, and left them there. Yossele was a man in his forties who had a busy office. He greeted them warmly in Hebrew but changed to English for their benefit, and welcomed them to Ma'barot. He told them he had been a soldier in the Jewish Brigade of the British Army, where he had learned more of his English vocabulary to add to what he had learned in school, as a child in Hungary.

He filled out information sheets with their personal data and told them they needed to have the current form of identification required by the Palestine government. Peter asked him how that could be done, since they were illegal immigrants. Yossele told him with a smile that he had a friend who worked in the local city administration who would procure the necessary papers for them. They would have to have photos taken, which could be done in the kibbutz, and when Yossele next went into the town, he would get the identity cards.

Yossele then told them something about Ma'barot, when it was started, and what they did. He offered them a book in French of the story of the kibbutz movement, which they eagerly agreed to read. He had been very impressed with their academic achievements and told them that he would try hard to find suitable work for them on the kibbutz.

Yossele said they would start as volunteers. Then, if they wanted to, after a probationary period, it was possible that they could be proposed for full membership in the kibbutz. He explained that each member of the kibbutz was a part owner of all the kibbutz assets, less its liabilities. Kibbutz members shared in all the services that the kibbutz offered, including housing, food, clothing, study facilities, health coverage, and even rest home vacations. There was even a possible third level of status, that of an employee, but it was problematic. The members were sociologically and philosophically against having paid employees, but there was much talk about possibly changing that article of kibbutz faith.

"But let's leave that matter for now," he said, "it's not urgent and we can talk about in the coming days."

He led them around the whole property and they saw the dairy barn, library, kitchen, infirmary, repair shop, the welding shop, garage, fish breeding ponds, the chicken house, the children's day care houses, the vegetable packing house, the orchards, and the fields.

After the tour, Yossele took them back to his office. He wanted to know if they had any plans and if there was any aspect of the kibbutz that particularly interested them. He also asked about their relationship and how long had they known each other.

Peter started to speak, but Miriam interrupted.

"Peter has been the leader of our entire group," she told Yossele. "This includes mostly concentration camp survivors. Using his own funds, he made all the arrangements to get us to Palestine. Without him, most of us would still be in different parts of Europe, trying vainly to pick up the pieces. As for our relationship, Peter is my deepest friend, and a Gentile."

Yossele listened intently to her story, smiled at the last statement and said, "Thank you, Miriam. Peter is not the first Gentile to come to this kibbutz, you know, and we welcome you both. Now, Peter, tell me what's in your head at this moment?"

"I'm thinking of how I can make some contribution to your kibbutz. I'm a linguist. I speak nine or ten languages and I'm ready to be a teacher in any of them, here in the kibbutz or elsewhere in Palestine. On the other hand, both Miriam and I want and need to learn Hebrew. We'll do anything we can do to contribute work to the kibbutz. By the way, I was a Scout Leader in Switzerland. After we settle down here, both Miriam and I want to get on with our doctorates in Linguistics, which we both started "in the old countries" and for that, we'll have to connect with the Linguistics Department of one of your universities. For the present, we want to settle in, meet people, make friends, learn Hebrew, and work in any area that you find for us."

"Thanks, Peter. Now Miriam, it's your turn to tell me something of what of you can offer and what you want."

"Well Yossele, I'm also a linguist but I only have five languages. I can teach any of them. I was a Youth Leader in Poland in the Bnei Akiva organization for seven years. I also need to learn Hebrew and after settling in I want to get on with my PhD. I also want to tell you that to be here in Palestine is a life-time dream come true."

"Impressive. In view of the fact that you both have very unusual qualifications, I'm going to discuss your cases with my Kibbutz Area Organization and try to find how we may best utilize your talents for the common good. We do have Hebrew instruction on a neighboring kibbutz close by, named Ha'ogen. We'll see about this and let you know in a day or two. Meanwhile, you should take it easy and rest up after your recent adventures. If you want to go into Netanya, I suggest you wait till I can first get the IDs I mentioned, in case you're stopped and questioned. As to the more practical matter of meals, breakfast is at 6:00 a.m., lunch from 12:00 to 2:00 p.m., and dinner at 5:00 to 6:00 p.m."

They knew they were being dismissed. Yossele was obviously a busy man and he had spent over two hours of his time with them already. They went back to their room to find someone just finishing replacing the broken window. It seemed Louis had let the appropriate person know that it was in need of repair. The man had said "Shalom" (hello) to them, but none of the languages either of them knew seemed to get the man's attention. In frustration, Peter used his Rumansh and the man nearly fell off his ladder in shock, tremendously excited. Peter had picked up that dialect when he spent three months in the Grisons, in eastern Switzerland. The man, who pointed to himself and said, "Avraham," was a member of the one Jewish family that lived in that valley, had come to Palestine in 1930 as a teenager, and never thought he would hear his own dialect ever spoken again. He fell on Peter with a great hug and a flood of words, and questions. Avraham asked them to come over to his house that afternoon for a cup of tea and to meet his wife. Peter and Miriam both accepted at once – an opportunity to get together with some members, socially, for the first time. Avraham said he would pick them up at four p.m. and, after fixing the window, left, mumbling how remarkable, no, unbelievable, it was, to meet someone who could speak Rumansh in the kibbutz!

Miriam and Peter found the dining room and sat down for lunch.

They started their meal with vegetable soup, hot and thick with vegetables, some of which were unknown to both of them. The main course was fried fish with hash-brown potatoes, then there was a dessert of bread pudding and coffee. It was an eye-opening meal to them, ample, tasty, hot, and very, very, filling. They realized that the kibbutz members got up very early, worked hard in the fields, orchards, or elsewhere, and were more than ready for a good, sustaining meal.

They met a number of people at their lunch table who spoke languages other than Hebrew. They found people to be very friendly, and most curious about Peter, with his Swiss/British background.

After lunch, Miriam led the way back to their room. They slept until four p.m., when Avraham arrived and led them to his home. He introduced them to his wife, Leah, as his "new friend from his old country" and his fiancée. She was from Belgium, a very beautiful young woman who had come to Palestine as a teenager in the Zionist Youth Movement just before the war. She and Avraham had met in the kibbutz movement and married in 1943 when she was twenty.

Their common language was Hebrew, but Leah spoke French and Dutch, her first languages, from Belgium. It was quickly decided that Peter and Avraham would speak in Rumansh, while Peter, Leah, and Miriam would converse in French. Their home consisted of a bedroom, a small living room, tiny bathroom and a minuscule corner for a tiny sink and cooker. In showing them around, Leah explained that all their meals were taken in the communal dining room, so they had no need for a kitchen. There was a covered patio outside, with half a dozen chairs and Leah explained that when they had friends visit, it was invariably outside, the predominant weather being dry and warm throughout the year.

While they were talking, Leah was busy making tea on her tiny stove and brought it out on her patio with some cookies. Miriam asked her what work she did on the kibbutz; they already knew that Avraham worked on the maintenance crew. Leah said she worked mainly in the dairy, but that in some seasons, she also worked in the orchards, pruning or picking fruit. She asked Miriam what work she was going to do there when they had settled in. Miriam told her that as yet she didn't know but maybe she might teach languages.

The new arrivals inquired as to what, if any, cultural activities took place in Ma'barot. Leah and Avraham exchanged a smile and explained to their guests that *every week* there were two or three events, some in their kibbutz and some in the neighboring kibbutzim, to which they were welcome. There were plays, concerts, lectures, and discussions on current national and international political and economic affairs. It was clear Miriam and Peter would need a fluency in Hebrew to get around and enjoy a cultural life in the kibbutz.

When it was time to go to dinner, they all walked along to the dining room, went in, chose their food, and sat down together at one of the long tables.

While they were seated, enjoying their meal and chatting to each other, in Rumansh and French, others seated at the same table inquired of Leah and Avraham about their new friends. Peter and Miriam invariably found a common language in which to speak to virtually all people at the table. Every person to whom they spoke gave them a welcome to the country and to the kibbutz, which again, helped to make Peter and Miriam feel comfortable among these multifarious strangers.

As they finished their meal and were returning their dishes to the kitchen, Yossele appeared.

"The very people I wanted to see," said Yossele, clearing his dishes as well. "Why don't you both come with me into the sitting room just at the end of the dining room." They all sat together in a private corner.

"I had a very interesting and long phone call this afternoon from a good friend of mine named Willem, who is originally from Holland," Yossele began. "We served together as soldiers in the Jewish Brigade, and we sometimes have business in common. Since he is the chairman in Palestine of the whole of Aliyah Bet, he had something to phone me about. I'm aware now that you have a practical knowledge of the activities of Aliyah Bet in Europe. Indeed, your own activities in Switzerland, Italy, Greece, and Spain have been intensely observed by their people in Europe, who informed their headquarters in Palestine. From the first time you contacted their agent in Zurich, you have apparently been an object of significant interest to Aliyah Bet headquarters here in Palestine.

"The truth is, it took a long time for them to accept you at face value as the leader and mentor of that Jewish group of survivors, since you are English and a Gentile. Aliyah Bet is a top-secret operation, and the greatest fear, right from the start, was that someone like you, on behalf of the British government, would be able to penetrate the organization and then "roll up" its activities. As a Britisher, then, and a Gentile, they naturally were apprehensive and kept a close watch on your movements.

"As time went on, however, they realized what a wonderful asset you were and your dedication and energies on behalf of Aliyah Bet soon dispelled their fears. I now know about your role in the *Helen's* arrival here and I want to tell you it would be our honor to have someone like you, and Miriam, of course, join our kibbutz. You are a true hero to the Jewish people, what some people have begun to call a Righteous Gentile.

"As I also previously said, now you have to recoup your strength. Soon, the kibbutz, and perhaps the nation of Israel as a whole, will approach you to continue your magnificent work."

Peter and Miriam were both astonished to hear such accolades. Miriam, for her part, told Yossele she approved of everything that he had just said about Peter. "It's hard to believe that one young person could have taken so much responsibility on his shoulders, and even with the help of others, accomplish so much so quickly."

Peter replied that he was quite embarrassed by what Yossele and Miriam had said and he felt that the language was excessive. He had done simply what was within his power to do and what he thought was right. He really didn't think what he did merited extravagant praise.

"I think that, if anything," Yossele said, "our praise hasn't nearly expressed what the Aliyah Bet people are feeling."

With that, everyone returned to their room. On the way along the pathway, Peter and Miriam were stopped by another young couple, who introduced themselves, in English, as Jack and Betty from Australia. They had recently become members of the kibbutz. They invited Miriam and Peter for "a cup of real coffee – my mom sends it to us from Sydney, and we use it on special occasions such as this is."

Betty and Jack led them to their home, which had the same layout as that of Avraham and Leah, but despite the basic interior, it was decorated with some attractive impressionist reproductions on the walls and some colorful curtains, which made the potentially drab apartment into both a homey and welcoming place.

Miriam commented on this immediately.

"Well thanks, Miriam," Betty said. "It's a pity that so many others here don't even bother to do this sort of minimum. In the kibbutz we do get a small kind of pocket money allowance, which we can use as we see fit."

Peter and Miriam had to tell their story again. They learned that Betty and Jack had come to Palestine together from Australia in 1937 in one of the youth organizations. Jack had worked with dairy cows and milk production in Australia and did similar work on the kibbutz. Betty worked with the children on the kibbutz.

When the war broke out in 1939, Jack left their first kibbutz to join the British Army and then, when the Jewish Brigade was formed, he was allowed to transfer into it.

As soon as the war was over, he came back to Palestine and married Betty. They joined this kibbutz, as their original one had closed down. So, as they were, themselves, relatively new members here, Jack and Betty felt they could comfortably advise and help this new couple.

Miriam joined Peter in thanking them for inviting them to their home. They assured Jack and Betty that they would take them up on their offer to help as soon as they got settled in.

When they returned to their room, Miriam grabbed a chair, jammed it under the door-handle, spun around, seized Peter with her arms around his neck and gave him a long kiss.

When they finally pulled away from each other, Peter said, "You know, my love, I feel we've now really started our life together, for the first time, in these modest surroundings, and I propose that whatever we may do in our future life, that this be our honeymoon and that we should refer to it as such and not just as 'the day we arrived in Palestine,' or 'Ma'barot.' What do you say, my dearest?"

"Absolutely," she answered, "that's simply a beautiful suggestion. I didn't realize you were such a romantic. So, today is the day we start our joint life together. You can't imagine how I dreamed of starting a new life with the man I love, when I was in Ravensbrueck. I see that miracles do happen. You don't know what incredible happiness you bring me, my sweetheart. I know this may sound a bit trite, but I feel that you are the one my soul has hungered for and that you make me complete."

The next morning, after they had just returned the breakfast dishes, they were greeted by Yossele.

"I've got to go into town today and I want to get you your IDs so I need your pictures. Will you come along with me?"

"Yes, of course," they replied and followed him out of the dining room. He led them to a hut, unlocked it, and they followed him in. It was dark inside, as the windows were blacked out, but Yossele switched on the light. They saw it was almost empty but for a camera on a tripod, a desk, a sink, and some equipment; one wall had a mural of a country scene. Yossele stood each of them in turn in front of the painted wall and took a picture.

He then said, "Thank you and you can go now. I shall now develop and print the pictures and take them with me and I'll print one extra of each for you."

They thanked him and left.

"That was a little surprising, wasn't it?" Peter said. "I never thought he'd be the photographer and the picture developer as well."

"Yes," "Miriam relied, "it was a bit strange. Maybe that's his own hobby. I wonder how long before we get the IDs?

"I'd like to go into Netanya and I really need to buy some clothes. I've only got this one outfit, which I got from the Swiss when I left the country. My trouble is, I only have twenty pesetas left from the Alicante allocation. So, can I get a loan from you?" she asked, with a smile.

"Of course, my love, and please never ask me for a loan. I'll give you whatever you need. It will give me the greatest joy in the world to go to Netanya on a shopping spree with you. I want to buy and buy until you have everything you need, and want. I can't believe I never noticed that you had nothing to wear. I suppose that's what love does to you – you only see the person, not her clothes. We'll also get you a suitcase and buy two backpacks as well. This is going to be such fun. Actually, I've never before been out shopping with a girl, especially my girl."

"Are you sure that you can do this? I mean after buying an airplane and a ship it's a wonder you have any funds left. I certainly don't want to create undue pressure for you. If I'm with you, I can wear the same thing every day forever."

"Not at all, my love," Peter answered. "Actually, I will greatly enjoy shopping with you and please don't worry about money. At this point, I – we – have enough funds to start out life comfortably in Israel."

They then decided to walk around the kibbutz. A short while later, they came to the dairy area, which consisted of a large milking shed and a building where the milk was processed and the equipment cleaned. In the milking shed, they were greeted with a loud Australian welcome of "Hullo, cobbers, come to pay us a visit then, have you?" It was, of course, Jack. He took a few minutes from his work to explain to them the routine of his work and that of his fellow workers. Afterward, on hearing they had met Leah, he passed them on to where she worked. She, too, was very pleased to see them, and happy to explain her job.

Before they left the dairy, Leah told them where the children's houses were, and they found their way there and met Betty. She, too, was very happy to see them and explained to them the whole philosophy at that time of having separate places where the children grew up, although, to be sure, the children spent a certain amount of quality time with their parents each week. She explained how children grew up in a sort of fraternity and sorority where they made close, life-long friends all the way to university or other centers of higher education. They saw the children's sleeping rooms and the schoolrooms for the younger children and learned that often, a high school might exist in one kibbutz and children from nearby kibbutzim would attend.

They also learned that different kibbutz organizations in the country followed different political party lines. They expressed their surprise at so many options being available in such a small country, but then Miriam pointed out that even in the "old country" there was more than one organization of Jewish youth groups, based on the political parties in Palestine.

Within the kibbutz's close community, there was little people didn't know about each other, and everyone was curious about the "Hero," Peter. Rumors started to appear and there was a vast amount of gossip and conjecture until, finally, a couple of the members, exasperated by the repetition, asked Yossele to tell them Peter's story. Yossele told them the facts, which, within a few days, had circulated to every member of the kibbutz and aborted the gossiping and questioning that was going on.

During those days, Peter and Miriam were quite unaware of how Peter had become the focus of attention of the kibbutz members. Actually, both Peter and Miriam were busy with Yossele, who had given them their IDs, which said they had entered the country legally, in the very minimal legal British quota, called Aliyah Aleph. He also enrolled them in a Hebrew class at Kibbutz Ha'ogen, which they would go to at 2:00 p.m. every Tuesday and Thursday.

Yossele wanted them to meet a kibbutz member named Aron, who was a professor at Tel Aviv University in the Arts Department. He would be able to advise them on their doctoral work. However, he was away that week, so Peter and Miriam went to pay a social call on Aron's wife.

Ruth was from Romania. French and Romanian were her mother tongues, so the pair had no trouble communicating with her. She had already heard about Peter and Miriam through the circulating gossip, was happy to meet them, and would gladly pass on their message to Aron upon his return.

Now that they had received their IDs from Yossele, Miriam and Peter were free to go out of the kibbutz and not be afraid of being asked for identification. They decided to go out the next day and went over to Jack and Betty's house to inquire about transportation. They were told there was a bus that went into Netanya and passed the kibbutz entrance at various times during the day. Jack asked Peter if he had money for the bus fare and for shopping.

Peter replied, "Well Jack, no, and yes. No, I don't have bus fare but yes, I've traveler's checks, which I will exchange at the first bank I see. Until then, can you give us a little help?"

"Yes, of course," Jack responded. "I'll give you five Palestine pound notes, which are equal to five pounds sterling and a few coins. That will get you started till you get to a bank. I recommend Bank Hapoalim, which is the Workers Bank, since it was formed by the same political movement that the kibbutz belongs to."

"Thanks very much Jack, and for the information about the bus. We've decided to go into Netanya tomorrow morning to do some shopping. Miriam is busy making up a shopping list in her mind, as she can't find a pencil to write one." They all had a good laugh at that, which exploded when Betty went into the other room, returning with a pencil, which she offered to Miriam, "in case your mind gets full!"

CHAPTER XX

The Brothers and a Town in Palestine

AFTER JAMES COMPLETED FLYING FOR PETER, HE RECEIVED an extraordinary letter from his English solicitor. It read as follows:

Dear James,

I hope all is well with you and that you are enjoying life while you wait to start your BOAC training. I have some rather surprising news for you. It seems that your father died, leaving an estate, and you are a legatee under his will, the extent of which I do not know as yet.

I am enclosing with this letter a document which I have received and which you have to sign before a notary public. In it, you are to acknowledge that you will accept a sum of money, as yet unstated, from your late father's estate on the condition that you renounce all and any claims which you may have against him, or his estate, now and in the future. This is a document which is in accordance with British law. I know this is sudden and I'm sorry I don't have more particulars, but it's all I know.

"Kindly have it signed as I indicated above and return it to me in the enclosed envelope.

"Yours very sincerely, Ivor Constant."

James was more than a little surprised to read of this legacy and he did not quite know how to take it. On the one hand, it was gratifying to him that his father, who had financed and obviously planned the whole of James's upbringing and education, had continued to think of him as his son, by leaving him something in his will. On the other hand, it remained to be determined if this legacy was only a nominal amount, which might not even cover the cost of the notary, or something a bit more substantial. "Oh well," he said to himself, "time will tell."

He arranged, in the course of the next few days, to seek out a local notary public and duly carried out the signature requirements and sent it off to Mr. Constant, the solicitor.

He more or less put the whole thing on the back burner and stopped thinking about it, but a month later, he received another letter from his solicitor; this time it came by recorded delivery mail, which he knew was something of a departure from his somewhat frugal solicitor's regular style.

What he then read in the first sentence made him fall precipitately into his favorite chair.

Dear James,
Further to my last letter to you and receipt of your letter of renunciation, duly signed, I now have the greatest pleasure to inform you that the sum of 1,000,000 (one million) pounds has been placed in your bank account. This constitutes the entire legacy from your late father.
I know what a great shock this must be to you and, like you, I had no idea that such a sum as this was involved. When you have settled down, if you would like to discuss this matter with me, I shall, of course, be at your service, as always.
Yours very sincerely,
Ivor Constant

For some days James's head was in a whirl. He had no intimate friends, male or female, with whom to discuss this matter, his four closest friends from college and the Royal Air Force having all been killed in the Battle of Britain in 1940.

A few weeks after receiving Mr. Constant's letter, James came to the conclusion that since he was not inclined to become an investor, he should simply put the money into a savings account at his bank and use the interest income to supplement his earnings. His bank manager warned him that he would have to pay income tax on the interest, but he also advised him that saving interest at five percent and paying tax on it would likely bring him about 30,000 pounds net a year, a very useful addition to his earnings.

One day, with the start of his engagement with BOAC still a month off, he came to a new decision. He would use part of this money to pay a firm of private detectives to identify and locate his parents, whom he had not seen in his whole life. He had always had this emptiness in his soul, but he knew that now he was in a position to use the legacy to try and find his antecedents.

He located a leading private detective firm and was happy to sign a contract to cover daily fees and out-of-pocket expenses of an operative, plus a substantial advance-payment to the company. There was also a final bonus if they were able to find his parents within an agreed-upon time.

Five weeks later he received a report from the company. Their man had started in Edinburgh, had quickly located his birth certificate, and had found the mother's name, she having registered the birth of the baby boy in 1916 in the name of James Roman. The mother's name was given as Lady Margaret Spencer, and her address as Westland Manor, Hampshire. The father's name was given as Richard Roman, and his address as Muddyford, Kent. James was informed that Lady Margaret Spencer, daughter of the Earl of Hampstead, had been killed, together with her friend, Lady Pamela White, in a motor car accident in Wiltshire, two years previously.

A week later the next report showed inquiries in Muddyford for Richard Roman were unsuccessful, but the parish register showed the birth of Richard Romaine. This name was close enough to Roman to follow up and the investigator found a diplomat of that name whose last posting was as ambassador to Switzerland. Inquiries by the agent found that Richard Romaine had lived near Berne, the capital, and that he had died one year ago, leaving a widow and a son named Peter.

The agent found that the widow, a Dr. Romaine, still lived there, and he called upon her. She received him graciously. He informed her that, acting for an unnamed client, he was seeking Peter's address so that his client could contact him. Dr. Romaine was intrigued and, after verifying the agent's credentials, told him that her son was living abroad. She refused to give the agent his address without her son's permission. She was willing to send a telegram to her son, asking for such permission.

The agent agreed to stay in the village to await the response, at a local, modest inn. Dr. Romaine had received a telegram from her son only a few days previous and so knew to send her telegram to Kibbutz Ma'barot.

When he received the cryptic telegram, Peter was intrigued by the request to give a private detective his address. He couldn't envision any reason not to agree, so he prevailed upon Yossele, the kibbutz secretary, to phone a telegram again to his mother, giving her permission to give his address to this agent. In his own mind, he was sure this request had something to do with either the boat or plane he had bought, either one of the lawyers he had encountered, or one of the agents.

Dr. Romaine received Peter's telegram, and gave the detective her son's address, although she felt uncomfortable not knowing his client's name. Back at the inn, he updated his supervisor and inquired whether he should go to Palestine.

Permission was withheld, and he was told to return to London. The supervisor then phoned James and told him the news and the address. Of course, as soon as he had heard the name Richard Romaine, he knew Peter must be his brother. He recalled Peter telling him he had been born in Switzerland.

Peter called up Ivor Constant and asked him to help him arrange for travel to Palestine. Constant told him he had made sure that his UK passport would be valid for entry into Palestine and he would be given a one-month visa stamp on arrival, with an option of further extension.

Next, James called BOAC and told them he had to leave the country suddenly on urgent family business and requested a stay on the training program. He was given a three-months' extension.

He flew to Cyprus two days later. On arrival at Nicosia, the capital, he waited three days and then was able to board a flight to Palestine.

On arrival at Lydda, the airport of Palestine, he was asked by a stern-faced British army officer his business in Palestine. He offered his pilot's log book and his discharge certificate from the RAF showing his rank as Group Captain, three levels of grade above that of the captain interviewing him. He was immediately shown great deference; someone was designated to help him with his modest luggage and procure a taxi. He was driven into Tel Aviv and found an unpretentious hotel close by the sea front, on Hayarkon Street.

At the hotel, the manager told him that Kibbutz Ma'barot was just up the Haifa Road and could be reached easily by taxi.

A taxi driver found the kibbutz without problem. James asked him to wait until he finished the business at hand. The driver found someone who could speak English and who agreed to take James to Peter's room.

James knocked on the door. After a few moments, Peter opened the door. Seeing his visitor, he roared "Good God, it's Jim, my pilot! Come on in, man. Miriam, we have a visitor."

"Not only your pilot," James smiled, "but I believe your half-brother, too!"

Peter was taken aback, and Miriam, who just walked into the room saw them frozen in a handshake, as though time had stopped. Jim turned to Miriam to shake her hand and then turned back to Peter.

"I don't understand?" Miriam said, trying to catch Peter's eye. But Peter was still dumbstruck.

Quietly, Jim asked Peter, "Was your father Richard Romaine?"

Peter replied, "Yes, he was."

"Well, Peter, he was my father, too."

"Jim, how do you know?"

Jim explained how he found his half-brother.

Peter said, shamefacedly, "I must now tell you, Jim, that for a while, I have actually believed you *were* my half-brother."

"What?" Jim said to Peter. "Why would you think so?"

Peter would have liked to tell Jim how he knew, in his own time, but that was not to be. He was glad to be able to assuage his conscience and proceeded to tell Jim what he had been told by his solicitor, and how he realized that the similarities were not coincidence. Indeed, by the time they were flying around Greece, Peter had been certain that the pilot Jim was also James, his half-brother. Why he didn't reveal himself was a complicated story, but at the time, he felt it would be better to finish the project at hand before moving forward with his personal life.

There was silence for a little while in that tiny room as everyone soaked in the experience of discovery. Jim couldn't help but feel a sense of betrayal at the way Peter had handled the situation. Peter, for his part, felt waves of guilt and pity for his brother, realizing that he should have trusted Jim, especially once he knew him.

It was Miriam who broke the silence. She went to Jim, gave him a long hard hug and kissed him repeatedly on his cheek, her eyes streaming with tears. She understood how embarrassed Peter was and how angry Jim must feel.

She said to Jim, with her arms around him still, "We all make mistakes, Jim. Mistakes of judgment are perhaps the hardest mistakes to correct. It's true, even heroes have feet of clay, but I know of twenty-eight men and women who Peter raised from the absolute depths of hell and despair, sick and weak and lost creatures that we were, to bring us back to life and health and hope. That is the side of Peter that you may know little about, but it is a side most men sorely lack."

Jim's anger melted away as he held out his hand to Peter. Peter seized it and they both hugged, patting each other on the back. Tears flowed freely as Jim announced: "It's all over, brother, it's all over."

Soon afterward, James, Peter, and Miriam left the visitors' room and went to James's waiting taxi driver, where Peter paid him off, arranging for him to return at 9:00 p.m. to take James back to Tel Aviv.

They then went to relax and talk at the kibbutz pool. Miriam filled in the blanks for James, recounting all their adventures and Peter's role in them. At the end, she asked James if, in the light of everything he had done, James was better able to see the real Peter, and forgive him completely.

"Yes, of course!" James said. He clapped Peter on the back and told him that what he had just heard made him proud indeed to be Peter's brother.

James was very interested in the kibbutz. Peter arranged for him to return the next day to see the kibbutz and escorted his brother to his taxi.

The pair returned to their room and discussed the entire episode for hours, until they both fell asleep.

James arrived at their room at 11:00 a.m. the following day, with a large bunch of flowers for Miriam, "For," as he said, "creating peace between the brothers." She was overcome with emotion, having never received flowers but only given them, once, to Peter at Camp Pietro.

The three spent the day touring the kibbutz, and Peter and Miriam introduced their new-found relative to the friends they had only recently made.

Before leaving, James told Peter that he had been astonished to receive a very substantial legacy from their father and Peter told him quietly that he was aware of it, and was very happy for him. James said he had tucked it away in a bank deposit account and it was there as a kind of security blanket for him, perhaps to buy a home for himself at some later time, when he might decide to settle down. Peter didn't volunteer any information about how their father had remembered him in his will. Nor did James ask.

"Well, I'm off now," James told the pair. "I've got to get back to England. I've got a job waiting for me."

"Please keep in touch," both Peter and Miriam said, together. "Yes," Peter continued, "I don't want to spend the next half of my life without a brother."

"Nor I," James said. "I'm sure our paths will cross again, very soon."

The next day, after breakfast, they walked through the kibbutz to the entrance. On the way, Miriam said, "This beautiful place is helping to complete the healing process which you started when you first visited me. I feel like I'm in the Garden of Eden."

"Perhaps we'll make this our home," Peter said. "But right now," he added, perking up, "we've got some shopping to do. Let's catch the eleven o'clock bus to Netanya, and develop a more mundane part of our lives."

They made their way to the entrance to the kibbutz and after some minutes, an *Egged* bus arrived and took them on a ten-minute ride to the center of Netanya.

Alighting from the bus, Peter and Miriam saw that they were on a wide street with shops on both sides. Peter's immediate need was for a bank. After walking three blocks, Peter saw a Bank Hapoalim and they went in. Accustomed to the tranquility and quiet of banks in Berne, in particular, and even in Salonika, Peter was astonished at the high noise level and animated activity of the customers inside the bank, almost all of whom seemed to be in motion, going from one bank teller to the next.

He saw that over each teller's place hung a card with something printed on it. The signs were in Hebrew, but he saw that each was different than the others. Which one was a cashier? he wondered. They both observed the activities going on at the various locations. Most of the tellers rubber-stamped the papers they were given and then their customers would move to another line, where, once again, their papers were stamped. Eventually, the majority of customers found their way to the teller on the extreme right, who would take their papers, stamp some and return some, and then count out money and give it to the customers.

They had tracked down the cashier! Peter joined a small queue in front of the cashier and after some minutes arrived at the grill protecting the man behind it.

"Do you speak English?" Peter asked.

The man shook his head. Peter then ran through a few of his languages and when he got to German, the man answered, "Of course, my friend, doesn't everybody?"

Peter smiled and then asked if he could cash some traveler's checks into Palestine pounds.

The cashier asked peter a series of questions:

"Do you have an account with the bank?"

"No."

"Do you have your passport?"

"Yes." Peter presented it to him.

"Do you live in Palestine?"

"Yes."

"Are you a legal immigrant?"

"Yes." Peter presented his ID.

"Please give me your traveler's checks," the cashier ordered. "Wait until I return."

Closing his window, to the consternation of the dozens of people on line in front of him, the cashier sauntered over to the bank manager's office with all of Peter's papers. Emerging a few minutes later, empty-handed, he told Peter to go into the manager's office.

Peter and Miriam entered the manager's room. This was a totally different scene. It was a sparsely-furnished, but tidy and quiet office with a well-dressed (suit and tie) man in his late thirties seated behind his desk. On seeing Peter and Miriam, he rose, offered his hand to Peter, and said, in impeccable English, "Good morning, Mr. Romaine, my name is Francois Leclerc and I'm the manager here. How can I help you?"

"Good morning, Mr. Leclerc. I'm pleased to meet you, and this is my fiancée, Miriam Polanski."

Miriam held out her hand with a smile to Francois, who shook it, saying, "I'm pleased to meet you, too, Miss Polanski."

Peter started by saying, "I see you have all my documents in front of you, Mr. Leclerc. I need to have some Palestinian currency to do some shopping, as we are new to the country."

"Your ID shows you came into the country only ten days ago," the bank manager observed. "Where are you currently residing?"

"We are volunteers at Kibbutz Ma'barot," Peter explained, "which is where we are living at present. A member of the kibbutz recommended your bank to us. If I may say so, Mr. Leclerc, neither your name nor your fluency with the English language seems to be typically Palestinian."

Francois gave a chuckle. "That's a fair comment. Well, as you may have guessed, I'm of French birth, and Jewish. I studied Economics before the war, in Paris, and then did my Doctorate in Finance at University College, London. That is where I learned the bulk of my English. Of course, having an English wife helped, as well. During the war, my parents were killed in France and since we had few other relations, last year my wife and I decided to make the move to Palestine. I served in the British Forces during the war. We had some small difficulties in entering this country, but who doesn't? Then I learned Hebrew, joined this bank, and voila!" he added, with a flourish.

"Now to business," Francois said. "I see you have some ten thousand pounds sterling in travelers checks issued in Switzerland, so please tell me what you want to do."

"I want to change two thousand pounds into Palestine currency and I would like to put the rest into a safe-deposit box, if you have one in this branch."

"Yes, we certainly do, Mr. Romaine, and I will be pleased to do that for you."

Peter went on to say, "I've here a letter from my banker in Switzerland attesting to my bona fides and worth. I would like you to make a copy for your file, so that you may know a bit more about me and can give a banker's reference for me in the future, should I need to have one."

So saying, he brought out the letter from Etoile Lambert, his Berne banker, which had established his credit-worthiness in Salonika. Francois opened it up and as he read it, his eyebrows rose, as had those of Yanis in Salonika.

After making a copy and handing back the original to Peter, Francois said, "Very well, Mr. Romaine, that seems to be in order, and now I'll get that safe-deposit box organized for you. Do you also want a checking account opened for you, while you are here?"

Peter replied, "I really don't know. In order to shop in Netanya, do you advise me pay in cash or by check?"

Francois said, "I would suggest you put, say, fifteen hundred pounds into a Palestine pounds checking account and keep five hundred pounds in cash, rather than to have two thousand pounds in cash on you. You could use checks for your shopping so that you will have a record in your bank account of what you are spending."

"Good advice, Francois. I'll do just that. Put 8,000 pounds sterling in traveler's checks into the safe-deposit box, 1,500 Palestinian pounds into a checking account, and 500 pounds into Palestine cash. By the way, I want Miriam here to be able to sign alone on my checking account."

"Very well, Mr. Romaine, I'll start the forms, and Miss Polanski, please let me have your ID and passport so that I can fill in your forms, too, as they are all in Hebrew, I'm afraid."

In ten minutes, Francois had prepared all the forms and presented them to Peter and Miriam for signature.

"Oh, I forgot something else, Francois, I would like Miriam to also have single signing authority on the bank safe-deposit box form."

"No problem, Mr. Romaine. Just add Miss Polanski's signature on this card and we are done. Here is your bank safe-deposit box key. Do you want a spare?"

"Yes, please," said Peter, "and please put the Palestine cash into two envelopes – 400 pounds in one and 100 pounds in the other.

"Also, Francois, perhaps you could tell us of some good shops in Netanya, for men's and women's clothing?"

"Certainly," he answered, and gave them directions.

They left Francois's office, happy with their choice of banks.

They found the shops recommended by Francois and, despite feeling uncomfortable using his resources on herself, Miriam bought what she needed.

While Miriam was dealing with her needs, Peter found a store that sold travel items. He bought one medium-sized and one large suitcase, and two backpacks, one medium-sized and one larger. After Miriam completed her purchases, they put everything into the smaller suitcase, then put that and the backpacks into the large suitcase. Peter paid the bill by check and saw that the shop manager phoned his bank, discreetly, to verify his check and came away from the phone smiling, having apparently been well satisfied with the confirmation.

Walking further along the street, they found clothes for Peter, and shoes and sandals for both of them. By this time they had filled both suitcases and returned to the bank.

Peter knocked on Francois's door, received a word in Hebrew, which he assumed (correctly) meant "enter," and went in. Francois greeted him warmly, smiled at the picture of Peter carrying the two cases, and invited him in.

"Everything is in order. I left orders with my subordinates to verify any purchases you may make. And by the looks of things, you're off to a good start."

"Thanks," Peter said, "I appreciate your swift and efficient service."

Like so many Israelis, Francois was anxious to give the couple his interpretation of the current political situation.

"I've been reading about those poor devils in the Cyprus detention camps, caught by the Royal Navy trying to cross the Mediterranean Sea," he lamented. "They're going to have to be released sooner or later. Palestine is like a cauldron slowly coming to the boil. Thank God there's a trained generation of people like myself, thousands of boys and girls who served as soldiers in the British Army or its allies in the war, plus the Haganah in training. Perhaps I've said too much, but even as new arrivals, you'll hear about these things in due course.

"Now," he went on, "it's just one o'clock. If you're finished your shopping, I suppose you want a bus or a taxi to take you back to the kibbutz. If you like I can phone for a taxi for you."

"A taxi is fine," Peter said.

CHAPTER XXI

Advice from Professor Weiss

ON RETURN TO THE KIBBUTZ, THEY UNPACKED THEIR PUR-
chases and went for a swim in the pool. On the way back, they met
Ruth and Aron, who were together. Ruth introduced Peter and Miriam to her husband, who had just returned from Jerusalem after
teaching there for a week. The two couples sat down on a grassy
knoll together. Peter said, "I'm in languages, Aron. Can you give me
some information about what you do at the University?"

"I specialize in the three levels of Ancient Egyptian and in the
east and northwest Semitic dialects of Akkadian, Old Akkadian, and
in Elamite, a connected language. These dialects include Old and
Middle Assyrian, Old and Middle Babylonian, and Neo-Assyrian.
But, I apologize about running on with my own stuff, as I want to
hear what *you* do and *want* to do, here in Palestine."

Peter replied, "Well I've French, German, Swiss-German, Ruma-
nian, Catalan, Italian, Romansh, and Spanish, and I need to pick up
Portuguese, Ladin, Friulian, Galician, and Provencal in order to have
all the principal languages of the western Italic branch, but I haven't
had time for the last ones yet. My long-term plan is to study the phonological topology of that group for my PhD. I studied the typography and ethnology of the group for my MA."

Aron replied, "Well, Peter, Tel Aviv and Jerusalem each have a university which, in turn, have extraordinary and broadly encompass-
ing departments of language studies. It would seem to me, with the
little knowledge I've of *your* field that you have the bedrock knowledge you need to start your doctoral studies."

"I hope so," replied Peter, "I already started my studies in that direction, at the University of Berne, in Switzerland. I worked on it
for six months before I left to embark on travels, which have so far

taken me to Palestine. It seems to me that I'm going to be here for some time, so I want to continue my doctoral work. I expect to have to carry out some teaching responsibilities in exchange for doing my research under the aegis of some university department. Oh, yes, I know, too, I shall have to learn Hebrew to live comfortably in this country, as will Miriam. Yossele has made arrangements for us to do that. I expect, too, that Miriam and I will have to do some teaching in return for living in Ma'barot."

"So," said Aron thoughtfully, "I'm fairly sure I know who to talk to at TAU (Tel Aviv University) about you."

"There's more," said Peter. "Miriam also started to work toward her PhD in Linguistics, oddly enough, back in Gdynia. But that was interrupted by four years in a concentration camp and one year making her way here. Do you foresee any problems for Miriam resuming her studies?"

"Absolutely not," said Aron. "In Palestine many have had their educational lives interrupted by the Nazis and we make it as comfortable as possible for each of them to pick up the threads again. And, what is your area of specialization, Miriam?"

"My intended area is to be Linguistic Anthropology, Aron, but I've this fear that so much time has passed since I was studying in Gdynia that I might not make it back to the academic world again."

"Have no fear, Miriam," he said. "We'll give you every help and encouragement to get back to it. I assume you received your MA?"

"Yes, I did," she replied, "under a false name, in the Polish language as well as the Slavic group, plus French and German."

Aron smiled at Peter and Miriam, saying, "I can see I've a most outstanding couple of young people here. I shall have much pleasure in bringing you along to meet the Dean of Students, who also happens to be the Distinguished Professor of Central African Languages. I'll make the appointment, giving you a few days' notice, and take you in with me one morning to the university. How does that sound?"

They both replied, "Wonderful, Aron, and thank you so much."

After dinner, Peter and Miriam walked along the road outside Ma'barot to the neighboring kibbutz, Ha'ogen, having picked up Jack and Betty. Peter told them they wanted to go over there and find out the details of the Hebrew instruction class for which Yossele had signed them up, and Jack and Betty had acquiesced at once. They all walked in, found the Kibbutz Institute, where meetings and classes were generally held, and met the Secretary of Ha'ogen, named Elijah, who was in the hall. Jack quickly explained in Hebrew who they were, where they were from, and introduced Peter and Miriam as the new arrivals, looking to learn Hebrew at Ha'ogen.

Elijah confirmed the classes were held in that Institute on Tuesdays and Thursdays at 7:00 p.m. for three or four hours each night, and a new series was to start in two weeks' time, for beginners. He also asked the newcomers if they knew any other languages than their mother-tongues. Peter admitted to eight and Miriam to four.

Elijah was duly impressed with those numbers and explained that people who have learned additional languages after their mother-tongue, usually had fewer problems than other people in learning Hebrew as adults, Hebrew being considered a difficult language to learn. He, himself, had been born in Palestine when it was held by the Ottoman Empire, so his mother-tongue was Hebrew, but he had learned Turkish and German in school.

Peter was most interested in hearing more about this, and speaking in German, he told Elijah the next languages he wanted to pick up were five Italic languages, but that he had always had a yen to learn Turkish, Persian, Aramaic, and Arabic.

"Perhaps Palestine will be a good place to learn from native speakers of those languages, after I've mastered Hebrew," Peter said.

"You talk about acquiring languages like other people talk about acquiring books, and seem to be able to go about it with almost equal ease," Elijah told Peter.

Neither Jack nor Betty knew German, so Jack asked Elijah in Hebrew what they were talking about and Elijah told him. The four walked back to Ma'barot and Jack asked Peter if he really had such a facility with languages. Without embarrassment, Peter confirmed it.

When Jack found out that Peter knew so many languages, he said, "You must be a genius to have learned all those tongues and talk of learning more, some of which I never heard of."

"No, not at all, Jack," said Peter. "But if you want to hear of a person who was really unusual in his ability to pick up languages, I'll tell you of one. When I was a post-grad in Berne, my own instructor told me of a professor at the Hebrew University of Jerusalem who was reputed to have acquired forty languages. His innate ability can best be understood by noting that he would go to a jungle country in Africa, live there for six or eight weeks – *weeks*, mind you – master their language, record, and make the first ever dictionary of the language. Now, that is what I would call genius level in the art or science of tongues."

By the time that the genius denial was fully expressed, they were back at Ma'barot and parted to go to their individual homes.

Two days later, Aron told them that he had made an appointment with the Dean of Students of the Arts Faculty of Tel Aviv University for the next day, at 9:00 a.m.

They were both excited at the prospect and Aron arranged to pick them up in a kibbutz-owned car at the kibbutz gate at 8:30 a.m. He also explained a small matter of kibbutz economics. The salary he earned at the university was paid entirely to the kibbutz. The kibbutz, on the other hand, was responsible for all his living expenses and, in addition, he received, as all kibbutz members did, a small weekly cash allowance, like pocket money. The kibbutz would also refund any expenses he was called upon to pay when earning his salary. Finally, as a kibbutz member working outside, he was allowed the use of a kibbutz-owned car.

The next day, Aron picked them up and brought them to TAU.

He led them directly to the Administration Building and to the office of the Dean of Students. He knocked, and led them in.

The Dean of Students was a clean-cut, bronzed, short-haired man of about forty-five years, who, in his shirt-sleeves (like most of the male members of the faculty), looked more like a professional wrestler, with his exposed huge biceps, than a senior professor in his specialty and the Dean of Students, a very high position.

He came from behind his desk to greet Aron and to be introduced to Miriam and Peter. Peter felt his hand crushed by the handshake of the dean. However, he resisted the instinct to wince and even managed something of a smile as he said, "I'm honored to meet you, Dean," in English.

Miriam, seeing this little occurrence, kept her hands behind her as she inclined her head graciously and, with a smile, said, "How nice to meet you, sir," in German.

The dean, seeing her reluctance to shake his hand, assumed she was Orthodox and would therefore not shake hands with a man not of her family. He offered comfortable chairs to all his visitors to sit around a table placed away from his desk.

"Well, Mr. Romaine and Miss Polanski, how can I help you? All I know from my friend, Professor Weiss, is that you two young people are newly arrived in Palestine, currently residing as volunteers in Kibbutz Ma'barot, and that I must see you. I know nothing of your backgrounds and having just met you both for the first time, all I can say about you is that despite your French name, you are clearly English with what I believe is a Swiss accent, and you, Miriam, despite your German, are Polish. Now, how accurate am I?"

"Since you know so much about Miriam and me already, sir, is there anything left to tell you?" Peter said, smiling.

"I'm sure there's a lot more about both of you," Dr. Katz answered, "so will you kindly tell me all about yourself – origin, educational achievements to date, how you came to be in Palestine and what you want of us here in TAU."

Peter told him how and when his forebears came to England and why he came to be born in Switzerland.

"Aha," said Dr. Katz, "that's the bit behind your otherwise perfect English accent; it's the French or Swiss-German influence from the schools you went to."

Peter also reviewed his desire to expand upon the eight languages he'd already acquired. He explained that he'd received his MA in ethnography and ethnology and that his doctoral work was to be a study of the phonological topology of the Romance group and that he had already done about six months' work so far toward it at Berne University.

Dr. Katz sat quietly for about two minutes while he reviewed and absorbed what he had just heard from Peter. Then, he cleared his throat and spoke very quietly:

"You remind me of myself at your age. I assume you're about twenty-five?"

"Exactly, sir," said Peter.

"Well, at the same age as you are now, I had also started to acquire various languages. Firstly, the European common ones, then my interests went to the Nilo-Saharan group of Central Africa, where I spent several years living among the tribes and studying the three groups of that family, Songhai, Saharan, and Chari-Nile. There are about 100 languages in that family, but I learned less than half of them.

"Then I came back here to teach them and research among them. Then, after that, they made me Dean of Students and I could stop being the world's greatest expert on a bunch of languages that few people were interested in. In my job as dean, I could influence incoming students never to go to Central Africa to waste years learning languages that very few are interested in."

He said the last sentence with a sort of twinkle in his eye and Peter could not be sure if he was laughing at himself.

"However, Peter, in your case, it is entirely different. I don't think you'll find it hard to find a tenured professor here in the European Modern Language Department to take you under his wing, and I'll speak to one or two to see how it goes and then I'll let you know via Professor Weiss. If you are accepted, you will have to do some teaching, but that will be arranged between you and your professor, and will take into account your other obligations.

"Now, to Miss Polanski. You have been sitting there quietly while Peter and I have had this long interview and I want to know how we might be of help to you, too."

She told the story of her life starting in Gdynia, and ended with having met Peter, all he did for her and the others in her group, and their lives together in Palestine.

Dr. Katz was quiet for minutes while he considered what he had just heard.

"Firstly," he said, "I see there's a lot more to Peter Romaine than just a man interested in linguistics. You're a man of action, Peter," he said looking at him. "A man who sets himself a difficult task and then fights it through to its successful completion.

"And you, Miriam," he turned to her. "Thank you for filling me in about your fiancé. I dare say you spent some time in concentration camp as well."

She nodded.

"I will be happy to recommend you to a professor in the Linguistics Department, and again, I will communicate with you via Professor Weiss.

"You can both expect to come for an interview in the next few days to your respective professors. I will try to get them on the same day at the same time.

"Aron, I want to thank you for bringing me two such outstanding applicants for doctoral studies. I'm far from prescient, but I think both these lovely young people have a wonderful future ahead of them. We'll do all we can to make sure that future includes TAU and this country."

They left the dean and, since they were in Tel Aviv, Aron suggested the two of them take a short tour. They found a taxi driver, Ebi, who spoke German and agreed to give them "the grand tour."

After discussing the price, the taxi took off. It turned out that Ebi had been a lawyer in Berlin until 1933, when Hitler came to power. He came to Palestine with his wife a year later. Because of his lack of fluency in Hebrew, he found it impossible to practice as a lawyer, but he had enough capital to buy a taxi, so that is what he had been doing to earn a living ever since. During the war years, he said, he had been fairly busy, with the influx of British troops on leave in Palestine for rest and rehabilitation. However, since the end of the war, a lot of British, Australian, and South African soldiers had gone home for demobilization, and things were very bleak economically for him in Palestine.

Ebi further told them that while he would love to take them to Jaffa, just a couple of miles south of Tel Aviv, there had been a lot of trouble there recently between the mixed populations of Jews and Arabs.

"There's all sorts of fighting going on; knifing, shooting, even kidnapping. Both parties want the country for themselves and the police and the army are trying to keep the peace."

"But what about the police and the British Army? Can't they keep it quiet?"

"No, the Palestine police are much more like soldiers or military police than civil police. They're here for adventure and a chance to knock about some Middle Eastern 'wogs' as they call us all. Their definition of a 'wog' is a 'westernized oriental gentleman.' So, we all have to be somewhat circumspect in dealing with them. When you're asked for identity papers, you must be outstandingly polite, not ask any questions, and remain silent unless you are asked a question. In effect, we're actually under an unwritten situation of martial law.

"There is, in fact, an appointed civilian Palestine government, which is located in Jerusalem, the head of which is appointed by London's Colonial Secretary, who works through the Palestine government's Chief Secretary and the Executive Council. He runs Palestine like he would an unruly English colony."

"What's the name of the head of this government?" Peter asked.

"He's called 'The High Commissioner' and his name is Sir Alan Cunningham. He was a British general and he's the seventh High Commissioner since the English created the title for Palestine in 1922, when the League of Nations approved the Mandate."

They continued their tour until it was time to return to the kibbutz. As requested, Ebi gave Peter a piece of paper with his name and number on it. Peter and Miriam both shook hands with Ebi and he drove off.

They went to their room and found an envelope on their bed. Inside was a note from Yossele telling them that the local committee of kibbutz secretaries had decided they should both teach two language classes. Miriam on Monday nights would teach Russian and

German, and Peter on Wednesdays, Spanish and Italian. They would both teach from 7:00 p.m. to 9:00 p.m. Those nights were selected to allow them both to join in the Hebrew classes at Kibbutz Haʾogen on Tuesdays and Thursdays. The note from Yossele went on to say that they were therefore free on Friday, Saturday, and Sunday nights to do their Hebrew homework, obviously meant as a humorous aside.

After reading the note, Peter and Miriam looked at each other and burst into hysterical laughter at the huge work loads being placed on them. Peter pointed out that their technical doctoral research work could be done during the day in the library at TAU, as they referred to Tel Aviv University, and as long as they could find text books in the languages to be taught, they could base their lessons on them. They felt certain there would be no problem getting textbooks for Hebrew studies.

That left them with the need to find textbooks for their doctoral work in Phonology and Topology for Peter, and Ethnography and Ethnology for Miriam.

"Let's not forget," Miriam reminded Peter, "that as doctoral students, we'll be required to do some university teaching as well, at least to the incoming undergraduates."

"Oh, my God, you're absolutely right," Peter realized. "But I remember the dean saying that our professors might have pity on us knowing we have a full load at the kibbutz, so we can pay our way."

"Yes, of course," Miriam said. "I don't suppose we're the first doctoral students who have to study and also have outside commitments. Looks like we'll have to wait and see how all these situations turn out and accommodate ourselves accordingly."

"Agreed," said Peter. "By the way, dear," he continued, "did you realize who we were talking to today at the university? Do you remember I was telling Jack as we walked back to Maʾbarot from Haʾogen about a story I heard in Berne from my professor?"

"About the professor who knew forty languages?" Miriam said.

"Well," he said, "we can now tell our children, when we have them, that we actually met that genius?!"

"I can't believe it," she replied. "A man with his knowledge and experience should be 100 years old. He looks comparatively young."

"It's probably all that time he spent in Africa," Peter joked. "They say those tribes have discovered the secret of youth."

Miriam touched her face. "Maybe we should plan on spending a few months there as well."

Peter held her face in his hands.

"Save your money. You'll never look old to me," he said and kissed her.

During the course of the next month, Peter and Miriam found their days and nights growing very busy. The process of learning Hebrew, for both of them, was anything but slow and steady. Within weeks, they were speaking Hebrew to each other and encouraging each other to write and read.

Within three months they were able to carry on conversations, and each had acquired a good working grammar and at least two thousand words of vocabulary. Their Hebrew teachers were exceedingly impressed, but when they learned that Peter and Miriam were linguists themselves, they understood how it was they had made such progress.

Meanwhile, Miriam had managed to borrow textbooks from the library at TAU in Russian and German, as Peter had in Spanish and Italian. They both found enthusiastic kibbutz groups to teach. They employed the system being used in their Hebrew class, which was to teach the language in that language, and they found their own groups responded well, as the students discovered they could start to use the new languages in their spoken form right away.

Both of them received invitations from Dr. Katz to visit him and to meet the two professors he had suggested to be their faculty advisors. When they met their professors, Peter and Miriam quickly realized that these were top researchers in their fields. Each professor was equally enthusiastic about working with their student.

Fortunately, both professors agreed not to add to the couple's work load for at least six months, to give them time to fully adjust to Hebrew and the kibbutz.

During the month of October 1946, Peter and Miriam were approached by a member of the kibbutz named Moshe, who told them of the existence of a Jewish underground military organization in Palestine, called the Haganah, that was being developed and trained surreptitiously, under the noses of the British occupying authority. It was created so that this army could defend the Jewish towns and villages against incursions and raids by the Arab population.

The Haganah came into being in 1920 and started to procure light arms and ammunition to train its members for defense. During the Second World War, when the German Army stood at the gates of Egypt at El Alamein, a formation of the Haganah was linked with the British military authorities and was given commando training by British officers, including Captain Charles Orde Wingate, of great fame. This unit, in association with the British Army, attempted to take Lebanon from the occupying Vichy French forces. It was during this episode, in 1941, that Moshe Dayan, who would go on to be Israel's Army Chief of Staff, Defense Minister, and Foreign Minister, lost an eye.

Peter and Miriam were invited to join. They agreed and undertook military training. In addition, Miriam was trained to run a field First Aid Unit. Occasionally, they took part in demonstrations against the British government's policy of restricting Jewish immigration to Palestine, and clashed with the Palestine Police and British Army. They soon discovered that most men in Ma'barot were members of the Haganah.

One Saturday morning they were delighted by a visit from Dov, their old friend from Camp Pietro. He arrived on a motorbike and told them he had obtained all the addresses of their group from Aliyah Bet headquarters and was traveling around the country to see how everybody was doing. He explained that Peter and Miriam were his last call, and he was ready to tell them all the news. Everyone he had visited wanted to know how and what Peter and Miriam were doing.

As for the group itself: Helen and Alex were married and had become members of an Orthodox Zionist Kibbutz. Helen had become pregnant a few months later. Max had given up on Judaism as a result of his experiences in concentration camp and had become an agnostic. He was engaged to Heide, and both were happy and farming in a Baptist Village in Palestine.

He also brought news of Peter's ship, which Captain Olaf had stored in Turkey at Iskenderun. Captain Olaf had sent a letter for Peter saying he had chosen Iskenderun to store Peter's ship, as that city was founded to commemorate the victory of Alexander the Great of Greece over Darius III of Persia, and to celebrate *their* victory over the Royal Navy. Olaf had notified Peter's attorney in Berne and had sent him the title documents of the ship.

Dov told them that a "get-together" had been proposed by many of the group. They wanted Peter to organize it at Ma'barot.

"I'm also most impressed with your joint knowledge of Hebrew. Do you know, we have been talking in that language ever since I got here?"

They both smiled. Of course, they knew.

Peter asked Dov what was happening with Aliyah Bet and were they "keeping busy?" Dov told him that, unfortunately, most of the illegal ships had been captured and this year, only two had managed to land in Palestine unscathed.

Peter then asked Dov whether AB could now make use of the *Helen*. After thinking a bit, Dov replied that he wasn't sure, since the *Helen* was such a small vessel and AB had been buying larger ships lately, to carry larger numbers; he would ask his chiefs at headquarters.

"Please ask the Aliyah Bet people if they can make use of the *Helen*, Peter said. "If they can, it's theirs."

Peter and Miriam took Dov over to Yossele.

When Dov and Yossele met, they first stared at one another then they both exclaimed, "Dov!" and "Joe!" at the same time. It turned out that Dov knew Yossele by the name of "Joe" when they were both in the Jewish Brigade of the British Army. Seeing that here were two old friends who wanted to talk together, Miriam suggested to Peter that they should leave and let them have some privacy.

CHAPTER XXII

Peter Makes an Important Decision

KIBBUTZ MA'BAROT BELONGED TO AN ASSOCIATION OF KIB-butzim that was totally secular and even anti-religious. However, Peter and Miriam had noticed that a number of the members continued to maintain some of their old ties to religion. This was indicated by the fact that some lit two candles in their homes on Friday nights and that a few met together on Saturday mornings in one home or another for a short religious service. Most of the men who attended those short services even wore a kippah, or skullcap.

The traditions and observances that bound people to their parents and grandparents was of intense interest to Peter, as well as to Miriam, who was familiar with the Jewish customs that she had seen in her home as a child.

When, on a couple of occasions, Peter had asked why a certain tradition was observed, most people had no idea, but insisted, "I want to keep the chain of Judaism unbroken, after all that has happened to us these past years." When pressed further, the usual response was, "Living in Palestine can't be like living in any other country. We have a culture that goes back thousands of years. We need to keep in touch with that culture if we want to have our own, special country."

These occasional discussions, together with what Peter had learned from time to time in Camp Pietro and from both Helen and Miriam, had sparked his interest about Judaism, very much as when he had first heard about Zionism in the hospital ward in Berne. Like any good intellectual whose curiosity was aroused, Peter began to read up on these subjects of interest.

He asked himself, "what is it in the background of these individual people which is so powerful that it causes them to carry on these customs so far from their roots, and in such notably different surroundings?"

He decided that, despite his heavy workload, he should do some research on this subject. He discussed it with Miriam, who very simply said, "Next time we go into Tel Aviv, we'll go to Steimatzky's bookshop and between us, we'll find the right books for you."

And that's exactly what they did. They found time to visit a number of small book stores as well, and purchased Jewish interest titles in German, English, French, and Hebrew. Gradually, as he continued to study, he developed an understanding and appreciation of how, historically, the Jewish People had clung to their beliefs despite the merciless brutality they suffered in country after country, by nation after nation. He learned about the Jewish experience in Egypt, Greece and Rome, and the Papacy-authorized Inquisition of Torquemada in Spain and Portugal. He read of pogroms and ghettos and the wandering Jews who managed to survive, even excel, in their adopted countries.

He was amazed to find that Miriam knew much of what he was learning and was even able to answer some of his many questions.

"I don't understand," he said, "how you're able to share your life with me, a Gentile, knowing what the Gentiles have done to your people?"

"My love," she answered him, "a Jew learns to differentiate between the Gentile governments and the Gentile masses on one side, and the individual Gentile on the other. We don't paint the world in one color. There were always a few Gentiles who were not like the rest. Even in Germany, under the Nazis, there were Righteous Gentiles who helped and hid Jews. Part of the reason we all look up to you is exactly because you are the antithesis of what we expected from the Gentile. You are compassionate and empathetic, and when you give of yourself, you hold nothing back. You have added a new, bright color to our palette of black in which many of us have painted the world.

"Can you see, Peter, with our people's global experience, how unlikely it was that we would imagine an Englishman in Switzerland caring for us? Can you begin to see how it would have seemed back in that known hospital?

"And then, in my own case, despite all that history behind me, the ineffable joy which came to me when I found I loved you and you loved me, made all the distrust, dislike, that I had amassed – before, during, and, for a short while, after the camps – melt away. In its stead I found a man with a Jewish soul, but without a Jewish blood-line."

Peter felt that it was time for him to speak of something he had kept hidden for some time.

"I've something to tell you, something I kept trying to organize in my mind, and in my heart. It wasn't until you spoke to me now that I realized I had made my decision without even knowing it. Having studied, researched, read, and listened to those about me, seen how you all conduct yourselves, I've come to the decision to convert to Judaism. I'm aware that it won't be easy and that the process may be long and tedious, but it's what I want to do.

"I was brought up in the Church of England and tried always to conduct myself as a good Christian in whatever task I set myself or despite whatever conundrum I was faced with. However, having now begun the study of the Old Testament and the Talmud, I believe that my soul is Jewish and it was only a matter of time before my mind and heart followed."

Miriam tried to connect and focus her spinning thoughts. After a few minutes, she responded.

"Peter, I had no inkling, no idea, that you were considering such a radical step as this. I knew you were studying Judaism, but I thought that this was to learn about the history and development of the Jewish people; just a philosophical and intellectual inquiry into the sources of my people's religion. I thought that since fate kind of pitch-forked you into such a maelstrom of extraordinary activity in the Jewish world, that you were just curious to learn more about Jewish traditions. But it seems it was in fact an inquiry to back up what you *felt* you wanted to do."

"No, no, Miriam, it wasn't that at all. It's true that I started out just to fill in the gaps of my knowledge about the Jewish people. But soon I started to feel how much the words and thoughts I was ingesting spoke to me. It was like a part of me that had been sleeping suddenly awoke – hungry, hungry for a better understanding of what I truly believe is my heritage as well as yours. So I continued to delve into the Tanach and the sea of the Talmud and I felt I had to drink more and more deeply of it. In due course a religious metamorphosis took over my life. I began to understand . . ." . ."

"I'm not sure I understand fully what you're feeling, but it makes me very happy that you have found what you felt was missing in your life. What can I say except, Welcome to my world."

The next day, Peter decided to discuss his decision with Yossele, asking him how to proceed. Yossele smiled at him and said, "First, I want you to know that we're honored, here in Ma'barot, to have you living among us. You're a real hero. As a matter of fact, I'm going to move you out of that rather simple volunteers' room you are living in and find you a real room. You deserve it and I also know it will make Miriam happy.

"Next, as to your decision to convert. In Palestine, matters of birth, marriages, divorce, conversion, and funerals are dealt with by the rabbis. Except in emergency matters, such as burials and circumcisions, we have a traveling rabbi who ministers to a number of kibbutzim, visiting each one on specific dates every year to deal with the non-urgent things.

"So, we frequently have two or more couples getting married when the rabbi comes 'round, and he holds a multiple wedding ceremony. However, your situation would qualify as one of emergency since, as far as I know, the process you're seeking can take some time.

"I'm going to phone the rabbi to ask him to make an urgent visit to meet you. I'll let you know when that will be. For now, I think you should continue studying Jewish law whenever you have a free moment."

Two days later, Peter and Miriam moved to a proper room, next door to Betty and Jack, the Australians who had already befriended them. The following week, Rabbi Rogosnitzky arrived to meet with Peter.

The rabbi was a huge man, six feet six inches tall, muscular but not fat, with twinkling, blue eyes, and a neatly trimmed goatee. He was brought 'round to their room by Yossele, who introduced him to Peter and Miriam. The rabbi held out his football-size hand to Peter, who took it a little cautiously.

"Rabbi, may I stay for your meeting with Peter, or would that be out of order?" Miriam asked.

The rabbi had not offered his hand to Miriam, nor did she offer her hand to him. "Yes," he said, "you certainly may stay, Miriam. I presume you are Jewish and I also presume you are a couple together?"

"Yes, I'm Jewish, from Gdynia, and yes, we are a couple," Miriam answered, looking at Peter.

"Very well," said this rabbi. "I want you to know first of all that I'm not your usual, run-of-the-mill rabbi. I mean by that, an Orthodox rabbi who just sticks to the rules and allows himself no flexibility. I believe that I have more compassion for Jews in difficult circumstances; for example, in the army at war, and living in a non-Orthodox community such as this kibbutz.

"In my own personal life, I observe the usual customs and ways of life as are laid down by our authorities. However, I was a military rabbi in the Jewish Brigade of the British Army during the war. In that capacity, I learned a lot of how to conduct religion in the field, and, in particular, to acquire a somewhat liberal tolerance that I had never suspected in my own make-up. For example, I told my men that in war, their main responsibility was to keep healthy and strong, even though they may have to eat non-kosher food in order to do it.

"Since I was appointed as rabbi to this association of kibbutzim, I've also found it necessary, in order to bring some religion and tradition to otherwise non-observant people, to temper my instinctive 'letter-of-the-law' upbringing with decisions more in line with the thinking of non-observant people. I can do this because of the numerous minority opinions of our rabbis, which may sometimes be used in just the kinds of situations I come into contact with on a regular basis. As my own rabbi often said, 'It is more meritorious to find leniency in the Law than strictness.'

"Now, tell me, Peter, is the reason that you wish to convert to Judaism because you wish to marry this beautiful Jewish young lady?"

"No, Rabbi. Miriam and I have never discussed marriage, but we are both extremely fond of each other and perhaps one day, down the road, we might marry. If marrying were the reason for my conversion, we would just go to Cyprus and get married there."

"So, what is your reason," asked the rabbi.

"Well, as fate would have it, for some time now I've been thrown into the company of Jewish people from other countries seeking to make a new life for themselves. Had you asked me even a year ago if I could ever see myself living in Palestine, I would have laughed and said absolutely not. Had you told me that I would be flying my own plane clandestinely around Europe and surreptitiously sailing my own ship to Palestine with a group of survivors of the Holocaust, I would probably have thrown you out of my house, or, at the very least, declared you insane. But here I am, having done all those things, and not only living in Palestine, but living on a non-religious kibbutz, working at Tel Aviv University, and learning Judaism.

"But to get back to your question. My reason for wanting to convert to Judaism is that I have begun to discover what it is that has kept the light of Judaism burning through millennia against all odds. I have seen, firsthand, the partially successful attempt of the Gentile world to obliterate the Jewish People, just because they are Jewish. All this has ignited a spark in me, a spark I never knew I had, a spark that seems to direct me to a path I didn't know existed before, the path to Judaism. The combination of what I've seen and what I've read," Peter pointed to their small library, "have led me to the improbable, yet undeniable conclusion that my soul is Jewish!" The rabbi was impressed as he inspected their library of thirty or so Jewish and other books in a dozen languages. "Do you say you've read all these?" he asked.

"Yes, all of them except those in Russian, Polish, and Ukrainian, which are Miriam's books."

"Hummmmm," said the rabbi. "Do you object if I ask you a few questions from any of your books?"

"Not at all," Peter said, "although I wasn't really prepared for an exam on them today."

The rabbi then picked up six of the books covering Jewish history, faith, festivals, Zionism, ethics, and the Day of Atonement prayers. He chose representative questions, trying to be more general than specific. To his total amazement, Peter answered every question, quoting "chapter and verse" to back up his statements.

The rabbi, who was himself a scholar, slowly replaced the books on the bookshelf. He then turned to Peter and asked him if he had ever attended a Jewish religious service. Peter had to admit he had not. He then talked to Peter about the requirements for conversion. He said in normal circumstances, a potential convert had to agree to maintain a kosher home and to bring up any children in the Jewish faith. However, he realized that at this point, it wasn't practicable to ask him to find kosher food in a non-kosher kibbutz, but he would ask that as the conversion process continued, Peter refrain from eating non-kosher meat until other provisions could be made for him.

He then asked Peter to step outside for a moment. When they were out of earshot of Miriam, the rabbi asked Peter if he was circumcised. Peter responded in the affirmative.

"Good, that will save you some grief," the rabbi told him.

"How do you handle circumcision where it was already done?" Peter inquired.

"It's done by just taking a drop of blood from that area, and that is considered as though it was a complete circumcision. In Hebrew it's called the "*Tipat Dam*" – the "drop of blood" ceremony."

They re-entered the house. Miriam greeted them with a smile and said, "Now, I wonder what you two have been discussing that a simple woman like me shouldn't be a party to?"

Peter smiled, saying, "Just men's stuff, my dear. When you're a little older, I'll share it with you, perhaps."

She laughed and let it go at that, knowing full well that Peter would tell her after the rabbi had left.

"Peter," the rabbi said, as he was leaving, "I must tell you that I'm more than a little impressed with the quality of your understanding of what you have studied and learned, as well as your sincerity. I believe you'd make an outstanding candidate for joining my people. However, there are some deficiencies in your practical knowledge of Judaism. I wish to discuss your case with a couple of my colleagues and I'll get back to you as quickly as possible. Be assured, however, that it is my desire that you become accepted at the earliest possible time and I will do my best for you."

Two weeks later, Peter received a letter from the rabbi inviting him to a meeting with three judges of the Beth Din (rabbinic Court of Law) of Tel Aviv, the Supreme Religious Authority of Tel Aviv and surrounding towns. It was a friendly letter, but in it, he suggested that Miriam shouldn't come with Peter. It could lead to unnecessary questions and since Peter had already stated to him that his reason for conversion had nothing to do with Miriam, it was better that she remain unconnected with this meeting.

On the appropriate date, Peter presented himself in the Beth Din offices in Tel Aviv, to three bearded, serious-looking gentlemen seated at one side of a table. Rabbi Rogosnitzky was also in attendance, and he and Peter were invited to sit on chairs facing the table.

One of the judges, speaking in Hebrew, asked Peter if he understood Hebrew. Peter replied that he had started to learn it about six months ago and had a beginner's knowledge. The judge turned to Rabbi Rogosnitzky and asked him to translate any words or phrases Peter might have difficulty understanding.

They continued in Hebrew.

One judge said that the applicant wrote that he had studied Jewish history and religion in depth. Was that so? Peter said that was true. The judge then asked him if he knew what was required of an applicant for conversion to Judaism.

"I believe so," answered Peter. "There are basically two conditions, sir. They are circumcision and immersion in a mikveh."

"And are you ready and willing to undertake those conditions?"

"I am, sir," Peter answered.

"Fine. But first we would like to examine you to understand how well you have mastered some of the technical *halacha* of Judaism."

Thereupon, the three judges proceeded in turn to ask Peter various questions. He was able to answer them all correctly.

Rabbi Rogosnitzky, sitting next to him, was aware that the questions started superficially, then progressed into further and further depth.

Some of the questions were:

Q: "What are the three foot festivals?"

A: "Passover, Pentecost, Tabernacles."

Q: "Who were the Matriarchs and Patriarchs?"

A: "Sarah, Rebecca, Leah, Rachel and Abraham, Isaac, and Jacob."

Q: "How many candles are lit on the first night of Hanukkah?"

A: "Two."

Q: "And how is that?"

A: "One is the attendant, the other is the candle of that night."

Q: "How many Temples did the Israelites have?"

A: "Two: Solomon's Temple, destroyed by Nebuchadnezzar, and the Second Temple, built by Zerrubavel, under the watchful eye of Ezra and Nechemia and destroyed by the Roman, Titus."

Q: "Why is there a fast on Tisha B'av?"

A: "To commemorate the destruction of the Temples on that date."

Q: "What is the meaning of the Kol Nidre prayer at the beginning of Yom Kippur?"

A: "To declare that all vows in the coming year between man and God are void."

Then the questions became deeper and more introspective, focusing in part on the laws of Shabbat and kashrut.

At length, the judges indicated that Peter should withdraw from the room. After ten minutes, Rabbi Rogosnitzky emerged, his face beaming.

"Peter, you have passed!" he exclaimed. "All that remains to be done now is to arrange for the "Tipat Dam" ceremony to be carried out by a mohel – an authorized circumciser – which I will arrange to take place privately in your home, and then, the immersion. This will be done at a ritual bath location in Tel Aviv in the presence of a Beth Din of three rabbis, which I will also arrange. The immersion, accompanied by certain prayers, in the presence of the three rabbis, will complete the conversion formalities in your case. But, as a result of your studies and learning, you have saved yourself the year of study under the tutelage of a rabbi."

Peter went back to the kibbutz and told Miriam the good news. She was overjoyed.

In the course of the next two weeks, the "Tipat Dam" and the immersion ceremony were completed. Rabbi Rogosnitzky arranged for it to be registered at the Beth Din and a certificate was issued to Peter to confirm that all religious requirements had been met.

Miriam and Peter's lives settled into a regular routine, but an extremely busy one. They were teaching two nights a week in the kibbutz and they were continuing their studies in the Hebrew language.

In addition to their university work, they had both been busy from time to time in the Haganah. Peter had become, to his own amazement, an excellent marksman and had been made sergeant, and given the title "sharpshooter." Miriam had become in charge of a field medical aid unit.

As the Jewish New Year approached, Miriam reminded Peter of Dov's request to arrange a get-together of the old group. Miriam went to Yossele and discussed it. He said he could see no problem, but it would have to be brought before the monthly members' meeting for approval, for, after all, he reminded Miriam, the kibbutz and its facilities belonged to all the members equally.

Since Peter and Miriam were not yet members, it was Yossele who brought their request up for discussion and a vote. By this time, every kibbutz member was aware of Peter's exploits and activities in bringing the group to Palestine. They also knew that their lectures and language classes were very popular, and, of course, they knew the important role the two were playing in the local branch of the Haganah. So it was no surprise that their request to have their friends remain in the kibbutz for three days was approved unanimously.

As soon as they heard, Peter and Miriam sent an invitation to Dov, asking him to send it to all the group, giving him the dates and suggesting they should all come as inconspicuously as possible, so as not to make the group arrival a noticeable event. They added an RSVP to the invitation, without really expecting any early responses.

Their first reply was from Helen, who said she and Alex would be coming with her baby boy. The next was from Heide and Max and Dov, and there were a few others. It seemed as though virtually all would come.

The date arrived. Peter and Miriam had canceled all their scheduled obligations and put together a written program for the three days to give out to the group as they arrived. All their meetings would be held in the institute meeting hall, where all kibbutz general activities took place.

There was, of course, great excitement as the group trickled in, in ones and twos. Helen and Alex, with their son, whom they had decided to call Peter, arrived first. There was a wonderful reunion between Helen and Miriam, and when Heide arrived, the three ladies were ecstatic.

Everyone had been in Palestine about a year and spoke at least passable Hebrew, and they all enjoyed teasing each other over their mistakes. By evening, twenty-five of the crew out of twenty-eight had shown up, plus Dov. The first program was for everyone to bring the group up-to-date on what they were doing. Peter spoke last and quite casually mentioned that he had converted and was now Jewish like everybody else. At that, there was tremendous and prolonged applause which went on until Peter put up his hand.

Max and Peter had a deep discussion; Max having given up his Judaism and Peter having taken it up. Max told Peter what had made him decide to do it. Peter said nobody who had not been through the horror of the camps had the right to comment on Max's decision and if he and Heide were happy with it, then that was all that mattered. Max told him that they were making plans to have a wedding in the Baptist Village in a few months' time, and invited Peter and Miriam to come. Peter said they would certainly try.

Peter and Miriam had invited Professor Aron and Ruth Weiss, Betty and Jack, Avraham and Leah, and Yossele, to come and meet their old group, and they all dropped in. Over the next few days, each member of the group found time to personally thank Peter for all he had personally done for them.

When the group finally left, their absence was felt keenly by Peter and Miriam. However, they agreed that it had been well worth the effort for everybody to meet up with each other again. They wrote a joint letter of thanks to Yossele, as administrator of the kibbutz, for having agreed to host the group for a reunion, and another to Dov for being the liaison man.

Soon after, Miriam came to Peter saying she needed to speak to him about something that was on her mind.

"Of course, my dear, what is it?" he said.

"I'm feeling tired all the time and although I keep to my schedule, it's getting harder and harder for me to do everything that I've agreed to. I realize that I must cut down somewhere. I've considered everything I'm doing and I really don't want to cut back on the things we've agreed to do for others, like teaching, so I've decided to suspend my doctoral work for the time being and resume it later on, when my life is less frantic. What do you think, Peter?"

"My love, if that's what you think you need to do, then by all means, you should do it. I've been so overwhelmed myself, I wasn't aware of the problem and thought you were coping well. And so, what you have said makes a lot of sense. I would just suggest that you organize your research in such a way that you'll be able to go right back to it when the time comes."

"Yes, I'll begin working on that at once. Perhaps a series of notes to remind me where I'm up to and how I plan to proceed. Who knows how long it will be until I go back to this."

A couple of weeks later, Miriam again asked Peter to hear her out.

"Have you decided to give something else up?" he asked.

"No, quite the contrary. I've decided to make add yet another layer to my life." Miriam was about to say more, and then stopped.

Peter had no idea what she was talking about, but encouraged her to go on.

"Well," she said, blurting out everything she had on her mind in one go, "I love you with all my heart and I know you love me too, and so, Peter, my dear, will you marry me?"

Peter was silent for a moment, then he got up, went to her, put his arms around her, put his lips to her ear and whispered, "Yes, of course, I thought you were never going to ask."

Then they hugged, rolling around on the bed, laughing and kissing each other.

"I don't understand," Miriam said, after they got up. "If you were waiting so long for me to propose to you, didn't it occur to you that you might ask me? I believe that's the conventional way that matter is handled."

"To tell you the truth, my love, I've been so happy just living together with you, it never occurred to me that we needed to extend our relationship in any other way. But since you've raised the subject, May I have the honor of your hand, fair maiden?"

They spoke to Yossele, who told them that the rabbi would be at the kibbutz in two months' time, the week before Chanukah, and he could marry them then.

Peter and Miriam sent invitations to James, Helen, Heide, Francois the bank manager, Peter's mother, Olaf, Dov, and Jean-Pierre Muraille, his lawyer/executor in Berne. They received "will come" replies from everybody except Alice Romaine, Peter's mother, who wrote that it would be too much effort for her in her present state of health. Peter had recently spoken with her and suspected there was more to the refusal than just a health issue.

Yossele explained that, after the wedding ceremony, there would be a party at the kibbutz, sponsored by the kibbutz, just as if they were full members of the kibbutz, because of the high regard everybody had for both of them.

The wedding took place, the invitees all came, including Captain Olaf. Rabbi Rogosnitzky officiated, food and wines flowed, a few bottles of whiskey – provided by Peter – circulated, a band played, and everybody danced.

As the saying goes, "A good time was had by all!"

CHAPTER XXIII

War

DURING 1947, THERE WAS CONTINUOUS UNREST IN PALEStine. There were mounting demonstrations against the occupying British authorities. The United Nations General Assembly decided on a partition of Palestine into Arab and Jewish areas. Although the decision involved three unconnected areas for the Jewish population, the Jews accepted this, as it was the first land offered to themselves in 3000 years. The Arab areas, including Gaza, were to be contiguous, but this plan was rejected by the Arabs, who demanded all the land for themselves. Instead, the Arab population began to attack the Jewish villages and kibbutzim. The Special Jewish Defense Units and the Night Squads, which were organized in 1938 by Captain Charles Orde Wingate, a serving British army officer in Palestine, were in frequent demand. The British searched for arms in the Jewish settlements. There were arrests and even the threat that the British might pull out, leaving the Jews to their fate and on their own, a theoretical scenario, which would, in fact, have been welcomed by the Jews.

In April 1947, the British Foreign Secretary, Ernest Bevin, turned to the United Nations and announced the British government's withdrawal from sole British responsibility for Palestine. The Soviet Union joined with the United States in supporting Partition and the creation of a Jewish State in Palestine.

In November 1947, the UN General Assembly adopted the resolution,referred to above, by thirty-three votes to thirteen, on the partition of Palestine. The plan was disadvantageous to the Jews, but they supported it. The Arabs rejected it immediately and declared war.

The Jews had to prepare for the approaching war clandestinely. The Palestinian Arabs had the support of the surrounding Arab states, Egypt, Syria, Lebanon, and Jordan, and the traditional sympathy of the British Foreign Service. There were major Arab riots in Jerusalem and elsewhere between December 1947 and May 1948, and there were skirmishes, road ambushes, riots, bombings, and massacres perpetrated by both sides, virtually on a daily basis.

The British eventually pulled out, the last troops boarding their ships in the port of Haifa, on May 14, 1948. On the same day, the Israeli Declaration of Independence was promulgated and the State of Israel declared.

War broke out the next day, May 15, 1948, when seven Arab countries declared war and invaded Palestine. They were Egypt, Jordan, Lebanon, Iraq, Syria, Saudi Arabia, and Libya. Additionally, the Arab Liberation Army was a separate army of irregulars led by Fawzi al Kaukji, which consisted of Syrians; Moslems from Bosnia who had served in the German SS; Moslem volunteers from Albania, who had also served in the German Army; and Moslem Yugoslavs and Croats.

Kaukji, born in Iraq, was a former soldier of the Ottoman Army, who had fought in the Arab Revolt in Palestine 1935/36 and again in 1939, when the Arabs attacked the British and the Jews. Kaukji's polyglot Arab Liberation Army (ALA), which numbered about 4,000 men, was allowed into Palestine in March 1947 by the British, following an ALA promise not to attack Jewish settlements. However, in January 1948, the ALA attacked two Jewish settlements in the north and were repulsed with the help of the British.

The UN, including the US, had placed an arms embargo on Palestine, but this only applied to the Jews: the independent Arab states were allowed to continue to acquire arms. Britain continued to supply Jordan with arms, including canons, until the actual invasion of Palestine in May 1948.

When the Jerusalem road was blockaded by the Arabs at Latrun, and further up the road, a major convoy of food, water, and supplies was cut off on April twentieth amid heavy Jewish casualties, no more provisions could be supplied to Jerusalem until a secret road through the hills was established, with humanitarian supplies carried up by men and mules.

Various units of the fledgling Haganah were brought in to fight to open the road. It was considered the highest priority to relieve Jerusalem, but all attempts failed, first against the Arab Liberation Army, then later again, when the ALA was replaced by the Jordanian Arab Legion, an army traditionally officered by the British and considered the best army in the Middle East.

The Haganah unit to which Peter and Miriam belonged was called up to take part in the battle for Latrun, at the start of the road up to Jerusalem, where bitter battles had already been fought, with no definitive outcome. The Jewish army was so short of soldiers that when a ship with immigrants landed in the port of Haifa, each able-bodied person aboard was to be issued a rifle and sent to take part in the forthcoming battle for Latrun. The commander of the unit involved knew of Peter's linguistic ability and decided to send him to Haifa to bring these fresh soldiers to Latrun. He was ordered to orient and lead them.

Peter was issued a rifle and ammunition and left the kibbutz with two buses containing rifles and ammunition, and instructions to pick up the estimated forty-five young immigrants in Haifa. He was just able to give a hurried kiss goodbye to Miriam as he left on the run. He knew that Miriam's medical unit had also been called up for the battle, as the Jewish soldiers were already taking heavy casualties.

Peter and his buses drove to the port area of Haifa, where he could see a freighter, about twice the size of the *Helen*, lying alongside the jetty. They drove to the ship and Peter went up the gangplank to be confronted by a Jewish soldier who asked him for identification and his purpose on board the ship. Peter told him he had come to pick up the new immigrants, at which point the soldier ran to the bridge and rang the ship's bell, obviously a planned signal, since immediately, groups of young men and girls appeared from every part of the ship.

Peter waved his arms to show them to get together so that he could talk to them. He asked them, in German, what languages they spoke and listened as they called out their answers. He was able to speak to over ninety percent of the immigrants in their own language and began to explain the situation and the fact that each one would be given a rifle and fifty bullets as they proceeded to Latrun. Peter knew that all the young people had already received some minimal training in shooting a rifle on board ship.

They were ordered to take their belongings and go to the buses waiting for them. There, they would pick up their rifles and ammunition, but not load the guns, and take their seats in the buses. The buses would then take them to Latrun and on arrival, they would be given new orders. They were part of the Jewish Army and had to obey their officers, including him.

One boy asked him the name of this army unit. Peter immediately replied, "Peter's Company."

There were some in the group who came from Poland and Lithuania, and Peter asked those who spoke Yiddish to explain his orders to them.

The group dashed off, picked up their meager possessions, and came back. Peter led them off the ship and marched them about 100 yards to the buses. They picked up their rifles and a bandolier of cartridges, and boarded the buses. The bus drivers counted them as they went on. There were forty boys and ten girls.

Peter walked through both buses, telling them again *not* to load the rifles. He wanted no accidents before they were to get into action.

Three hours later, they arrived at the outskirts of the Latrun area, where the buses were stopped at a military area. A uniformed officer got on Peter's bus and asked for Lieutenant Romaine. Astonished, Peter said, "My name's Romaine."

The officer said, "You've just come from Haifa, have you?" Peter said, "Yes, I picked them up from the ship."

The other man told Peter he had been given a field commission and was, indeed, now a lieutenant. He told Peter to get his group off the buses, line them up, inspect their weapons, appoint one of them as a sergeant, and march them north to Peter's headquarters, which was next to a Red Cross tent, about a kilometer away.

Peter got his people off the buses, lined them up, inspected their rifles, showed them how to use the slings and carry the rifles with the slings on their right shoulder, so they should at least look like soldiers. There was to be no talking and everyone had to keep in step with him. Peter noticed one man who looked particularly alert, understood Peter's instructions, and carried himself well. He was about six foot six inches tall and his name was Moshe. Peter told the group that Moshe was the sergeant and second-in-command of Peter's Company.

Peter led off, with Moshe calling the step, in German, "*Eins zwei, eins zwei,*" until they all got into the cadence. Soon, the unit started to feel that they were, indeed, a real military formation.

A short while later, Peter saw some tents clustered together, one of which had a Red Cross flag outside. Next to it was a larger tent, guarded by two soldiers.

Peter halted his group and entered the tent, after a cursory check by a guard. There were six officers inside. A Colonel Avraham introduced himself and asked what Peter was doing there. "I'm Lieutenant Romaine," Peter replied. "I've just brought fifty new recruits here from Haifa, right off a ship."

"Bless you, Lieutenant," said the Colonel. "We need reinforcements very badly. Are they fit and ready to fight?"

"I believe they are," said Peter, "but I've only known them for three hours. However, they have rifles and fifty rounds of ammunition each, they know why they're here, and I think they'll do as well as can be expected."

"Good," said the Colonel. "Have you had Haganah training, and for how long?" he asked.

"Yes," Peter answered, "two nights a week for fifteen months."

"Wait here," said the Colonel.

He went and spoke to the others, who were all clustered around a table with maps on it. They spoke for a minute or two, then the Colonel signaled for Peter to join them.

One of the other officers made room for Peter and said, "Shalom, Peter, I'm General Arnie. I've just been hearing about your group from Haifa. By the way, what language do they speak?"

"Well, they speak about six languages, but I can talk to them all except the Poles, who have friends who translate what I say into Yiddish." Peter said.

"What, Lieutenant, you're a linguist too?" said the General.

"Yes," said Peter.

"How many languages do you speak?"

"About ten," said Peter, matter-of-factly.

"Excellent," said the General. "Now, I want you to look at this map. This is where we are now and this is our line of soldiers. I want you to take your group along this way to the end of our line, which is up against these trees. Your people are to take cover at the edge of these trees. We have information that the Arab Legion will be attacking all along our line as soon as it gets light, in about one hour. You must get your people to fix bayonets and wait it out. Any questions?"

"Yes, sir," Peter answered, looking at the map. "Who is in command of the troops on my right?" he said, pointing.

"You're quite right, Peter, I should have told you. His name is Francois and he speaks French, English, and Hebrew."

"I believe I know him, sir. Is he Francois Leclerc with Bank Hapoalim?"

"Right again, Peter. I'll let him know you're coming. Good luck, and off you go."

Peter left the tent, rejoined his Company, and marched them off 200 meters from headquarters. He briefed the unit on what he had learned from his own briefing.

"I know many of you feel like this situation is surreal," he told the soldiers around him, "but I assure you this is very real, and very dangerous. There will be no sleep for the weary tonight, and as far as food is concerned, you'll eat after the battle. We're fighting the Jordanian Arab Legion, which is commanded by many English officers. They are Bedouin and have fought before. They have experience on their side, but we have the knowledge that what we're fighting for is our future and the future of the Jewish People. There's no way we can lose if we keep our wits about us and our guns trained on the enemy."

Eventually, they reached Francois's unit.

"Hello, Francois," Peter said as he saw the bank manager. "I bet you didn't expect to see me here. Remember me, Peter Romaine; and my unit is going to be just past yours, backing onto the trees up the hill."

"Well, well, well," said Francois, "fancy meeting you here, Peter. I'm happy to have you as my next door neighbor, my esteemed customer. How many do you have?"

"I've fifty," said Peter, "Forty boys and ten girls, all with rifles and fifty rounds of ammo. I picked them up off their ship in Haifa last evening and here they are. I want to get to my position soon so they can sit down and get a rest before dawn. I understand from General Arnie, he expects an attack as soon as it gets light."

"You got a briefing from General Arnie, himself?" asked Francois, impressed.

"Doesn't everyone?" Peter said. They shared a laugh as Francois showed Peter where his position started, then Francois went back to his own unit.

Peter examined his area, then spread out his troops along a line just in the trees facing the field, which sloped uphill from his position. He made sure they were grouped in twos and went around with Moshe. He checked that all rifles were loaded and bayonets were fixed. He or Moshe went around every half-hour to make sure that at least one of each pair was awake and alert. His own position, with Sergeant Moshe, was in the middle of the line.

As dawn approached, Peter went one way along his line and Moshe the other way, to make sure everybody was awake and their safety catches were set to "off."

As they finished reviewing their troops and went back to their position, the bombardment started, beginning with three-inch mortars. Peter's troops had some small protection as they pressed against the tree trunks, but those units who were out in the open had no cover and soon cries were heard and calls for "medic!"

It seemed to Peter and Moshe that the mortars were landing closer and closer to their position. "I would guess," said Peter, "that their troops are also moving in a line abreast, following the mortar bombs, but not too closely."

Soon, as expected, the mortar rounds stopped and whistles and calls were heard from the enemy, not far away. Figures began to materialize, 50 to 100 yards away. Peter took aim and began firing, as did his infantrymen. He had told them that they should only fire when they had a target in their sights, otherwise they would just be wasting ammunition. He moved out from the shelter of the trees to give himself a better field of view. With the increasing light, he could now see down along the whole Jewish line, which was taking heavy firing from the enemy. The Arab Legion had hundreds of men, some carrying light machine guns, but most firing their rifles, led by their officers in front, firing pistols.

He called out to his unit, "Let them have it!" in one language after another, while crawling ahead of them and shooting at one target after another, seeing one enemy soldier after another go down. Suddenly, he was lying flat on the ground with pain searing his chest. Then he passed out.

The next thing he knew, he was lying on his back, looking up at a tent roof, and hearing Miriam's voice saying, "Peter, what happened?"

He was quite sure he was hallucinating until a familiar face drifted into his vision and a cool hand was placed on his forehead.

"Can you focus on me, my beloved? You've been wounded. You took a bullet in your left collarbone. We've stopped the bleeding, temporarily, but they are going to send you to the hospital for surgery to take out that nasty bullet and repair your collarbone. They don't think your lung is affected, but your left arm will have to be in a sling for a little while. I'll come and see you in the hospital after we've dealt with all our wounded."

"How did I get here?" he asked.

"That enormous Moshe of yours, who said he was your sergeant, he carried you here all the way from the battlefield after all the shooting was over. He came bursting in, shouting, in German –

"This Peter of ours, the leader of our unit – he is a terrific leader. In the battle, he spoke to each of us in our own language and kept us

264

shooting at the enemy. I've never seen such bravery – you must save him! You must save our Peter!"

Peter smiled, and then fell asleep. He was taken to Tel Hashomer Hospital.

An hour later, there was a lot of murmuring among the doctors and medics as the imposing presence of General Arnie was seen entering the First Aid tent. He went around to all the wounded and spoke to each one. Then Miriam heard him say to the doctor in charge, "Did you happen to see a Lieutenant Peter? I spoke to him before the battle and sent him to his battle station."

Before the doctor could answer, Miriam spoke to the General: "Excuse me, sir, I heard your question and I dealt with him. He is my husband. He was wounded and was taken to Tel Hashomer Hospital for surgery."

"Well, I'm just now going to Tel Hashomer Hospital, to visit other people who were wounded. If I will see him there I'll be sure to give him your regards."

Before Miriam could say any more, the general left the tent. And off he went.

Late in the day, the medical tent was closed down and the staff was sent home. Having heard one of the doctors say he was then going to Tel Hashomer Hospital "to see what he could do over there," Miriam asked him for a lift.

"Of course, Miriam," he said. "I suppose you're going to visit your young man there?"

"Yes," she said. "I'm terribly concerned."

"Well, don't worry, I checked his wound. It didn't seem life-threatening," the doctor assured her. "He'll be just fine, especially after he sees you."

When they arrived at the hospital, the doctor immediately found out where Peter was located and he accompanied Miriam to see him.

Miriam found Peter awake, and his eyes lit up with joy as she came to his bed and kissed him gently, saying loving words.

He returned her kisses, then burst out laughing.

"What on earth are you laughing at, you strange young man?" she asked.

"My darling, I was just thinking how our present roles were reversed since we first saw each other," he said.

"Of course, I know, but this situation is not funny. Oh, and I want you to meet Paul, the doctor from my medical unit. Paul brought me here and attended to you when you were brought in by your sergeant."

"Hello, Peter," said Paul, "and have they taken out your bullet yet?"

"Yes," said Peter, "and here it is." He brought it from beneath his pillow, wrapped in some cotton.

"I don't want to see it, ever," said Miriam.

"So, how are your feeling, Peter? I suppose you have your left arm in a sling under the blankets?" asked Paul.

"Yes, I do," he answered, "and I'm feeling quite okay. I had a good sleep after the surgery and I'm ready now, Miriam, to go back to Ma'barot for dinner, or are we late?"

"Very comical, my love," she answered. "But I've the impression that you're going to be kept here for some little time, wouldn't you think, Paul?"

"That's up to your surgeon here. I would expect them to want to watch your recovery after the surgery quite carefully before they discharge you. And now I must leave you both. I'm going to find out what I can do to help here and I'm going to telephone my wife to let her know where I am. I'll try to drop in to see you later, Peter."

"What a nice man," Peter commented to Miriam after he walked away.

"Yes, he is," she replied. "While he was driving me here, I heard on his mobile radio that just as we were fighting at Latrun, a convoy of 200 trucks was attempting to bring food to Jerusalem, but it was ambushed at Shaar Hagai. Fifteen were killed and forty-four wounded, including some of our top leaders. It seems that no more supplies will get through there."

At that moment, a nurse came over to feed Peter some soup. Miriam offered to do it for her, freeing her for more important matters. The nurse was very grateful.

"Do you think I could stay the night with my husband?" Miriam asked.

Looking at her armband, the nurse said, "I don't know why not. It will do him good to have his own nurse on call," she smiled. "I'll find you a chair of some sort to rest on."

Thus, she stayed the rest of that night. In the morning she bid Peter goodbye and was on the way out when she met the same nurse again.

"Thank you so much, nurse," Miriam said. "I'm headed back to my kibbutz, Ma'barot, to change and then return to my unit."

"Wait," said the nurse. "One of the doctors just went off duty and he's headed to Haifa. Perhaps he can give you a lift?"

The doctor was glad to have company, as he hadn't slept all night and wanted someone to keep him awake in the car. He gave Miriam a lift all the way to the kibbutz.

Miriam returned to her unit on the front lines, unable to see Peter for three days. On the third day, Miriam went to the hospital. Still in pain, Peter was pronounced fit to go home, where Miriam could look after him and the kibbutz doctor could take over, and Peter's bed could be released for another patient.

On the fourteenth of May 1948, the British High Commissioner left the country and on the next day, the State of Israel was declared, to be immediately recognized by the USA, and on May seventeenth by the Soviet Union.

The War of Independence raged until various armistices were signed, between February and June, 1949, separately between Israel and Egypt, Syria, Lebanon, and Jordan. Israel gained about fifty percent more territory than was allotted to it by the UN Partition Plan, which the Arabs had previously rejected.

The war created about 726,000 Palestinian refugees, who either fled or were evicted from Jewish-held areas. Gaza was controlled by Egypt. The West Bank of the River Jordan was occupied by Jordan and subsequently annexed to it.

Between April and September 1949, abortive Israel-Arab truce negotiations took place in Lausanne, Switzerland. No substantive agreements were reached.

CHAPTER XXIV

Back to Civilian Life

PETER, IN DUE COURSE, COMPLETELY RECOVERED FROM HIS war wounds and within a few months, was back to teaching in the kibbutz and TAU, continuing his research at TAU and still officially in the army reserves, where he was promoted to captain. He was frequently called up for short periods to give crash courses in Hebrew to new immigrants, especially those who needed to know the army lingo while in the service. He soon wrote specific but simplified lexicons for specific trades and professions, such as law and accounting, which became "best sellers" among new immigrants.

Miriam, with her nursing/medical unit experiences behind her, and having stopped her doctoral work, also continued teaching. The TAU authorities couldn't understand why this was so. She explained that she felt it was her duty to make a contribution to the university that had opened its arms to her and her husband. Upon hearing this, the Board insisted that she receive a salary for her erstwhile and current efforts, and promoted her to professor, with the job of teaching seven languages, including Hebrew.

One day, Miriam came to Peter with an announcement.

"Peter," she said, "you haven't been treating me with proper respect as befits my status."

"Really?" Peter said, smiling. "Don't tell me they've made you Prime Minister already," he joked.

"Better than that," she said, taking out a letter from the university. "Read this!" she commanded.

She gave him the letter which started, "Dear Professor Polanski . . ."

"Everything seems to be in order," Peter said, folding the letter and returning it to her. "So, what is the important news you want to share with me?"

"Didn't you see the salutation? 'Professor Polanski.' I'm a professor now and I think you should accord me a certain amount of respect, if not reverence," she mockingly said.

"Oh," Peter scoffed, "is that all? I've had that title for some months now. It was something to do with the number of languages I teach, I think."

Miriam was crestfallen and began to pout. Peter put his arms around her and gave her a hug. "Okay, *professor*, but I still think Prime Minister suits you better." And they both laughed.

Three years later, Peter received his doctorate, with first-class honors. His outstanding abilities were closely observed in the university and one month following his doctorate, he was appointed to a new department within the faculty, created especially for him, with an appropriate title: Professor of Phonological Topology of Romance Languages.

Peter now was expert in fifteen languages including Portuguese, Ladin, Friulian, Galician, and Provencal, and, of course, Hebrew. Now he felt ready to master other Semitic languages including Arabic, Aramaic, and Amharic, as well as Turkish, Balkan Turkic, and Farsi.

"How on earth are you going to have time to study those five new languages while you are running your department and teaching Phonological Topology?" Miriam wondered, out loud.

"Oh," Peter exclaimed, "didn't I tell you? The University established my department more or less as an honor to me. They don't expect many, if any, students to sign up for my courses, unless there are other crazy people like me who want to study the entire family of Romance languages. So, I suspect I'll have plenty of time to study other languages. And of course, as a full professor, I get a full professor's salary, so that's useful too.

"By the way," he went on, "it's time I told you my financial story, of what I'm worth, how I came to it, and the whole history of my family at least for the last 900 years, since I don't have any information earlier than 1066 AD"

"Wow," she exclaimed, "can you really go back in your family history so far?"

"Certainly," he said.

Peter proceeded to recount his history, starting from 1066 with the invasion of England by the Normans, up to his grandfather, then his father's death and his will, and finally, how he was able to buy the *Helen* and *Richard's Renown*. After finishing his story, culminating with his present worth, he sat back and waited for her reaction.

Miriam was speechless – for a few moments.

"I've been married to a multi-millionaire all these years and you never told me?" she said, astonished. "This is incredible, amazing. And you work and work just as though you have to, when you could stop working tomorrow and live a life of luxury and relaxation with me."

"I suppose that's quite true," he admitted, "though it never occurred to me to do it. You see, I've come to love teaching and I love studying new languages, or, I should say, very old ones, and we have everything we need here. Over the years, you've decorated our little home beautifully, we have all the gadgets we want here, and we love the kibbutz. What more do you want?"

"My dearest one, I love you even more than before, not because you're rich, but because you have such good values and humility. I, too, am very happy here. And that explains why you turned down the kibbutz's offer of membership a few years ago. I was never quite sure why you did that, but since you were so firm about it, I went along with you. Now I understand. If we had no money in the world, then the peace and relative serenity and financial security to old age which comes with membership of an old-established and solvent kibbutz would be attractive and tempting. But as it is, I presume from now on your professorial salary from TAU will go to the kibbutz."

"Yes, it will, Miriam, I've already arranged it."

"What about your other subject, Peter – the technique you developed for quick teaching of Hebrew to new immigrants? Are you going to do anything with that?"

"I've already presented it to the Ministry of Absorption for them to use in the new immigrant language schools, called Ulpans; they're now setting up all over the country."

"You never tell me about such interesting things, Peter, my love. Why is it?"

"Because I didn't think it was important, my dear."

"Well, I do, my dear Peter and I think the State of Israel should give you a medal for that."

The following year, 1953, Peter received his first award of many, the Israel Prize "for outstanding work in the field of education, in particular for his unique program for teaching Hebrew to new immigrants." At the same time, Peter was awarded the Meritorious Service Medal for outstanding leadership and valor while taking part in a military action in the War of Independence, in which he was wounded and given a field commission. He was also promoted to Lieutenant Colonel (Reserves) in the Army.

Kibbutz Ma'barot threw a big party; all the original group who had come to the country with Peter on the *Helen* were invited, plus his brother James – and they all came, together with Dov, Shlomo, Georg, and Olaf.

The faculty of TAU threw a cocktail party for Peter who, at Miriam's behest, bought a suit and a tie, which he also was to wear for the prize award ceremony. Miriam was his glowing companion at these functions, whereas Peter was his usual imperturbable, polite, and urbane British self.

During the cocktail party at the University, Peter was approached by Professor Katz, the perennial TAU Dean of Students and now his close friend, who asked him and Miriam to accompany him to another room, where a world-renowned professor was waiting to meet them. Katz led them to an anteroom off the reception lounge.

"Peter and Miriam, I would like to introduce Professor Sydney David to you. Sydney, this is Professor Peter Romaine and his beautiful wife, Miriam." They all shook hands.

"Professor David is my opposite number at the University of Southern California in Los Angeles and despite being a Yankee, is a good friend. He's also a linguist of sorts."

"What's your field, Professor?" Peter asked.

"Similar to yours, I should think," answered the professor. "Linguistics, but I specialize in a totally different branch, in Sanskrit and the Indo-Iranian group of the Indian sub-continent."

"Then I think that, geographically speaking, we may meet, if you go as far as Afghanistan?"

"Well, yes, I do," said David.

"Then I suppose you have Persian and Pushto?"

"Yes, I do," he said.

"Well, then we do meet, because I learned Farsi and Turkish last year."

They all laughed at the coincidence.

David said, "I thought you were Romance, Peter."

"Yes, that's so, Sidney, but I've a few others too."

"How many, if you don't mind me asking?"

"I've seventeen, and working on Arabic, Aramaic, and Amharic at the moment," he replied.

"Impressive. But before I forget, let me add my congratulations on the award of the Israel Prize, plus your war medal, as well as your promotion in the Army Reserves."

"Thank you very much, Sidney," Peter responded.

"Now to get to why I asked Isaac to bring you over here. Awards aside, it so happens that in Los Angeles, we are short of a head of department in precisely your field. We have a number of post-doc people who want to go on with their studies in phonological science. I'm here to ask you whether it might be of any interest to you to consider coming to Los Angeles to head up such a department? I hardly have to mention that, in your case, tenure would go with the position, and the salary would be substantially greater than you get here?"

Peter suspected that Sidney had been interrogating him for a purpose, and wasn't totally surprised when the offer was made. Miriam, however, hadn't had any premonition of where the conversation was headed and was taken by surprise.

"Thank you very much for your offer," Peter said. "I'm aware that it was serious and that's precisely why I must talk it over with my wife. May I ask you how long you plan on staying here?"

"Today is Thursday. I'm staying over the weekend, though I know your weekend is one day, and I'm leaving on Tuesday next. Peter, may I ask you your country of origin, since in this country, everybody seems to come from somewhere else!"

Peter said, "I'm English actually, but I was born in Switzerland and I've triple citizenships: Swiss, British, and Israeli. How can I get in touch with you?"

"I'm staying at the Hilton in Tel Aviv, but I will be in Jerusalem until Sunday night. I return to Los Angeles on Tuesday."

"Fine, Sidney, I'll be in touch."

And with that, Peter and Miriam returned to the party, where it seemed nobody knew what had happened to the guest of honor.

Peter and Miriam had no opportunity to discuss this momentous conversation until they were in a taxi on their way back to Ma'barot.

"Quick, tell me, my love," said Miriam, clutching his arm. "Did you suspect he was going to make this offer early on?"

"No, my love, I didn't even know the University had a department of Phonological Science. Why?"

"Well, dear, you were so unbelievably cool that I thought you might have been given some warning by Isaac. Now tell me, what is your first impression of this situation? Is it real?"

"Of course. Isaac would never have introduced us unless Sidney

David was for real. And I must tell you, it is something I want to think about, with you, my love, for this is a two-person decision. What do *you* think about it?"

"I think it is exciting, and tempting," Miriam admitted, "subject to visiting there, seeing the campus, meeting the University people, seeing where we might be living, and of course, settling your conditions of employment."

"I'll tell you what I'm thinking, Miriam. This adventure, which is our lives together, has been exciting, rewarding, and filled with the kind of love few people encounter, let alone take hold of.

"I propose we continue our adventures at this time by telling Sidney David that yes, it is of interest to me to consider moving to Los Angeles." Peter looked at his wife, waiting for her final decision.

"What can I say, my dear, except, 'Where you go, I go, where you sleep, I sleep,' or in plain lingo – Let's go!"

On their return to Ma'barot that evening, Peter went to visit Yossele and told him about Professor Sidney David and his offer and his proposed response to it.

Yossele expressed regret that Peter and Miriam were leaving the kibbutz and Israel, but he was by no means surprised. "You have become a world figure in your field and it is in the nature of world figures to be sought after by other institutions. So congratulations, and rest assured I won't divulge this to anyone until you tell me I may."

Late Sunday night, using Yossele's office phone, Peter called the Hilton Hotel in Tel Aviv and spoke to Sidney David. Sidney was happy to hear such a positive response. He told Peter he would be back in Los Angeles by Tuesday and would get a letter off to him by the end of the week.

Peter told Miriam of Sidney's response, but told her not to pack until a letter came from Los Angeles.

The two of them could talk of little else for a day or two, then they had to pack and go up to Jerusalem on Monday, where they stayed at the King David Hotel, at the kind expense of the Jerusalem Municipality, to prepare for the Israel Prize ceremonial award on Wednesday. In the hotel, they were given the presidential suite. As they entered the palatial rooms, they looked at each other and both smiled; they were both thinking of the humble kibbutz home they had left just that morning.

"Just stick with me, baby," said Peter, in an exaggeratedly James Cagney accent, "and I'm gonna show you de woild." Miriam looked at him in horror – reminding him that was *no* way to speak in the holy City of Jerusalem, where he had come to be honored for his exemplary knowledge of languages, including English. He acknowledged his departure from his usual self, and promised that as long as they were in Jerusalem, he would never speak in such a tone again. And reminded her that California is not Jerusalem . . .

"Just as long as you remember to speak in Hebrew, good Hebrew, during the awards ceremony," she said.

"Well, if that's the case, perhaps I should speak with a Yemenite accent, as that seems to be the most authentic form of Hebrew." He began to talk in that accent, and Miriam responded in kind. After a few moments, they started to laugh and collapsed into each other's arms.

Wednesday came in a whirl of non-stop activity, starting early, when the Israeli press corps invaded their breakfast area on the hotel terrace overlooking the beautiful pool and gardens. Peter made a deal with them, agreeing to give a press conference if they would leave him and Miriam alone long enough to finish their breakfast, to which the press corps agreed.

At the press conference, most of the foreign reporters asked their questions in their own language, and Peter answered them appropriately. Those viewing the proceedings were fascinated by the ease in which Peter was able to switch from language to language, once in a while even correcting a grammatical error made by the reporter asking the question.

One reporter asked Peter why he had been given a field commission. Peter thought for a moment, then said, "They must have been very short of officers on that day," which made the reporters laugh.

At one point, when Peter told the audience that learning languages had always come easily to him and that his talent for language was really nothing more than that, a God-given gift, a reporter got up and said:

"There you go again, Professor Romaine, being unpretentiously unostentatious, which we comprehend is your predominating characteristic."

"And which paper do you represent?" Peter asked.

"The Times of London, Professor," the reporter answered.

"I might have known," said Peter.

"Why did you say that?" asked the reporter.

"Because the Times never uses a short word when a long one will do!" said Peter, to a great gust of laughter from the whole press corps.

The ceremony took place at 11:00 a.m. that day, in accordance with the State Ceremony protocol in the presence of the Parliamentary Chairperson, the President of the State, the Prime Minister, and the President of the Supreme Court.

After the award ceremony, Peter and Miriam were invited to lunch with the President of the State. As soon as he entered the President's residence, the President invited him to take off his jacket if he felt like it. It was a typically warm day in Israel and Peter, seeing the President remove his own jacket, was happy to take his off.

The President asked him to recount his life story. He explained that everybody of whom he had asked that question had told him a different story and he looked forward to hearing a similarly dissimilar story, from him.

Peter hadn't expected the President's request and was silent for a long time, trying to collect his thoughts, not sure where to begin.

To his relief, Miriam spoke up.

"I really think I should tell Peter's story. I think I have more of a flair for it, don't I Peter?"

"She does, Mr. President. But also bear in mind that she has a vivid imagination as well," he said smiling.

"Very well," said the President, "I always enjoy a good story, and a little imagination never hurt a tale. So, please go ahead, my dear."

When she had finished, without too many flourishes, there was silence for quite some time in the dining room. Peter was looking intently at his plate, Miriam was beaming, the President's wife was blowing her nose and wiping her eyes, and the President had his mouth partially open, as though having heard or seen a miracle.

At length, the President spoke, "Well, this was certainly an outstanding tale to add to my collection. If it were possible, I think Professor, Lieutenant Colonel Peter Romaine, should receive yet another Israel Prize for what he has done, especially as so many of his marvelous adventures were carried out when he was still a Gentile. Peter, I meet many heroes here in the President's House, but I think what you have done to help Jews, this country, our People, is not only amazing, but makes us all proud to call you '*yehudie*' (Jew). Thank you, on behalf of all of us."

Then the President rose from his chair, crossed around the table to Peter, took his hand in two of his own and said, "Thank you."

After lunch, Peter and Miriam were driven back to Ma'barot. At dinner, every kibbutz member came over to shake Peter's hand or slap him on the back and give him congratulations. They knew he had single-handedly put Kibbutz Ma'barot really on the map.

The following Sunday, the mail delivery brought an envelope addressed to Peter from the University of Southern California. It contained a letter and two first-class tickets from the Dean of The College of Letters, Arts, and Sciences, inviting him to visit the University in three weeks' time. It also contained a detailed form regarding his academic history, as well as his qualifications, for him to complete and return by mail as soon as possible.

Peter wasted no time in filling out the form and sent it off by return mail.

Everything was set. They now had a specific date to be in California, including hotel reservations, which, the letter assured them, were made in their name. Then a thought occurred to Peter. "Miriam, neither of us has been to the United States. Let's leave a few days early, stop in New York for a visit, and then go on to Los Angeles."

"What a great idea," she said. "We'll have a chance to see New York in a leisurely fashion, rather than wait until the way back, when we'll have who knows what pressures on us, either from Tel Aviv University or the University of Southern California."

"Agreed, then," Peter said, happily. "I'll see about changing the tickets so we can spend time in New York and let the university here know about our plans. You make a list of the places you'd like to go to. New York is brimming with culture, and I think at this point, we could both use a little world-class culture in our lives, n'est-ce pas?"

"Absolutely, my love," Miriam answered, beaming.

CHAPTER XXV

Los Angeles

TWO WEEKS LATER, THEY ARRIVED IN NEW YORK. FIRST, they took an organized one-day trip around Manhattan, which taught them the layout of the streets and avenues. They also learned that it was enclosed by the East River and the Hudson River. They shopped a little on Fifth Avenue, Miriam having decided to buy two or three new outfits to wear in Los Angeles, while Peter bought two sport coats and shirts to match. As Peter's wife, Miriam had long ago lost any embarrassment in spending money, since he had continued to encourage her to spend on whatever she wanted. In Israel, her needs had been very modest, but here, in the big city, she found shopping an exciting experience and hardly had to be encouraged by Peter.

Eight days later, having arrived in Los Angeles as planned, Peter showed up at USC and met Dean William Jones. They had a short, fifteen-minute chat, during which time, Peter learned that the dean had read and absorbed all the details he had sent with his inquiry form.

Then a half-dozen men and women joined them, all of whom were keen to meet Peter. As they were introduced to Peter, each one gave him a business card. He apologized that he didn't have any cards of his own yet, but the dean brushed that aside and said they had all seen a copy of his curriculum vitae and nothing further was necessary.

He learned that they were all members of the faculty, each was head of a department, so that if he joined, they would be his equals in rank. There was one additional woman who joined the group a little later, from the legal department, who would be drawing up an employment agreement, were he to join USC. They were all anxious to talk with Peter.

Peter got the impression that this was really more of a social meeting. The dean quieted everyone and asked if a few of those in attendance would like to join him and Professor Romaine and his wife for dinner that night. Two men, plus Sidney David and the lady from the legal department said they would like to, and dinner arrangements were made at Peter's hotel. The meeting broke up and Dean Jones said he would be happy to walk Peter around the campus for an hour or so. Peter accepted and he had a pleasant tour of the campus. Afterward, the dean procured him a university car and driver, which returned him to the hotel. Miriam wasn't in their room, but when he inquired at the switchboard, he found she had left a message for him that she would be at the swimming pool. He made his way there and found her on a lounge chair, resplendent in a sexy two-piece swimsuit that he had not seen before.

She had not noticed him, so he decided to play a trick. He walked quietly behind her, crouched down behind the head of the lounge chair, slowly advanced his arms on either side of her head and then quickly placed his hands on her shoulders, simultaneously saying "boo" in her ear. She grabbed his left hand with her right hand, pulled forward, and sank her teeth into his hand. As she screamed in fright, he yelled in pain. When she recognized her assailant, she was furious.

"What do you think you're doing, you horrible man. You're lucky I didn't bite your finger off. It so happens I was blissfully asleep and dreaming of you. I demand an immediate and full apology," and then, softening, "and a glass of champagne. Right now!"

Peter, holding his hand, signaled to a waiter working at the pool and said to Miriam, "A thousand apologies, but you got your revenge – just look at my hand." It was already showing a half-moon bruise but the skin wasn't broken.

The waiter arrived and Peter ordered two champagne cocktails.

Miriam still pretended she was put out by the way he woke her, but when the champagne cocktails arrived, she kissed him to show she had recovered her good spirits, clutched his injured hand in her own hands, adding, "I'm sorry, though you deserved it," and asked him how he had got on at USC.

He gave her a report of what had transpired, telling her that this was just a preliminary meeting and nothing much would be settled until everyone had the lie of the land, so to speak.

"Now, some news. We are invited to dinner, here in the hotel, at 7:30 tonight with the dean, two heads of departments with their wives, and a pretty single lady from their legal department, plus Sidney David."

At this news, Miriam quickly finished her drink and got up, saying, "You should have told me that at once. Now I have to run to the beauty parlor to make appointments for a hairdo, a manicure, and a pedicure, for I've some rather pretty evening sandals I got in New York for such an evening as this. And I've got to look my best as the wife of the new head-of-department-to-be-at-usc." So saying, she swept away, with her bathrobe flowing behind her.

She left Peter with something of a feeling of shock, as it seemed to him she had suddenly, and with one key word, "dinner," been transfigured into the epitome of an American upper-class woman. And what made her immediately think of "hair-do, manicure, and pedicure?" Truly this was an amazing metamorphosis considering that one week ago, living in their little, simple, kibbutz home of two rooms and no kitchen, the only sandals she owned were the very basic plain, leather ones, such as what everybody wore. And the only hair-do she ever had was the shower in the communal shower house, followed by brushing with a little hand-held hair drier in their living room. It seemed to him that she would easily fit into an American life.

Suddenly, Miriam re-appeared, happy and bubbly.

"I was able to get an appointment for all the things I wanted at the beauty shop," she announced joyously. "I met with the hair stylist too, and told her I needed to be ravishing tonight, as we were going to have dinner with your new boss that I haven't seen yet, and she promised to do such a special job on me so that not even you will recognize me."

"But I do want to recognize you tonight, my love, otherwise how will I be able to know who to sleep with later? You know how I feel about lawyers," he mused.

"Have no fear, my dearest Peter. I didn't come with you from Switzerland, to Italy, Spain, Greece, and finally to Israel, just to lose you to the first single woman you meet in Los Angeles."

"Fair enough, my love, but I did tell you she was pretty, didn't I?"

"Yes, but after the way I look tonight, you won't even notice she's there."

"Well, the truth is, when you're around, I don't notice any other woman, pretty or not. And, just for the record, I lied. She's not pretty at all."

Miriam kissed him, whispering "I guessed as much" in his ear, as she went to the room to prepare for her make-over.

A couple of hours later, Miriam crept into their room, found Peter asleep, and, carefully, so as not to mess up her hair, placed her lips on his to wake him up.

He duly awakened and said, "Is it over? Have you been transformed? Let me look at you."

Miriam dutifully moved away, displaying her hands and twirling around so he could see her new look. Peter examined her fingernails and toes and said, "Absolutely beautiful! You should always have manicures and pedicures when we come to live here."

"You'll get no objection from me, my love," she replied.

Then he scrutinized her hair-do. "Well, I must tell you," he said, hesitantly.

"Yes? Yes?" Miriam prodded. "Oh, don't tell me you don't like it. I don't –"

"Well, I've never seen your hair like this before, but I absolutely love it!"

"Wonderful!" she said. "I just wonder how those university wives will dress tonight."

"Please, Miriam, don't think about it. No matter how they look and what they wear, I know you'll stand out."

At 7:30 p.m., they made their way down to the dining room and met their party, all having just arrived, except the lawyer and Sidney David. Peter introduced Miriam to everyone and the two men introduced their wives to Peter. Then, Sidney and the lawyer arrived and Sidney introduced the lawyer, whose name was Nancy, to Miriam. The two wives were expensively-dressed, but somehow succeeded in looking dowdy. Miriam was happy that none of the women wore a long dress, but they all wore various items of jewelry, something Miriam never thought to buy on her trip to New York. Peter saw the way Miriam was looking at the jewelry and made a mental note to rectify the inequality as soon as they moved to California.

Peter was comfortable in this setting, as the men all talked about their hobbies and interests unconnected with work. It put him at ease.

The two wives were both involved in charitable activities, one was in a choir and the other had stables and rode a lot.

Altogether, it wasn't a boring evening, but it was apparent that all the others knew each other pretty well and they wanted to know as much as possible about Peter and Miriam. Miriam recounted some of her trials at Ravensbrueck, while both Peter and Miriam spoke about their exploits getting to Israel, as well as their experiences in the War of Independence.

Sidney raised the subject of Peter's Israel Prize and Miriam spoke about lunch with the President of Israel. This led to some inquiries about Peter's unique way of teaching Hebrew, which he was glad to talk about. Everyone was duly impressed.

Before they parted, the dean suggested that Peter take the next day off and get down to business only the day after by coming to his office and discussing contractual matters. Of course, Peter assented.

As everyone left, Nancy leaned over to Miriam and said, "Sidney was quite right, you know."

"Right about what?" asked Miriam

"Sidney described you to me as like a beautiful film star."

"Thank you, Nancy, but I'm so made up now, I hardly recognize myself."

"Miriam, believe me, you are a most attractive woman, and when you come here, which I'm sure you will, you'll set a new sartorial standard too. By the way, where did you find those *fabulous* sandals?"

"Oh, these things," she answered, casually, "I picked them up in New York on our way here."

"You know, Miriam, I thought I knew what people on a kibbutz looked like, but you have certainly disabused me from my preconceived notions."

"You must understand, Nancy, I wasn't milking cows and plowing every day; I was teaching post-grads languages of the Slavic Group at Tel Aviv University, and French and German in the kibbutz. We continued to live in the kibbutz after we were brought there as illegal immigrants, and we were fortunate that we had the expertise to pull our weight without doing the manual labor much of the kibbutz do. Our status in the kibbutz was never as members, although we were offered; we always lived there as volunteers."

"Still, whether as members or volunteers, you are excellent representatives of your community and your country." And with that, Nancy kissed Miriam and left.

On his next visit to usc, Peter sat with the dean and Nancy. There was discussion of salary, status, title, tenure, and health benefits. They reviewed his teaching sessions and hours of supervision of doctoral candidates as well as all the clauses dealing with vacations, publishing, home loans, etc. He was shown his office, complete with lavatory and shower, and asked about the number of desks and chairs he would require in the office.

Then, Nancy told him she would have a completed draft of his contract in two days. The dean asked, "When can you start?" to which Peter replied, "When do you want me to start?"

"Well, we want to give you enough time to put your affairs together and still come early enough to prepare for the next semester. Would a month be long enough?"

"Sounds reasonable," Peter said. "Before going back to pack, I would prefer to spend time now to look around for somewhere to set up house. I think what I need is a good estate agent. Can you suggest one? I would like to spend some time on that before I return to Israel."

"As a matter of fact, I do know somebody in that line of business," the dean told him. "Let me make a phone call right away." He made a call and apparently got the person right away. "Hold on, Mike," the dean said, "I've got him here and I'll put him on the phone."

The agent was Mike Johnston and he agreed to meet Peter at his hotel at 3:00.

"Glad that's settled," said the dean. "Keep in touch with my office, please."

When Peter got back to the hotel, he located Miriam in the shopping area. "Let's get lunch and sit down to talk. I've much to say."

When they were sitting down in the coffee shop and had ordered lunch, Miriam said, "Well, Peter, do you have the position?"

He said, "Nobody said 'You're hired' in so many words, but I've been negotiating my employment contract; they've shown me my office, complete with lavatory and shower; they've asked me when I can start; the dean has put me in touch with an estate agent who is coming over here at 3:00 to meet us; so yes, I suppose that I've been hired. Nancy will have the contract ready in two days for me to sign, but I told the dean that I want to get a home under way before we go back to Israel to close things down and move our stuff. What do you think, my love?"

"I think that yes, you've most assuredly been hired." She got up and came around the table, put her arms around him, and gave him a long kiss. "That was to say congratulations, my love. Now, let's enjoy lunch."

After lunch, they went to the room to freshen up and at 3:00 p.m., they met Mike Johnston, who, with a beaming face, presented them with two business cards: "I'm your friendly local real estate broker, very much at your service, and I didn't catch your names."

Peter, who hated effusiveness, said, "Probably because I didn't throw them, Mike, but we are Miriam and Peter Romaine."

"I'm delighted to meet you, Miriam and Peter, and how can I help you?" said Mike.

Peter, who never quite got used to the custom in Israel of calling everyone by their first name, and certainly wouldn't broach such a disdain for etiquette in the United States, said, pointedly, "Well, Mr. Johnston, we are looking to buy a home, within a mile or two of usc, with at least three bedrooms, three bathrooms, two reception rooms, and, hopefully, great views."

Mike Johnston, who was nobody's fool, realized his buddy-boy style wasn't working here, and changed tactics immediately.

"Very well, sir," he answered, respectfully, "and can you tell me the price range you have in mind?"

Peter appreciated Mike's new-found awareness, thinking, *Leave it to an American to change his demeanor on a dime.*

"Since we are in Los Angeles for the first time, we have no idea how prices run here, so perhaps you can go through a few properties with us and we'll soon learn the range of prices which can work with us. I presume you have some properties in your briefcase, Mr. Johnston?"

"Yes, I do, Mr. Romaine. Can we find a quiet place to sit down?"

"Yes, of course. Just hold on a minute," said Peter. He went over to the concierge.

The concierge led them all to a very private, beautifully furnished sitting room. They sat down around a table and Mike brought out some brochures.

"I don't know whether you prefer a single family house or a condominium, Mr. Romaine, but I've a few homes in the flats of Beverly Hills which are in the price range of $3 to $5 million. Might those be of interest?"

"Possibly, Mr. Johnston, but talk about some condominiums, too."

"Well, I've got one or two in a brand new building, which vary between $400,000 on the second floor to $1,750,000 at the penthouse level."

"Does penthouse mean the top floor, Mr. Johnston? Pardon my ignorance, but we are new to the United States."

"Yes, indeed, Mr. Romaine, and this penthouse is on the eighteenth floor and has a great view overlooking a golf course, so natu-rally that will be a permanent feature. It so happens that my firm is the exclusive agent for this building. Would you like to see it?"

Miriam and Peter got up from the table and went over to the win-dow together. She put her mouth close to his ear, "Peter, darling, are you sure you're even willing to consider a home at that price?"

"Absolutely, my love, I couldn't think of using our money for a better cause. And please come back to the table with a smile on your face."

They returned to the table, where Peter said to Mike, "Well, the answer to your questions is yes. Can we see it today?"

Mike picked up a phone and made a call. "Yes," he told them, "we can go right over now and see it. May I give you a ride in my car?"

"Yes, please," Peter replied.

It was rush hour on Wilshire Boulevard, a new phenomenon to both of them, having never seen nose-to-tail traffic on six lanes, but in half an hour, their car drove into the drive-way of an imposing, very new building. Mike ushered them into the elegant entrance lobby, where he was met by the doorman, who handed him a key. As they alighted from Mike's car, Miriam noticed the name-plate of the building. It was called "The Diplomat."

They all entered an elevator, which took them up to the penthouse level. Mike unlocked the door to one of the apartments and showed them in. Miriam immediately went to the window of the large re-ception room and looked out. It was a most dramatic view, much greenery of the golf club to the east and mainly two- and three-story buildings to the south, leading to some high-rise buildings, which seemed to be offices.

"Peter, come and see this view!" she called.

He came over and joined her, "My word," he said, "this is really dramatic. Mike," he said, "tell us what we are looking at."

Mike said, "Looking east, you'll always see grass and trees because it is the Los Angeles Country Club, which will be green in perpetu-ity. South, you look at Century City offices, an entertainment center, and a shopping mall."

"And look Peter, there's a little balcony," Miriam said. "Let's see the rest of the apartment." Mike walked them around the rest of the apartment, pointing out the features.

After they had seen everything, Peter asked Mike, "What else do we have to know about it?"

Mike answered, "Well, there's the price. The building has just opened up – that means it's just got its Certificate of Occupancy from the City and the price is not cut in stone yet. I would imagine that a firm offer with a secure bank account would maybe get a bit off."

Peter took Miriam into another room to talk privately. "What do you think of it?" he asked.

"What can I say?" she said. "It's fabulous, it's gorgeous, it's a dream place."

He said, "I agree. I feel like making an offer right away before it slips away."

Going back to Mike, Peter said, "After the price, what more?"

Mike said, "There's a monthly maintenance fee to pay; that covers building maintenance and insurance, staff wages, expenses of the common areas, manager's and building engineer's salaries, and such things. It's paid by every homeowner based on the square footage of each apartment. I'll have to look this up."

Miriam asked, "Is it available for move in now?"

Mike said, "As soon as you've bought it, it's yours. When you move in is your business."

Peter said to Mike, "We both like it. I can afford it and I can prove it. We have to sleep on it and I'll call you tomorrow morning. We have your card. It would be an easy cash transaction – no mortgage. We'll, of course, need a decorator. Do you know of one who is experienced in this high-rise area?"

"Yes, I do," he said, "and I would be happy to recommend her to you. I happen to know she has done a number of condos on this street."

"Very well, Mike," he said, watching Mike's face break into a smile. "I'll call you tomorrow morning."

They parted back at their hotel, Peter still calling him "Mike," and Mike – not taking any chances – still saying "Mr. Romaine."

Peter and Miriam talked into the small hours, but finally fell asleep in each other's arms, murmuring to each other, "I love our new home."

The following day Peter signed an "Offer to Buy" at the price of $1,500,000 and attached to it a copy of his Swiss banker's letter, setting out his bank worth. He had had it updated every year "just in case" he needed it. Now, finally, he needed it. He gave it to Mike at the same time as he signed the "Offer to Buy" and he and Miriam enjoyed watching Mike's face change colors as he suddenly realized that this young couple, who were planning on working for the university, had the cash to finish the transaction at once.

They put a thirty-day period to close in the "Offer to Buy," and Mike had to instruct the two of them in that peculiarly American institution, the escrow. That period was time for the seller to verify the banker's letter and the buyer to satisfy himself about the ownership of the title to the property. Peter also sent an urgent letter to his banker in Berne, instructing him to send a dollar check to the escrow company for $150,000, being a ten percent deposit of the offer price.

In two days, Mike called Peter to say he had received a counter-offer from the Seller in the amount of $1,625,000. Peter instructed him to prepare a counter-counter offer in the amount of $1,562,500. Mike came over in an hour for Peter to sign that and left in a hurry to get it to the escrow. Two more days later, Mike called him to say that (1) the deposit of $150,000 had arrived at the escrow, and (2) the Seller had agreed the price of his counter-counter offer amount, and the closing of escrow was set for three weeks' time and re-registration of the new owner by the County Recorder would follow shortly after. However, Peter would be satisfied at the close of escrow that he was, indeed, the new owner.

By this time, Peter had already agreed verbally to his contract of employment with the university, and called Nancy to tell her he had bought a home, the escrow of which would close in three weeks' time. He, therefore, suggested the start date for his employment contract should be in six weeks' time, which Nancy duly entered into the contract. Peter then made an appointment to sign the contract in two days.

Peter notified the dean of his plans. The dean was happy to hear the news, but said he was quite amazed that Peter had bought a home so quickly. "Is that how you perform, Peter?" he asked.

"Yes," Peter replied, "I believe if you see something which you know you want, and you ascertain that the price is fair and equitable, you should seize it while you can."

The dean was very impressed with Peter's financial acumen, wondering out-loud if Peter might not like to teach business as well.

"I'm quite happy doing what I do best," Peter answered. "But thanks for the thought."

Next, Peter called up his banker and asked him to send a further remittance of $1,600,000 to the same escrow account. Peter knew that would leave him about $190,000 surplus in the escrow, which he would transfer to a new bank account he would have to open. He knew there would be expenses on the sale and then there would be decorating costs and, finally, there would be furnishing expenses. Probably they would need to buy two cars, but only after their return.

Meanwhile, Peter called up the decorator mentioned by Mike and made an appointment at The Diplomat for the following day. He then reported to Miriam, who was a little overwhelmed with the speed at which everything was taking place. "And this for a fellow who took forever to propose," she said to him.

They visited some of the apartments that the decorator had finished and were duly impressed. They instructed her to prepare a complete decorating proposal for the apartment while they were away, including provision for a parquet floor throughout the apartment, since the developer had left bare concrete, leaving buyers to decide what they wanted to do to finish. The decorator was to present a furnishing plan, too, within a budget for their approval or amendment.

Peter told Miriam that although they would both be involved with the decorating and furnishing, he would rely on Miriam to mainly deal with the matter. He could see that on their return, he was quite likely to be immediately involved with his new position in the university.

Miriam was quite happy to take charge of the decorating. Then she suggested that on the way back to Israel they stop in Switzerland and say farewell to his mother, especially since she probably couldn't attend his award ceremony because of her health. And, as long as they were going to fly via Zurich, perhaps they could arrange to stay over for a few days, to sight-see.

"I've been so obsessed with our move here, I didn't even think of the possibilities you mention. Of course, how insensitive of me. We'll see my mother and I'll show you the real Zurich, as well as Berne.

"Which brings me to yet another thought. While we're in Israel, I should make inquiries of Aliyah Bet as to whether they would like to take over the *Helen* and the DC3, too, which I'm very happy to transfer to them."

The next day, they met with the interior designer, Yenta, at their new apartment. She was middle-aged, a real personality, and gave them an immediate feeling of confidence. She inspected the apartment, had picked up a plan at the reception desk in the lobby, and expressed herself ready to sit down with the Romaines and discuss business. She had her car downstairs and suggested they go with her, if they didn't have one, to the Hilton Hotel, very close by, where they could sit down in comfort with some coffee and talk.

When they were settled in at the coffee shop of the Hilton, Peter asked her, how would she be recompensed? She replied with a smile that it would be very simple. There would be a commission to her of forty percent on top of the actual cost of the labor and materials.

They were both shocked at this, recognizing immediately that as a "cost plus" contract, the more pricey the work…. Peter then asked her to give him a rough estimate of the decorating part without her commission. For the furnishing, he asked her to give an estimated range of cost, knowing that each client has their own ideas. She wasn't happy at that request but she came up – after doing some figuring on a notebook, and knowing the square footage of the apartment – with total amounts. Since neither Peter nor Miriam had much idea of what it should cost, it certainly seemed a lot of money.

Peter had a proposition for her. He rapidly calculated thirty-five percent of the decorating part and thirty-five percent of the mid-range of the furnishing part.

He added those two together then said, "I can offer you the following: Thirty-five percent as a flat fee for the whole job, to be presented to us as a proposal in one month from today. We'll pay you one third down today, one third when the decorating – including the parquet floor – is finished, and a third when the agreed furnishing schedule is fully installed."

Both Yenta and Miriam were in shock. Yenta had been getting away with her formula for a long time and had never been faced with such a cut-and-dried proposal, which was tempting, as a third would be paid to her today. Miriam was seeing Peter perform for the first time like a businessman, very much as he, in turn, had seen Olaf.

Yenta pretended to do some more figuring in her notebook while thinking furiously. Finally, she said, "Very well, Mr. Romaine, I'll do it. Now, how do you want to set it up?"

Peter said, "If you give me one of your sheets of business stationery, I will write up a simple agreement, exactly as we have just said, we'll both sign it, we'll get it copied at the front desk, I will give you a check for the first third, and we'll part: You, to go away and work very hard on the proposal and give it to us in a month when we meet, and we'll prepare to make this city our home. I will call you when we return. We shall be staying in this hotel again. okay?"

Yenta swallowed hard and then said, "okay." She gave Peter a sheet of her stationery. He sat down and rapidly wrote up a straight-forward agreement for services to be rendered. It also contained a statement that it was to be automatically canceled and the full down pay-ment returned if the proposal wasn't rendered in a month's time.

Yenta read it carefully, word by word, then after they both signed, Miriam took it and had it copied, giving one to Yenta and keeping one herself. Peter wrote out a check and gave it to her, they all shook hands and then Yenta left.

They took a taxi back to their hotel, then had a discussion with the concierge about flights. He took a note of their requirements for their trip: Los Angeles-New York-Zurich (four nights' hold over), Berne-Zurich-Israel-London (two nights' hold over), New York-Los Angeles, in a total of thirty-two days.

They left it with him and had dinner. Toward the end, a beaming concierge came over and informed them he had booked every flight, "First class, of course, sir and madam." He said he would get a writ-ten itinerary in the morning and would send it up. They would be-gin their first flight in two days. Peter thanked him and toasted this next stage in their lives with their drink of choice: two champagne cocktails.

Next day, Peter met Nancy and signed his employee agreement with the University, receiving a copy signed by both parties. Then he notified the dean that he was leaving the following day.

They packed, leaving one case with the concierge with clothing they didn't require on their trip, together with a good tip for his ser-vices, and confirmed a reservation for their return with a start date, but no conclusion, as they knew they couldn't move in to their new home until all the work was done, including a big library shelving area for their immense joint collection of books.

They arrived in Zurich in the early evening, allowing them to have dinner in their hotel room and then go to bed to sleep off the very long flights from Los Angeles.

The next morning, after breakfast, Peter called his mother to tell her they would be visiting within the week. Then they left the hotel on foot to start to explore Zurich's shopping availabilities and pos-sibilities on the main street, Bahnhofstrasse. As they passed one el-egant women's clothing shop after another, the now-worldly Miriam clutched Peter's arm, saying, "Look at that!" or "Isn't that beautiful?" until Peter said, "Let's go in a few and take a better look inside."

She immediately led the way into half a dozen women's clothing shops she had been eyeing, sat him down in each, and proceeded to examine the inventory for style and price.

After a while, Peter said, "Haven't you found anything you'd like to buy yet, my dear?"

"Anything?" she replied. "I'd really like to buy almost everything I've seen. I love looking around in these elegant boutiques and I think soon I shall find something I absolutely must have. Just a little more patience, my dear."

Miriam was very comfortable in the shops, speaking French or English or German according to how she was addressed, by the salesladies. Eventually, she decided to put a full wardrobe together while Peter sat in the chairs provided by the stores for the respective husbands of their patrons, happily indulging Miriam as she bought what she needed.

In every store, Miriam had the purchases sent to their hotel.

At length, Miriam pronounced herself satisfied "for today" but said she was willing to look again tomorrow, as she was feeling a bit tired after trying on all those garments.

Meanwhile, Peter had also been looking at the shops and had seen the many jewelry shops. He recalled his promise to himself about getting jewelry for Miriam and decided to correct that oversight immediately. But first, he led her to the famous Confiserie Sprüngli, where they had the most delicious hot chocolate and the most luscious pastries she could have ever imagined.

When they both sat back, relaxed and replete, he said to her, "Miriam, my love, it's now time for me to do some shopping."

"Of course," she cried, "how thoughtless and selfish of me not to have thought of you. Tell me, what do you want to buy for yourself, my love?"

"I'll tell you what, let's just go out and walk along the street, then when I see something I fancy, we'll go in and inquire.

"That's fine, Peter," she said, but a little puzzled that he had not told her *what* he wanted to buy.

They left the cafe and continued to walk on Bahnhofstrasse. After passing a few shops, Peter stopped at a richly displayed jewelry shop whose window was filled with an assortment of rings, bracelets, earrings, necklaces, and clips, all of which were with diamonds of various sizes. "Ah," he said to Miriam, "this looks like the perfect place to have what I want."

"But Peter," she said, "what *is* it that you want?"

"I want to buy you two diamond rings, a diamond necklace or two, a pair of earrings to match, a couple of pairs of diamond clips, and maybe a diamond brooch if we see one we like."

"Are you joking, Peter?" she said.

"I've never been more serious, Miriam. Let's go in and see what they have that we like and then we'll buy it. You know very well that I can afford it and this is something that I want to do, right now.

"Don't think I don't know that you've never once asked me for anything of a luxury nature. I don't want to start arguing with you now about what you need and what you don't need. I want to buy you what I need to buy you. I've decided that it's more than time that I can indulge myself and give you a few trinkets that you will like." So saying, he seized her arm and led her, gently, into the store.

It was really old-world. All the assistants in the shop were men, every one of them impeccably dressed in morning suits. The tone was hushed, like in a ceremonial setting; each assistant, unless working with a customer, was standing at attention behind a showcase. In front of each showcase were two exquisite tub chairs and on the top of each showcase was a pair of French bouillote lamps with tole shades, a most elegant ensemble.

An even better-dressed man, presumably the manager, in a white tie and tails, met them at the entrance and greeted them. "Good afternoon, sir and madame, may I be of assistance to you?" he asked.

Peter responded, "Yes, we'd like to see rings, necklaces, earrings, clips, diamond brooches, but not all at once."

"Certainly, sir. My name is Chanson and I'm the manager. If you will kindly come this way," he said, leading them to the first showcase. "And this is Claude, my chief assistant. May I know your name, sir?"

"We are M. and Madame Romaine."

"May I assume, sir, that you are Swiss?"

"I was born here, yes, but if it is more expensive to be Swiss, then I can be a foreign tourist."

Mr. Chanson laughed at that and said, "No, sir, it is more expensive to be a tourist, they have to pay the tax, but you don't have to."

And with that, he withdrew, leaving them to Claude. "Would you like to start off with rings, sir?" he asked.

Peter nodded. While Claude went away to bring a selection, Peter said, "I would like, my love, to buy you a diamond ring for your left hand and a plain band of white gold or platinum to go with it, and a diamond eternity ring for your right hand. Would you like that?"

"Are you sure that's what you want me to have, Peter?" she asked. She was staggered by this.

"Yes, I'm sure, my love."

Claude returned with a large tray of various diamond rings set in platinum, white gold, yellow gold, and rose gold.

Peter said, "Tell us what we are looking at."

Claude approved of a customer not pretending to know what he was looking at and explained they were all 18- or 24-karat gold and platinum, and the diamonds varied from 1 to 3 carats. He would be happy to tell him the prices of any item.

Peter said he wanted a white gold or platinum diamond ring with a matching unadorned wedding band for his wife's left hand and a matching diamond eternity ring for her right hand.

After Claude told him some prices, he said he would go for a diamond between 2 and 3 carats, but he wanted his wife to choose the shape of the diamond she liked.

Miriam examined the diamond shapes and settled for a marquise-cut, 2.5-ct., pure white diamond on a platinum shank, and an octagonal-cut exterior wedding band. She chose a 3-ct., emerald-cut white diamond for the eternity ring.

The manager took away the three items to polish them up and box them. Claude asked Peter what he wanted next. Peter answered, "A diamond necklace, earrings, and bracelet."

Claude hurried off to put away the rings and bring out the next items. He displayed the diamond necklaces on a black velvet cloth for Miriam to see. She said to Peter, "I think they are all beautiful and I would love any one of those four. What do you think, Peter?"

"You choose, my dear," Peter said. She spent a great deal of time looking over the necklaces and the matching earrings and finally chose one. Next were the diamond bracelets. Claude brought about ten for her to see and she had great fun putting them on her wrist one after another. Finally, she chose a square 18K white gold, diamond bracelet. Peter smiled lovingly at her. Claude said, "Bravo, Madame! It looks perfect on your wrist."

Again, the manager took it away to polish and box while Claude took away the other bracelets and produced a tray of about fifty diamond brooches of hugely varying sizes and designs, virtually all mounted on platinum or white gold.

It took Miriam half an hour to choose two, one was white gold, butterfly shaped, with 3–6 point, round, prong-set diamonds. The other was a platinum, 18 kt., rose-gold bow dress clip in a retro style, featuring fourteen round, rose-cut diamonds and seven round and faceted prong-set rubies.

The last item was dress clips in diamonds. Claude brought a dozen pairs and she picked two pairs, diamonds on platinum for each: one, a pair of triangles, the other, a pair of interlocking circles.

After the manager took those away, Peter said to Claude, "May I see the bill now, Claude?" Claude's reply was, "If you like, Monsieur, or I can send it to your hotel if you prefer. I presume you are staying at the Central Plaza Hotel?"

Peter said, "How on earth did you know that?"

Claude replied, "Well, sir, I'm an avid reader of the Sherlock Holmes books and I can learn a great deal about a person simply by observation and listening. In your case, it was relatively easy. That you are Swiss is easy, your French has the slightest Swiss accent. That you don't live in Switzerland was easy; you don't live in Zurich, that was for sure – nobody living in this city ever comes in and buys like you have – but I don't think you live in Switzerland at all. Your sports jacket and shoes don't look Swiss, so I guess you live in some other country. If you are financially comfortably off enough to come in here today and do such shopping, then I guess you are staying in Zurich's best hotel, which is, of course, the Central Plaza. And, as Sherlock Holmes used to say, 'Quod Erat Demonstrandum, my dear Watson.'"

Peter burst out laughing at this flow of literature and logic from the formal-looking sales assistant. He said, "I'll take the bill here, Sherlock, and give you a check."

"So how long will you be staying at the Central Plaza, Monsieur Romaine?"

"Another three nights. But why do you want to know?"

"Well, frankly, tomorrow we'll call your bank to make sure the check is good, while you are still in Zurich. I see the check is on your bank in Berne, so that is just a formality. I'm sure you don't object to our doing that. After all, the bill is for $150,000, so we would be very remiss in not taking that simple precaution."

"No objection, Claude, none at all. And thank you for your services."

Just then the manager appeared with all the purchases in one elegant box, which wasn't closed up. He asked Peter if he wished to check the individual boxes against his invoice. Peter declined, but said they would like to take a taxi back to their hotel with their purchases. The manager said they would phone for one right away.

When they arrived at the hotel, Peter put the jewelry into the hotel safe.

The next day, they walked again on Bahnhofstrasse, Miriam having said on the previous day that she was satisfied with the wardrobe that she had bought, but willing to look again. However, that day, Peter decided he would start the shopping expedition.

Accordingly, when they came to an important-looking shop that had a great front window, behind which there were examples of just about every watchmaker in Switzerland, he took Miriam's arm again and said to her, "Look, watches."

"Yes?" she said, "I can see, and what a huge number of makes."

He said, "We're going in here to buy at least two watches, for you and for me. Do you know, my love, only yesterday I awakened myself to the fact that you don't even have a watch, and mine is a cheap watch that I've had since the scouts? So, after you, Madame."

An eager assistant came to them and asked if she could help them.

"I want a Rolex for myself and I want to see a lady's Rolex and also a lady's Patek Phillipe, please," Peter said.

"Yes, sir," said the assistant. "Please take a seat and I will bring a selection." In a few minutes, she returned with a selection of Rolex watches. He made up his mind immediately, as he knew exactly what model he wanted. Miriam chose one exactly like his, but for ladies, and although she knew quickly what she wanted, she had to eliminate all the other models to be sure.

Then, they saw a selection of the "fancy" models of Patek Phillipe, with and without diamonds around the face, and various beautiful variations. At length, she selected and Peter approved. After buying the watches, Peter said he decided he needed to buy a whole new wardrobe for himself. He spoke to the manager and asked for a recommendation to a good men's emporium. The manager told him of a superior shop a hundred meters along the street.

They walked there and Peter bought a completely new wardrobe of suits, sports jackets, trousers, shirts, and ties, and two suitcases to contain Miriam's and his new purchases. Miriam helped him to select materials and ties, and he decided that unknowingly, she was possessed of natural good taste, which made his own task that much easier.

They returned to their room at the Central Plaza and were aghast at the number of boxes already stacked against the walls.

Having decided to go and visit Peter's mother, Alice Romaine, in Berne, and then having to return to Zurich in order to fly to Israel, they decided to keep their room at the Central Plaza and pack their possessions when they returned from Berne.

They had bought two additional suitcases, true, but if even that was insufficient, they could always buy one more in Zurich on their return. Since they could fly from Israel to Los Angeles via Zurich, they could also leave in this hotel the possessions that they wouldn't need until Los Angeles and pick them up from the concierge on their final way back to Los Angeles.

Peter called his mother to tell her he was coming with his wife to see her earlier than expected and would be in Berne the next day. They would stay at a local hotel overnight. Peter called the Schweitzerhof-Bern Hotel and reserved a room for the next night.

After paying in advance for the use of the room in Zurich, he had security lock the room with specific instruction that no one was to enter until they returned.

They arrived in Berne at 9:00 a.m. Peter said, "Since we're early, I'll call Berne Aviation and check on my airplane." Jacques, the manager, was delighted to hear from Peter and offered to pick him up and take him to the plane.

Within ten minutes, Jacques picked up Peter and Miriam and drove them over to his hangar area, and re-introduced Peter to his DC3, *Richard's Renown*, after years of not seeing it. It looked clean and tidy. Peter entered and looked around. The cockpit and passenger compartment were immaculate. Jacques told him that once a month, the plane was taxied around the airport to make sure everything was in order and batteries charged, his monthly bills were sent to the banker and were always paid promptly. Jacques asked Peter if he could give him a lift anywhere and Peter accepted, telling Jacques he was going to visit his mother at the family home.

Arriving at his home, Peter thanked Jacques and, with Miriam, walked up to the front door. His mother opened the door, gave him a peck on his cheek, and on being introduced to Miriam, held out her hand to be shaken and said, "Pleased to meet you, Miriam," in her clipped, English way.

Peter was thinking that although his mother was quite a remote, cool person, he thought that after a six-year absence, considering this was the first time she saw his wife, she might have given them a warmer reception. He felt sorry and apologetic for the way his mother treated Miriam. Of course, part of this was his fault, he realized. He had never told Miriam anything about his mother; for example, he could not remember her hugging and kissing him, ever, when he was a child. On the other hand, he hadn't thought it would have been proper to "warn" his wife about his mother.

They entered the family living room and seated themselves. His mother rang a little bell, the housekeeper entered, and Alice ordered tea to be brought in. They had a cup of tea and little quartered salmon- and-cucumber sandwiches with the crusts trimmed off, and then there was an interval of silence. His mother asked nothing about his life or where he was living or what he was doing. Has she completely retreated into herself? he wondered. Is this how she is all the time, or just when I'm around?

"Mother, I'd like to show Miriam around the house, if that's okay with you," Peter said, breaking the ice.

"Of course, dear," his mother answered, stirring her tea and staring blankly at him. "I'm afraid the gardener has been late in coming this year," she added.

Peter showed Miriam around the house, which was a large, 100-year-old, typical Swiss house. He looked at the back garden, which he could remember as being ablaze with flowers. It was unkempt, and the few flowers that tried to poke their petals out of the overgrown shrubs had lost their color. He made a mental note to call the gardener and make sure he resuscitated the garden.

They entered his father's study. Everything was exactly as he remembered, including his father's pipe lying precariously on an ashtray.

"I've got to make a few phone calls, Miriam. Do you want to wait here or go downstairs to the parlor?"

"I think I'll try my hand at thawing your mother out of her doldrums. She seems so sad, so listless and unresponsive. I do hope it's not because of me.

"Nonsense, my dear. My mother started escaping reality, as it were, soon after my father passed away. None of her friends could drag her out of the house, and she made a sort of cocoon for herself within these four walls. But by all means, see if she will respond to your charms. Certainly, everyone else we've ever met has," he smiled.

Peter got busy making his calls. He agreed to meet with Jean-Pierre Muraille, his lawyer, and Etoile Lambert, his banker, later in the day. He suspected that he wouldn't be coming to Berne again any time soon and wanted to keep the lines of communication open with these two important people in his life, especially as he might need them to handle future long-distance dealings.

Then Peter went downstairs to see his mother and Miriam. To his surprise, he found Alice was sniffing and wiping her eyes while Miriam had her arm around her shoulders. "What's going on?" he said, trying to sound as cheerful as he could. The effect of his cheerful demeanor was to cause Alice to burst out in loud sobs. Miriam looked at Peter and beckoned him over to the couch.

"Your poor mother," Miriam began, "when I came down she smiled and asked me, 'where do your parents live?' I told her they were murdered by the Nazis in Poland in the war. She looked at me, as though seeing me for the first time, held her hands out, and when I sat next to her she put her arms around me and started to cry. It was so heartbreaking, Peter. She's been murmuring since. As though trying to remember something or perhaps recalling an old memory."

"You know, my love, you are probably the first person she's met who lost her family because of the Nazis," Peter explained.

"I see," she said thoughtfully, "just as you are the first person I ever talked to who didn't lose somebody during the war. How insensitive of me. I just never realized that there are people like your mother who were basically untouched by the horrors of the war, perhaps didn't even realize the extent of the effect of the death camps. What a blessing it must be to have lived those years in relative peace and tranquility."

"And perhaps, also," Peter suggested, "what a feeling of guilt some people must feel knowing that while they were safe and enjoying life, millions were wretched and dying."

His mother had been sitting quietly, listening to their conversation. Alice said to Miriam, "You know, dear, I remember when I came to see you in your hospital ward in the Berne Hospital; it never occurred to me that you and the other girl who was with you there –"

"Heide," said Miriam, quietly.

"Yes, that was it, Heide," said Alice. "How clever of you to remember. Are you still in touch with her?"

"Mrs. Romaine, Heide and I lived together for four years in a concentration camp in Germany. She saved my life every day and I saved her life every day. She couldn't be closer to me if she was a twin sister. So yes, I'm still in touch with her, I'll always be in touch with her."

"Of course, how silly of me, Miriam, I'm so sorry. There's something about you, my child, that breathes life into these old bones. I don't know how long you and my dear son, Peter, are going to be in Berne, but I've decided that I would like to know you before you leave. You are a beautiful and clever young woman, and I'm sure Peter made a wonderful choice in marrying you. I'm sorry I've been so absorbed in feeling sorry for myself that I've missed these last years. Now how are we going to arrange for us to spend more time together?"

Amazed at his mother's total about-face, Peter said, "Right now, Mother, we have to leave. I've two appointments this afternoon. But we'll come over first thing tomorrow, after breakfast. Is that okay?"

"Wonderful," said Alice, "and thank you both for your understanding."

"I'm just going to call a taxi and we'll be off," Peter said.

"No, Peter, take the car," said his mother, "then you can return it in the morning."

Thanking her, Peter and Miriam hugged Alice, and left.

As they got in the car, Peter said to her, "Congratulations, you really succeeded in getting through to her, my love. I knew that if anyone could reach her, you would.

"I just remembered one more person I've got to call, my old professor, Dr. DuPont. I want to tell him how his drop-out doctoral student has fared in the intervening years. He'll especially appreciate my work regarding the Israel prize."

After they renewed connections with their lawyer, Jean-Pierre Muraille, they went to meet his banker, Etoille Lambert. Peter asked for, and received, a bank draft for one million dollars. "Settling-down money," he told the banker. "We're buying a home in Los Angeles, USA, and don't want to come up short."

"Well," Etoile said, "you know where to come for more." He also presented Peter with an accounting of his monies earned and spent.

After the two visits, they returned to the hotel. Peter made a call to Professor DuPont, who immediately asked, "When are you coming back to finish your doctorate, Peter?" Peter laughed and told him he finished that some years ago in Israel. "In what language, Peter?" the professor wondered. "As a matter of fact, I wrote the thesis in Hebrew, then translated it and had it reprinted in English."

"Splendid," DuPont said, enthusiastically. "And what did you call it?"

I called it "A Study of the Phonological Topology of Ten Romance Languages."

"Bravo," said DuPont. "Would you be kind enough to send me a copy, the English translation, please?"

"Of course," said Peter. "It so happens I'm staying here in Berne for one night, I've a copy in English with me, and I'll get the hotel to mail it to you."

"Thank you very much. And what else can you tell me?"

"Well, I'm a professor at TAU *and* I've just been appointed a professor at USC in California, and I recently received the Israel Prize for developing a better teaching method in Hebrew for new immigrants, and I'm married to a wonderful woman who's also a professor of linguistics. Could anything be grander, Professor?"

"I always knew you'd come to a bad end, Peter," he quipped, "but congratulations for all those things. And will you also kindly let me have a copy of your 'Better Teaching Methods of Teaching Hebrew to New Immigrants'?"

"Yes, I will, but it will have to be in Hebrew."

"Don't worry about that. I know I can get it translated somewhere in this great university of ours. And thank you so much for calling me, Peter. I used to know a linguistics man at USC – we met at one or two international seminars. His name is Isaac Katz."

"Oh, I know him. He is now Dean of Students."

"Give him my regards, will you, when you see him next."

"Yes, of course. Well, goodbye professor."

"Goodbye professor."

"Well," said Miriam, "you obviously had a great deal of respect for Professor DuPont."

"Well, when I dropped out of my doctoral studies, he was my supervisor and, in my eyes, a superman. I dropped out because I had started to get very involved with the Aliyah Bet thing and your group. He asked my reason and I told him only that I had become involved in a life-saving project, which was going to take all my time and energy for a long time. He was such a gentleman. He realized that I couldn't confide in him and he just wished me well and hoped that I would return to my doctoral studies when my outside interests concluded. That's why I've such a special feeling for him.

"Now Miriam, my love, let's go down and have dinner and I'll get the concierge to send off this English copy of my thesis to Professor DuPont at the University and book us flights to Zurich for late afternoon tomorrow. That will give us time to spend the morning with my mother, then maybe she'll come out for lunch with us."

Next day, they visited Alice Romaine again, but this time she was a changed and recovered woman. She even managed to smile at them and to kiss them both. Peter and Miriam, in turn, recounted the stories of Camp Pietro, Alicante, Salonika, Kavala, the voyage of the *Helen* and the purchase of the DC3, and finally, the arrival of the group of illegal immigrants by night on the coast of Palestine. They spoke in generalities of the War of Independence of Israel, as they didn't want her to know they were both active in it. Then they filled her in on their present lives on kibbutz and university.

The only thing the couple didn't mention was Peter's conversion: they knew she would never understand his emotional feelings for Judaism, let alone his desire to learn more and more about what she always referred to as the "passé" Testament.

She showed no interest in the other members of the group besides Heide, but Peter let her know that both Heide and Helen Phillips from Berne had married and continued to live in Israel, and that undoubtedly, Peter and Miriam would have continued to live there if Peter had not received the offer of a professorship and head of a department at USC in California.

When they had talked themselves out, Peter asked his mother if she would like to go out for lunch with them at their hotel.

"You're such dears," his mother said, "but I'm still not ready to face the world, as it were. Perhaps I'll start by resurrecting my relationships with some of my old cronies, maybe even take more interest in the garden and the upkeep of the house. Then, slowly, I make my way back into society. I hope you understand."

"But Mother," Peter implored, "we'll be living in California and who knows when we'll see each other again? Are you sure you can't leave just for a short time?"

"Thank you. But I simply can't. Hopefully, you two young people will be traveling back to Berne some day soon, and then, well, then things will be different and I'll be the talk of the town," she teased.

For the first time since Peter could remember, he left his mother, teary-eyed. She was obviously very sad at their departure.

Later that day, they flew back to Zurich and went to their hotel. After going to their room, they started to unpack their purchases, got rid of the boxes and bags and carefully repacked everything in cases that would remain in the hotel until they returned from Israel. They would take with them to Israel on this final trip just one case, with minimal toiletries and casual clothing for both of them.

The next day, they left three cases with the concierge, checked the jewelry into the hotel safe-deposit, and boarded their flight for Israel.

On arrival, they went to the kibbutz, to their old room, changed into casual kibbutz clothes, and went to see Yossele. They told him of their plans and that they would be staying for about three weeks while they made their farewells to their friends in the university and the kibbutz. They also asked permission to invite two couples from their immigrant group to spend a couple of days in the kibbutz, if that would be in order.

"First, congratulations to both of you," Yossele said, "and of course,

I'll be happy to arrange for your two couples to stay here for a few days to say goodbye."

The next day, Peter and Miriam went to TAU to let Isaac Katz, the Dean of Students, know what was going on, and that Peter had to resign his position there, due to his appointment as head of a department at USC in Los Angeles. Miriam, too, had to relinquish her job, as well as her appointment as a professor.

They also went around the university to say goodbye to the friends they had made. Everybody congratulated Peter on his appointment at USC, clearly understanding that this was an appointment that he could not decline.

They sent letters to Heide and Helen, telling them they were leaving Israel due to Peter's appointment, and inviting them, plus their families, to spend a long weekend with them at Ma'barot in two weeks' time.

Back in the kibbutz, they made a point to spend some time with their friends Avraham and Leah, Jack and Betty, Aron and Ruth Weiss, the professor from TAU and his wife, and not forgetting the kibbutz driver who first picked them up on the beach at Nahariya.

They went into Netanya to see their bank manager and army friend, Francois Leclerc, and to bid him farewell. Peter closed his foreign-currency and local accounts and took away a cashier's check, which he would deposit in due course in Los Angeles.

They didn't omit going down the road to Kibbutz Ha'ogen to bid farewell to the secretary, Elijah. He was very sorry to see them go, as they had both been popular teachers and Hebrew students in his kibbutz.

While in Netanya, they made arrangements with a shipping company to pack and ship their books and other belongings to Los Angeles.

Peter telephoned to Yossele's friend from his British Army days, Willem, who was the chairman of Aliyah Bet in Israel. Peter formally offered him the *Helen* and *Richard's Renown*, the DC3, if Aliyah Bet could use them. He told them that the ship was stored in Iskenderun, in Turkey, and the DC3 was stored in Berne, in Switzerland. Both were in full operating condition. Their documents of title were with his lawyer in Berne. If Aliyah Bet wanted them, he would instruct his lawyer to make arrangements for Willem to take them over. Willem said he'd let him know tomorrow.

Instead of calling, the next day Willem showed up in person at the kibbutz, and knocked at Peter and Miriam's home.

"I just had to come myself to thank you for your magnanimous offer, which, on behalf of Aliyah Bet, I'm happy to accept. On a personal note, I want you to know that for many in this country, including myself, you are a living legend and I'm humbled by what you, one single man, have done for my organization and my country."

Willem then presented Peter with a beautiful, colorfully inscribed Certificate of Appreciation from Aliyah Bet, signed both by Willem and the President of the State of Israel, and written both in Hebrew and English.

In two weeks, Heide, noticeably pregnant, and Max arrived, as did Helen, also pregnant, and Alex, with their firstborn, Peter. They were put up in the volunteers' rooms, where Peter and Miriam had started their kibbutz life, but spent most of the time either in Peter and Miriam's house or at the swimming pool.

The six old friends had a good time together, but Heide was very sad that her "sister" Miriam was leaving Israel. They hugged and cried. Helen felt the same bond with Peter as they hugged for the last time. When she kissed him goodbye, Peter realized that leaving her would leave a vacuum in his heart that could never be filled. They had had a special relationship at a special time in their lives and a spiritual bond entwined them both.

"This isn't good-bye, you know," Peter said. "We'll be visiting Israel in the future, for vacations if nothing else. Let's just call this *au revoir* – or *lehitraot*, as we say in Hebrew."

Then it was time for them to pack up their belongings, and the next day, Yossele arranged for Louis to take them to the airport at Lod. When they arrived in Zurich, they checked in again at the Central Plaza, collected their three large cases from the concierge, the jewelry from the safe-deposit, put it together with whatever they had arrived with, sat down on the bed, and contemplated their possessions.

"It looks like a lot," Miriam ventured.

"It *is* a lot," Peter acknowledged. "Reminds me of the rabbinic adage, 'Many possessions bring many worries.'"

"Do you think it's too much?" she asked, looking around her.

"How could it be too much for two young, well-to-do people on their second honeymoon, moving into their first real home and purchasing their first real wardrobes?"

"Should we stop feeling embarrassed, then?" she asked.

"Let's always be a little embarrassed, knowing how lucky we are, not only to have our wealth, but to have each other."

"You always know what to say, my darling," Miriam told him. "Let's start our honeymoon right now, by going downstairs to the bar, having two champagne cocktails, dinner, and an early bed."

"That's a great proposal, which I enthusiastically second."

The next day, Peter said to Miriam over breakfast, "Look, my love, our itinerary goes from here to London, New York, then Los Angeles. We have a couple of days in London, then what about a couple of days in New York before we return to Los Angeles and a busy time for both of us?"

"Great idea, my love, but we have to pack accordingly."

"What do you mean?"

"We should repack one case of items we'll both need for London and New York. That way, we won't spend half our time packing and repacking everything."

"You're absolutely right! You have such a practical view of things. I'll speak to the concierge and get him to make changes in our flight itinerary. We'll do the tourist thing and perhaps see a play in each city."

"Okay," Miriam said, "now I've got a better idea of what to pack for both of us in our one suitcase. Day clothes, evening a bit dressy, and toiletries."

They had a great time in London, although they found most of the activities of a historical nature rather than a contemporary one. They took in a play at the Lyric Theatre in London's West End, and toured a number of inns dating back to the fifteenth century, including the venerable and celebrated *Prospect of Whitby* and *The Guinea*. The Tower of London and the Changing of the Guard at Buckingham Palace were especially captivating, the former for its grisly history and the latter for its pomp and splendor.

In New York, they hired a car and driver to take them around and get an idea again of the avenues and the cross-streets, Central Park, the bridges, and Welfare Island, which they visited. They could not believe that such a small, bustling island existed in the heart of New York.

They went to Radio City Music Hall and were amazed at the sight of so many girls kicking up their heels at the same time, on stage.

At last, they arrived in Los Angeles, somewhat travel-worn, but ready to start a new life, together. They were awed by the hotel suite Peter had reserved. This would be their home until their condo was finished.

Before they tumbled into bed, he put in a call to Yenta, the decorator, to let her know they were back and wanted to get together with her.

"Have you finished our proposal?" he innocently asked.

"Of course, Mr. Romaine," she answered indignantly. "The month was up yesterday and I had it ready then."

He couldn't repress a short laugh. "That's fine Yenta, can we meet tomorrow at 11:00 a.m. in my suite at the Beverly Wilshire?"

"I'll be there at 11:00," she said, and hung up.

When they went down for breakfast, they left instructions to clean the suite immediately, as they would be coming back after breakfast.

They returned to find everything in place and Yenta arrived precisely at 11:00. She was beaming as she gave a beautiful bouquet of flowers to Miriam and said, "Welcome back, Mrs. Romaine."

The three people settled down around a table in the sitting room of the suite. Yenta passed out two copies of her proposal to Miriam and Peter. Miriam started to read it from the beginning and Peter looked at the foot of the last page, the bottom line – clearly reflecting their different approaches.

They then went through the proposal line by line, asking questions and checking to see how long the project itself would take.

They found the entire process orderly and thoroughly professional, as expected. There were some decisions to be made by them, about colors, plumbing fixtures, lighting fixtures, and locations of outlets for electrical appliances, TV, security, and telephones.

Yenta had brought dozens of brochures to help with the choice of lighting and plumbing fixtures and types of electrical and phone outlets. This allowed Peter and Miriam to come to decisions at once, even settling on the wooden parquet pattern for the floors.

Within the next two months, the flooring and all the electrical and plumbing and decoration was finished. At the same time, Miriam was working with Yenta on furnishings. Some items had to be manufactured and some had to be shipped from across the country and, rarely, from Europe. After a further two months, the Persian rugs, the electrically operated drapes, the safe, and the furniture for all rooms was in place and, though they lived in the lap of hotel luxury, as Peter said, "It's time we went home."

CHAPTER XXVI

The Condo; The Party

THEY MOVED INTO THE CONDO WITH THEIR LUGGAGE, AND were happy to unpack it into their respective voluminous clothes closets, which Peter had designed. The only thing left to do was to go shopping for food and groceries, which Miriam volunteered to do the following day.

The first night, they went out to an Indian restaurant they had previously discovered and enjoyed. They found they had a liking for both Indian and Persian food.

While getting the condo decorated and furnished, their books and belongings arrived from Israel and Peter started his life at USC. He drove there daily in the two-seater sports car he had bought, which he enjoyed immensely. Miriam drove a more sedate Mercedes Benz sedan, which she also enjoyed, having learned to drive quickly and well.

After a few months in the condo, Miriam thought it was time to join a synagogue, having found there were two within three blocks of their home. She would go mostly on Saturday mornings to services and after a little time, she decided to join the Ladies' Club. There, she quickly made friends with some other members. At first she dragged Peter to some of their social functions, and in time, Peter met a number of interesting men whose company he enjoyed, so they fairly soon had quite a social circle.

One day Miriam said, "Peter, I don't think you've ever been to a synagogue service. You prepared yourself so well for the Jewish side of your life, but you've never entered what is arguably the center of Jewish worship, the synagogue. How about coming with me next Saturday to see for yourself how those ancient traditions, which you were so intrigued to find extant, are carried on today in the modern world? What do you say?"

"Very well, my love. You're right, you know. It's certainly time for me to put into practice what I learned from the books. What do I have to do?"

Miriam told him that the synagogue she'd chosen permitted men and women to sit together, unlike in Orthodox synagogues, so she would be right by his side all the time. He would understand the Hebrew prayers, but he might find some of the old Hebrew words and phrases a novel experience, and one well worth exploring.

That next Saturday saw them both in Miriam's synagogue. He found that, to his surprise, he was enjoying the experience, and after the service, Miriam was able to introduce him to the synagogue's rabbi and the members, some of whom he already knew. He felt comfortable there, was able to follow and understand what the service was all about, and appreciated the warm welcome he received from those he met.

Soon he found himself accompanying Miriam on many of her synagogue visits, and after a few months, decided to join the synagogue himself. He was soon approached by one of the Board members, who asked him to run for election to the Board, having heard of Peter's academic prominence both in USC and in Israel.

Peter discussed the matter with Miriam at length, and he agreed to run. By the time his curriculum vitae, both academic and military, were displayed to the synagogue membership, his friends on the membership committee told him he was a shoo-in to be elected to the Board.

Sure enough, despite his relative newness to this prestigious synagogue, Peter was duly elected and took his place in the community.

At the same time, Peter and Miriam were deemed lively and interesting guests and had a busy schedule accepting invitations to the homes of some of his faculty associates.

However, for her part, Miriam started to feel that she needed more than a fulfilling social life; she needed to nourish her intellectual side as well. She discussed this with Peter, who suggested that she might consider going back to her thesis, in her long-lost subject of Linguistic Anthropology. She thought it was an excellent idea and asked Peter to inquire for her in his faculty.

He found, among his colleagues, one professor, James Wilson, whose subject was close to the core of Miriam's thesis. He was willing to discuss it with her.

They had had a very positive meeting. She brought all her previous multilingual certificates, which Wilson was most intrigued to see

He also discussed the work she had done in Hebrew at Tel Aviv University, but told her that she would have to rewrite what she had done, in English. She quite understood, laughed it off, and said it was no problem, because after all, she was a linguist. So they agreed she would continue her studies under his supervision.

Miriam then settled into a routine of going to the University two or three days a week with Peter, working away at her studies, in the library, first finishing up her research, and then, rewriting her thesis in English. From time to time, she would have a meeting with Professor Wilson, who would see how she was progressing and encourage her to keep going. He told her he very much approved of her choice of thesis subject as an original and significant topic. He thought it would be well received in the profession and wouldn't be surprised if she was offered a professorial position, either here or in another university in southern California. All this made her feel great about herself and her work.

It took her two years from the time she restarted her work with Professor Wilson to finish. Then, one day, when they were having lunch in the faculty lounge, she told Peter she had finished the thesis.

He jumped up, and forgetting his English reserve, yelled out "Whoopee" at the top of his lungs. One of his colleagues came over, patted Peter on the back and said, "I don't know what this is all about, Peter, but that's the most exciting thing that's happened in this lounge in years!"

"Miriam has finished her thesis," Peter shouted.

"Then whoopee, indeed," whooped his colleague, "and congratulations to Miriam."

She went through the defense of her thesis in front of a panel of professors, who passed her with acclaim and congratulated her, much as had Professor Wilson, on the choice of a significant topic for the literature in her subject.

That night, at home, Peter said, "I want to throw a party to celebrate this outstanding event in our lives. We'll have it catered, with a barman, and really have a great time."

"Who would we invite?" she asked.

"We have a whole lot of friends to whom we owe invitations, from the Synagogue Ladies' Guild, Synagogue Board Members, and our colleagues at the University. I don't think we'll have any difficulty in inviting a hundred people."

"That's more people than we had on the kibbutz," Miriam joked. "What a wonderful idea!"

And, indeed, they had a great party.

A Party at the Romaines

The year was 1960 and the location was a penthouse on the twenty-fourth floor of a condominium building on Wilshire Boulevard in Los Angeles, California. A large and boisterous party was being given by the owners, Peter Romaine and his wife, to celebrate her having recently received a PhD, which she had started twenty years previously . . .

An Historical Note

IN 1922, THE LEAGUE OF NATIONS RATIFIED AND CONFERRED upon Great Britain an official Mandate to administer Palestine, which had been part of the Ottoman Empire until 1917, when the British Army drove out the Ottomans from Palestine.

The Palestine Mandate specifically obligated Britain to implement the terms of the Balfour Declaration of November 2, 1917, and to "place the country under such political, administrative, and economic conditions as will secure the establishment of the Jewish National Home."

The events of 1946–1948, partially referred to in the Epilogue, seem to have been somewhat at variance with the Mandate obligation referred to above.

Epilogue

THE BACKGROUND TO THE STORY IN THIS BOOK IS BASED ON the efforts of the British Government to prevent Jewish survivors of Hitler's concentration camps from leaving Europe and immigrating to Palestine.

Information has only recently come to light about the extent of the extraordinary measures taken by agents of the British Government with the full knowledge and intention of that government during the period 1946–1948.

In a book published by Bloomsbury Publishing PLC in September, 2010, titled *The Secret History of MI6: 1909–1949*, written by the distinguished British historian Dr. Keith Jeffery, he exposed the British Government's incredible actions to prevent this so-called illegal immigration, and described their tactics in detail:

They plotted to implement combinations of bombs with delay timers, intended to explode after ships sailed out to sea; limpet mines attached to ships; poisoning a ship's water supply or the crew's food; and even setting fire to ships while in port. With typical British tongue-in-cheek understatement, the combination of plans was titled "Operation Embarrass."

The facts cited above are certainly authentic: the book was published "with the permission of the Secret Intelligence Service and the Controller of Her Majesty's Stationery Office." In addition, it seems that Dr. Jeffery was made an offer to explore the remaining archives and write the official history of MI6. It is therefore apparent that the book is based on his officially approved research, however negative it may appear, concerning the British Government of the time.

In late 1946, the British Labor Government, led by Clement Attlee, actually requested MI6 to propose a plan of action:

"to deter ships' masters and crews from engaging in illegal Jewish immigration" to Palestine. Action of the contemplated nature was stated to be particularly effective "if some people"(undefined) "actually suffer unpleasant consequences." This very "proper" English phraseology obviously meant causing casualties by death or injury were not to be thought of as abhorrent; on the contrary, they were to be considered necessary to be effective.

The long-time chief of the MI6, Major General Stewart Menzies, suggested that following these planned attacks, they could be blamed on a fictitious Arab group, "The Defenders of Arab Palestine." If that had come about, it would obviously have created even more bloodshed between Arabs and Jews in Palestine than had already taken place in plenty, during the 1920s and 1930s.

"Operation Embarrass" was launched following a meeting held on February 14, 1947, at which were present representatives of MI6, the War Office, the Colonial Office (responsible for operation and control of the Palestine Mandate), and the Foreign Office (known by political observers for decades as being traditionally anti-semitic).

The "Embarrass" team was set up with a special communication network, named "Ocean" and a substantial budget of its own. A primary instruction was that no link shall ever be able to be proved between this clandestine organization, designed to murder and injure, and its creator, the British Government.

Three major objectives were given: (1) direct action against refugee ships and personnel;(2) a "black" propaganda and disinformation campaign; (3) a deception scheme to disrupt refugee activity from the Black Sea ports.

British spies with bombing equipment were sent to Italian and French ports. Their cover story, if captured, was to say they had been recruited in New York by wealthy right-wing Americans from the oil and aircraft industries.

It was expressly made clear that the British Government would give no help, overtly or covertly, if they (the operatives) were caught in action, by any country.

During a period of nine months, from the summer of 1947 to early 1948, "Embarrass" attacks were made on suspected ships in Italian ports by bombs and limpet mines. Thought was given to blowing up "*The S.S. President Warfield*" (later named "*The Exodus*") in a French port.

Britain, which aimed and plotted to blow up and otherwise prevent ships from their truly humanitarian task of carrying concentration camp survivors to Palestine in 1946–1948, was, sadly, among those countries who immediately and forcefully condemned Israel out of hand for halting a politically-inspired voyage of ships from Turkey to Gaza on May 31, 2010, denigrating Israel's right to legitimate self-defense, which is the first and primary duty of the government of any country. The British Prime Minister described the Israeli action to prevent the Turkish ships entering Gaza port as "completely unacceptable."

It would seem, to a neutral and dispassionate observer, who examines and considers those events of 1946–1948 and compares them with recent opprobrium heaped on Israel following the Gaza episode, by Britain, among others, that nothing much has changed in the British Foreign Office's traditional animosity toward the Jews of Europe in trying to find refuge in Palestine, and the response involving Israel today.

GLOSSARY

Anthropology   The science of humankind, in the widest sense

Anthropological Linguistics   Linguistic research based on the science of humankind

Bnei Akiva   A Jewish religious youth organization

Chanukah   A Jewish festival commemorating the defeat of the Greeks by the Jews in the second century, BCE

Ethnography   The scientific description of races and peoples, with their habits, customs, and mutual differences

Ethnology   The branch of knowledge which deals with the characteristics of different people and the differences and relationships between them

Haganah   The Jewish underground army

Kippah (Yarmulka)   Small head-covering worn by male Jews, in religious services mainly, and by Orthodox Jews generally

Linguistics   The knowledge or study of languages

Moshe Dayan   Born in Palestine, a Haganah officer, later an army general in Israel; subsequently a politician and Minister of Defense, an avid collector of antiquities

Linguistic Anthropology   Anthropological research based on the study of the language of a selected group

Phonology   The branch of science that deals with speech sounds and pronunciation in particular languages

Phonological Topology   Grammatical structure in a language emanating from or relating to speech sounds or pronunciation

313

Safed   A town in the north of Israel

Shaar Hagai   The start of the main road up to Jerusalem

Topology   Sharing certain predominant features of grammatical structure in a language

Typography   Appearance of the printed language

Yeshivah   A Jewish religious school

ABOUT THE AUTHOR

EDGAR MISKIN has spent most of his working life as an accountant, both in private practice and in commerce, including some years as Financial Controller in a large aircraft company. He was a British Army Officer in World War II, and has been a lifeguard, a center lathe operator in an engineering factory, a film actor, and a real estate developer. However, if he had to do it over again, he would probably have chosen to be an antiquarian, due to his interests in ancient history and languages, anthropology and archaeology.

This is Edgar's second book, his first being The Exchange, published in October 2007, also an historical novel. It starts in the Second World War and tells the story of three British soldiers, their extraordinary exploits, and their remarkable successes after the war.

Edgar Miskin lives in Porter Ranch, California.

ABOUT THE COVER IMAGE

The image on the front cover is a copy of a photograph taken on April 14, 1947. The ship pictured had been captured by the Royal Navy in the Mediterranean Sea and then towed to the port of Haifa, in Palestine.

The ship's official name was the *Guardian*. It was purchased by the Aliyah Bet organization, renamed the *Theodore Herzl*, overhauled and loaded with 2,641 Jewish Holocaust survivors.

It sailed from Sete, a port about seventy miles west of Marseille, on the south coast of France, in late March of 1947.

It was stopped and boarded by armed personnel of HMS *St. Brides Bay*, a frigate of the Royal Navy, in the Mediterranean.

Resistance was given by the survivors; two were killed immediately and one died of wounds subsequently. The picture shows the shrouded bodies of the two dead being carried on stretchers, through the passengers, toward the ship's side.

The story in this book relates to a similar journey, also undertaken by survivors endeavoring to escape from Europe and hoping to find refuge in Palestine, at precisely that time in history.